TRY DARKNESS

ALSO BY JAMES SCOTT BELL

Try Dying

JAMES SCOTT BELL

TRY DARKNESS

A NOVEL

CENTER
STREET®

NEW YORK BOSTON NASHVILLE

Center Street
Hachette Book Group USA
237 Park Avenue
New York, NY 10017

Visit our Web site at www.centerstreet.com

Center Street is a division of Hachette Book Group USA, Inc.
The Center Street name and logo are registered trademarks of Hachette Book Group USA, Inc.

Printed in the United States of America

First Edition: July 2008
10 9 8 7 6 5 4 3 2 1

Library of Congress Cataloging-in-Publication Data
Bell, James Scott.
    Try darkness / James Scott Bell. — 1st ed.
        p. cm.
    Summary: "In the second novel featuring trial lawyer Ty Buchanan, the murder of a client will force Ty into the underbelly of L.A. to protect the child she left behind."—Provided by the publisher.
    ISBN 978-1-59995-685-5
    1. Lawyers—Fiction. 2. Los Angeles (Calif.)—Fiction. I. Title.

PS3552.E5158T787 2008
813'.54—dc22

2008000499

To the memory of John D. MacDonald

TRY DARKNESS

1

THE NUN HIT me in the mouth and said, "Get out of my house."

Jaw throbbing, I said, "I can't believe you just did that."

"This is my house," she said. "You want more? Come on back in."

Sister Mary Veritas is a shade over five and a half feet. She was playing in gray sweats, of course. Most of the time she wears the full habit. Her pixie face is usually a picture of innocence. She has short chestnut hair and blue eyes. I had just discovered those eyes hid an animal ruthlessness.

It was the first Friday in April, and we were playing what I thought was some friendly one-on-one on the basketball court of St. Monica's, a Benedictine community in the Santa Susana mountains. The morning was bright, the sky clear. Should have meant peace like a river.

Not a nun like a mugger.

Backing into the key for a spin hook, I was surprised to find not just the basket but a holy Catholic elbow waiting for my face. I'm six-three, so it took some effort for her to pop me.

"That's a foul," I said.

"So take it out," she said.

"I thought the Benedictines were known for their hospitality."

"For the hungry pilgrim," Sister Mary said. "Not for a guy looking for an easy bucket."

"What would the pope say to you?"

"Probably, *Well done, thou good and faithful servant.*"

"For a smash to the chops?"

"You're a pagan. It probably did you some good."

"A trash-talking sister." I shook my head. "So this is organized religion in the twenty-first century."

"Play."

Okay, she wanted my outside game? She'd get it. True, I hadn't played a whole lot of ball since college. A couple of stints on a lawyer league team. But I could still shoot. I was deadly from twenty feet in.

Not this morning. I clanked one from the free throw line and Sister Mary got the rebound.

Before becoming a nun, she played high school ball in Oklahoma. On a championship team, no less. Knew her way around a court.

But I also had the size advantage and gave her a cushion on defense. She took it and shot over me from fifteen feet.

Swish.

Pride is a sin, so Sister Mary tells me. But it's a good motivator when a little nun is schooling you. I kicked up the aggression factor a notch.

She tried a fadeaway next. I got a little bit of her wrist as she shot.

Air ball.

Sister Mary waited for me to call a foul.

"Nice try," I said.

"Where'd you learn to play," she said. "County jail?"

"You talking or playing?"

She got the animal look again. I hoped that wouldn't interfere with her morning prayers. *Holy Mary, Mother of God, pray for us sinners, now and at the hour we talk smack.*

I took the ball to the top of the key. Did a beautiful crossover dribble. Sister Mary swiped at the ball. Got my arm instead with a loud *thwack.* I stopped and threw up a jumper.

It hit the side of the rim and bounced left.

I thought I'd surprise her by hustling for the rebound.

She had the same idea.

We were side by side going for the ball. I could feel her body language. There was no way she was going to let me get it.

There was no way I was going to let *her* get it.

I was going to body a nun into the weeds.

2

WE WENT DOWN. The brown grasses at the edge of the blacktop padded our fall.

I had both hands on the ball. So did Sister Mary.

She grunted and pulled. By this time we were out of bounds.

I started to laugh. The absurdity of a frantic postulant and a macho lawyer in a death grip over a basketball was hilarious.

Sister Mary didn't laugh. She wanted the ball.

I had to admire her doggedness. She's the type who'd go to the mat with the devil himself if she had to.

But I still wouldn't let her get the ball.

Then I was on my back, holding the ball to my chest. Sister Mary was on top of me, refusing to let her hands slip off the ball.

Her body was firm and fit and I looked at her face thinking thoughts one should not think of a woman pledged to a life of chastity.

I stopped laughing and let her have the ball.

She took it and rolled off me.

Neither of us said anything.

Then a voice said, "Now, isn't that a pretty picture?"

Father Bob stood at the other end of the court, hands on hips.

One displeased priest.

I shot up, helped Sister Mary to her feet. "Nothing to see here," I said. "Just a little hustle and flow."

"Or grab and go," Father Bob said.

Sister Mary said nothing. Her face was flushed and she was breathing hard.

"A friendly game of one-on," I said. "You see? I'm doing my part to help the community stay in shape. You want a piece of me next?"

Father Bob, who looks like Morgan Freeman's stand-in, said, "I know a few tricks even Sister Mary hasn't learned yet."

"I have to go now," she said. Without her characteristic smile, she dropped the ball in the grass and jogged toward her quarters.

Father Bob motioned me over. "Tread carefully," he said.

"I know," I said.

"Do you?"

"What's not to know?"

He picked up the ball and spun it on his finger. Like a Globetrotter.

"Not bad," I said.

"God created the world to spin on its axis," he said. "Perfectly. And he created man to be in perfect communion with him. Only man messed up. He messed up the way things are supposed to spin." He grabbed the ball with both hands. "In the garden, you know the story."

"A snake got Eve to eat an apple."

"Don't know if it was an apple," Father Bob said. "It just says 'the fruit of the knowledge of good and evil.'"

"Was that such a bad thing to want?"

"If a serpent's offering it to you, it is. Now, we've come a long way trying to get things to spin right again. That's the reason for the church. That's the reason for people taking holy vows. And that's the reason you have to tread carefully around here."

I took the ball from him and tried to spin it on my finger. It fell to the ground and bounced.

"See?" Father Bob said.

"Fine."

"Then are you ready to earn your daily bread?"

3

THE WOMAN CAME in holding hands with a little girl. The girl was maybe six years old. They were both dressed in thrift store casual. The woman had shoulder-length brown hair and a face that would have been nice if you could take the pain out of it. Her expression was grim and resolute, as if she'd been hit a few times and knew she'd get hit some more.

She was about thirty-five but carried an extra decade around like a peasant with a load of bricks.

The little girl had dirty-blond hair worn in a ponytail fastened with a green rubber band. The rubber band matched her eyes. She held a small backpack with a pink unicorn on it.

Father Bob got up and greeted them, showed them to our table.

We were at the Ultimate Sip, a coffee bar in a strip mall on Rinaldi. The Sip is an inspiration in our Starbucks-saturated world. A wholly owned independent subsidiary of the mind of one Barton C. McNitt. He's a Vietnam vet, a little older than Father Bob. Father Bob affectionately refers to Barton C. McNitt as "Pick."

"Because if there's a nit, McNitt will pick it," Father Bob told me. "He likes to argue."

Pick McNitt had been a philosophy professor at Cal State Northridge until he went crazy. He spent some time in a sanitarium, where Father Bob met him by walking into the wrong room.

They argued then and have been friends ever since.

I pay McNitt a little chunk each month for the use of the Sip as an office. And for a p.o. box in the franchise McNitt owns next door.

"This is Reatta," Father Bob said, introducing the woman. She nodded at me. "And this is Kylie."

The girl looked at me, then put her head behind her mother.

"Garçon," I called out to Pick McNitt. "How about three specials and a hot chocolate with lots of whipped cream for the girl?"

McNitt was behind the bar. He wore a billowing red Hawaiian shirt to cover his substantial girth. With his white beard and bald head, he was a perfect department store Santa, but for one thing—he'd scare the kids.

"All glory is fleeting," McNitt called back.

"Can I color?" the girl asked Reatta. Reatta nodded. The girl plopped her unicorn bag on the table and took out some paper and crayons.

"Reatta came to me when I was doing some rounds downtown," Father Bob said. "She's just gotten a room at the Lindbrook Hotel on Sixth. But she's facing life on the street again."

"They won't take my rent for next month," Reatta said.

"What are they charging?" I asked.

"Four hundred a month. For a hundred and fifty square feet." Her brown eyes scanned my face. They were searching, maybe for somebody to trust.

"And they've told you that you have to move out?"

She nodded.

"Why don't they just take the rent money?" Father Bob asked me.

"It's called the twenty-eight-day shuffle," I said.

"Sounds like a dance."

"It's a dance around the law, is what it is. Here's how it works. Downtown hotel owners shuffle their people in and out, to try to establish that they're a commercial tourist hotel, not a residential hotel. That way tenant protection laws don't kick in. So they say to people like Reatta here that she has to move out, stay out for a week, and then she can come back."

"So this is better financially for them?"

"Not necessarily."

"So why do it?" Father Bob asked.

"Because, my mass-saying friend, a commercial hotel property can be sold to a developer with very little red tape. Said developer can then turn said hotel into fancy lofts for sale to downtown professionals. That way, everyone makes money. Except the people who used to live there. They end up on Skid Row."

"Very nice. And you say this is illegal?"

"If you can get somebody to do something about it."

"What about the DA or the city attorney?"

"They've sued a couple of owners. But that's it. The downtown developers have a lot of power. So it's left to public interest law firms to try to take up the cases. But the hotels have big firms behind them. I know. I used to work for one of those firms."

"Is there anything you can do for her?" Father Bob asked.

I looked at the girl who was busy coloring her paper. To Reatta I said, "Do you have anyplace to go if they don't accept your rent?"

She shook her head. "A shelter is all. I hate those places."

She had good reason to.

"How many more days do you have?"

"Seven."

McNitt delivered the drinks. The little girl perked up at the sight of a cup with a mound of whipped cream on it, a Pike's Peak of delight.

The other three coffees were McNitt specials. He called them Gandhi lattes. Said they promoted nonviolent resistance.

Kylie took a lick and got a little whipped cream on her chin.

"Tell you what," I said. "I'll take a trip down there later this afternoon and talk to the manager. See what I can find out. But if I do this, I'll need a retainer."

Reatta frowned.

"I'd like to have that picture Kylie's been drawing," I said.

The girl looked at me and smiled. "Okay," she said. "But it's a secret."

"I can keep secrets," I said.

She pushed the paper across the table to me. It showed two stick figures, one big and one small, holding hands in the upper part of the paper. My razor-sharp mind figured that to be Kylie and Reatta. A squiggly line came out from them and snaked all across the page, down to the right hand corner. In this corner Kylie had drawn several items of what I took to be candy.

Because she had written *Candyland* there.

"A map to Candyland," I said. Razor-sharp mind again.

Kylie put a finger to her lips. "Shh! It's a secret."

4

BEFORE HEADING DOWNTOWN, I stopped at the Van Nuys jail. Earlier that week I'd agreed to see Gilbert Calderón, twenty-eight. His mother, who came to mass at St. Monica's almost every day, found out about me from Sister Mary.

Señora Calderón, a cheerful woman the shape of a gas pump, begged me to take the case. Gilbert was in for murder and she didn't trust the PD's office. They let her son go to prison once before, she said. Didn't put up a fight, she said.

Maybe your son does bad things, I almost said, but didn't.

So I went to see him. He was being held without bail. Soon he'd be transferred to the Twin Towers, near Chinatown, to await the preliminary hearing.

They brought Gilbert into the attorney room, shackled and in his carrot suit—the orange coveralls reserved for high-power inmates. Those accused of murder, mostly. They sat him down and attached him to the table.

Gilbert Calderón had all the marks of a gang *veterano*. Dark prison tats on his neck. Survival eyes. Lines at the corners from beatings taken and given. A hardness around the cheeks, as if his skin had been stretched by strong hands. A white scar under the chin.

But he was smiling. One of his front teeth was gold.

"Hey man, thanks for coming," Gilbert said.

"Don't thank me yet," I said.

I took out a copy of the police report I got from the PD's office. Five days before his arrest a couple of robberies were committed in the Valley in the span of half an hour.

The first robbery occurred at Fornay's Flower Store on Sherman Way at 11:38 a.m. Twenty minutes later a Baskin-Robbins store on Topanga was hit.

It wasn't ice cream they found on the floor.

When police arrived at the scene they found Simindokht Roshdieh, forty-two, dead, and her husband, Firooz Roshdieh, bleeding from the head.

Witnesses from both locations filled in the facts. An employee of Fornay's, Denise Barr, described the robber as Hispanic, with short black hair and brown eyes. She thought he was in his early to mid-twenties, around five feet, ten inches in height, weighing between 140 and 170 pounds.

She told investigators the man wore a long black trench coat, tan pants, a tan scarf, and black and white Nike running shoes. She stated he had tattoos on his neck, possibly letters. At the time, Barr thought the man was dressed "inappropriately for the weather," which she described as "warm."

According to Barr, the man approached her at the cash register and politely asked, "Will you open the register, please?" Barr did not immediately respond and the man repeated his statement. At the same time he removed a gun and pointed it at her. Barr then opened the register and the man stepped around the counter, reached into the register, took the money. On his way out of the store, he grabbed a balloon from one of the displays.

"What about that?" I asked Gilbert.

His smile was long gone. "I wouldn't do no dumb thing like that if I'm robbin' a store."

"What dumb thing would you do?"

"Hey man, ain't you my lawyer?"

"Not yet. Let's go through the rest of this."

Heather Dowling, another Fornay's employee, told police she had just returned from her break when she noticed a Hispanic man with a short haircut standing behind the counter. The man told her to "stop, stay" and pointed a gun at her. As he left the store, Dowling noticed a tattoo on the back of his neck that "looked like a name of someone or something."

"What's it say on the back of your neck?" I asked him.

"Consuelo." He turned around so I could see the tat. Then back to me. "High school, man. Love. Lasted all summer."

"So this witness Dowling was right about that."

"You know how many *vatos* got names?"

"Let's keep going."

At the Baskin-Robbins store a customer named Byron Horne said he was about ten yards from the entrance when he noticed a Hispanic man wearing a black trench coat walk in. He saw several tattoos on his neck. He described the man as five feet, six to eight inches tall and weighing around 160 pounds. He heard two shots and saw the man run out of the store. Horne ran into the store and saw a bleeding Firooz Roshdieh, who was screaming, "Call nine-one-one!"

Horne called and a team was dispatched. No suspect was arrested that day.

Relying on the wits' descriptions a homicide detective named Sean Plunkett searched a law enforcement database containing records of convicted criminals with tattoos. Gilbert's name surfaced in connection with his detention at the Mexican border in February 2001. Border authorities had arrested Gilbert and photographed his tattoos. Plunkett learned that Gilbert had been detained with a woman named Nydessa Perry. He checked on Perry and found out she was on federal probation following a conviction for distributing crack.

A day later, Plunkett assembled a six-man photographic lineup. One of the photos was of Gilbert, taken from the California Department of Corrections.

Firooz Roshdieh identified another man, saying, "I never forget those two eyes." Barr identified Gilbert. Horne was unable to identify anyone.

Nydessa Perry was called in to look at the security camera images from the Baskin-Robbins store. She gave a positive ID on Gilbert.

Who was not surprised, considering what he told me about Nydessa Perry. No love lost there. He had dumped her because of her drug use, he said, and she swore she'd get him someday.

5

"SO YOU GIVE me your side now," I said. "Start with where you were that morning, when the murder took place. Can you do that?"

"Yeah," Gilbert said. "Got it clear in my mind, man. I was with Jesus."

I rubbed the bridge of my nose. "Gilbert, you have to trust me, okay? It's a lawyer client thing. Client trusts lawyer—"

"Hey, last time I did that, I ended up in the slams."

"And you probably lied to that lawyer too, am I right?"

He smiled again. "You're pretty good. I like you."

"Well that just makes my day, Gilbert. Now let's forget about Jesus for the time being and you tell me exactly where you were in the late morning hours of March twenty-ninth?"

"Under a tree, man."

"Tree?"

"In the park."

"What park?"

"I don't know, the one over there." He nodded with his head, having no idea which direction he was looking.

"Did anybody see you at this park?"

"Jesus." He smiled again.

"Anybody else?"

"I don't know, man. I was out."

"Why were you out?"

"*Cerveza.*"

"Did you drink alone? And don't say you were with Jesus."

"God and the Holy Ghost, too."

I rubbed my whole head now. Here is a retirement plan for criminal defense lawyers: Get a dime for every client who finds Jesus behind bars. And a nickel for every one who gets paroled then goes back to being what they were before.

"Focus, Gilbert. It's the morning and you're drinking beer, right?"

"It was still dark when I started."

"Why were you drinking?"

"Chase away the demons, man."

"Did it work?"

He shook his head. "I didn't kill nobody. You got to know that."

"But the DA, Gilbert. He thinks you did do it, and he's got some pretty strong evidence."

"What evidence?"

"Nydessa Perry, for one."

"Oh man!" Gilbert jerked his hands in the desk restraints. "She's a liar and crackhead!"

"Quiet down," the room deputy said. He was standing at the interview room door.

"So is that all you got?" I said. "You were asleep under a tree, no one saw you, and your ex-girlfriend is lying to get you?"

"Does that sound bad?"

"Like a garage band without the garage."

"Eh?"

"Just sounds bad."

Gilbert frowned.

"But we'll see what we can do," I said.

"You taking the case?"

"I said *we*, didn't I?" I stood up.

"Where you going?" Gilbert said.

"I do have other clients."

"You got trouble, is what you got."

I just looked at him.

"I see it in your face," Gilbert said. "So I want you to take care of yourself out there. You need any help, let me know."

I almost choked to keep from laughing.

"Just keep it in mind," Gilbert said. "We can talk. God talks to me and told me you were gonna get me out of here. Told me you were the man."

I stood up. "Then ask him where I can find a witness who'll corroborate your story. Get back to me on what he says."

6

I PULLED OUT onto Van Nuys Boulevard, getting a friendly wave from a guy standing on the corner with a cardboard sign. The sign read "WHY LIE? I WANT A BEER." I admired his honesty. He wouldn't have lasted long in the law game.

And he'd probably make more than I would for the foreseeable future. There are lots of ways to make more than I do. A woman once tried to sell me some gravel from Michael Jackson's driveway. She didn't need my green. I knew she'd find someone else who'd give it to her.

This land of dreams never lacks for schemes, and quick thinking to go with them.

Once, outside the Galleria, a guy in a dirty fatigue jacket with a gas can asked me for a few bucks. I said I'd go with him to fill up the can. He said no.

Three weeks later I was there again, and the same guy came up to me. I said, "Your car sure runs out of gas a lot. You hit me up last time I was here."

He blinked a couple of times. "That was my other car," he said.

In many ways, this town is an inspiration.

I guided my silver Cabriolet to the 101 Freeway. Fought the traffic downtown. Got to Sixth Street and Main around four-thirty. I parked at an overpriced meter and walked a block to the Lindbrook Hotel.

The Lindbrook was one of many single-room occupancy hotels for people on the economic fringe. It had a facade that looked like a movie theater from the twenties. It was six stories and had a fresh coat of dark gray paint. The fire escapes were candy apple red. Somebody'd had some fun.

Several of the windows that looked out on Main had little American flags taped on them or stuck in window planters. That told me that this was home to some vets. Viet Nam and Gulf War guys who never made it all the way back. There were a lot of them around the city.

The inside of the Lindbrook did not have a fresh coat of paint. As I walked into the lobby, I got a whiff of an odor no human being should have to endure. The nearest thing to it was the time I sat downwind of a three-hundred-pound Jabba at Dodger Stadium one fine summer night. He plowed down four Dodger dogs with onions and relish before the first inning was over. By the bottom of the second, my row was engulfed in a noxious cloud that could have bleached our shirts.

That was bad, but this was worse. A struck match would have blown the place up. The source had to be either the collection of old men sitting on old furniture in the old foyer, or a sulfur manufacturer next door burning down his factory for the insurance.

Afternoon light filtered in through the front windows, throwing weak beams of yellow on the black and white Chiclet floor. An old chandelier hung from a dark green chain in the beamed ceiling. A brown moisture stain spread out from where the chain was attached.

I was making for the reception desk, enclosed in Plexiglas like a bank teller's window, when I heard "MumbuddynomakenomubbamindGeneKelly" behind me.

I turned around. A tall, thin guy, maybe seventy years old, with beard stubble and a blue scarf around his head, made wild eyes at me.

"MumbuddynomakenomubbamindGeneKelly," he said.

"Sure," I said, and went back to my business.

The guy ran around in front of me. "Disco Freddy," he said.

"What?"

"Disco Freddy! Mr. Gene Kelly!"

His arms started whirligigging and his head shook like he was having a fit. Then he spun around three times fast and put his arms out in a "Tah-dah!" gesture.

"Gene Kelly!" he said.

An older gentleman in one of the chairs in the lobby clapped his hands.

"Terrific," I said and tried once more to go by him.

He jumped in front of me again. "Disco Freddy! Mumbuddynomake-nomubbamindFredAstaire!"

"Oh, I get it. Now you're going to imitate Fred Astaire."

Disco Freddy smiled and went into the same helicopter routine with his arms, spun around three times, and finished just as before. It was not an imitation that would have been recognized as a dancer in any known universe.

"Mr. Fred Astaire!" he said.

"That's just great," I said. "You do Donald O'Connor?"

"Disco Freddy!" he shouted.

"Paula Abdul?"

I tried again to get past him. Disco Freddy was too quick. He put his hand out.

"You want me to pay you for that?" I said.

"Disco Freddy," Disco Freddy said.

"Got to pay the man," the old gentleman in the chair said. He looked like James Earl Jones. Big, with a booming voice. Not bad for a guy who must have been seventy-five.

"Do you do birthdays?" I asked Disco Freddy. "Bar mitzvahs?"

"Disco Freddy!"

I fished out a dollar just to save myself some time. Disco Freddy took it, pocketed it, spun around three times.

"Mr. Rudolf Nureyev!" he said.

7

THROUGH THE HOLES in the Plexiglas I said, "I represent the tenant in room 414."

The fortyish man in the booth was about a hat taller than a Munchkin, with a slanted mouth that reminded me of the Lollypop Guild. His long hair was stringy and dark brown, like wheat pasta. He squinted at me like he didn't understand. A sign taped to the window said,

> *Rent Payable in Advance.*
> *Check Out On Time.*
> *No Refunds.*

I pulled out a business card, which Sister Mary had lasered for me. a couple of days before. All it said was *Ty Buchanan, Lawyer*, along with the p.o. box I rented from McNitt and a cell phone number. I put it in the metal tray. The Munchkin took it and squinted even more.

He shrugged. Turned to a big flat book on the table in front of him, like something out of Dickens. Opened it, flipped to a page, ran his little finger down the side, closed the book, and shook his head.

"Moving out," he said.

"Change of plans," I said. "They've decided to stay. I'm going to write you a check."

He shook his head.

"Yes," I said. "I'm going to give you the check for 414."

"Won't take it."

"You don't take it, you're in violation of the law. You understand that, right?"

His eyes opened wide and he gave me a steady look. Not friendly. Not wishing to welcome me to Munchkin Land. Like he knew more than he was letting on but wasn't going to let on that he did.

"You wait," he said, then scurried through a door next to the mailboxes.

I turned around and surveyed the lobby again. Disco Freddy was by the front window, sitting on the floor, his knees at his chest and arms around his knees. Resting before the next big show.

There were a lot of shows in L.A. these days. Especially down here near Skid Row. Hospitals were coming down at night, dumping mentals out on the street so the missions and private facilities could deal with them. That was also illegal, but the dumpers were good at picking their spots.

What it did was put more mentals on the streets of the city, to fend for themselves. Most preferred the street, where they could get drugs. This was a world far removed from the one I used to run around in.

That world was a big litigation firm on the west side and a nice house in the Sepulveda Pass.

And a woman I was going to marry.

Then she was killed. And I got set up for murder.

Suddenly I was one of the shows. You stay in this town long enough, it happens.

The man came back into the booth. He shook his head and slid a card through the tray to me.

When I looked at it I almost spun around like Disco Freddy.

8

IT WAS A business card. For a lawyer. The Lindbrook's lawyer.

Al Bradshaw.

My former colleague at Gunther, McDonough. We came up the ranks together. He used to be one of my best friends. Used to be.

I called him. His assistant put me right through.

"Ty? Is it really you?"

"Really and truly and in the flesh and wandering through downtown Oz."

"Howzat?"

"It's very strange here, Al."

He paused. "Boy, how are you?"

"Peachy," I said. "There's a karma thing going on."

"You coming back? You know McDonough would love—"

"I'm talking good karma. Like dragging your sorry client into court and stepping all over his face."

Pause.

"You're kidding, right?" he said.

"No," I said.

"You want to explain?"

"I'm in the lobby of the Lindbrook Hotel."

Pause.

"Can't say much for the bar here," I said. "But the floor show is aces. They got a guy here does Gene Kelly."

"You're at the Lindbrook right now?"

"Right now. And they're trying to give my client the twenty-eight-day bum's rush. You ought to tell them they can't do that."

Pause.

"Ty, this is really weird. How'd you get involved in this?"

"I have a client. I'm setting up shop on my own."

"Solo?"

"My bar dues are all paid up."

"Why don't you come on down and we'll talk?"

"Why don't you tell the management to take a check or the next stop'll be superior court?"

Pause.

"You're not being real congenial here, Ty."

"Why should I be? It's not complicated. Now I'm trying to think which client would be the one to own the Lindbrook. It must be one of yours, or Longyear's. I'm trying to remember. Would it be Orpheus? Somebody like that?"

Snort from Al. "Tyler, my friend, what are we doing, huh? What is all this? We've been through too much together. Let's go to Sombrero. Now. Just like old times. I'll buy."

"Al—"

"We'll work it out. The way all legal matters should be worked out, over a couple maggies and some chips."

"Al—"

"One hour."

9

ON THE DRIVE over I called Sister Mary. She works the office and is the best nun on the computer. She has a cell phone, too. St. Monica's is making a pilgrimage into the twenty-first century.

"Hello, Mr. Buchanan."

"Ty. Please."

"How can I help you?"

"What is this, Jack-in-the-Box all of a sudden?"

"Is there something you need?"

"I need to apologize for this morning. I got a little competitive out there. Didn't mean to get all March Madness on you."

"That's quite all right. I allowed myself to . . . I was partly to blame."

"But I saw a little of that Oklahoma stardom. You should've played college ball."

"Mr. Buchanan—"

"Ty."

"How can I help you?"

"I need you to look something up for me. The Lindbrook Hotel downtown. Find out about Orpheus Development Group, an LLC. My old firm handles them, through an associate there named Al Bradshaw. I don't know who the players are. But I recall a lawsuit filed against them about two years ago that may have named the parties. I want to find as many names associated with Orpheus as I can. Try the name Rood, too. You may not be able to turn anything up but—"

"Mr. Buchanan, I was programming computers when you were working on a manual typewriter."

"Sister Mary, may I remind you I'm not that much older than you? That they actually had real computers when I was a kid?"

"Oh yes. I saw some of those machines in a museum once."

"You're a credit to your religion, Sister."

"As you are to yours."

"You're a sweetheart."

"We don't often hear that one," she said, and hung up.

10

SOMBRERO ON PICO. A place Al and I used to frequent to get frequently hammered. Al because he was not happy at home. Me for a variety of reasons that didn't apply anymore.

It's the place where I first met Jacqueline Dwyer. And where things started that I couldn't stop. Where life fell off a cliff. Which is why my nerves were on high alert as I went inside.

Al was waiting for me at a table, his coat off and tie loosened. Already working on his first margarita.

"Hey, look at you," he said, offering his hand. "No work clothes for you, huh?"

"These are my work clothes," I said. "I'm working right now."

"For a tenant at the Lindbrook. A woman calls herself Reatta."

"Well *too shay*," I said. "You actually did some work for a change."

"Love you, too. What are you drinking?"

"Straight Coke."

"Come on."

"With lemon."

Al motioned for the waiter, who came over in his white shirt, black vest uniform. "A large Coke with lemon slices," Al said. "Chips and guac."

The waiter scurried away.

"How you making out?" Al said.

"Like the Lincoln conspirators."

"Huh?"

"Hanging in there."

"Good," Al said. An embarrassed pause thudded into his margarita. "I know this place has a lot of memories for—"

"Let's talk about Orpheus Development Group," I said.

Al tried not to flinch. "You guessing or telling?"

"Educated guess. Orpheus has plans to gentrify the Lindbrook. Am I right?"

"You know I can't say anything about that."

"Then why'd you get me down here? Ply me with chips? You think I'd lie on my back and let you rub my tummy?"

"No—"

"Who's the guy, the front man for Orpheus? I'm trying to remember the names, but I never worked with them. Somebody named Rood or Rod or something."

"Ty, you know I can't talk about that."

"You'd be yapping loud if I filed and got to depose him."

"Come on! You're not threatening to file now, are you?"

"Why not? I have to keep fresh. Seems to me a good way to do it is to pierce the sham corporate veil and get some people before a judge."

"We could get you bounced like that." He snapped his fingers, but the sound was pretty limp. "You have a classic conflict of interest, having worked for the firm."

"I'd still have it before a judge."

"You're taking this awfully personal, Ty. Why?"

I ate a chip.

"You want me to tell you why?" Al said.

"No."

"Okay, here it is. You got shaken up pretty bad when Jacqueline died. I know that. Everybody knows that. You wind up in jail and you almost get killed yourself. It's like being in war. You have post-traumatic stress. You're not supposed to have your midlife crisis for another ten years or so. But you take it on early because of what happened. You wonder if you're doing the right thing at Gunther, McDonough. Maybe now—"

"Why don't you catch a breath."

"…maybe now you think you have to go out and rep the"—Al made quote marks with his fingers—"downtrodden. That's fine for a while, but sooner or later you have to come back to reality and common sense and shuffling the cards around on the table so everything works out."

"Are the cards marked?"

"Ty—"

"When did you go into psych, Al?"

The waiter returned with a fresh basket of chips, a bowl of guacamole, and my Coke and asked if we were ready to order. Al said yes. I said no. The waiter said he'd be back.

"Is that the way it's going to be?" Al said.

"I came here to listen. It's your show."

"All right. This is because you're a friend, okay? This is not a fight you want to get into. This is not something you can win. You know how it works. You know what we can do if we want to play hard. You know we can grind you down. We can make your life a living hell."

"Better to reign in hell than serve at Gunther, McDonough."

"What?"

"Nothing."

"Ty, be reasonable."

"Why don't *you* try it? You have a client who is breaking the law. Breaking. The. Law. Because he doesn't want the hassle of dealing with tenants who have actual rights. And he has you on a leash, the attack dog, and thinks he can scare people off."

"Don't do this, Ty. I'd hate to see us end up at each other's throats."

"We're there already." I took a chip and scooped up a golf ball–size chunk of guac. Pushed the whole thing in my mouth, washed it down with Coke. Stood and said, "Thanks for the dinner."

"Ty, wait."

I didn't.

11

IT WAS DARK when I got back to St. Monica's.

I'm still trying to get the hang of the community here. You don't find a lot of monasteries in L.A. You don't bump into a lot of monks at Trader Joe's.

This is a community of nuns who follows the Rule of St. Benedict, which is around fifteen hundred years old. They take vows of poverty, chastity, and obedience. They also have a vow of stability and try to be as self-contained as possible. One way they do this is by baking and selling fruitcake.

Frankly, I don't know how they stay in business.

They have a vow of "conversion of manners," which sort of turns the normal way people look at things upside down. You give instead of get, give up instead of smash the other guy.

Except, apparently, when playing basketball.

But the thing that sets them apart is a vow of hospitality, and that's where I come in. When I needed a place to hide out, here they were. Right in the mountains overlooking the San Fernando Valley. A nice big plot of land these Benedictines scored in the early days of the great ranchos.

Father Bob is the sort of resident priest, to say mass and hear confession and those sorts of things. Things I'm clueless on.

There are three types of nuns here. The nuns in charge are the baby boom generation, represented by the superior, Sister Hildegarde. These nuns don't wear habits, like you see on Ingrid Bergman in *The Bells of St. Mary's*. They wear, well, K-Mart style. Modest and right off the rack.

Then there's the younger ones, like Sister Mary Veritas. She's the youngest one here, in fact. They do wear the habit and don't like the Vatican II slide. They identify more with the third type, the older nuns, the ones Sister Mary calls "the greatest generation."

These are the nuns who gave their all to make religious life happen and they are largely forgotten now.

Once I asked Sister Mary why there were all these types of nuns running around. She said, "In community, there is room for diverse lifestyles and gifts. People think there's only one way to be a nun or sister or monk, but there isn't. St. Paul said there are different kinds of gifts, or charisms. And each one is given by the Lord for the good of the church."

"You know," I replied, " the legal system is sort of like that, only without the praying and without God."

Sister Mary says human weakness interferes with any system, even religious communities. The biggest tension being how the older nuns are going to be taken care of as they get closer to meeting their Maker. These abbeys never have enough money and—at least according to Sister Mary—there's not a big move to take care of their own.

The older nuns occupy a wing on the grounds of St. Monica's. Sister Mary and some of the young nuns spend a good part of their day there ministering to the graying veterans.

This does not always sit well with Sister Hildegarde. She just can't seem to wrap her head around the yutes. Why, she reasons, after all the reforms, would anyone want to go back before Vatican II? She looks at the younger nuns the same way an aging professor at Berkeley looks at campus Republicans.

12

"IS THAT THE young man about the toilet?" Sister Perpetua said.

She was sitting in the plain wooden chair in the middle of her tiny room. The room had a bed, a crucifix on the wall, a desk with a lamp, and that was about it. A window looked out to the night. From the direction I figured it was the eastern view, which was a large plot of undeveloped land owned by the abbey.

Land Sister Mary said ought to be used to build better facilities for nuns like Sister Perpetua.

Sister Mary had a folding tray with a wash basin behind Sister Perpetua's chair. The older nun's hair was short and full of soap as Sister Mary washed it.

"No," Sister Mary said, "this is Mr. Buchanan. He's a guest here." She looked at me. "A guest who should not be in a nun's quarters at this hour."

"I knocked," I protested. "What was I—"

"Does he know about the toilet?" Sister Perpetua was at least eighty and had brown eyes that looked like windows to a glorious past.

"Something wrong with the toilet?" I asked, sharp as ever.

"We'll take care of it tomorrow," Sister Mary said.

"Do you know about it?" Sister Perpetua asked me.

"Hey, I used to own a house," I said. "I know toilets."

Sister Mary scowled at me. "I don't think you want—"

"No problemo," I said. "I need to earn my keep around here—"

"You don't have to," Sister Mary said. "Believe me."

I took Sister Perpetua's hand. It was delicate, bony. "Sister, glad to meet you. I'm going to try to help you out."

"He's a nice young man," Sister Perpetua said.

"Yes," said Sister Mary, "but I don't think he wants to—"

"Of course I do," I said. "You just leave it to me."

"Mr. Buchanan—"

I touched my lips with my finger and went to the small bathroom.

Sister Mary had nailed it. I didn't want to.

The toilet bowl looked like a Jackson Pollock. Not something an amateur plumber should be mucking around in.

"No problemo!" I said. The only instrument available was a well-worn plumber's helper. I took up the plunger and held it over the bowl.

"He seems a nice young man," Sister Perpetua said in a stage whisper. "I hope he knows about toilets."

We're all about to find out, I thought.

I gave the plunger its baptism and started pumping. From the bowl came a gooshing sound, like an orc sucking flesh. This was why you go into law.

"Okay in there?" Sister Mary called.

I worked it a few more times and heard the same sound. The level of the Jackson Pollock went down a little. Success.

I pushed the flush handle. A pause of agonizing length followed. And then, Vesuvius.

"Uh-oh," I said. "A little help."

The contents came flowing out over the rim, like something out of a Technicolor fifties sci-fi movie. *The Blob That Ate St. Monica's.*

Sister Mary appeared at the door. I think she had a smirk. She grabbed the towel on the rack, threw it on the floor, then found another in a cupboard and used that too.

"Oops," I said.

"Christian charity does not permit me to reply," Sister Mary said. "I'll clean it up."

"No, let me—"

"You've done enough. Why don't you wait outside until I'm finished here. I have some information for you."

"You sure? I mean about me not helping."

"Oh yes. Quite sure."

I wasn't all that upset about getting out of the room of foul things. I was too embarrassed to say anything to Sister Perpetua. I just waved.

Just before I closed the door I did hear her say, "And he looked like a nice young man."

13

THE NIGHT WAS clear and a warm wind blew in from the canyon. I sat on the patchy grass in front of the unit and looked at the stars.

I remembered how my dad tried to teach me the constellations when I was eight or nine. He was a cop in Miami. He got me to see the Big Dipper and Orion's belt, but after that I was pretty lost. I didn't see how anybody could connect the dots and come up with a bear.

My dad was killed in the line of duty when I was a kid. For a couple years after that I used to try to find a constellation that might have been him.

Sister Mary came out and sat on the grass with me.

"So how bad was it?" I asked.

"Pretty bad," she said. "Remind me not to ask you to fix anything here."

"If it makes any difference, I really was trying."

"Sister Perpetua thinks you're the new janitor. She's a little worried the job may be too much for you."

"Maybe we can change the subject. Were you able to find anything out about Orpheus?"

"Yes. He was a Greek."

"What?"

"In Greek mythology. Orpheus descending."

"Son of Mr. and Mrs. Descending?"

"That toilet must have done a number on you."

"You have no idea."

"Orpheus was married to a woman named Eurydice. She died and was taken to the underworld. Orpheus went after her. He was a musician and was able to use his music to charm Hades, ruler of the underworld, who gave him permission to take Eurydice back up to the world."

"Must have been some good kind of music, like Duke Ellington."

"Whatever. Hades had a condition, though. He warned Orpheus not to look back to see if Eurydice was still there. Orpheus couldn't stand it and did look back before he got to the world. So Eurydice was snatched away from him. Later Orpheus angered some women of his city because he took no interest in them, and they ended up tearing him to pieces and throwing his head into the River Hebrus."

"Nice."

"So the question I have is, Why would a land development company name itself after Orpheus?"

"You have a guess?"

"I do."

"Go for it." I was more than a little interested. In the matter involving my murdered fiancée, Sister Mary had provided a crucial insight. She'd told me about the seven deadly sins and how at least one of them was going to be at the heart of any crime, and she named the two she thought it might be. She was right.

"Whoever is running Orpheus," she said, "or whoever dreamed it up, believes he can charm anyone with his music. Not literally, of course. But with whatever he uses to get people to do what he wants."

"Or she," I said. "Maybe it's a woman."

"How likely is that in the world of large development companies?"

"Not very," I said. "But just to keep the options open."

"I did find one name," Sister Mary said. "Hyrum Roddy. He is some sort of agent for Orpheus. Agent for service or something like that."

"Agent for service of process," I said. "Every corporation is required to have someone designated for official contact. Did you get an address?"

"Of course," she said. I could not see her face clearly in the dark, but enough of it was visible to show that little half smile. The one she got when she challenged me to around-the-world on the basketball court. Knowing she could shoot lights out.

"Sister Mary, if I ever get my own office, and you ever get out of this gig, maybe you'd come work for me."

The smile left her. "Mr. Buchanan, a calling is not a *gig*. It's not something I entered on a whim."

"I didn't mean—"

"I know you didn't."

"Dumb thing to say. Forget it."

She stood. "You need a calling, too. Everyone does."

"Who says I don't have a calling?"

"Well?"

"It's from the Latin. *Carpe denim.*"

Pause.

"Seize the jeans," I said.

She rolled her eyes. "Good night, Mr. Buchanan."

"Good night, Sister."

14

I DREAMED THAT night in my trailer.

They have two pretty functional trailers on the grounds here. One is for Father Bob. The other was empty and they let me use it. I can cook a little, wash a little, run a little electricity. I had a nice house near the 405 once. But stuff happens. At least I had some money in the bank. But money doesn't stop bad dreams.

In this one I was running away from a limo. It was chasing me down Hollywood Boulevard and even though there was traffic, it kept finding me. I even ran along the sidewalk, and the limo followed, scattering people.

It felt like I was running with ankle weights on. I ran down an alley that ended at a wall about a hundred feet high. The wall had caricatures on it of old movie stars. They were grotesque caricatures. Charlie Chaplin looked like a serial killer. Gable had a wicked smile.

The limo caught up with me. The door opened.

Someone got out.

It was the pope.

He was dressed in a tux. He asked me if I wanted to go to the Oscars with him. He opened the door of the limo and motioned me to get in.

Then I woke up.

And lay there for about an hour, listening to the night, wondering who I was and what I was doing here.

You're a real treasure, Buchanan. Taking up these fine people who actually believe in something, taking up their space and their good wishes. They want to save your soul, that's all, and you want to eat their food and live in their trailer. It can't end well.

Outside, the sound of the wind was the only thing I heard and it seemed like the only sound in the universe I'd ever hear.

15

MONDAY MORNING I went to see Fran Dwyer, Jacqueline's mother. Fran is the only person resembling a relative I have in L.A. She likes it when

I drop by. I make sure she has enough in the refrigerator and some books to read. She likes mysteries. Likes that Stephanie Plum.

When her daughter died, Fran had a pretty hard time of it. But she was getting stronger, month by month. She'd even taken on a part-time job, Tuesdays and Thursdays, with the media department at Cal State Northridge. She went in and filed and answered phones and entered data on the computer. Good for her.

She was tending her garden when I pulled up to the little house, fifties vintage, mid-century modern. Probably cost ten grand when it was first built. Now you could get half a mil for it.

Fran waved at me. She was wearing a sun hat and yellow cotton dress. She told me to go in the house and wait. Said she'd just be a minute with the zinnias.

I went in and got a strange feeling. As if Jacqueline were going to walk out into the living room, as vibrant and beautiful as ever. She'd run up and kiss me on the mouth and ask me where I'd been. I'd crack wise and she would laugh. We'd talk about marriage plans as we held hands.

My chest caved in as the feeling passed. I almost ran out to my car to get away.

Fran came in, wiping her hands on her dress. "Something to drink?"

"No thanks."

"Mind if I?" She went into the kitchen. Her energy level was up. A good thing.

I followed her. "How you getting along, Fran?"

"Fine," she said. "It's good to be around young people."

"Oh yeah? What are they into these days?"

Fran opened the refrigerator, took out a pitcher of what looked like iced tea. "Oh, you know, that stuff they call music. Whatever happened to the Beach Boys?"

"Sunburned," I said.

"Or some of the great singers. When I was little you know who I liked?"

"Who?"

She paused in the middle of pouring tea in a glass. "Don't laugh."

"Promise."

"Connie Francis. Now she could sing. *Where the Boys Are*—I was in love with that movie. She could eke out the sad notes in her voice. Oh my. Did you ever hear Connie Francis?"

"Sure," I said. "On an oldies sta—I mean, yeah."

Fran laughed. "I'm pushing sixty, kid. You can put me in the oldies category."

"Never."

She took a sip of tea and looked out the kitchen window. Sun dappled the yard through the spreading fruitless mulberry out there.

"Any big plans tonight?" I said. "Movies? Friends?"

Fran said nothing. For a minute I thought she saw something out there. A bird or squirrel. But then her head went down. She dropped her glass on the counter, spilling it.

I went to her. She was crying. She turned to me and put her head on my chest. I put my arms around her.

"I'm sorry," she said.

"No, no—"

"I just…"

"I know."

I held her like that for a moment. Then she gently pulled away and grabbed a dish towel from the rack. Put it to her face. I took the other dish towel and started mopping up the iced tea.

"I'm so sorry," she said. "I haven't done that in a while. I was just remembering. She used to like to go out in the yard by herself."

"I remember you telling me that," I said. "She'd eat oyster crackers."

"And grapes."

"Yes."

"And look at the sky and think and read. I can't even think how many times I'd see her there. I'd feel so good. She was so good."

"She came from good stock," I said.

16

I STAYED WITH Fran another half hour or so. She went back to her garden. I didn't like her being alone so much. Wished she'd socialize more. But grief takes its own bitter time.

I took Victory across the Valley and stopped in to see Hyrum Roddy.

He had a modest office in a once fashionable section of Studio City. There are several two- and three-story professional buildings there from the fifties and sixties. The fancier firms had long since moved west to Warner Center or south into Century City or Westwood.

Roddy's office was on Ventura just east of Laurel Canyon. It was a law building, one where sole practitioners rented offices and shared a receptionist. I passed one of them with a diamond tie clip on the way in—he was on the way out. There was a sign for available space. Maybe when I finished raking Roddy over the hot coals of moral outrage, I could see about moving in. I was sure Roddy would be thrilled.

The receptionist looked like she'd rather be hanging out at the Galleria than answering phones. I told her to announce me as Buchanan, a lawyer for a tenant at the Lindbrook.

She did. Put down the phone and told me to wait.

I sat on the couch and picked up an old *Sports Illustrated*. Read about a golf tournament Tiger Woods had won two months ago. And about the latest troubled life of a kid football player who had come out of college early, got the huge bucks, had a great rookie season, made the Pro Bowl, and raped a concierge in a Honolulu hotel room.

He grew up on the streets, they said. His father, who wasn't married to his mother, was killed when he was nine. His mother did drugs. Only football saved him. So you could understand that when he had it all, the demons would come roaring back. The demons never really left you, they said.

Tell that to the concierge, I thought.

A man in a white shirt and red power tie came into the reception area.

"Mr. Buchanan? I'm Hy Roddy."

He shook my hand. He was about forty, with a full head of salt-and-pepper hair and the practiced manner of a car salesman. "Come on back. I've been expecting you."

Expecting me? Al. Must have thought ahead, must have called him. That was Al.

Roddy had me sit in a black leather client chair in his office. There were papers and files all over. He used half his floor as filing space. Brown accordian folders overstuffed with manila tabs were jammed against each other like old phone books.

"I thought I might get a call first," he said. "I talked to Al Bradshaw yesterday."

"Good old Al," I said.

Roddy smiled. Again, practiced. "Yeah! Al's a great guy. Great guy. Golfing buddy. You golf?"

"Windmill-and-clown courses only."

"You ought to take it up. Great game. Great game."

He reached for something on his desk and picked it up. Absently, like it was something he twiddled with when talking on the phone. His eyes never left mine.

"Basketball's my game," I said. "The little white ball doesn't really do it for me."

"You get used to it. First few years I had a nasty slice. Last few years I've had a nasty hook. Eventually it evens out, if you work at it."

Now he was squeezing and unsqueezing the thing in his hands. I couldn't quite tell, but it looked like a little rubber animal of some kind. When he squeezed, something light brown protruded from the back end of the animal, then sucked back in when he let go.

"Well, I'd love to talk about Tiger and Phil," I said, "but that's not why I'm here."

"I know. You're here because you have a client, one of the Lindbrook people."

"You talk about them as if they were zombies."

"You ever been to the Lindbrook?"

"As a matter of fact."

"It's what they used to call the last stop." Squeeze. Back end outcropping. Unsqueeze. "The people in there aren't going anywhere, so it doesn't really matter if they are transferred out onto the street for a while and then come back."

"Except, of course, that it's illegal."

Squeeze.

I said, "Can I ask what that is?"

He held the animal up. "This? It's a pooping bear. Got it in Alaska."

"A pooping bear…"

He leaned forward. "Yeah, see? You squeeze it, and a little poop pops out." He demonstrated. "You let go, and it pops back in."

"Sweet."

"It's a gag thing, but it relaxes me."

"Bear poop'll do that."

Roddy set the bear back down. "Look, you practiced law over at Gunther, McDonough. You know how it works. The system is a machine. What is legal or illegal doesn't really matter. All that matters is that the machine runs, and as few people as possible get crushed."

"Except my client doesn't want to move, and she doesn't want to get crushed, either."

"That is so unreasonable. Talk some sense into her. Al filled me in on who she is. We're not running blind here. She's got a kid."

"She doesn't want to go out on the street," I said. "There's nothing unreasonable about that. You ever been on the street?"

"I know what it's like."

"You know about being on the street the way I know about golf."

He just looked at me for a moment. "Al tells me you're thinking of filing."

"If I have to."

"Then we just move to another part of the machine. And it all comes down to money. So let's go there now. What will it take to make this go away?"

"What if I told you it's not a matter of money?"

"It is always a matter of money."

He was right, of course. We both knew it. I was running around trying to be some white knight on a horse, and it didn't take much to return to the real world. He was making an offer, and I would have to go over this with my client. She'd probably end up taking the money, and the twenty-eight-day shuffle would continue to turn in downtown Los Angeles.

"What are you authorized to offer?" I asked.

"I'm not that far along yet, but what if we make it a month's rent? She can come back in a couple weeks and that will be that."

"And then?"

"We'll cross that bridge, so to speak."

"Maybe we should cross it now."

"Mr. Buchanan, let me tell you something. In golf, when you hit a shot out in a hazard, or miss a fairway and you're in the trees, there's an old saying. When you're in trouble, get out of trouble. Don't try to make the big shot, be a hero, try to get it all at once. Chip out onto the fairway and take your lumps and go from there. Why don't you take this little chip shot. Get out of trouble. You can continue the game later on, if you feel like it."

"I'm a full-swing kind of guy," I said.

"You can break a club that way," he said.

"Or whack somebody who gets too close."

He smiled. "Crazy sport, huh?"

"No crazier than squeezing poop from a bear, I guess."

His smile left.

So did I.

17

I DROVE DOWN to the Lindbrook and walked into the lobby. A different Munchkin was behind the glass. A woman this time. But she didn't look like a member of the Lullaby League. She was Asian-American and all business.

Nor did I see Disco Freddy. I was actually a little disappointed at that.

I took the stairs four flights and knocked on the door.

The little girl was glad to see me. Maybe having a visitor was a nice little break in their routine. She had been reading a book on the floor. I wondered why she wasn't in school. There were still truancy laws if they found you. Maybe the mother didn't want to be found. Or maybe she was doing her version of home schooling. Whatever it was, I didn't ask.

"I went to see a representative of the owners of the hotel," I said. "They don't want to have a big legal fight. They have offered to give you a month's rent if you won't make a stink."

"I'm not interested," Reatta said, her eyes flashing like a Spanish dancer.

"I can always go back, give them another number. Is there a number that would work for you?"

"No."

I was surprised but a little pleased by her attitude. "You mean you would rather fight this thing?"

"Mr. Buchanan, as you can see, I don't have much of anything. I never have. The only thing I have is Kylie."

"What about her father? What ever happened to him?"

"He went away," Kylie said offhandedly.

Reatta nodded.

"Do you know where he is?" I said.

Reatta looked like she didn't want to talk about it. I decided to ask her later.

"What about family?" I said. "Or friends?"

"Nothing," Reatta said. "We have no one else. It's just the two of us. I guess I'm tired of being pushed around. Just because people have more. More money. It isn't right. I want a TRO and then an injunction."

"Wow, you've really thought this through. You didn't happen to go to law school, did you?"

She laughed. "Hardly."

"You mind if I ask what kind of work you do?"

"I'm not right now. Looking." Clipped, like she didn't want this to go any further.

Then she added, "Can you help us? I don't have money to hire a lawyer. I feel bad about asking you. If you decide you can't, I won't hold it against you."

"Don't worry about that. Just think long and hard. This trouble is something that can go away quite easily."

She looked at her daughter. "But what will that be teaching her? I want her to learn to stick up for herself. I want her to learn how to fight."

I liked her.

Kylie looked up from her book and said, "I want to fight."

I liked her, too.

"Okay," I said. "We fight."

18

TUESDAY MORNING I put on a suit and tie. I was going to court.

In California a defendant is entitled to a preliminary hearing within ten days of arraignment or plea. In a murder case it's usual to continue the prelim, which means to put it off until everybody's happy enough to go forward.

The only unhappy one is the defendant, who gets to cool buns in jail while the lawyers dance around.

When the prelim finally rolls around, the DA tosses in some evidence and the judge almost always says there's enough to justify a trial. The legal threshold is low and judges don't like letting defendants off the harpoon without a trial. It doesn't do their election prospects any good to be sending defendants home without a trial or plea deal.

They hope that setting a trial date will be a good incentive for a defendant to cop a plea and take the paperwork off the rolls.

Which is good for most defendants, who are, in fact, guilty. They get a lesser sentence and everybody goes home.

But if you're innocent it's a different matter.

I didn't know what Gilbert was at this point, but I decided not to waive time, for two reasons.

The first reason was a little inside information on the judge in Division 104. Her name was Noreen Anderberry and she had once been a public defender. This is rare among judges, who these days are usually drawn from the ranks of the prosecution.

I thought if I could cast enough doubt in Judge Anderberry's mind about the lineup ID, there was an off chance she might let the thing go. That didn't mean Gilbert would be off the hook. The prosecutor could always refile. But they'd have to refile with more than they had here, and they wouldn't be able to get it.

The other reason I wanted to go forward was so the prosecution didn't have more time to get ready. Catch them with their knickers down, so to speak.

In other words, roll the dice and look for that seven.

Then the deputy DA walked in.

19

HIS NAME WAS Mitch Roberts. He was my height and had toxic eyes. The prosecutors who handle capital cases are like that, I was told by a law school friend, one who worked for the Public Defender's Office. They mean business, he said. They mean to put people on death row, on the gurney with the needle. They don't play around. And what are you doing trying criminal cases, you idiot?

Good point. When Roberts came over to me and stuck his hand out, I thought, this is a guy who owns courtrooms.

"Buchanan?" he said.

"How you doing?" I said.

He smiled. "Saw you on TV." Lots of people saw me on TV when I was accused of murder. That profile was not going to go away.

"How'd I look?" I said.

"Like you do now. Nervous."

"Once I get going I'll be okay."

"You were a civil lawyer. Ever do criminal?"

"Some."

"Trials?"

"Once. Small company, a CFO cooking the books."

"Criminal's a different gig. Homicide's different than that. Capital is a world all its own. Think you're up to it?"

All right, the macho game had begun. Chest thumping. Looking for the advantage. That was right in my wheelhouse.

"Just call me Fast Eddie," I said.

"What?"

"Ever see *The Hustler*? Paul Newman?"

"What's that got to do—"

"There's a scene where he's going to play billiards with a guy, only he's never played it before. He plays the pocket game. So his manager, played by George C. Scott—"

"Look, Buchanan—"

"…tells him they're leaving, but Fast Eddie says, Hey, it's the same. It's a table and it's balls, you just have to get the feel of it. And he wins."

Roberts looked at me, unimpressed. "You want to plead him out now?" he said. "We'll take off the special circumstances—he can do life."

"That's some sweet deal," I said.

"It's not going to get any better."

"Let's shoot some pool."

20

JUDGE ANDERBERRY WAS reed thin. Not workout thin. Almost anorexic. She was in her late fifties and had been on the bench fifteen years. My research also turned up that she liked the theater. She was on some board connected with the Taper. Maybe I'd do a little acting.

She had glasses on a beaded string around her neck and a big blue copy of the California Evidence Code in front of her on the bench.

Gilbert Calderón was sitting next to me at the counsel table. I'd gotten him some clothes to wear so he wouldn't be in orange for the hearing. The shirt was long-sleeved to cover the gang tats.

Just before the judge spoke Gilbert whispered, "Everything's gonna be all right."

I looked straight ahead.

The judge put her reading glasses on and called for the lawyers to state their appearances. We did. Then Roberts called the LAPD detective who investigated the crimes to the stand. Sean Plunkett was fifty-one and resembled a Rottweiler.

I knew what he'd say because I had his report. He went over the events meticulously, like he was trained to. After forty-five minutes I got to cross-examine.

Most lawyers don't know how to do cross well. They let the witness repeat the direct testimony, or ask open-ended questions that invite the wit to explain to his heart's content.

Which is why I wince when I see TV lawyers asking, "Why did you do that, Mr. Johnson?" on cross. Mr. Johnson usually folds on the show. In real life, Mr. Johnson will likely put another nail in the coffin of your dying case.

So I had a focus for my cross, and it went like this.

"Detective Plunkett," I said, "you are the one who interviewed Firooz Roshdieh, is that right?"

"Yes," he said.

"And that was at one-thirty-two p.m. on the day of the incident, correct?"

"Yes."

"At which time you asked Mr. Roshdieh for a description of the shooter, correct?"

"Correct."

"According to your report, Mr. Roshdieh said the shooter was over six feet tall, is that right?"

"Sometimes the stress of a—"

"It's a yes-or-no question, Detective."

"Objection," Mitch Roberts said. "Let the witness finish his answer."

"The answer is nonresponsive," I said.

Judge Anderberry, her reading glasses perched on the end of her nose, said, "This is a prelim. I'll allow some leeway. The witness may answer."

Looking like he'd just scored a Milk-Bone, the Rottweiler said, "The stress of having a gun in your face, of having your wife shot, sometimes renders the description skewed toward a larger recollection."

"Ah," I said, "sort of like a shaving mirror?"

"It's just stress. In all other aspects, his identification was consistent with the defendant."

"That calls for a conclusion," I said. "Her Honor will make that determination, not you."

"Your Honor," Roberts said, "does defense counsel have to lecture the witness and curry favor with you?"

"Ooh, *curry*," I said.

"Approach, please," Judge Anderberry said. "Without the reporter."

The DDA and I went up to the bench, where the judge peered down at us like an owl. "Now, Mr. Roberts, let's try to keep the personal out of this. And the same goes for you, Mr. Buchanan. I understand you're both trial tested, but remember, this is just a prelim and you don't have to pose for a jury. In fact, you don't have to pose for anybody. I don't even think the press is…"

She stopped and looked toward the back of the courtroom.

Roberts and I turned around.

Everybody in the courtroom seemed to do the same.

At an attractive nun, in full habit.

21

"WHAT IS GOING on?" Judge Anderberry whispered.

"I know her," I said.

"You know this nun?"

"Yes. She's like an assistant."

Roberts and Anderberry looked at me, astonished.

"What can I say?" I shrugged. "She's good."

"Well, is she here to talk to you?" the judge said. "You want to have her at counsel table?"

"Talk about currying favor," Roberts said.

"Not to worry," Anderberry said. "I'm Episcopalian." She called for a ten-minute recess and told me to straighten out what I wanted to do with the nun.

22

"WHAT ARE YOU doing here?" I asked Sister Mary. We were seated at the counsel table. Gilbert had been taken to lockup.

"I wanted to see you in action," she said. "And maybe I can help."

"You want to see me…"

"In action."

I felt like Tom Sawyer in front of Becky Thatcher. I wanted to show off. Then I reminded myself that this was the Superior Court of the State of California and a man's life was on the line.

"This is a public building," I said. "I guess I can't keep you out."

"Do you want to?" she asked. "Do you want me to leave?"

"Don't you have prayers or something? Or fruitcake duty?"

"I am using my discretion here. Besides, I have been praying for you this morning. I wanted to come down and see some of them answered."

"Oh yeah? Well maybe you can pray me up the real killer, huh?"

"It's worth a try."

"Try."

"Anything else?"

"Lunch."

"Excuse me?"

"We'll have a lunch meeting," I said. "I am going to treat you to the finest meal you've ever had. Get ready for it."

23

WHEN THE JUDGE came back everyone seemed to have accepted the presence of the holy spectator, and we got right back to it.

"When we left off," I said to Plunkett, who was back on the stand, "I was asking you if Mr. Roshdieh said the shooter was over six feet tall. Did he?"

"Yes."

"Now, you arranged for a photographic lineup, did you not?"

"Yeah," Plunkett said.

I took a copy of the photo lineup from my briefcase. The photographs were numbered one through six. Gilbert's photo was number four.

"I show you what is marked as Defense Exhibit 1. Do you recognize that?"

"Yes. It's a copy of the photographic lineup I put together for the witnesses."

"And what number is Mr. Calderón in this lineup?"

"Four."

"Did you have Mr. Roshdieh look at the lineup?"

"Yes."

"And this was one day after the shooting, was it not?"

"Yes."

"Not under the stress of having a gun in his face. You didn't have a gun in his face, did you?"

Judge Anderberry warned, "Mr. Buchanan."

I put my hand up. "Sorry, Your Honor. Let me ask it this way. Detective Plunkett, you brought this lineup to Mr. Roshdieh at his residence, is that right?"

"Right."

"He was not under stress then, was he?"

"His wife was killed the day before."

"Did you note in your report that he was under some stress?"

"No. It's a given."

"Unfortunately," I said, "it's not. What you don't have in the report doesn't get to come in now."

"Mr. Buchanan," the judge said, "the witness may offer another recollection. I can decide what weight to give it."

"Of course, Your Honor. I was just pointing out that the witness may be adding some recollections now under...great stress."

"Objection," Roberts said.

"Sustained," Anderberry said.

"Detective Plunkett," I said, "according to your report, Mr. Roshdieh identified photograph number six, isn't that correct?"

"Yes."

"And he said to you—and I quote"—I got the report from counsel table and read it—"'I never forget those two eyes.' Is that what Mr. Roshdieh said?"

"That's what he said."

"No further questions."

24

ROBERTS CALLED DENISE Barr to the stand next. She was the For-nay's Flower Store employee who had given the most direct identification of Gilbert based on the photo lineup. From this I guessed that Roberts was going to wait to call Nydessa Perry. If he could avoid it, he would.

So the cross of Ms. Barr would be crucial.

She was a thoroughly credible witness. Thirty years old, pleasant look-ing, even tempered. She ran through the events of that day without a hitch. A Hispanic male, dressed too warmly for the weather, with short hair and brown eyes. According to Barr, he "politely" asked for money, and when she didn't immediately respond, he asked again and pulled a gun on her. That's when he stepped around the counter, took the money, and walked out of the store, grabbing a balloon on the way.

Roberts asked her if that man was in the courtroom. She pointed at Gilbert.

Then the witness was turned over to me.

Another rule of cross, one that is constantly violated, is that direct at-tacks are almost always counterproductive. Unless you have the witness dead to rights, caught in a lie, or someone so unsympathetic no one cares what you do, it's best to be as gentle as Mr. Rogers.

"Good morning, Ms. Barr," I said.

"Good morning."

"I'd like to ask you just a few questions about the incident, all right?"

"All right."

Of course it was all right. But I wanted her to know I wasn't going to try to chew her foot off.

"Now, according to the police report, you stated that the robber had tat-toos on his neck, possibly letters, is that correct?"

"Yes, I saw letters."

I frowned—a well-placed frown is good—and looked at the police re-port. "According to the report, your words were 'possibly letters.' Do you recall telling that to the police?"

"I thought I just said 'letters.'"

"Do you think maybe the police got it wrong?"

"Objection," Roberts said. "Calls for speculation."

"Sustained."

"Let me ask it this way," I said. "What is in the police report is at odds with your testimony, isn't it?"

"I don't know."

"You have seen neck tattoos before, haven't you, Ms. Barr?"

"Yes."

"Now, when the suspect drew a gun, we know from the testimony of Detective Plunkett that you must have been under great stress."

"Objection."

"Sustained."

"You were under great stress, weren't you?" I said.

"I suppose I was."

"You suppose?"

"Yes."

"Have you ever had a gun pointed at you before that day, Ms. Barr?"

"No."

"It surprised you, didn't it?"

"Of course. Yes."

I looked at the police report once more. "Now, when you looked at the photo lineup, you did not immediately identify Gilbert Calderón, did you?"

"No, I—"

Before she could finish, Roberts was on his feet objecting again.

"On what grounds?" Judge Anderberry said.

"We'd better approach," Roberts said.

25

BACK WE TROTTED to the bench. Roberts was hot. "Mr. Buchanan has asked a question of the witness which he knows there is no basis for."

"What's he mean, Mr. Buchanan?"

"I have no idea, Your Honor."

"Oh please," Roberts said. "There is nothing in the police report stating she did not *immediately* identify the photo. He made it seem like there was. He deceived the witness and he asked a question that has no basis in fact."

"But it did have a basis in fact," I said. "You heard the witness say *no* when I asked her the question."

"And I want that answer stricken, Your Honor."

"Wait," I said. "I have an idea. Let's make a movie of this little charade and call it *An Inconvenient Truth*."

I caught a little smile on Judge Anderberry's face, then a quick attempt to stop it. "All right, Counsel, let's calm down. It seems, Mr. Roberts, that Mr. Buchanan did something we see too little in criminal court these days. It's called good lawyering. There's always a little theatricality involved in a good cross-examination. Personally, I'd like to hear where Mr. Buchanan is going with this witness. Your objection is overruled, Mr. Roberts."

Very few times in my career have I wanted to kiss a judge. This was one of them.

I went back to Ms. Barr like the gentle kitten I was. "I had just asked you, Ms. Barr, your hesitation in identifying Mr. Calderón. It took you several minutes, correct?"

"Yes, I—"

"Thank you. I have no further questions."

"I do," Roberts said. "May I redirect?"

"Yes," the judge said.

"Ms. Barr, you took several minutes because you were being careful, isn't that right?"

I shot to my feet. "What's not right is leading the witness. Your Honor, why don't we just have Mr. Roberts take the stand?"

"That's quite enough," Judge Anderberry said. "Mr. Roberts, that question was improper and you know it. But somehow I have a feeling I know what you're going to say now."

I loved it. The judge was having fun with the prosecutor.

Roberts didn't flinch. Instead he asked the obvious follow-up. "Ms. Barr, why did you take several minutes to identify the defendant?"

"Because I was being careful?"

The judge smiled. I smiled. Instead of just answering as she had been all but instructed by Roberts, the witness answered with a question. Like she wasn't sure what to say or how to please the prosecutor.

I looked out into the gallery at Sister Mary. And winked.

Did I just wink at a nun? There's got be some divine judgment for that.

"One more question," Roberts said. "Is there any doubt that the man who robbed you at Fornay's Flower Shop is the defendant?"

"None," she said.

"No more questions," Roberts said and quickly sat down.

26

ROBERTS CONFERRED WITH someone sitting next to him at the counsel table, a blond-haired woman in a blue suit who had come in halfway through the prelim.

Then, with a look of some resignation, Roberts stood and said to the court, "We are ready to submit this, Your Honor."

Judge Anderberry looked at me. "Do you have any witnesses to call?"

I knew the rule was you didn't call your defendant at the prelim. But I toyed with calling Gilbert to the stand. If the case did go to trial, there wasn't much in his account that could hurt him, other than the fact that no one could vouch for him. And then—

Gilbert leaned over and said to Roberts, "Scum."

The judge slapped her hand on the Evidence Code in front of her.

A couple of people in the front row snickered.

I worked hard not to put my head in my hands. At least it wasn't something worse.

"The defendant is not permitted to speak," the judge said. "Unless he is under oath on the stand."

"Your Honor," I said, "Mr. Calderón won't be taking the stand."

27

I WAS READY with a citation for the judge. I read from a copy I'd made. "The evidence at the preliminary hearing must establish reasonable or probable cause, that is, 'a state of facts that would lead a person of ordinary caution or prudence to believe and conscientiously entertain a strong suspicion of the guilt of the accused.' The quoted language is from *People v. Slaughter,* Your Honor."

The judge nodded. "Continue."

"The language says '*strong suspicion.*' Not mere suspicion. I submit, Your Honor, that the People have not presented enough evidence to meet that standard. In both cases, the identification is suspect. Mr. Roshdieh identified a different photo. Ms. Barr finally did, but you saw how she testified. It wasn't exactly airtight assurance. She pointed at Mr. Calderón here in court, but she was more sure now than when she looked at the photo lineup. A memory does not get fresher with time, Your Honor. In short, there is no reasonable cause here to entertain a *strong suspicion* that Mr. Calderón is guilty of the crime charged."

When I sat, Gilbert Calderón leaned over to me and whispered, "You're not scum."

I leaned over to Gilbert Calderón. "Just don't talk."

Mitch Roberts argued his side and he was sharp, informed, persuasive.

Judge Anderberry slipped her reading glasses off her nose and let them fall to her chest on the beaded string.

"I would like to compliment both counsel," she said. "Strong arguments on both sides. Mr. Buchanan, you are an able lawyer, and if you can keep your client in control it will be a pleasure to have you. You have presented a very strong argument here. I have considered it. I have considered the testimony and demeanor of the witnesses and…"

Dramatic pause. She had to be a frustrated actress.

"…I find there is probable cause to bind the defendant over for trial. Let's set a date."

28

"SO YOU LOST?" Sister Mary said.

"It's only round one," I said.

We were in the courtyard outside the building and had just stopped at my desired location—the Chicago-style hot dog stand.

Sister Mary looked at me, at the stand, and at the umbrella over the stand. "This is the finest meal you were talking about?" she said.

"You ever had a real Chicago-style dog?" I said.

"I don't think so."

The vendor was a short gray man with a walrus moustache. In a thick Chicago brogue he said, "You haven't lived, Sister."

"Drag 'em through the garden," I told him.

The vendor smiled. "Here's a guy who knows whereof he talks. This is my kind of guy."

He pulled out a bun and plopped a dog on it and started with the condiments, in the right order, starting with the mustard. When he got to the onions Sister Mary said, "I'd like some ketchup with that, please."

The vendor reacted like he'd been shot. He stopped his work, holding the half-finished dog in his left hand. He looked at me. "You better explain life to the sister. Because I am not givin' one a these up if that's what she's thinkin'."

Sister Mary looked stunned.

"You don't put ketchup on a dog," I whispered.

"Why not?"

"It's just not done," I said. "It ruins it. It's like…"

"It's like kissin' your boyfriend and he's got B.O.," the vendor said. Then quickly added, "With all due respect, Sister."

"Trust us on this one," I said.

"Aren't you allowed to have your own hot dog the way you want it?" she said.

"*No*," the vendor and I said at the same time.

"Do I finish?" the vendor said, holding up the bun. "Or do I dump it?"

"By all means, finish," Sister Mary said. "Far be it from me to cause a disturbance in the Force."

"That's the ticket," the vendor said. "I like her."

The man gave us two of the nicest-looking Chicago dogs I've ever seen, along with a couple of Cokes. We went to a bench.

I was about to take my first bite when Sister Mary said, "Hold it, bub." Then she crossed herself and said, "Bless us, O Lord, and these your gifts, which we are about to receive from your bounty. Through Christ our Lord. Amen."

She nodded at me and we began to nosh. After that first bite she made a face. It was a mix of beatific vision and fright. I figured it was the peppers.

She recovered and said, "Not bad."

"You'll get used to it. Once you do, you'll never look back."

"I thought you did well in there," she said. "Very *L.A. Law.*"

"*L.A. Law?* You were just a little thing."

"I had a poster of Corbin Bernsen in my room."

"Arnie Becker? He wasn't exactly a model of chastity."

"But he was so cute. Who did you have a poster of in your room?"

"Magic."

"Johnson?"

"Is there any other? He played like I wanted to play. But my mind kept writing checks my body couldn't cash."

"You still have a move or two."

"Thanks, I—"

The tinny sound of an ancient hymn interrupted us. It was Sister Mary's cell phone. She begged my pardon and flicked it open.

I took a huge bite and thought about Magic Johnson in game four of the 1987 championship against the Celtics. The baby sky hook. The ultimate game winner. I wondered if I had one in me for Calderón. I thought I'd had a chance with Judge Anderberry...

Sister Mary's face lost all color. Frozen expression.

"What is it?" I said.

Tears started to trickle, then stream down her face.

29

WE GOT TO the Lindbrook an hour later. Two black-and-whites were parked in front on Sixth. Father Bob and several others were milling around on the sidewalk. Gawkers passed by and paused, looking in. Free show.

"I haven't been able to get any information," Father Bob said. "They herded us out and won't talk to us. I told them I was a priest, but they didn't let me in. All we know is that she's dead and no one knows where Kylie is."

Father Bob had come here to visit Reatta, to see how she was getting along. He'd managed to ask several of the other residents if they'd seen the little girl, but they hadn't.

"Wait here," I said.

"I'll come with you," Sister Mary said.

Father Bob nodded. "Me too. Tell them we're clergy. Do your lawyer thing."

That's the noise I was trained for, so I waved them along. The moment we stepped into the lobby a uniform stopped us. "No entry, sir," he said.

At least he called me *sir*. I was still in my court clothes. "I'm the lawyer for the victim," I said. "Who's in charge?" I showed him my card.

"You're the lawyer for somebody at this hotel?"

"Who do I talk to?"

"This is a secured site, sir," the officer said. Polite but firm.

"There's a girl involved, a little girl. Do you know where she is?"

"I don't know that, sir. If you'd like to wait—"

"I wouldn't like to wait. I want to know where the girl is. And I want access to room 414. Now."

The cop looked behind me. "Who are they?"

"Clergy," I said. "This is her priest. He wants to administer the last rites. You cannot keep them out."

"Sir, I can't—"

"Do you want me to cite the California Code on this? And State and Federal Constitution? But worse, do you want this splashed all over the news? How you let a soul go to hell because you denied the victim her—"

"All right, all right. Just wait." He turned around and spoke into a handheld.

I looked at Father Bob. "Was that enough noise for you?"

He smiled. "Well done, though technically it's not the last rites. It would be a prayer after death."

"So sue me," I said.

"That's your job," he said.

The uniform turned back to me and said, "Come with me."

30

THE DETECTIVE IN charge introduced himself as Lieutenant Brosia. He was around fifty and wore a beige coat over a white shirt and dark blue tie. His brown hair was neatly combed. He looked like he pushed weights to keep in shape.

We were just outside the door of room 414. I could see a couple of other people moving in the room. Crime scene team.

"I don't appreciate you throwing your weight around," Brosia said. "We can't release the body. We're treating this as a homicide and there'll be an autopsy."

"I'm here with her priest," I said. "He wants to…do what he does."

"Which is what?" Brosia asked.

"A prayer for the dead, if you please," Father Bob said.

I said, "There's a little girl. Named Kylie. Six years old. Do you have her?"

"I'm afraid not. We've spoken to a couple of the residents and they have no idea where she is, either."

"You figure she was taken?"

"We don't know. You were representing this woman?"

"Yes."

"You can give us a full identification then? She had no ID."

"All I knew was her first name, Reatta."

"May I go in?" Father Bob said.

"I'm sorry, Father," the detective said. "This is a crime scene."

"This is a matter of a soul," Father Bob said. "I have a right to go in."

"I don't know about that," Brosia said.

Frankly, I wasn't sure what the law was on this. I said to Brosia, "Look, do you really want to draw a line in the sand over this? You want it to get out that the LAPD denied a poor dead woman a prayer?"

"Is that some kind of threat, sir?"

"Not at all. I'm looking out for both our interests here."

Brosia thought about it. "How long will it take?"

"Not long," Father Bob said.

"All right," Brosia said. "I'll allow you in. You will not touch anything. You will pray and then leave."

Father Bob and Sister Mary moved past me. Brosia let them in. When I tried to get in he put a hand on my chest.

"Not you," he said.

"She's my client," I said.

"You're a lawyer, not a priest, and that's a big difference." Brosia smiled.

I rolled my eyes and tried to think of a legal argument to get myself in there, but then decided it wasn't worth the effort. Maybe I'd need help from Brosia later on.

Brosia went in and I watched through the open door. I could see Reatta's body lying on the bed, fully clothed. Her head was at a slight angle, eyes open in death. I could see no blood. One of the CS team was clicking digital photos.

Father Bob knelt at the side of the bed, as did Sister Mary. As if they were taking over the room. Everybody stopped what they were doing.

Crossing himself, Father Bob said, "May Christ, who called you, take you to himself. May angels lead you to Abraham's side."

Sister Mary said, "Receive her soul and present her to God the Most High."

"Give her eternal rest, O Lord," Father Bob continued. "And may your light shine upon her forever. In your mercy and love, blot out all sins she has committed through human weakness. In this world she has died. Let her live with you forever. We ask this through Christ our Lord."

Sister Mary and Father Bob said, "Amen." So did the photographer.

They came back out and joined Brosia and me.

"Now," Brosia said, "who was she, Father?"

"I only knew her first name," Father Bob said.

"I thought you were her priest."

"I am."

"But you don't know anything else?"

"Maybe that was her full name," I said. "Reatta. No last name."

"Maybe," Brosia said. "But that doesn't help me much."

"Can you run prints?" I said.

"That'll be done," he said. "But they'll have to be in our system for a match. Sometimes people like this just fall through the cracks." He handed me his card.

I gave him one of mine. "We have to find the girl," I said.

"We have somebody on that," he said.

I looked at the body. "How was she killed?"

"I'm not going to get into that," Brosia said. "I would like you all to come down and make a statement for me. Anything will help."

"I want to know what you're going to do to find the girl," I said.

"I told you. We're doing what we can. Of course."

"I know what that means," I said. "She's not going to be high priority—"

Sister Mary touched my arm. "He said he would do whatever he could," she told me. "I think you should take him at his word."

31

HEADING DOWN THE stairs, I said to the nun, "You don't need to interrupt me again."

"You needed it," she said. "You were going to say something you'd regret."

"I can handle my own commentary."

"Just trying to help."

"Well don't."

"Listen." She stopped in front of me. "I care about finding her as much as you do."

Father Bob, farther along, said, "Come on, now. We can settle this outside."

When we got back out to the sidewalk I saw Disco Freddy. He was twirling in the street, right off the curb. The old guy who'd applauded for him was there, too. He looked at me with recognition.

I spoke out loud to everyone who could hear me. "Have any of you seen the little girl who lived in 414? Any idea where she could be?"

A few heads shook.

The old guy came to me and said, "I asked about her first thing. Nobody knows, man. She just up and disappeared."

"You see anybody around here who didn't look like he belonged lately?" I asked.

"Only like ever' day. This place is looser'n goose grease. My name's Oscar. I'll help if I can."

A guy with a gray ponytail and jeans and a large gut pushing a Western-style shirt said, "She was a quiet kid. I remember that."

Disco Freddy shouted, "NumbuddynomakenomubbamindDebbieReynolds!"

"Shut up, Disco!" Oscar shouted.

"Disco Freddy!"

"He thinks he's doin' a show at Candyland," Oscar said.

"Why'd you say Candyland?" I said.

"That's just the room downstairs. There's vending machines. Cokes and candy. We call it Candyland sometimes. Disco thinks it's a theater. Like Broadway."

32

I BLEW BY the uniform with a wave. He didn't try to stop me. Only this time I went for the stairwell and down to the basement.

It was a rec room of sorts. A few chairs and tables. Some cards spread on one of the tables. An old, warped Ping-Pong table in the middle. And against the far wall, two vending machines. One had candy and snacks. The other was courtesy of the Coca-Cola Company.

One corner of the room was taken up with a chaos of old furniture—upturned tables, cushions, benches—half of it covered with an old paint-spattered tarp. It was like someone had once decided to clean the place up then forgot about it halfway through.

It was also a place where a kid could make a fort or hiding place.

"Kylie?" I said. "Are you in here?"

No answer. I didn't get too close to the clutter. "It's me, Ty, the lawyer you and your mom met. Remember? Where you got a hot chocolate? And you gave me a secret map?"

Silence.

"I'm all alone. I'm not going to let anyone hurt you. I was trying to help your mom, and I'll help you. That's what I do. Are you in there? You want me to help you get out?"

A long pause. Then I heard a movement. A creaking under the tarp. Then the tarp itself moved.

"It's okay, Kylie. It's going to be okay."

A foot peeked out of the enclosure, in a little tennis shoe. Followed by the other, then Kylie's tiny form backing out and into the open. She was covered with dirt and dust. She had her little pink backpack on one shoulder. She rubbed her eyes. "I'm hungry," she said.

"Then we'll get something to eat," I said. "Come on." I went over and picked her up. She let me, leaning her head on my shoulder.

"My mommy's dead," she whispered.

"Yes," I said. "I know."

"Don't let him get me."

"No. I won't."

Then she started to cry. Softly at first. Then it grew. Her body shook and I was the only thing she had to hold on to, so she held. I stroked her hair and let her cry it out. Her warm arms squeezed my neck. As they did, a rippling heat expanded outward from inside me. It made me nervous, like I'd been hand selected for an elite team I wasn't qualified for, some Delta Force dropping into a jungle battle zone. Then nerves melted into resolve. I'd never been a father. But now, filled with something primal, I knew what it must be like to have a daughter who comes to you in the night, frightened of darkness or dream, and you are the one she seeks, and you know you will do anything to protect her. Anything.

I knew this without pause or analysis or Dr. Phil.

I just knew.

Then I carried her upstairs.

33

I ALMOST MADE it outside without getting stopped. My aim was to gather Father Bob and Sister Mary and get out of there. I could call Brosia later.

But the uniform saw me on the sidewalk and ordered me to stop. A crowd quickly gathered around, the denizens of the Lindbrook, even Disco Freddy, and started making noises toward Kylie. Some cheering.

She buried her head deeper in my chest.

"Back off!" I shouted.

Father Bob stepped in with a little more patience and gently pushed the people back.

A moment later Brosia appeared. "Let's get her out of here," he said.

"Where?" I said.

"My office. Central. It's a couple blocks away."

"I want to get her something to eat first. Calm her down."

"I want her at the station, now."

"In a little while," I said.

"She's a witness."

"She's also my client. I'll get her to you soon enough."

34

THE FOUR OF us—Father Bob, Sister Mary, Kylie, and I—convened at a corner diner. Sister Mary took Kylie into the bathroom and cleaned her up. She came back tired and a little cranky. Kylie, that is.

She wanted pancakes. I ordered her pancakes.

"We'll go talk to the policeman in a little while," I said to her. "I'll be with you the whole time, okay?"

Kylie nodded.

"And then we'll go to a place where all three of us live, and you can stay there with us."

I gave a quick look to Father Bob and Sister Mary. Both had *Wait till Sister Hildegarde hears about this* looks on their faces.

Kylie said, "Will the man find me?"

"No," I said. "We won't let him find you. The police will catch him."

That was going to be the thing now, keeping Kylie safe and calm until we could decide what to do.

After we ate I sent Sister Mary back to St. Monica's with Father Bob. She said she'd get a room ready for Kylie.

Then I drove Kylie to Central Division on Sixth Street, parking in front.

"Is this where the police live?" Kylie asked.

"Some of them," I said.

She held my hand as we walked in.

35

DETECTIVE BROSIA WAS accommodating. He didn't fight me about being with Kylie during the interview.

She sat on my lap in the interview room. Had her arms around my neck and held on to me. I put her little pink backpack on the table.

"A couple of things," I said, "before you start."

"Go," Brosia said.

"If she gets tired, we end the interview."

"Fine."

"You need to know some things. I was at the Lindbrook last Friday. The victim was a tenant and they weren't going to let her stay. It's illegal, and I called them on it. They put me in touch with their lawyer. His name's Al Bradshaw, works for Gunther, McDonough & Longyear. Now she's dead."

"You saying there's a connection?"

"I'm saying that's what happened. You can follow up."

"Thanks. Anything else?"

I asked Kylie if she needed anything to drink. She said she would like some orange juice, please.

Detective Brosia brought her a Styrofoam cup with orange juice in it, and a cup of coffee for me. He sat at the table.

"Kylie," he said, "can I ask you some questions now?"

She nodded tentatively.

"You don't have to be scared. Your friend Mr. Buchanan is here. Okay?"

Nodded again.

"I'm a policeman and I have to try to find the person who did the terrible thing to your mommy, okay?"

Nod.

"Can you help me?"

Nod.

"Can I look in your backpack?"

Nod.

Brosia took the backpack, opened it. Poured out the contents. Some crayons and paper fell out. "Is that all?" he asked.

Kylie nodded once more.

Brosia put the things back in the pack and said, "All right. Were you in your room when your mommy got…hurt?"

Nod.

"Where were you?"

Kylie thought a moment, then whispered in my ear, "The closet."

"She says she was in the closet," I said.

"Can she talk to me?"

Kylie shook her head.

"I think I'd better translate," I said.

Brosia frowned. "Now that's a new one on me. Doesn't that present a hearsay problem?"

"Not for investigatory purposes," I said. "It'll be all right. I'll swear to everything on the statement."

Brosia shrugged. "We'll go with it, then. So Kylie, you were in the closet?"

Kylie nodded.

"Why were you in the closet?"

She whispered to me. I said, "She plays and sleeps in the closet. It's like her room."

"Did you see what happened to your mommy?"

Kylie whispered that she saw a man. I told Detective Brosia. It continued that way, with me as the go-between.

"How did you see the man?"

"There's a crack in the door."

"You mean the closet door has a crack down the middle because it folds, right?"

Kylie nodded.

"Was it dark in the room?"

"Mommy had lights on."

"So you could see what was going on?"

"Some."

"Do you know how this man got inside the room? Did he walk in or knock on the door?"

"Mommy let him in."

"So your mommy knew him?"

She shrugged.

"Had you seen this man before?"

She shook her head.

"Can you describe this man?"

Kylie looked at me, confused.

"Can you tell me what he looked like?" Brosia said.

At this point Kylie drew some strength and faced Brosia. She answered him directly now. "I only saw his back. He had black clothes and a rainbow hat."

"A rainbow hat?" Brosia said. "Can you tell me anything else about the hat?"

Kylie shrugged. "Rainbowy."

"Lots of colors on it?"

Kylie nodded.

"Anything else?"

She shook her head. Brosia seemed frustrated.

Then Kylie said, "I can draw it."

Brosia scratched his chin. "That's not a bad idea. Do you want to use your crayons, Kylie?"

"I'm tired," Kylie said.

"You're doing great," I said. "A real champ."

36

KYLIE TOOK HER crayons and drew a pretty good rendition of a man in a hat. She drew green and red and yellow rings on the hat.

"It looks like one of those Rasta hats," Brosia said. "I think we have one in the evidence locker. Hold on another minute."

He left again.

Kylie sighed.

"Almost done," I said. "Then we'll go to a place where you can see the mountains and the sky for miles."

"Really?"

"Yep."

"Is it a hiding place?"

"Sort of," I said. "It's not a place a lot of people know about. It's where I'm staying right now."

"I want to stay with you."

"Then that's how it'll be."

Brosia came back in holding a knit Rasta hat with the distinctive color rings.

"That's it!" Kylie said, surprised and a little scared. "Is the man here?"

"No," Brosia said softly. "This isn't the same hat. But this is like the one the man in the room wore?"

"Uh-huh."

"That's pretty distinctive," I said. "Somebody at the hotel should have noticed that. Somebody sitting in the lobby, or the desk clerk."

Brosia said, "What color skin did the man have?"

Kylie thought about it. "I stopped looking."

"I think she's about through," I said.

"Just a few more questions." Brosia leaned forward. "Did you see the man hurt your mommy?"

Kylie shook her head.

"Could you hear what was happening? Was there an argument or a fight?"

"There was talking but I couldn't hear."

"Then what happened?"

"There wasn't talking for a long time. I went to sleep."

"How long did you sleep?"

Kylie shrugged.

"When you woke up, what did you do?"

"I came out and saw Mommy on the bed. I said her name. But she didn't wake up. I ran to Mr. Hoover."

"Mr. Hoover who lives across from you," Brosia said.

"Uh-huh. And he came in and he said Mommy was dead and he went to get the police."

"What did you do?"

"I got scared and I went to Candyland and I hid."

"Candyland?"

"It's the lower-floor room," I said. "With a candy machine. She had a little hideout there. That's where I found her."

"How'd you know she'd be there?" Brosia said.

The question was a little too pointed for my taste. "I figured it out," I said.

"We'll have to talk about that," he said. Then to Kylie, "Did your mommy have many men friends who came to visit?"

She shook her head.

"Did your mommy and you ever talk about men coming to see her?"

Kylie shook her head.

"How long were you living in the hotel?"

"I don't know." She had started whispering the answers for me to repeat again.

"Was it longer than a year?"

"I don't know."

"How old are you, Kylie?"

"Six."

"Did you have a birthday party when you turned six?"

"My mommy gave me some cake with a candle in it."

"Just your mommy?"

"Uh-huh."

"Were you living in the hotel when your mommy gave you that cake?"

Kylie nodded.

"What's your last name, Kylie?"

She shrugged.

"What was your mommy's whole name?"

"Just Mommy."

"She didn't have a last name?"

"She said we could just be Mommy and Kylie."

Brosia frowned, wrote something down. "What about your daddy?"

Kylie whispered to me, "I'm tired."

"That's it for now," I told Brosia. "She needs some sleep."

"I'm not finished yet," he said.

"Kylie is," I said. "I'll be in touch."

He paused, then nodded. "See that you are. What about notifying Family Services?"

I shook my head. "I'm her counsel and guardian-in-fact. Last thing she needs is county services."

"Can't argue with you there," Brosia said.

"You wouldn't want to," I said.

37

OUTSIDE THE STATION, just before we got in the car, Kylie tapped my leg. She motioned with her finger for me to bend down.

"I didn't tell him about the picture," she said.

"What picture?"

"Of Mommy. I didn't want him to take it away. Am I bad?"

"Show me the picture," I said.

Kylie took her backpack and unzipped a pocket. Pulled out a photograph. It was a little wrinkled around the edges.

Showed a smiling, attractive woman.

"Your mommy?"

Kylie nodded. "Can I keep it?"

"Sure you can," I said. I'd make a copy of it and send it to Brosia. It didn't have any evidentiary value that I could see. "But can I keep it for you for a little while?"

"Okay," Kylie said. "If you promise to give it back."

"I promise."

She started crying then, into my hip. In her little muffled voice she kept saying she wanted her mommy. I knelt down and let her cry it out for a while, then wiped her tears away with my thumb.

"You did real good today," I told her. "You're brave, did you know that?"

She sniffed and shook her head.

"Well you are," I said. "You need to know that."

38

I DROVE HER back to St. Monica's. She fell asleep on the way. I carried her onto the grounds and found Sister Mary in the office.

Sister Mary said she had a cot in her room. "It's better if someone's around when she wakes up," she said.

I agreed and carried Kylie to Sister Mary's small room and put her on the cot, then covered her with a blanket.

"What's going to happen now?" Sister Mary said.

"I start making trouble for some very rich people."

39

I GOT TO the Starbucks in Westwood Village at ten the next morning.

They were playing "L.A. Woman," by the Doors. I hadn't grown up with the Doors and knew about Jim Morrison only by watching that movie Val Kilmer was in. Didn't much care for the gastric squeal of "mojo risin'" over and over. I would have preferred shoving pencils in my ear.

Al came in about ten-fifteen. All smiles.

"This is more like it, bud," he said. "Just like old times. Glad you called."

"I figured I'd buy you a foamy frothy white chocolate froufrou," I said. "That was your drink, wasn't it?"

"Triple venti white chocolate mocha."

"What's that do to your heart?"

"Makes me know I'm alive. When I'm at home I'm not so sure."

"And how is the lovely wife these days?"

"Same old."

"Still not the Norman Rockwell type, are you?"

He shrugged. "Norman Rockwell was probably a serial killer. You never know."

I got him his drink and refilled my regular and paid the ransom. At least by this time the Doors were gone and some good jazz was going.

"So I was sorry to hear about the death of that woman," Al said.

"The murder, you mean."

"Sorry to hear about it. Really."

"Sure."

"Sorry because she was your client, bud. And a human being."

"She was a human being that had to live like a rat. In a hellhole your client owns. Only you don't let the rats stay in the hole a full thirty days, and that makes it illegal."

"There are several issues to that—"

"Don't start getting all lawyerly on me, Al. I was always better at it than you anyway. There's *issues* when you don't want to do what's right. When everything's on your side, the law and the facts, suddenly the issues go away. That's the way the game is played."

Al bit down gently on his lower lip, like an amateur poker player hoping to fill a straight. It was the slightest tic but enough to give me a sense of well-being. Truth was, I didn't mind playing a little hold-'em with Al, just to see him sweat.

"What did you call me down here for?" he finally said. "Lecture me about the law? Way I see it, anything we had to say to each other is now moot. You had a client and that client is, unfortunately, dead. Yes, she was a tenant at the Lindbrook, and you could have filed something, but now that's gone."

"Convenient, isn't it?" I said. "If I were of an Oliver Stone bent, I might even say your client had an interest in making the problem go away."

"Tyler, my friend, don't do this. Don't go getting yourself into a lunatic state of mind. This is the big city—stuff happens. It happens a lot to people like that woman, out there on the streets. We wish it wouldn't but it does."

"She has a little girl," I said.

Al frowned. "Did I know that?"

"You should have."

"How old's the girl?"

"Six."

"Where is she?"

"I've got her."

"You? What are you going to do?"

"Protect her. And her rights."

"She's your client?"

"I'm guardian ad litem." That's a fancy Latin phrase for someone who stands in for an infant or child in a legal matter.

"Well that's just great, Ty." Al picked up his drink as if he were making a toast. "You are a good man, taking care of the little ones. Where's she living? With you?"

"Her permanent residence is the Lindbrook."

Al froze with his cup halfway to his face.

"Yeah," I said. "Isn't the law great? She can assert her right, by way of yours truly, to continue to occupy room 414 at the Lindbrook Hotel. The law is *wonderful*." I toasted him with my cup.

"You are not serious."

"Do I look like Adam Sandler to you?"

Al's hand was actually shaking a little when he put his cup down. "Don't do that," he said. "You don't need to do that. We can work out a settlement right now. You and me. You can get a nice chunk for the girl. Think about that. Better than—"

"Who's behind all this, Al?"

"What?"

"You're going to a lot of trouble to protect somebody. And you're worried what'll happen if I find out. You're worried that this Lindbrook thing is going to blow up in somebody's face, and maybe you'll get singed yourself. Is that about it?"

He shook his head. "You were a lot easier to work with when you weren't so sold on yourself."

"Maybe I'm just not for sale," I said. I wanted to believe that.

Al tapped his cup lid with his index finger. "What's with all this nickel-and-diming now? There's no future in that, not for you."

"And you know what's for me, is that it?"

"We've known each other a long time," Al said. "We've worked together before."

"Yeah. Remember the Morocco suit?"

"Sure," Al beamed, as if he was proud of it.

The Morocco case was a lawsuit fueled by two monstrous egos with enough money to thump their chests like twin Kongs. Arn Bunting, the billionaire oil man from Texas who had made inroads as a Hollywood producer. And Duane Dollinger, the best-selling author on whose novel the movie *Morocco* was based.

The movie's budget ballooned to a staggering $170 million. The critics massacred it. On opening weekend it took in a mere $18 million, finishing third behind the latest Pixar animation and a Will Ferrell comedy. The movie never got legs, even though it had two A-list stars for the leads.

Dollinger threw a fit and blamed Bunting for the loss, which hurt Dollinger's hope for a franchise based on his series character. Bunting shot back that Dollinger had abused his right of approval over the script. Seven writers had worked on it at one time or another, and Dollinger had hated them all.

Our firm represented Dollinger, a sixty-five-year-old fireplug who told us he would keep on throwing money at us until he had cut off the two things that Bunting, as a man, would rather keep.

"What I remember about that," I said, "was the week Dollinger testified. Here was a guy who was living large in Arizona, had a loyal following, who messed up his own movie and was now spending his time in a spite fight. He wouldn't settle. He wanted to get to a jury, tell his story. His greatest story ever, starring himself. And he had the money to do it and we gladly took it, didn't we?"

"And why not?"

"I thought, as I watched this guy, what would it be like if he was just some average doofus who really got ripped off? He'd never be able to be here, to get the representation we could give him. Even if he was in the right. It galled me then but I pushed that aside. I wasn't supposed to think about it. Well, I've been thinking about it. Money shouldn't be the only thing that talks."

"You're being naive now, Ty. In the law, costs and benefits are the only thing that matter. You can put a value on anything, and that's the way it should be. It's more efficient that way."

"Well, as the great philosopher Steven Wright once asked, if one synchronized swimmer drowns, do all the rest have to drown too?"

Al just looked at me.

"I don't like drowning, Al."

"Wait a minute," he said, now looking like he'd drawn that straight and was ready to go all in. "I see. You think there could be some connection between this chick's murder and Orpheus. You really do, don't you?"

I said nothing.

Al was happy to go on, tilting his head back as if telling a joke to a packed house. "Yeah! You got this idea you're some kind of Bogart or something, and you're gonna find a conspiracy. Yeah, Ty Buchanan, supercop."

"I want Depp to play me in the movie," I said.

"This is so funny except that it's not."

"Then let's get a serious offer on the table. Here it is. You instruct whoever is calling the shots at the Lindbrook to accept rent on behalf of room 414, and every other renter who makes the request. You have until four-thirty today to give me your answer. If it's not the answer I want to hear, then I'll be at the courthouse tomorrow morning when it opens for business and present the clerk with a complaint that names Orpheus and Roddy. Have I made myself clear?"

Shaking his head, Al said, "Sad. Really sad."

"Four-thirty," I said.

"You have a tank of gas?" Al said.

"What's that supposed to mean?"

"I think you'll be taking a drive."

40

HE STEPPED OUTSIDE with his cell on his ear. I listened to the Ray Charles track, happy. That was more like it. That was real music and artistry.

Law was like that, too. A lot of art and jazz to it, despite what they tried to tell me at Gunther, McDonough. You can have all the law on your side, but unless you know what to do with it you can come off like a rube holding live wires in his hands. You might be the one who gets electrocuted. Or more likely your client.

Which is why you need to get past the games played at a place like Gunther, and the lawyers like Al Bradshaw who practice there. They've become like the machines in *The Matrix*, running off the juice of humanity. And draining it in the process.

To be a great lawyer, it was occurring to me, you have to feel something. You can't sleepwalk through a case or cause. You have to find the thing you'll die for.

A criminal defense lawyer has the hardest job, because he usually reps the guilty and the damned. So what's he supposed to feel? The Constitution, that's what—the guarantee that the government can't just shut you away because they don't like the way you look or what you say, but they have to overcome a big burden of proof, and if we lose that, boys and girls, we lose the only thing that stands between us and the exercise of pure will and mob rule.

This was the one thing Gilbert Calderón had going for him. His lawyer actually believed that.

But Al was right about one thing. I did think I could smoke something out by keeping Kylie on as a tenant at the Lindbrook. I did think there was more going on. It was a long shot, but the Red Sox finally won a World Series, right?

And a little part of me, the selfish part, the part Father Bob and Sister Mary hadn't been able to excise, just plain loved sticking it to Al Bradshaw.

Al came back in and sat down.

"You are being given one more shot."

"Of espresso?"

"Listen to me. You are getting a privilege not many people get. All I can say to you is, don't blow it."

"I'm all atwitter."

"You should be. You better be. You've got fifteen minutes to get to the top of Linda Flora Drive."

41

IN LOS ANGELES, the rich have always been able to carve out slices of exclusive heaven for their nests. They've always been able, with little effort, to hold back the hordes of merely well off and not-doing-too-well. The gates of their restricted habitations did not have to be made of iron bars. Time and land values do just as well.

Mostly land. L.A. was never a crowded hub of European immigrants in stuffy tenements working factory jobs. Early on, it was a sprawl of fashionable neighborhoods like Angeleno Heights and Bunker Hill and the Adams district. As these began to fray, wealthy developers expanded outward, to Beverly Hills and the new burg called Hollywood, with handy deed restrictions built in. No blacks. No Asians. No Mexicans.

By the time the courts stepped in and put the kibosh on such restrictions, the land had appreciated so much the "undesirable element" just plain couldn't buy in. Thus, the rich had erected barriers of gold every bit as effective as the impenetrable gate that met me just off Linda Flora Drive, at the home of one Sam DeCosse.

Or I should say, *one* of the homes of one Sam DeCosse, the billionaire land developer.

That was who I was going to see. That was the shot Al said I had. The one not to blow.

To blow it with Sam DeCosse was a one-way ticket to big trouble in little Catalina, which is the island you could see from the DeCosse property, along with a big stretch of ocean, the Getty museum, and about one-fourth of the world.

The gate at the end of the drive was like the one in *King Kong*. No one was getting in without the king letting you. Three security cameras in various positions stuck up from behind the gate, like those aliens from *War of the Worlds.*

I had to get out of my car and announce myself at the little box outside the gate. And wait. One of the security cameras moved, scanned me. I smiled at it.

Another minute ticked by. Then the gates swung open. I got back in the car and drove up to Valhalla.

That's right. That's what Sam DeCosse called his place.

42

FROM THE OUTSIDE, I guessed the house was maybe fifteen thousand square feet, Spanish architecture. Palm trees on the outside, almost like a mansion from the crazy twenties in Hollywood.

A weight-lifter type in a gray suit with pink tie was standing outside the front, waiting for me to pull up. He had brown buzz-cut hair and squinty eyes. As if he spent too much time in the sun.

If you were to open a catalog for mail-order bodyguards, he'd be the picture they'd have. He was not the valet. He did not offer to park my car.

I got out and nodded. "My name's Buchanan. I have an—"

"I know," the guy said. "I'll show you in."

I walked toward him and he requested that I stop. I stopped.

"I need to pat-search you," he said.

"Excuse me?"

"We have to be careful."

"So do I," I said. "I won't be patted by anyone I'm not engaged to."

The squint got squintier. "Sir, it's just a standard pat search."

"And this is just a standard 'you're not going to touch me,' pal. Deal with it."

For a moment he looked like he wanted to deal with it. Personally. But before he could, a voice said, "That won't be necessary."

In front of the door stood Sam DeCosse. I recognized him from the hair. DeCosse had one of the most recognizable pates in the country. His hair was the color of a polished penny, and no one knew if that was natural or not. He combed it in an impossible way that seemed to defy the laws of physics. The front swept halfway down his forehead, then back over itself, like a Malibu wave in reverse. Only an industrial-type lacquer could have kept it all in place.

When combined with his olive skin, the effect was striking. He was one of those people who walks in a room and sucks in all the energy. There was even a rumor going around a few years ago that Bill Clinton refused to be in a gathering with Sam DeCosse because he couldn't get the attention away from him.

"Come on up, Mr. Buchanan," DeCosse said. "Thank you, Devlin."

The bodyguard's jaw muscles twitched.

I smiled and walked up the path toward Sam DeCosse. He was wearing a fairway green golf shirt tucked into black slacks.

"Welcome to my home," he said.

43

THE FIRST THING I saw as I walked through the front door was a large bronze piece of what someone in an LSD flashback would have called art. It was a tangle of what looked like eyes and arms, looking or reaching toward stars and moons. It was Lucky Charms meets a fatal crash on the 101 Freeway.

"Like it?" DeCosse asked, striding into the foyer.

"Friendly," I said.

"I hate it. It's my wife's idea. Instead of a flower arrangement, you see, you get this, which is supposed to give a sense of the divine. She's the spiritual one in the family. A feng shui maniac."

"Maniac?"

He nodded, resigned.

"Doesn't being a maniac sort of defeat the purpose of feng shui?"

"Come in, won't you?"

He led me into a huge living room with lots of glass and light. The walls were painted fresh blood red, a little too garish for my taste.

As if reading my mind, DeCosse said, "The color is my wife's idea of her inner self. She's fiery and spontaneous. I'm the serious one."

"Should be at least one in every family."

"You should see the kitchen. It's a color called *robust eggplant.* Can you imagine that?"

"I can hardly imagine eggplant."

Another voice, a woman's, said, "Oh, I think you can."

I turned and saw a tall, striking honey blonde, mid-thirties. She wore a strappy orange top that was barely adequate to hold her most stunning feature. The feature was either nature's gift or the work of a surgeon, but most men would not care. She wore black yoga pants tucked into Koolaburra boots. Her eyes were green and her skin about as perfect as a baby's behind, if the baby were made of porcelain.

She came to me with hand extended. "I'm Ariel," she said in a breathy voice.

"My wife," DeCosse said. He was probably twenty years older than she was. Maybe he felt the need to explain.

"Glad to meet you," I said. "Ty Buchanan."

"Buchanan. Good strong name," she said. "You would be a sort of metal horse trough."

"Excuse me?"

"Yes, with running water for charisma and prosperity."

"I'm sorry?"

"Feng shui," DeCosse said.

Ariel said. "Do you have a passion, Mr. Buchanan?"

"Really good pastrami," I said.

Her face froze a moment. As if she didn't know what to make of me. Then she tilted her head back and laughed. A little too hard.

"I'll see if Maria can come up with something for lunch," she said. "You are staying for lunch?"

"I don't think so," I said. "But thanks. Maybe another time, when I need to get shuied."

She froze again. Then laughed again. Then said good-bye and left the room.

"She's something, isn't she?" DeCosse said. "She's got a life force going on. Wants to act."

"She's got the looks." Which put me in mind of the Anna Nicole Smith syndrome. Blond Venus marries older man for money, tries to get career in show business. Maybe that was unfair. Maybe they loved each other and she was the next Streep.

"She wants to do character work," DeCosse said. "She wants to be known for more than her looks. She did a play at one of these little theaters in Hollywood, some Russian play, by Gorky I think it was. She was totally into it. But I wouldn't mind if she landed a role on a hit series. It'd keep her occupied."

He turned his back as if to signal the end of that part of the conversation and walked me into a sun room. He motioned for me to sit, which I did on a futon covered in jade green silk.

"Thanks for coming on such short notice," DeCosse said. "I'm glad I happened to be in town."

"My luck."

"Luck has very little to do with anything, Mr. Buchanan. Luck is the coin of the loser, whether it's Las Vegas or life."

"Wow, did you just come up with that? Because that's pretty good."

"Maybe it's in one of my books," he said. "Which I write myself, by the way. I don't use ghost writers like certain other…"

"Billionaire authors?"

"Got no respect for that. You farm out your project to some hack for a fee, then you sign off on it and the publisher runs with it and everybody goes away happy. But you die a little inside. You have taken a slice out of your soul."

"That's very metaphysical of you."

"Surprised?"

"A little."

"Why?"

I shrugged. "It's not exactly what you're known for. You're known as the Chainsaw. You're known to cut down any and all obstacles in your path to clear the area for whatever you want to do."

DeCosse smiled. Perfect teeth, of course. "Did that come out of one of my PR kits or something?"

"Maybe you should hire me."

"Don't think I might not. You've got *huevos*. It takes 'em to work for me, and it takes 'em for you to be doing what you're doing. You used to work over at Gunther with Al Bradshaw."

"That's right."

"Why'd you leave? You sure you won't have something to drink? Let me make you a DeCosse."

"You have a drink named after you?"

"Would you expect anything less?" He walked to an oak credenza and pushed a button. The credenza opened like the Red Sea, and a bar setup appeared. Silver and crystal and clinking things.

"The secret ingredient is love," he said.

Okay.

He did some mixology, then came to me with two glasses with ice and something amber and fizzy. He handed me one and raised his.

We drank. Whatever it was had a gentle kick, like an eight-year-old girl soccer player.

"Bourbon's at the base," DeCosse said. "Bourbon built this country, did you know that?"

"Um, no."

"Not the overindulgence of it. That's for weak men. It's the men who could handle it, coming home after World War Two, who started in New York and proceeded to build the greatest nation on earth. They did it on bourbon and gin and guts. That was my father's generation. The greatest generation."

"Your father was a builder, too, wasn't he?"

"The best. Came back from the South Pacific and started kicking everybody's butt in New York. Bourbon was his drink, too. He knew how much he could hold."

DeCosse drank again and sat in a chair opposite me. "So you were going to tell me why you left Gunther, McDonough."

"Were you around last year when I had my little run-in with the law?"

"Run-in?"

"A minor tiff. I was accused of murder."

DeCosse paused mid-sip, squinted. "Ah! Now I remember. You're that guy."

"I'm that guy."

DeCosse shook his head. "Now I admire you even more. You beat that rap. That's hard to do."

"It's easier if you're innocent," I said. "The firm, of course, didn't believe in the presumption of innocence, and sent me packing. After the charges were dropped, Pierce McDonough asked me if I'd come back to the firm. I wasn't interested."

"What interests you now?"

"The hotel business."

He put his drink on the table next to his chair. "Then let's get down to the hotel business. Key word that, business. It means offering something that people will want to pay for, and doing it in a way that they keep wanting to pay for it. That's what I do, Mr. Buchanan. I create things people want and they pay me for it. Are you with me so far?"

"So far it's simple economics."

"But economics is rarely simple these days. You've got government interference and media interference. And then there's the worst sort of interference, the kind that gets really irritating."

"And that is?"

"The legal kind. You lawyers. I don't know what it is about law school, but there's brain damage inflicted there—takes away all your objectivity. I guess, like the mosquito, there's nothing you can really do about it. All you can do is swat at the individual mosquitoes as they try to suck your blood."

He made a picking motion off his arm and pretended he was squeezing something between his fingers.

"Now," he continued, "I have my own pond of mosquitoes that bite for me. You can't avoid it in this world. So when I come across a bright young bloodsucker like you, I say to myself, what would it take to have him in my pond? Surely that's a matter of economics, too."

He swirled the ice in his glass and took a sip, waiting for me to answer.

"Is there anything," I said, "that isn't a matter of economics?"

"Can't think of anything."

"You know, right and wrong."

"You can put a price on that, too. Now as I understand it, there's a minor problem involving one of my properties, and you represent that problem. What if I were to offer this interest one million dollars?"

"We'll take it."

"You see? And what if I were to offer ten dollars?"

"We'd say, Take a hike."

"So there you have it. Somewhere in between is an arrangement that can work for both of us. Quaint notions of right and wrong—these only get in the way of sensible men working for the best interest of all combined."

"I'll take nine hundred and ninety-nine thousand," I said.

DeCosse smiled and drank.

"And one other thing," I said. "I want whoever killed the girl's mother."

The smile melted. "What are you talking about?"

"Let's see if we can put an economic value on that," I said. "My client is a six-year-old girl who lived in the Lindbrook with her mother. A couple of nights ago somebody killed her mother. I want to know who."

"The police are certainly involved, are they not?"

"Yeah." I said nothing else, let the heaviness linger in the air.

"Well I don't see how that has anything to do with me or our talks."

"I thought you might be able to help."

"Why?"

"Maybe you know things I'd like to know."

"Mr. Buchanan." DeCosse put his drink on the table then rubbed his hands together, as if he were rolling clay snakes. "I don't know what implications there are in your attitude, but I find them to be counterproductive and rude. Doesn't have any place in our talks."

"Mr. DeCosse, you run a huge company and you sit up here on a very nice piece of property with your wife, fenging your shui through life. Maybe you don't know all that's done on your behalf. Maybe you have ways of finding out."

"You can't seriously be suggesting that someone associated with me would murder a flophouse tenant over some dispute about rent."

"I'm not suggesting anything. I just want you to know there's more to this than economics. Yes, I'll entertain a settlement offer on behalf of my client. You can have Al Bradshaw give me a call when you're ready. But it better be a good number, one that can take care of the needs of a girl for a long, long time. And it's not going to stop there. I'm going to find out who killed her mother."

"Fair enough," DeCosse said. He whipped a cell phone off his belt and pressed a button, then put it back in the holster. "You talk straight up. I like that. Reminds me a little of myself when I was your age."

I didn't quite know how to take that. "One thing," I said. "Your developments are huge. Why the interest in a crummy little hotel downtown? Even turning it into lofts, that seems smaller than what you're into."

"You're perceptive, Mr. Buchanan. Another point in your favor. I'll only say my reasons are my own, and leave it at that."

The door opened and Devlin the weight-lifting bodyguard—sounds like a kids' show—came in.

"See Mr. Buchanan to his car," DeCosse said. We stood. DeCosse did not offer to shake hands.

44

DEVLIN WALKED ME out to the drive. He kept half a step behind me, to my right.

I slowed down once. He slowed down.

"You don't act like an MBA," I said.

"Never played in the NBA," he said.

"I'm talking master of business administration. You don't have a basketball look."

"What sort of look do I have?"

I stopped. He stopped. I turned toward him. He didn't move.

"You look like a guy who enjoys hurting people," I said.

He smiled. His capped teeth glistened in the sun. In L.A. even the bodyguards get cosmetic surgery. "I enjoy a lot of things. Tennis. Women."

"And hurting people."

"Especially that."

A squeal of tires broke up the friendly chat. Coming up the drive was a red Ferrari, going way too fast. Just to be safe I jumped three feet to my left. Devlin didn't move, but he cursed real fine.

The Ferrari skidded to a dead stop, leaving about a foot of space between the grill and Devlin's knees.

Out of the Ferrari popped a guy with red hair. He wore dark aviator shades and a fawn-skin jacket open over a black knit shirt and blue jeans. A practiced casual look. I guessed him to be hovering around thirty.

"Hey Dev, what up?" Red said.

"Mr. DeCosse." Dev nodded but did not look pleased about having to do so.

Red looked at me and said, "How's it goin'?"

"Like a rapper with a new expletive."

Red blinked. "Who is this, Dev?"

"A lawyer."

I looked at Devlin. "Who is *this*, Dev?"

He said nothing. Red didn't look amused. "I'm Sam DeCosse."

"Junior," Devlin added.

"Hi, Junior," I said.

This clearly teed off Junior. His cheeks got rosy and blotchy. His freckles stood out like little pancakes.

"You're just leaving, I hope," he said.

"He's leaving," Devlin said.

"Good," Junior said, and blew on past me to the house.

Pregnant pause. "He seems like a fine lad," I said. "Cultured."

Devlin took a step toward me. "We may have a real talk sometime soon."

"I'll try to make it a two-way conversation."

"Look forward to it."

As I drove away, my body was buzzing. I'd been knocked around a few times in the past months, and a revenge lust was bubbling inside me like Charles Bronson's ghost. My adrenal glands got working whenever I thought this way. My heart pumped and my hands got sweaty.

This was not normal. Part of me didn't want to be, because normal got you kicked in the teeth.

But another part was fighting against Bronson's ghost. Against revenge. It was the part Father Bob said was my better angel.

I didn't believe in angels.

45

I DROVE DOWNTOWN to the county law library and did a few hours of research on landlord-tenant law. When I got back to St. Monica's, Sister Hildegarde was out in front of the office. She called to me.

Sister Hildegarde was from Our Lady of the Perpetually Put Out. She wore her gray hair short and her expression long.

"The little girl who's here," she said.

"Kylie," I said.

"Yes. She's been crying for you."

"For me?"

Sister Hildegarde nodded. "It's not uncommon in a situation like this. She has attached herself to you because she sees you as a savior."

I said nothing.

"Have you thought about how you might attend to her needs?"

"Needs?"

"She's a little girl. And she's now an orphan. As far as we know, she has no family, is that correct?"

"Right."

"There's her schooling, her medical needs, her long term. We'll have to get Family Services involved."

I shook my head.

"What's the alternative? Are you going to become her permanent legal guardian?"

"To be honest, I haven't thought that far ahead."

"Mr. Buchanan, one of the things I have to do, as the abbess here, is think ahead. We all must. I will offer you any help I can placing the girl in the proper—"

"What if she stays here? For the time being."

"How long would that be?"

"Until we can think this through a little more."

"She needs care. She needs someone dedicated to her well-being."

"We can all pitch in."

Sister Hildegarde frowned. Owlish. Like I was a field mouse. "Think about what you're doing. You'll simply be putting off the inevitable. Meanwhile, if she grows more attached to you—or anyone here—it will make the change, when it comes, all the more difficult."

She was right, of course. I just wasn't ready to admit it.

"I don't want the county involved," I said. "Everything they touch turns to—doesn't work out. Let's see if we can find a family on our own."

"And how do you propose to do that?"

"Hey, why don't you pray about it? And I'll look into the alternative? What a team, huh?"

Her stolid expression was a Rushmore of nonresponse.

"Thanks for your patience," I said softly. "Saint Benedict must be looking down now with a big smile on his face."

"Oh, you are smooth," she said. "No wonder you were such a good lawyer."

"Were?"

She didn't respond.

46

KYLIE WAS WITH Sister Mary in the conference room. When Kylie saw me she ran to me and threw her arms around my left leg.

"How you doing there, kid?"

"Okay," Kylie said.

"Sister Mary been taking good care of you?"

Kylie nodded. "We've been drawing pictures. I drew a horse."

"Yeah? I can't draw horses. Fact, I can't draw much of anything."

"I'll show you."

"Okay," I said. "You show me how to draw a horse."

I sat at the desk and watched Kylie work with the pencil. It was not a bad horse. A horse from a six-year-old, but you could tell what it was.

Mine was not so good. Kylie handed me the pencil and a blank piece of paper and I tried to make it look like what she had drawn. It looked like a giant pig.

"That's okay," Kylie said. "I wasn't very good at first."

I looked at Sister Mary. "She gives me hope."

"Hope is good," Sister Mary said.

"Let's try again," Kylie said.

We drew another round of horses. Kylie instructed me on how to do the ears and the tail. It worked. I was getting closer. At least I moved out of the pork zone.

The bells in the chapel started up and Sister Mary excused herself to pray. I took Kylie to the one comfortable piece of furniture in the office, a green sofa, and sat her down.

"You doing okay?" I asked.

"What's going to happen to me?" Kylie asked.

I sat next to her. "We're going to figure that out," I said.

"Can I stay with you?"

"For a while."

"I mean always."

"Me? Well, you wouldn't want to stick around with me. I'm too…flaky. Messy, too. And I'm a lawyer. You want to steer clear of lawyers if you can."

"I want to stay with you," she said.

"We'll do what's best, I promise." I hoped I could follow through on that. "Kylie, where did you and your mommy live before the hotel?"

She furrowed her brow. "In Avisha's house."

"Avisha?"

She nodded.

"Who's Avisha?"

"Mommy's friend."

"Do you remember where the house is?"

"By the ocean."

"Avisha lives by the ocean?"

Kylie nodded.

"Does Avisha have a last name?"

"I think so."

"Can you remember what it is?"

She shook her head, looking worried and disappointed. Like she had wanted to please me.

I patted her hand. "Don't worry. Just tell me what you can remember and it'll be okay. Tell me everything you can about Avisha."

"Avisha's nice."

"What does Avisha look like?"

"She has bright hair."

"Bright?"

"Uh-huh."

"What color?"

"Um, white."

"Is Avisha old?"

"Uh-uh."

"But she has white hair?"

Kylie nodded.

"How long did you live with Avisha?"

Kylie shrugged.

"If you needed to talk to Avisha, could you find her?" I asked.

"I don't know how."

"Did Avisha ever come visit you at the hotel?"

She shook her head.

"What kind of a house did Avisha live in? A big house?"

Kylie shrugged.

"Did anyone else live with Avisha?"

"James."

"Who's James?"

Kylie whispered, "Her boyfriend."

"What did James look like?"

"He just looked regular."

"He didn't color his hair?"

Kylie shook her head. "Except at the party."

"There was a party?"

"Uh-huh. We walked over to the beach."

"And James colored his hair at this party on the beach?"

"All of us."

"All of you colored your hair at the party?"

"We colored all of ourselves."

"You colored...with what, paint?"

She shook her head. "Just colored stuff. We threw it. It was fun. Everybody was laughing and hugging."

A picture of this wasn't really coming together for me. And it wasn't getting any closer to someone who could tell me more about Kylie's mother.

"I'm tired," she said.

"Okay," I said. "We won't talk anymore."

She leaned her head on my chest then and started to cry.

47

I PICKED HER up and held her and went outside.

I carried her to the parking lot, up to the edge, where we could look down at the Valley. The freeway stretched in front of us, headlights coming and going, red taillights the same. Beyond that the lights of the city were starting to appear. We could see all the way across to the Santa Monica range.

I said, "You know, I lost someone very close to me, too." I waited a moment and she started to calm. When she went to sniffling only, I went on. "Her name was Jacqueline and I loved her very much. We were going to get married. But then she died. And I cried, too."

Kylie wiped her nose with the back of her hand. "What did you do?"

"I found some people to help me. I found Sister Mary and Father Bob. And they've been real good to me. That's what's going to happen with you. You have some friends now, and we'll stick together and figure out what to do, okay?"

She paused, then nodded tentatively.

"Now look out there," I said. "Isn't that a great view? If you could fly straight out there you'd go over those mountains right to the Pacific Ocean."

"I like the ocean," she said.

"Maybe we'll drive over there soon. We'll play in the sand."

She put her head on my chest again and sighed. We were silent for a while. Then I put her down and we sat on the ground.

"What was your mommy like? I mean, what do you think about when you think about her?"

"Sad."

"What was she sad about?"

Kylie shrugged.

"Was she ever happy?" I asked.

Kylie nodded.

"What made her happy?"

"When I color. She likes to look at my pictures."

"They're good pictures."

She smiled.

"What else do you remember about your mom?"

Her smile faded and she shrugged.

"If I told you it might help us catch the man," I said. "Do you think you could tell me some more about her?"

She didn't say anything.

"Do you know anything about your daddy?"

Kylie shook her head.

"Do you know what his name is?"

"Uh-uh. Mommy never said. Only Avisha."

"Avisha?"

"Avisha said my daddy was odd."

There were a lot of daddies out there who were odd.

Kylie said, "Do you have a daddy?"

"I did."

"Where is he?"

"He died," I said. "When I was a boy."

"Were you sad?"

"Very sad. He was a policeman."

"I don't like policemen."

"Some of them are very nice," I said. "Some of them are trying to help us."

"I hope you're not sad anymore. It's not good to be sad."

"No," I agreed. "No good at all."

48

LATER, WHEN KYLIE was about to go to bed in the room Sister Mary had prepared, I went to check on her. She asked if I would stay and tell her a story. Sister Mary kissed her good night and went to the office, leaving me holding the story bag.

The bag was empty for a moment. Then I thought of one. It came from way back when my mom told me stories when I was about Kylie's age. She used to tell me about King Arthur and the knights of the Round Table. Always liked those.

"There was this boy in England, the son of the king, but he was taken care of by a magician named Merlin."

"Merlin?"

"Yeah. He had a long white beard. Anyway, the king died, and there had to be a new king. And there was this sword stuck into a stone. And whoever could pull that sword out of the stone was the king."

"Who pulled it out?"

"The boy. He was the only one who could do it. His name was Arthur, so he got to be the king. King Arthur."

"Wow."

"He was a good king. Do you know what a king does?"

"Sort of."

"In the old days, he ran things in his own country. He was the boss. Whatever he said, you had to do. So you could have bad kings who'd tell you to do bad stuff, and good kings who would tell you to do good stuff. And the good kings would also go around and fight bad guys."

"Bad guys?"

"Oh yeah. There's always bad guys. Even now. So King Arthur needed a special sword to fight with, so Merlin took him to this magic lake, and there was a lady of the lake."

"A lady?"

"Of the lake."

"Was she swimming?"

"No, she lived there."

"She lived in the water?"

"No, I think she had a condo. Anyway, she got a boat for King Arthur and he went out on the lake where there was this arm sticking up with a sword."

"An arm?"

"Remember, this was a magic lake. So the arm gave King Arthur this magic sword, and the sword had a name."

"A name?"

"Excalibur."

"Wow."

"Now," I said, "King Arthur gathered some very special knights. Do you know what a knight is?"

"I think."

"Like a soldier. A fighter. They had swords and horses and fought bad guys. So King Arthur built this big round table for all his knights to sit at. Knights got to be called Sir. So he had knights like Sir Lancelot, Sir Galahad, and Sir Loin of Beef."

I added that last one courtesy of Bugs Bunny.

"And they had this code," I said.

"Cold?" Kylie said.

"No, code. It's like rules. They did things that were right and didn't do things that were wrong."

"Like lying?"

"Yes. Like lying. And not being cruel. If somebody asked for mercy, they'd give them mercy."

"Mercy?"

"Yeah, it's like somebody says they're sorry, so you don't hurt them."

"That's nice."

I thought about the justice system. I thought about how nice it wasn't.

She fell asleep soon after that. I stood up and looked at her. If the word angelic means anything, it meant Kylie's face.

I'd never thought about having kids until Jacqueline. When I did, the idea of it seemed inevitable. The most natural thing in the world. A way to get complete, myself and the rest of the world.

I'd spent a long time living out the big hole my dad's death left in me. Jacqueline was the first person I ever met who could fill it. And then she died, too.

For a while I thought that was it—I'd never get back to humanity again.

Looking at Kylie, I had a glimmer that there was something alive in me still. A good thing. And I wanted it to last. I didn't want it to go away.

I tucked her in and went looking for Sister Mary. I found her in the office and filled her in on what Kylie had told me about Avisha and James and the colors and the ocean. Did it make any sense?

"No," she said. "But I'll chew on it."

"Chew well."

"It's what I live for."

49

FATHER BOB WAS enjoying a cigar on the front step of his trailer, which is next to the one they let me use. I saw the red tip of the stogie glowing in the dark. I sat next to him and he offered me one and I said not tonight.

"Winston Churchill almost single-handedly saved Western civilization," Father Bob said. "Do you think he could have done that without smoking ten cigars a day?"

"Gee, I don't know."

"A good cigar always helps. Relaxes and focuses the mind. Cuts through the clutter. You once told me you took a lot of philosophy in college."

"Yeah."

"So the great questions must interest you."

I snorted. "You want to know what I found out about philosophy? I'll tell you. I took a class in epistemology from an associate prof, a young guy working on his doctorate. He liked to hold class outside so he could smoke. He'd put a coffin nail in his mouth as he talked, and he'd light a match, and he'd keep talking and he'd hold the match out there as he followed what-ever tangent he was on, until the match burned down to his fingers. Then he'd shake and drop the match, keep talking, light another match. None of us ever heard what he was saying—we'd all just be watching each new match, watching for the moment when it'd burn him. And that is about all the good philosophy will do you."

Father Bob shook his head. "What about theology then?"

"Same difference," I said.

"Not so," he said. "With theology you have a basis for moral knowledge. Philosophy without God leads only to narcissism."

"If I didn't love myself so much I'd probably agree with you."

He puffed his cigar, then said, "Let's not get derailed tonight. I'm sincere. I only have McNitt to talk to about these things, and you know what that can lead to. Constipation."

"So what does that make me? A laxative?"

"An inquirer. A seeker of truth."

"I don't know what I am. Maybe I'm just an atheist and we should leave it at that."

"No. The one thing you're not is an atheist."

"How do you know?"

"Because you're rational. Atheists aren't rational."

"How's that?"

Father Bob waved his cigar in the air, like a professor with a pointer. "In order to be an atheist—one who claims to know that God does not exist—you'd have to be in possession of all the knowledge in the universe. Have to know every single fact and factoid throughout the cosmos, since God's existence, if true, would be a fact. But since you don't know every fact in the universe and don't even know how much you don't know, you can't possibly claim to know there is no God. You'd have to be God to know there wasn't a God. And then, in an ironic twist, you would have defeated yourself by being God. Isn't this wild?"

"That sounds just a little too convenient."

"Can you defeat the logic? Can you disprove the existence of God?"

I thought about that one for a second, my brain doing flips. "If I recall my philosophy, you can't prove the nonexistence of anything."

"Case closed. You can't be a dogmatic atheist."

"You can be a strong agnostic, though."

"Oh, you don't want to be an agnostic."

"Why not?"

"Because some night you'll wake up and find a flaming question mark on your front lawn."

I winced.

Father Bob said, "You want to make more bad jokes, or shall we keep talking?"

"Not tonight," I said. "Tonight I am one with my doubts."

And I was. Living right here in a religious community was odd enough for me. The way the world worked didn't make sense. Not the way any God worth knowing would have set it up. Good people dying and bad people living. Kids without mothers. Not the way I would have done it.

But maybe that's the point. Not being God is one thing I specialize in.

And then you get people like Father Bob and Sister Mary, who are in this world and just doing what they do, bringing good to people in spite of all the chaos.

That question mark. It was on fire all right.

50

THURSDAY MORNING I parked at Universal City and took the Red Line downtown. Los Angeles has a subway now, but it's not like New York's or Chicago's. The city is too spread out. You usually can't take the train and walk to where you want to go.

The geniuses who deal with rapid transit in this city always get it wrong. Always. When they had a chance to do what Ray Bradbury suggested, criss-crossing monorails, they chose instead to dig holes. Down in the holes the ticket machines don't always work. When the weather is moist they won't take the bills. And don't talk to me about the buses that hack and wheeze across the asphalt arteries of our fair city. I'd rather be riding in a chicken poacher's truck on a dirt road up to Machu Picchu.

It's all about the money and local politics. Train holes bring money, and so does roadwork. However you slice it, cars continue to be the lifeblood of L.A. travel, only that bloodstream clots six, seven times a day in what is laughingly called *commuter traffic.*

On the Red Line, the Tom Bradley/Civic Center station is one of the more convenient stops. It spits you out into historic downtown. The two courthouses, criminal and civil, are close to where they once were when L.A. was growing up. Back when Earl Rogers became the greatest trial lawyer of his day. A handsome, theatrical, sartorially resplendent mouthpiece who performed legal miracles in the criminal courts. Until drink brought him down.

Clarence Darrow once tried a case here. Then Darrow was indicted for jury tampering and got Rogers to defend him. Darrow was acquitted.

Here, Errol Flynn was tried for statutory rape and acquitted. Mitchum for smoking weed, convicted. Famous divorces have been played out on this stage. And, of course, there was the Manson family, the Hillside Strangler, and the Night Stalker.

And O. J., Robert Blake, and Phil Spector.

And me. Once.

The L.A. County Superior Court is across from the Music Center and just up the street from the Disney Concert Hall, the one designed by Frank Gehry. The Disney is a mass of metallic swoops that has been variously described as a modern architectural marvel and an acid trip in the land of aluminum foil.

It seems like a perfect metaphor for the city itself. Weird and chaotic, but with plenty of nice moments inside.

I went to the court clerk's office and I filed a TRO—a temporary restraining order—to stop the Lindbrook from evicting the lawful tenant of room 414, my six-year-old client.

The papers would be served later that day.

I knew the saliva would hit the fan then.

I just wasn't ready for how hard.

51

WHEN I EMERGED from the lower intestine of Los Angeles at Universal City, I saw I had a message from Sister Mary. I called back.

"I talked to Kylie some more, about the color party," she said.

"And?"

"She talked about throwing colors, like you'd throw dirt, and a big fire. It triggered something in me, so I did a little surfing. I think she may have meant Holi."

"Holy what?"

"Holi. H-O-L-I. It's a Hindu festival. The festival of colors. Usually happens in March. They have celebrations in L.A. With bonfires, people throwing powdered colors. Sounds the same."

"And there was one at the beach?"

"Yep. I pulled up a story from the *Times*. Last year they had one near Leo Carrillo. About a hundred and fifty people."

"You are good."

She said nothing, but the nothing sounded like someone smiling.

"How about we take Kylie for a ride?" I said.

52

LEO CARRILLO STATE Beach is a one-and-a-half-mile stretch of sand on the "wrong side of the pier" section of Malibu. It's the wrong side because real people can get to it. Even though the law says the coastline belongs to the public, the Malibuers to the south like to discourage just anyone from walking in front of their homes. So access is, well, made a little more difficult by way of fences and locks.

But not here at this state beach, named for an old character actor who played a Mexican sidekick in an old TV Western series called *The Cisco Kid*. You could do a lot if you were on TV in the 1950s. Even get a beach named after you. This is the land of dreams.

We turned right off of Kanan Dume Road and drove up Pacific Coast

Highway. Took it slow. I wanted Kylie to see if anything looked familiar. She peered out the window like a good soldier. Concentrating.

We passed Zuma Beach with its lifeguard towers and parking lot. Green hills and housing tracts to the right. The ocean on our left was whitecapped with the wind.

I remembered a time when I was a kid and went to a beach in Florida with my mom and dad. Dad showed me how to make a sand castle. We formed this semicircle wall, then made a moat and dug a little hole in front so the water from the waves would go inside the wall.

"Always dig a good, deep hole," Dad said. "So the water passes through and the wall stays up."

I thought that was very cool. Like we were in control of the forces of nature. Like we were showing the ocean who was boss.

As a final touch, Dad showed me how to drip watery sand from my fingertips, forming little pointed turrets on top of the wall.

That was very cool, too. An artistic touch.

It was the last time I went to the beach with my dad. The last time I made a sand castle, too.

We drove past County Line, where a knot of surfers looked for waves. It was a good day for riding. Nice breaks. I was half watching a guy catch one when Kylie suddenly said, "There!"

She pointed to a mobile home park on the right. I slowed, then turned into the gravel drive and headed in. There was a kiosk off to the side, empty, so I kept on going.

The mobile homes were in rows, eclectic in style and color schemes. Some looked newly painted, others weather worn. I drove halfway up the road parallel to PCH and pulled over next to some rocks.

We got out and looked at the ocean. Kylie giggled and jumped up and down. She held my hand.

Sister Mary said, "How can anyone look at this and not believe in God?"

"God is beautiful," Kylie said.

Sister Mary smiled at me.

A voice said, "Help you?"

I turned around to face a security guard, a kid maybe twenty-five trying hard to look forty.

"How you doing?" I said.

"What can I do for you?" He had a high, whiny voice. One that could be very annoying in very little time.

"We're looking for a tenant here," I said. "Someone this girl and her mom stayed with about a year ago. Were you here then?"

"You have the name?"

"Avisha is all we know. You have anyone named Avisha here?"

"I can't give you that information, sir. If you don't know anyone, you'll have to leave."

"Well that's just it, son." I love calling security guards *son*. "We do know someone here—we just don't know the whole name or exactly where she is. And that's where you and your training come in."

He just looked at me, then at Sister Mary, then back at me.

"Let me put it to you this way," I said. "I'm an attorney and I represent this girl and her mother. They were invited guests of Avisha's and we need to get some information from her about that period of time."

"Your name is…?"

"Tyler Buchanan."

The guard took out a pad and pen and wrote. "And the name of the mother?"

"Reatta."

"Is that first or last?"

"First."

"Last name?"

"That's actually the information we're looking for," I said.

"You don't know the last name?"

"No."

"Doesn't the girl know?"

"It's complicated," I said. "So do you want to ask Avisha if she'll talk with us? I'm sure she'll want to."

"I'm sorry, I can't do that. This is private property."

"Just give her the message, how about that? If you want we'll wait down at the office."

The guard shook his head. "I'll have to ask you to leave, sir."

"Well, thank you for asking," I said. "Now, can you tell her we're here?"

"Sir, I'm asking for the last time."

I shook my head. The guard flipped his official Captain America super-security-guard pad closed and walked with purpose toward the front of the property.

A crunch of footsteps behind me. It was an old guy in a denim jacket with floral designs stitched into it. He wore two braids, Native American style, woven from his gray hair and tied off with paisley fabric. He had on wraparound shades and a cowboy hat. He was either Willie Nelson's evil twin or the great grandson of Sitting Bull.

"Been a long time since I seen a nun," he said.

Sister Mary smiled. "Sort of like spotting a great pied hornbill, isn't it?"

Mr. Braids paused, then bent over and looked at Kylie. "Well, hi there, honey," he said.

Kylie hid behind my leg.

"Don't you remember your old pal Fly?" he said.

Fly?

"Heard you mention Avisha," he said, as if having the name Fly was the most natural thing in the world. "That'd have to be the little girl who was here about a year ago. Kelly, wasn't it?"

Kylie's head pushed against my hamstring.

"You folks come on up to my place," Fly said. "Petey there, the security guy, he insists that you be seeing somebody. Well that somebody'd be me. Fly Charles. Maybe I can help you out."

53

FLY'S MOBILE HOME was paneled with faux pine and held old venetian blinds, a well used sofa, TV, and glass-topped coffee table with a Domino's pizza box and two empty Corona bottles. On the wall over the sofa was a glass-encased electric bass. And next to that, framed, a gold record.

"Musician?" I said.

Fly grunted.

I went to the gold record for a closer look. "Detritus and the Electric Yaks?"

Fly grunted again.

Sister Mary said, "Oh wow! My dad had your album!"

"Thank you," Fly said.

"I guess I never heard it," I said. "Sorry."

Fly shook his head. "The second one didn't do so hot. Then we broke up. Old story."

"Were you Detritus?"

"Not then. Now maybe."

"You played bass?"

"Still do, man."

"Like Flea?"

"Don't even say that name!" Fly erupted. "He *stole* that name! He took it from me, just like he took my style!"

"Flea took your style?"

"He was a punk kid, and I mean punk in the worst way, out of Fairfax High, when he came to me for a lesson, and I was messing around and slapping my bass, and the next thing you know…" His voice trailed off in disgust.

"Red Hot Chili Peppers," I said.

"Don't say that name either!"

"But the Electric Yaks," I said, "you still had that album."

"One song on that album. That was it! They called us a one-hit wonder, and once that happens, man, you can't ever get back. You want a beer or something?"

"No thanks," I said. "Sister Mary, you want a beer or something?"

She made a face at me.

"So how's Kelly doin'?" Fly said. "Come on out, honey. You don't have to be afraid of ol' Fly."

Kylie stayed close to me. I said, "Kylie is her name. Kylie. You knew her mother?"

"Oh yeah, sure."

"And Avisha?"

"Yeah."

"I'd like to talk to her," I said. "Can you tell me where I can find her?"

"She's in number 27, just down a couple. So where's the mother? What was her name—Reanne, something like that?"

"Something like that."

"Uh-huh. How's she doing?"

I put my hand around Kylie's shoulder. "She's dead."

Fly took off his sunglasses, which aged his face about ten years. His gray eyes were tired, his skin sallow. It was the Keith Richards look, the kind that could make Botox nervous. "Bummer," he said.

"How well did you know Reatta?" I said.

"Reatta. That's it. Yeah."

"How well?"

"How well did *you* know her?"

"She was a client of mine," I said. "I was her lawyer."

"She had a lawyer?"

"It's not like a rash," I said.

"Most of the time," Sister Mary said.

Fly said, "Maybe I should to talk to you, outside the hearing of…" He glanced at Kylie.

"Why don't you take Kylie outside for a look at the ocean?" I said to Sister Mary. "I'll be right out."

54

WHEN WE WERE alone, Fly said, "You know much about Reatta? And Avisha?"

"That's why I'm here."

"I sure could use that beer. You sure?"

"I'm good."

"Hold on." He went to the kitchenette, talking as he went. "Yeah, I been doin' studio work for thirty years. I still got it. Don't' let 'em say any different." He opened the refrigerator, pulled out a Corona.

"You were about to tell me about Reatta," I said.

He came back in, sucking suds. "Reatta and Avisha. Pros, you know what I'm saying?"

"Hookers?"

"Escorts, man. High end."

"High-end hookers living here?"

"What's wrong with living here?"

"Nothing, I—"

"Yeah, nothing. Got the ocean right outside the door, man. You know what this spot's worth?"

"I get it. So Reatta was working for an escort service?"

"L.A. Night Silk. Heard of it?"

"No."

"I don't know what the deal was, to be honest. Avisha I know for a long time."

"You know her boyfriend James?" I asked.

Fly hunched his shoulders and took another pull on his Corona, shaking his head as he did.

"What do you know about Reatta? What can you remember?"

He shrugged. "I just got the impression she knew Avisha from the service, and had this kid and needed a place to stay awhile."

"How long was she here for?"

"I don't know, two, three months maybe."

"Why'd she need to stay here?"

"You'll have to ask Avisha. The kid, she okay?"

"As okay as a kid can be who lost her mother."

"How'd it happen?"

"It's under investigation."

"Murder?"

"It happens."

"Stinkin' world. I wrote a song called 'Stinkin' World.'"

I was afraid he was going to offer to sing it for me. "Anything else you can tell me about Reatta? Where she was from, anything like that she may have mentioned?"

Fly shook his head. "I really feel sorry for the kid. She being taken care of okay?"

"Yeah."

"Living with nuns, huh? I didn't know they were still minting 'em. She's a young one. Where she from? They got a coven around here?"

"I think you mean *convent*."

"What'd I say?"

"Coven."

Fly slapped himself on the side of the head. "Sex, drugs, and rock 'n' roll, man."

55

SISTER MARY AND Kylie were standing on a couple of rocks looking out over PCH to the ocean. The wind was still whipping up whitecaps. My pants and Sister Mary's habit were flapping in the breeze.

"Windy!" Kylie shouted, laughing, her hair flowing. I was glad for her. Glad for a little bit of happiness. Like gas, the price of happiness was going up. This was a freebie.

I heard tires on the gravel drive. A sheriff's car heading our way, slow. Behind it walked the security guard, like a kid who had just called on his big brother to beat up a bully.

The car stopped and a deputy emerged. A David Caruso type, trying to look cool. His six-point star glinted in the sun. I thought I heard the theme from *The Good, the Bad and the Ugly.*

"How you doing, sir?" he said, meaning he didn't care at all how I was doing.

"Great," I said. "Taking in the view."

"You'll have to take it in somewhere else," he said. "This is private property."

"I'm visiting."

"Who are you visiting, sir?"

"That's private, just like the property."

"Doesn't work that way, sir. If you and the sister will please—"

"All right," I said. "I confess. I'm a raving fan of Detritus and the Electric Yaks."

"Sir—"

"Are you into Detritus?"

"Sir—"

"Because I was visiting their bass player, the legendary Fly. He lives right there."

The deputy looked at the security guard. "Is there anything to that?"

"Well, yeah."

To me, the deputy said, "I take it your visit is over."

"There's just one more stop I want to make," I said.

"Where?"

"Just over there," I said as vaguely as possible.

"The name."

"Avisha."

"Do you know the last name?"

"I think she's undercover," I said. "If I tell you the name I'll have to kill you."

The deputy said, "You have to leave now."

56

"NOT VERY FRIENDLY," Sister Mary said as we pulled out of the mobile home park. "I thought Malibu was laid back."

"You didn't think Fly was laid back?" I said.

"He was a piece of work."

"He was also lying," I said.

"He was?"

"Not giving up everything he knew. Just enough to get me to talk."

"How could you tell?"

"It's a gift."

"So now what?"

"So now we stop off at Zuma. We take off our shoes and stomp around in the water. Then I take you home and I come back tonight."

"Why?"

"Find Avisha," I said.

I drove us to Zuma and parked in the lot. We got out and Kylie ran to the sand. Sister Mary took off her shoes—they were not the "sensible shoes" I always thought they had to wear, but black Nikes—and hitched up her habit and went after Kylie.

I tagged along, watching the two of them laughing at the water's edge. They drew some looks from people on the beach but didn't care. Kylie, barefoot now in her yellow dress, jumped and splashed as the waves slapped down and ran up to her ankles.

Sister Mary joined in. A jumping, splashing nun. Which made Kylie laugh all the louder. Then they held hands and went out a little further. The water came up to Kylie's knees.

They were perfectly happy there.

So I took off my shoes and got on my knees and made a sand castle. Made it the only way I knew how, with a hole in the front for the water to pass through.

57

THAT NIGHT I came back in the car Sister Mary drives for St. Monica's. It's an ancient Taurus. It still runs.

The nuns must have blessed the thing a hundred times over. Put holy water in the radiator. Imported carpet from the Vatican. Whatever they did, the thing's a miracle on wheels.

Also good cover. I knew the deputy and security guard would have recorded my license plate. The Taurus gave me a little anonymity.

There was a stretch along PCH where a few cars were parked. People on the beach who had watched the sun go down. A half-moon was out. Some mobile home porch lights were on.

These mobile parks are not gated communities. It's not hard to slip in if that's what you really felt like doing. I felt like it. I didn't have to go in through the front but could cut right in around the same spot Kylie and Sister Mary had been looking out at the ocean. The only thing between me and the park were some rocks.

When I got in I saw a light on in Fly's place. I ignored it.

I walked past numbers 25 and 26. Twenty-seven was at the end of the row. There was no light on inside or out.

Some headlights flashed from down the road. I slipped along the side, between 26 and 27. A couple of large plastic trash receptacles were against 27's wall. I squatted behind them, waiting for the car to pass. Could have been a patrol. I didn't need to answer any more questions from security guards or deputy sheriffs.

After it passed I waited a second or two, then tapped on the back door of 27. No response.

I knocked again, just make sure. I went up some stairs to the other door—sliding glass. Knocked on the glass. And again.

Tried the glass door.

It slid.

I pushed the curtain aside and poked my head in. "Avisha?"

No sound.

"Candygram for Avisha."

Nothing.

I went inside. My eyes were used to the dark but that didn't help much. The kitchenette had to be close by, so I walked like a blind man, hands out in front, palms inward so I wouldn't leave a print. The place smelled of perfume and sea.

I could vaguely make out the contours of the kitchenette. Got to the sink area and found a dish towel hanging by the window. Took it down and used it to open the refrigerator.

The light was enough to give some illumination, and not enough, I hoped, to call any attention to the place. In the refrigerator was a half-drunk bottle of white wine, the cork stuck in it and the bottle on its side. Next to that, a Baggie with some white pills in it. And an open pack of Oreo cookies.

I needed to move quick to find…I had no idea what. Maybe an address book, if she kept one that wasn't electronic. Something that would lead somewhere closer to Reatta.

Five minutes. I gave myself five minutes to find something or get out.

I went back out to the living room and pulled back a window curtain for some light. The place was neatly kept. Flowered pillows on the sofa. House plants and a bookshelf, with books neatly stacked. On a coffee table was a large statue, Hindu variety. A woman was kicking up her left foot. Like she was leading dance aerobics.

At least I thought it was a woman. Later I found out it was a guy, a god actually. Shiva, creator of all things. Also the destroyer.

Busy guy.

But not giving me much of anything I needed. I thought about flicking on a light but decided against it. Which meant that looking around wasn't going to bring up anything. Breaking and entering is the same, whether it's a house or trailer or room in a motel. I needed to get out before a guard—or Avisha or James—popped in.

I walked slowly back to the kitchenette and was about to elbow the refrigerator closed when I saw the body.

58

SHE WAS FACEDOWN in the small corridor to the left of the kitchenette. I'd missed her the first time by turning the other way at the start. The refrigerator light was enough to show me two things. A corpse that was shapely, black, and scantily dressed. And a puddle of blood on the light carpet, looking like the source was the back of her head.

My throat clenched as I backed up. I bumped into the counter.

I made the sliding door in about three steps, got out, didn't bother to close it. Jumped the three stairs. Landed like a tree sloth and found I was looking right into the kitchenette window of number 27. An old face stared at me.

Naturally I ran.

I did not pass Go. I did not collect two hundred dollars. I did not look back or slow down. When I jumped the rocks on the side of the hill I fell and rolled the distance to the shoulder of PCH. Rocks, sticks, and grit bit every part of me. When I got up I was bleeding.

That was not good. Not good for me, not good for the Taurus.

But we were both better off than Avisha.

59

WHEN I GOT back to St. Monica's I parked the Taurus and went to Father Bob's trailer. He let me in and I told him what happened. He started cleaning me up.

"You have to report this," Father Bob said.

"No, I don't," I said.

"There's a dead woman."

"She's not going anywhere. She'll be found. I'm not going to help them out. Because they'll be asking me questions. They're going to be asking me questions anyway, and I've got to think up a good lie."

"You can't lie!"

"Why not?"

Father Bob stopped what he was doing and faced me. "Are you honestly asking me that question?"

"What's got your collar in a knot?"

"You cannot lie. It is categorical."

"Come on, Father. You don't think there's lies in the church?"

"If there are, they are sin. A sin one place does not justify sin in another. It is an affront to the very nature of God."

I stood up, knocking my chair over. "Tell God he's got some affronts going on, too. What does he expect from us?"

"Ty, don't."

"He hasn't been doing such a great job lately, so I don't want to hear from him or you about life, okay? Can we agree on that much?"

Father Bob's face reflected more hurt than disapproval. Which only made things worse.

"Thanks for the cleanup," I said, and left. I walked past my trailer and up the hill. In back of St. Monica's it was all undeveloped land. I thought about walking out into it as far as I could.

Almost did.

I cursed out loud. Cursed Father Bob for the way he could get his teeth in me.

Then I walked back to the grounds and got my phone and called the Malibu/Lost Hills sheriff's station. I told them where they could find the body. I told them who I was and that I'd come down tomorrow and tell them exactly what happened.

Then I called Detective Brosia, got his voice mail, and spilled the story to him, too.

When I finally clicked off I looked up at the sky and said, "Satisfied?"

60

THE NEXT DAY was Friday. I drove to the Malibu/Lost Hills sheriff's station on Agoura Road. They were expecting me. I got directed to a small, spare county nondesign conference room and sat for about fifteen minutes.

Finally a middle-aged deputy sheriff entered and introduced himself as Sergeant Mike Browne. He had a yellow pad and pen with him. He sat down opposite me.

"We found the body," Browne said. "Just as you told us we would. Now we need to figure out why you knew and why you decided to tell us about it."

"Because I found her. I thought you should know. I wasn't going to tell you at first."

"Why not?"

"Because it wouldn't look very good, would it?"

"What changed your mind?"

"A friend."

"A friend?"

"He's got scruples. He scruped me. So I'm telling you. Here's the whole thing. I had a client who was murdered sometime Monday night. The LAPD detective in charge of that is Brosia, at Central Division, if you want to check with him."

Browne wrote it down.

"She has a daughter, six years old. From the daughter I learned they'd stayed with someone named Avisha, about a year ago, near the ocean. She remembered some things, and based on that a friend and I drove the girl down here and she spotted the mobile home park. She remembered it.

I found out Avisha lived there. But one of your stalwart deputies ran me off."

Browne nodded but said nothing.

"So I came back at night. I wanted to try to find her without anybody getting in my face. It was dark at her place but the sliding door was open. I went in. I found her body and I left. I called you later."

"Why'd you wait?"

"I was nervous about it."

"What time was it when you found her?" Browne said.

"Probably eight-thirty or so. I remember parking about eight-fifteen, eight-twenty."

"Where were you before that?"

"I was eating. Then I was driving."

"Where did you eat?"

"Is that important?"

"It might be."

"Arby's," I said.

"Did you talk with anyone?"

"The girl who took the order. I sat at a table by myself."

"Did you make any calls or get any?"

I shook my head.

"There's another thing," I said. "A guy named Fly Charles is a neighbor of Avisha's. I talked to him."

"Fly Charles?"

"Remember Detritus and the Electric Yaks?"

Browne shook his head.

"Before our time," I said. "They had one hit years ago. He was their bass player. He told me Avisha had a boyfriend named James. You may want to follow up on that."

Browne scribbled some more, then said, "This isn't the first time you've been around a murder."

"And charges against me were dropped because they found the real murderer. I helped them. I'm helping now."

"I hope you're not planning on leaving the country anytime soon."

"Nope."

"I'll probably need to talk to you again."

"Of course." I gave him my phone number and my address as St. Monica's.

"That's a monastery, right?"

"Yes," I said. "You like fruitcake?"

"No."

"Too bad. I can get you as much as you want."

61

SISTER MARY WAS at prayer when I got back. I waited in the courtyard, sitting on a bench and looking at the statue of the woman the place was named for. St. Monica had her head cocked and was looking up.

A brass plate on the base of the statue told how St. Monica agonized and prayed for seventeen years for her son, Augustine. She was told by a bishop that "the child of those tears shall never perish."

There was nothing in there about Augustine saying, "Thanks, Mom."

But there was this inscription:

> *Exemplary Mother of the great Augustine, you perseveringly pursued your wayward son not with wild threats but with prayerful cries to heaven. Intercede for all mothers in our day so that they may learn to draw their children to God. Teach them how to remain close to their children, even the prodigal sons and daughters who have sadly gone astray. Amen*

Astray. Now that I could relate to.

I caught some movement out of the corner of my eye and turned. Sister Hildegarde was closing the door to the office, walking with a man in a suit toward the parking lot.

The man in the suit had perfect black hair, neat and trim and moussed. I couldn't see his face, but he walked like a lawyer. He walked like somebody with billable hours.

They went out to the parking lot and the guy got in a black Mercedes and drove off. Sister Hildegarde came back, saw me sitting in the courtyard.

She headed my way.

When Sister Hildegarde heads your way, look out. A tsetse fly going for a cow does not move with such single-mindedness.

"Mr. Buchanan," she buzzed.

"How you doing?" I said.

"Can I help you?" she said.

"Help me what?"

"Find a place to move into?"

"And don't let the church door hit me on the way out?"

"It's not that," she said.

I stood up. "Did you know, Sister, that there is one private lawyer for every two hundred fifty Californians?"

"Why is—"

"But only one legal aid attorney for every eight thousand, three hundred and sixty-one low-income Californians?"

"Is that true?"

"You bet it's true. If you bet. What I'm saying is, there are people who are getting the living snot beat out of them because they can't afford a lawyer, and you, Sister Hildegarde, are in a position to help them. I am that helper."

She said nothing.

"And I'm certainly here to help you with any legal matters that may arise. And I won't charge you, unlike that lawyer you were just talking to."

Sister Hildegarde reacted like she'd been stung. "How could you know that?"

"We sense these things," I said. "We're all part of the same circle of hell."

"Thank you for your interest, Mr. Buchanan."

"You're not going to tell me who he was?"

"I don't know that it is any of your affair, if I may put it that way."

"Good way to put it. I was just asking. Maybe I can do the same work for a fraction of the cost. With the money you save, you could help out some of those old sisters."

Stiffening, Sister Hildegarde said, "You've been talking to Sister Mary again."

"Is she a bad influence on me?"

"That is an opinion I shall keep to myself."

"What have you got against her?"

Sister Hildegarde's eyes got a cold steel look. "I don't like the implication of that question."

"I just thought, you're all on the same team, right? But there's some underlying tension going on and maybe that's why I'm here."

"Excuse me?"

"Maybe God sent me to negotiate a settlement."

With a heavy sigh, the head sister said, "I don't expect you to understand all the dynamics of an order like ours, of life in community, of the many facets it entails. I think it would be best if you would refrain from interjecting yourself into our processes and concerns."

"In other words, you want me to butt out."

"I wouldn't put it that way..."

"But it's shorter and sweeter."

"Yes," she said. "It certainly is."

I nodded stiffly. Sister Hildegarde nodded stiffly. I went back to the statue, which was still looking up.

Stiffly.

62

SISTER MARY CAME out to the courtyard, with Kylie in tow. She'd had the girl drawing pictures in the mess hall—what I called the mess hall—and now was out for a walk.

Several of the other sisters were on their way to various places on the grounds. A few wore habits, but most did not.

"How you guys doing?" I said.

"It's been a while since I've been called a guy," Sister Mary said.

"Generically speaking," I said. "A human race kind of thing."

Kylie said, "We're having s'mores tonight."

"S'mores?" I said. "What is this, camp?"

"I thought it would be fun," Sister Mary said.

"I'll be there. I'm a s'more guy from way back." I patted Kylie on the head. "Kylie, would you mind if I spoke to Sister Mary alone for a second?"

"Okay," Kylie said. "Can I go look at the rose garden?"

Sister Mary said, "Sure." And Kylie skipped off.

That was nice to see. "How's she doing?"

"Children are amazingly resilient," Sister Mary said. "She cried last night. I held her until she stopped."

"You're really important to her," I said.

"So are you."

That brought an unexpected knot to my throat, so I sat Sister Mary on the bench. "I found Avisha," I said. "Dead."

"What?"

"Execution style."

"Why, do you think?"

"Will you hop online and check an escort service named L.A. Night Silk?"

"I beg your pardon?"

"Escort service."

"You mean…"

"Yeah."

"You want me to do what with that?"

"Find me a hooker," I said.

Pink starbursts popped onto her cheeks.

"I want to talk to somebody from the service, that's all. They won't unless I make it look like an actual transaction."

"Let me get this straight," she said. "You want me to use the abbey's computer to search for a prostitute?"

"Escort."

"And what if Sister Hildegarde should happen to walk in and see what I'm doing?"

"Wouldn't you just love to see her face?"

Sister Mary broke into a smile. "You are tempting me to sin, Mr. Buchanan." She paused. "I'll get right on it."

63

WHILE SHE DID I drove to the Van Nuys courthouse for an afternoon meeting with Mitch Roberts.

The DA's branch office is on the second floor of the old court building on Sylmar. The reception area had a framed photo of the current DA, smiling down on all as if nothing was wrong. As if the city was a well-oiled machine and he the conductor, the fireman, the suited superhero of the justice set.

But under his watch were about a thousand deputies, each with their own personalities, quirks, agendas, axes, and ambitions.

According to the American Bar Association's model rules of ethics, a prosecutor's supposed to be a "minister" of justice, not simply an advocate. His job is not just to convict but, in the words of that great legal philosopher Spike Lee, to do the right thing.

But the L.A. office of the DA is a pressure cooker. The people on the street want to see convictions. They don't give a rip about justice. They just want their neighborhood cleaned up. Unless it's their son or daughter or cousin on trial, of course.

So the DDAs do the cleanup. Most of the time it's really dirt they're after, but every now and then...

"This doesn't have to be a long-drawn-out thing," Roberts said after I'd been shown to his office. "We'll drop the special circs. He can plead and get straight life. That's the best he can do. If he goes to trial, he faces death or L WOP."

L WOP means *life without parole.*

"Such a deal," I said. "But considering the man may actually be innocent, why would that be something we'd even think about?"

"You honestly want to take this to trial?"

"Your case is weak."

"Tell me again how many capital cases you've done?"

"You keep bringing that up, like you don't want me to try this case. I like trying cases. I like juries. They are the great equalizers."

"Not in this environment, buddy. People shooting the mom from a mom-and-pop business is not something people like, especially in the Valley. You're a west side guy, right?"

"Used to be."

"You'll find out. It's like tipping."

"Tipping?"

Roberts leaned back and crossed his legs. "When I was going to law school, at night I worked as a waiter, first in Westwood, then in the Valley. We used to talk about Valley tippers. Cheap. It was an exciting night when you got ten percent out of 'em. They're that way with defense lawyers. You'll be lucky to get 'em to buy fifteen percent of your case. That's not a way to win."

"Were you a good waiter?"

"Yeah."

"And did you give your customers a menu?"

"Of course."

"And on that menu, I bet there was more than one choice."

"Your point?"

"You're not giving us much choice."

"It just seems a shame. You want to start your criminal career with a guy going to death row?"

"Tell you what," I said. "I'll relay your offer to my client. I'll let him make the call. And he'll tell me to tell you where to put your offer. That's just his way, you understand. And then I'll make *you* a deal."

"I'm listening."

"If I can prove to you you've got the wrong guy, you'll move to dismiss."

"Knock yourself out," Roberts said.

64

I SPENT THE weekend working on my closing argument in Gilbert's case.

One of the best lessons I learned from Pierce McDonough, a great trial lawyer in his day, was that you begin with the end in mind. You formulate your closing argument first and then work your evidence presentation around that.

Most big firms use focus groups now and test-market their theories before deciding what direction to take.

I didn't have those resources available to me, so I did the next best thing. On Saturday at the Ultimate Sip I ran the evidence by Father Bob, Sister Mary, and Barton C. McNitt. Kylie was with us, sipping a hot chocolate and coloring.

It all came down to two things. The trouble with eyewitness testimony and a motive to lie on the part of one of the witnesses.

McNitt, wearing a big black shirt that looked like a whale skin with arm holes, said, "Eyewitness testimony is the thing most people rely on, but it's got a whole lot of problems."

"Which is why I'll begin right at the top," I said, "by telling the jury how unreliable eyewitness testimony is. I'll take them to school—"

"No," Father Bob said.

"No?"

"I wouldn't do it that way."

"You're going to tell me how to try cases now?"

"You must prepare the soil of their hearts," he said.

I shook my head. "What is that even supposed to mean?"

"Allow me?"

"Go for it," I said.

"I would begin like this: Ladies and gentlemen, I am tempted at this time not even to make an argument. I have a sense that if you were going to go into to the jury room right now, just based on my cross-examination of the witnesses, you would vote not guilty."

"Now that's not bad," I said. "Where'd you get that?"

"I read books, son," Father Bob said. "Books on the law I especially like. Great closing arguments. Like Clarence Darrow in the Leopold and Loeb case. Or Louis Nizer in John Henry Faulk. You can learn, son, so listen." He cleared his throat and stood. He faced us as if we were in the jury box.

"But I have the duty to marshal all of the evidence. And I don't think there is any question that the eyewitnesses actually *think* that it is Mr. Calderón who robbed them, Mr. Calderón who pulled the trigger of that gun. But in our system of government it is not they who try the defendant. We have you twelve people and you are the jury. You're here for a reason."

"Can't wait to hear this one," McNitt said.

"Quiet down and you will," Father Bob said. "You are here to stand between the government and the defendant. You listen to the evidence. You weigh it. You are the ones to judge it in terms of your own common sense and your own experience. That's what makes this country different from most other countries. In our country it is not the prosecutor who gets to vote. He must prove his case to you, beyond a reasonable doubt. If he is not able to do that, you must find the defendant not guilty. The defendant doesn't have to prove anything."

"Solid," I said.

"In most other countries that is not true. But in this country it is the foundation of our system of justice, and thank God for that, ladies and gentlemen."

"Thank who?" McNitt said.

"Throughout the history of the criminal law there runs a sacred trust, a monument to the dignity of all mankind. This sacred trust is now placed in your hands, I am talking about the presumption of innocence."

I applauded. So did Sister Mary.

Pick McNitt grumbled. "You've convinced me," he said. "The eyewitnesses in the Bible were unreliable and there's a presumption they don't know what they're talking about."

Sister Mary looked at me with a *here we go again* expression.

So McNitt and Father Bob went around and around awhile. I tuned them out and looked at what Kylie was drawing.

"It's me and you and Sister Mary," she said. "Standing by the ocean. And that's a shark coming out of the water."

"A shark, huh?" I said. She had drawn me bigger, between them and the shark, with my arms out in a gesture of protection.

The shark looked hungry.

65

MONDAY MORNING I went to the Twin Towers downtown to see Gilbert Calderón and give him Roberts's offer.

"You mean I say I did it?" he asked.

"And you get to keep your life. They could go for the DP here."

"I ain't afraid of no death penalty, man. I know where I'm going."

"That would be San Quentin."

"No. To be with the Lord."

"Fine. But I don't want to be your travel agent. I have an offer from the DA, I'm obligated to—"

"I can't say I did it when I didn't."

"Okay."

"And I'm gonna walk. I got real faith in you."

"Hey, you know what? That and five grand'll get you Dodger season tickets."

Gilbert paused, then said, "Could you do something for me?"

"If I can."

"Thanks." He cleared his throat. "Would you tell the DA I'm sorry I said he was scum? That was just my old man asserting himself."

"I'm sure Mr. Roberts has gotten over it."

"No, man, this is important. Bad talk, coming out of my mouth. I got to make that right."

"Okay, Gilbert. When I see him, I'll pass that along."

"Thanks, that's a weight off my shoulders."

Gilbert was troubled by telling a DA he was scum, but not by the death penalty. Jail did some crazy things to people. This was a new one on me.

66

OUTSIDE I BOUGHT an *L.A. Times* and gave it a quick scan.

Another toddler was dead, shot in gang crossfire in South Los Angeles.

The city's chief of police made a PR statement about it. Local politicians were falling all over themselves to be next.

Nothing much better inside. A neighborhood with a bad homeless problem was getting "cleaned up," which only meant the homeless were being hassled to other parts of the city. And *those* neighborhoods were really, really happy about that.

Foster care was suffering because payment rates lagged behind the cost of living and were, in fact, lower than the price to kennel a dog. People were dropping out of the duty, leaving more kids without a place to go.

Two people died when a big rig crashed into a tractor-trailer on the westbound 210 and caught fire. And the ACLU was suing a local college for denying a male student the right to attend classes in the nude.

Just another day in the naked city, as they used to say.

But the biggest news had to be the panda droppings. The Chinese were into recycling panda poop, fibrous from the bamboo diet, and making paper goods out of it.

Now that was enterprise. That was the mind of man at work for the betterment of all.

Which put me right in the mood for the big one-page ad for a huge success seminar at Staples Center.

The ad was dominated by a photo of Roland Funk, the New York speculator who had become a national celebrity after divorcing his first wife and taking up with an Olympic skier from Switzerland. Now he was pitching his "magic way to become a millionaire," joined by a bunch of his "friends."

There was Robbie Abston, a "life performance coach," whatever that meant. His photo showed a mouthful of teeth as white and large as elephant tusks. In three hours, the ad promised, he would change your life forever.

Yes, and then came Pug Robinson, former heavyweight boxer, now a skin cream entrepreneur, on "How to Punch Up Your Business and Sex Life."

Next was the latest power couple, coauthors of the hot new book *The Key*, who promised to teach you how to harness all the laws of success and attract love and money into your life after just one hour. In the photo they stood back to back, arms folded, flashing pearlies.

What a lineup! Here you would learn about businesses you could start on a shoestring budget and build into an empire. How to increase any sale 350 percent with a little-known trick. Of course, there was the standard promise of real estate profits with no money down.

Then, adding a bit of spirituality to the mix, was Oz Julian, the "people's pastor" from Denver, who promised to place you at the pinnacle of life *right now.* His smile looked like a transplant from the land of cookware infomercials.

Finally, to top it all off like Cool Whip on a brownie, was a session with the "fastest-rising star in the world of real estate development," Sam De-Cosse Jr.

Junior.

Rising star. Sure. Riding daddy's coattails maybe.

That's when it hit me. I'd thought the Lindbrook was a little too small for Sam Senior. But maybe it was Junior's deal, his starter kit.

Maybe it was Junior I needed to talk to about what happened in the Lindbrook.

Tickets were only forty-nine bucks, and what the heck? Maybe I could have a word with Junior. Maybe I could learn how to start a business. Maybe I could corner the U.S. market in panda poop.

I put the event on my calendar.

67

USUALLY, YOU DON'T go to a nun to get connected to a call girl. But in this case Sister Mary had gotten some names off of L.A. Night Silk. She handed me a list of four based, she said, on their profiles. She did this at my trailer, as far from the office as she could get and still be on the grounds of St. Monica's.

"What sort of profiles?" I asked.

"Please don't ask," she said. She looked upset. Or concerned.

"Thanks," I said. "You've been a great help."

"And I'm going to continue to be," she said. "When do we go?"

"Go?"

"To talk to them."

"You want to go with me?"

"You think I'm going to let you be alone with a prostitute?"

"I'm just going to be talking, paying for their time."

"Sez you."

"Sister Mary, you wound me."

"I'll see that Sister Judith looks after Kylie."

"And after that you'll look after me?"

"Sharp, Mr. Buchanan," she said. "Very sharp."

68

PROSTITUTION.

They call it the world's oldest profession but I think lawyers were there first. When a caveman made a move on somebody else's woman, there was no payment involved. But there was the law. The law of the club. And lawyers have always been about clubs. At Gunther, McDonough, I loved to swing 'em hard.

Then the prostitutes came along and it was all a matter of exchange. Society tried to stop it, but the demand was too great.

Lawyers and prostitutes have been running some nice scams ever since.

Escort services is one of them. Technically, the service only rents out "companions." A woman on the arm to take to dinner or a function or the crap tables in Vegas. That's what is negotiated and paid for. Any sex, the services say, is purely a voluntary thing that may or may not happen. And if it does, well, that's what adults do.

Right.

The salesman from Chicago, the field hockey jock from UCLA, the stockbroker from New York—these guys are not paying for a night of jocular conversation or Yahtzee.

And everyone knows it. The cops, the politicians, the clinicians who administer the HIV tests. There's not a lot of call to shut these things down, of course. Because the local government gets to tax the business, and it's a business that never runs out of customers.

69

SISTER MARY HAD determined that three of the escorts had been working for Silk for over six years. That's a long time in the trade. Without a retirement plan, too.

But with seniority comes cost, and this cost wasn't cheap. Five hundred for four hours for the first one on the list, named Lana. I called, got a voice mail, and she returned my call an hour later. I told her I'd meet her in the lobby of the Bonaventure Hotel and we'd go to dinner and see what happened after that.

She said fine and quoted me the price. Then I gave her my credit card number. It was easier than ordering from Amazon.com.

70

THE BONAVENTURE HOTEL is on Figueroa in L.A.'s financial district. Seemed fitting, as I was about to make a financial transaction myself. Of sorts.

Lana told me she would be wearing red and holding a *Wall Street Journal*. Honest. Just like the movies. Or maybe she was into investing. Whatever it was, I made her immediately. She was sitting in one of the big chairs by the fountain.

She was tall and slender and packed into her red dress. Her hair was light strawberry and shoulder length. Her face, while perfectly made up, seemed to carry an added weight, as if time had attached lead pellets to her cheeks. When she smiled at me, it looked like it took effort.

"Mr. Buchanan?" She had a gentle voice with a practiced, come-hither nuance.

"How are you?" I said, and then felt completely flustered. What do you do when you meet your escort for the first time? Shaking hands seemed completely unacceptable, and lip lock a bit over the top.

She answered with a kiss on the cheek and I caught a whiff of cigarette smoke and perfume in her hair.

"I'm Lana." She took my hand. "I'm looking forward to our evening."

"Me too." And I was, if she'd talk to me.

"Where's our first stop?"

"My car. Come on."

We went to the elevator and down to the garage. I opened the door for her and she got in. And saw Sister Mary sitting in the back.

"What is this?" Lana snapped. "I don't do three-way and I don't do RP."

I wished Sister Mary didn't have to hear that. "I'll explain," I said. "I actually want to take you out to dinner. That's what I paid for."

"What's RP?" Sister Mary said.

"I'll handle this," I said.

"Role-play," said Lana. "I don't do role-play."

"Lana," I said, "let's go to a nice place and eat and talk. That's it. That's what I want."

"This isn't a role," Sister Mary said.

"Wait a second," Lana said. "Are you telling me this is an actual nun here?"

"Nice to meet you," Sister Mary said.

Lana shook her head. "I don't get it."

"She's going to eat with us," I said. "She's a real nun and she's a friend of mine, and all I want to do is talk. Really."

"You want to convert me," Lana said. "This is some kind of rescue deal going on. Well, I—"

"Hardly," I said. "This is the easiest money you're ever going to make. And I'll remind you, I've paid up front."

Lana looked at Sister Mary, then back at me. Then she started to laugh. It went on for a while. When she caught her breath, she said, "I've had a couple of street preachers use that same line. Never a nun. I guess variety's the spice of gumbo, so let's go eat."

71

I HAD A place in mind. Bruno's on Wilshire, a place I used to go all the time when I was a high-flying litigator. It wasn't cheap—nothing about this night was cheap. But I hoped the combination would be good enough to loosen some information.

Junius was the maitre d' and he smiled at me. "Nice to see you again. It's been a long time."

His expression changed from delight to mystification when he saw Sister Mary. "We're together," I said.

He smiled again and showed us to a booth with a half-moon table covered with crisp white linen. One wall of the place was a wine rack and another wall held contemporary art, by which I mean many colors that didn't add up to anything. There was a golden hue to the lighting, which was in keeping with the prices on the menu.

I asked Lana if she'd like a drink and she said she didn't drink when she was "out." So I ordered us Pellegrino and the duck vol-au-vent appetizer, one of their specialties.

"So, we just talk?" Lana said.

"Yep," I said.

Lana nodded at Sister Mary. "And exactly what is her role?"

"She's my assistant," I said.

"Assistant? Are you a priest or something?"

Sister Mary snorted.

"Not a priest," I said. "Sort of a lawyer."

"Sort of? What does that mean? You are or you aren't, right? I'm not sort of an escort, if you know what I mean."

"I know," I said. "I used to be with a firm and now I'm out on my own. By the way, if you ever need a lawyer…"

"What would I need a lawyer for?"

"Who *doesn't* need a lawyer?"

"Can I answer that?" Sister Mary said.

Lana's face turned somber. "I'm perfectly happy doing what I'm doing."

It would have been clear to every person in the place that she wasn't happy at all. But what we needed was for her to relax.

"You from L.A.?" I asked.

"Louisiana," Lana said. "Shreveport."

"Shreveport? Really?"

"C. E. Byrd High School. Go Yellow Jackets."

"You don't have an accent," I said.

"I can turn it on and off. If somebody wants a Southern gal, I"—Lana switched to Blanche DuBois—"am so happy to help." She gave the last word two syllables. *Hay-ulp.*

"Not bad," I said. "What brought you out this way?"

"Fame, of course. I was homecoming queen and won the talent contest. Sang 'Grand Old Flag' and twirled batons. That gets you front page in the *Shreveport Times.*"

"Came out here right after high school?"

"Nothing to keep me there. Good reason to leave. But I don't want to get into that. Why spoil a perfectly fine evening with sordid tales from the Deep South?"

"So you came out for movies or modeling or something and got a little sidetracked."

"Who says I got sidetracked? Maybe I just decided on a career change. Maybe you're making a whole lot of assumptions and…Why are we talking this way? You didn't bring me here for a life story session, did you?"

"I'm interested," Sister Mary said.

"Why?"

"I just am. I'm always interested in life stories."

"Yeah? Then tell me yours. How's that, lawyer? She tells me hers first."

I looked at Sister Mary. "We are on the clock here."

"Oh that's a hoot," Sister Mary said. "A guy who used to bill in seven-and-a-half-minute increments."

"Go ahead," Lana said to Sister Mary. "I'd like to know."

72

"I GREW UP in Oklahoma," Sister Mary said.

"Not just Oklahoma," I said. "Oklahoma City itself!"

"This is my story. Kindly put a cork in it."

Lana laughed.

"Anyway, I had a good home life. Nothing to complain about. Really got into sports, especially basketball. Got to be pretty good at it."

"She cheats," I said.

"She said put a cork in it," Lana said. "Please do, or I'll charge you double."

I put a cork in it.

Sister Mary said, "We went to church, but it was so familiar to me. I never really felt it in my bones, so to speak. Then one day we were at my grandparents' place by a lake, and I took a little boat out by myself. The sun was starting to set and there was an orange glow in the sky and over the trees. And I just started crying. I didn't know why. But it was because of the sky. When I came back in I asked my mom about it. Why did I cry? And she said, 'Because you're homesick for heaven.'"

For a moment nobody said anything.

"That's when I started to see God in my life," Sister Mary said. "Not as something I'd been brought up with, but something real—and not just real, but somebody who knew my name and wants me in heaven with him. Later, after college, I decided to become a nun."

Lana thought about it. "I never felt that way. Homesick for anything. I'd like to sometime."

73

"LET ME TELL you why I wanted an escort tonight," I said.

"Finally," Lana said.

"Another escort from L.A. Night Silk was murdered a week ago."

Lana tried hard not to look stunned. She took up her water glass for a sip. I saw the water trembling.

"Who was it?" she said.

"I think you know," I said.

"So what?"

"Ever think it might happen to you?"

"Look—"

"Easy," Sister Mary said to me, then put her hand on Lana's arm. The gesture sent a signal to Lana's brain, softening her.

Sister Mary said, "Don't say anything you don't want to. Just relax."

I kicked Sister Mary under the table.

"Don't kick me under the table," Sister Mary said.

Lana laughed. "I don't believe this whole conversation."

Looking at Sister Mary, I said, "If I had a little cooperation here, maybe we could all believe it."

"I'll cooperate you right in the chops," Sister Mary said.

"What kind of nun are you?" Lana asked.

"Good question," I said.

"Have a bread stick," Sister Mary said.

"There aren't any," I said.

"Have one anyway." To Lana, Sister Mary said, "Did you know Avisha?"

"Yes. She was someone I was close to, in fact. Good kid. Do the police know who did it?"

"I thought you might know," I said.

"Why should I?"

"You know her boyfriend? James?"

"He didn't do it."

"How do you know?"

She shrugged. "I just don't think he's that kind."

The waiter returned with the duck. Lana said she wasn't hungry and didn't want anything else. Sister Mary, probably to keep Lana from feeling bad, said she wouldn't eat, either.

The waiter looked hacked. And I was hungry. So I ordered up a bone-in rib eye and half a dozen oysters on the halfshell. Resist that, ladies.

"At least try to answer some questions," I said. "Confidentially. Sister Mary will attest to my ability to keep a secret."

Lana looked at Sister Mary, then at me. "About what?"

"Did you know another girl in the service, named Reatta?"

She thought a moment, shook her head.

I took out the picture Kylie had given me.

"Tawni," she said. "That's Tawni."

"And she's with your same service?"

Lana nodded. "A few years ago."

"Any idea who'd want to kill her?" I asked.

"What?"

"She's dead, too."

Putting her head in her hands, Lana let out a big sigh.

"Somebody—cops don't know who—got to her," I said. "They haven't released cause of death yet, but it was definitely a homicide."

"Where?"

"Just down the street. The Lindbrook Hotel."

Lana shook her head. "She wanted to get out of the life. She had a kid. She thought she had something better, but it didn't turn out that way, did it?"

"What was the better thing?"

She shook her head. "No."

"Why not?"

"I have to go." She slid out of the booth. "I'll call a taxi."

"Wait…" But she was already heading for the door. I started to get up but Sister Mary pushed me back.

"Let me," she said.

74

EVENTUALLY THE WAITER came with my rib eye and the oysters. "Is everything all right?" he asked.

"Sure," I said. "The ladies just stepped out for some air. I sucked it out of the room. They'll be back. Bring me a glass of your best California Cab. You pick it."

"Of course."

He delivered the wine before Sister Mary got back. Alone.

"I told her where she could get in touch with me," she said.

"Where is she?"

"She wanted to go."

"What did you do, scare her off?"

"No, I—"

"Who was paying for this? Me or the archdiocese?"

"Do you want to hear what she told me?"

"That'd be real nice."

"Then cool off," Sister Mary said. "Have another bite of cow."

"Just talk. What's it about?"

"The better thing Reatta thought she was getting."

"You got her to tell you?"

Sister Mary nodded. "Never underestimate the power of an understanding ear."

"And maybe being a woman?"

"That would help."

"Unfair advantage."

Sister Mary helped herself to an oyster from the plate of ice on the table. Put the shell on her own plate.

"This is strictly confidential," Sister Mary said.

"Of course. Give."

"I don't watch television. Much, anyway. Do you know a show called *Men in Pants*?"

"I know of it. Todd McLarty is in it." Todd McLarty, of course, being the hot "next movie star" of ten years ago, now dying on the career vine and being resurrected in a hit ABC sitcom.

Sister Mary dappled some cocktail sauce on her oyster and used the little fork to eat it.

"Okay," I said. "Enough with the marine life. Tell me what it is about the show."

"And Todd McLarty," she said. "He was the one. He was the one she thought was the good thing."

In this day when almost anyone could be the father of any given baby, where possible fathers of numerous babies crawl out of or into the woodwork, the news didn't seem all that earth-shattering.

That could have been. McLarty was known in his day as a guy who liked high-priced call girls and coke. Today these things are also used to get careers going again. The standard visit to rehab, combined with a name leak from some madam's black book, is sure to garner a lot of ink and talk. It did for McLarty, and look at him now. A hit show. A mil an episode.

Not bad for a bad boy from Tarzana.

"How sure is she about this?" I asked.

"Tawni told Lana she was going to marry McLarty. That didn't happen, of course. She lost track of Tawni after that."

As I tossed a little sauce on an oyster, a few thoughts jumbled around in my head and reached for each other.

"Todd," I said. "Rhymes with odd."

"You're good," Sister Mary said.

"Kylie told me that Avisha said her father was odd."

Sister Mary raised her eyebrows. "You don't think…"

"I do too think, thank you very much."

"No, I mean, that he could be Kylie's father?"

"Maybe I'll ask him. Right now we eat."

75

LATER, BACK AT St. Monica's, Father Bob offered me a stogie. We sat outside the trailers smelling the mix of sage and laurel and Dominican tobacco.

"Last time I smoked one of these I'd just won a two-million-dollar verdict," I said.

"You miss that?" Father Bob asked. "The power lawyer business?"

"Not at all. Kind of surprises me. I liked going to court for high stakes, yeah, but there doesn't seem to be much point in that anymore. It's all about shuffling around millions of dollars from here to there. The insurance companies pass it on to their customers in higher premiums. The companies pass that along to consumers in higher prices. Around and around you go."

"What made you see it that way?"

"I don't know."

We paused. Father Bob said, "It was Jacqueline, wasn't it?"

"Yeah. Of course," I said. "You don't see things the same after something like that. If you did, you'd be made of stone." I took a draw on the robusto. "Maybe that'd be better. Didn't Dylan once write a song about that?"

"Not that kind of stoned."

We were quiet for a while after that and I thought about how I used to get baked in college and law school. How Jacqueline convinced me it was not a good thing to do that ever again.

I missed her face and her love, the hurt coming on fresh. I thought then that her loss was going to be like that thing amputees get. Shadow pain. Your foot hurts but you have no foot, it was cut off, but the pain is there just the same. You don't know when it's coming on, it just does. You wince and bear it and hope it doesn't return too often.

"You okay?" Father Bob said.

"Sure," I said.

"Doesn't sound all that convincing to me."

"Am I paying you to be a shrink?"

"I'm a shrink for free. Or a friend."

"Right."

"And you have a friend in God."

"Friend? He has a strange way of showing it."

"In what way?"

"Okay," I said. "You remember once at the Sip, when McNitt was talking about God and evil? You kind of brushed it off."

"Did I? I don't remember."

"You made some comment about at least McNitt admitting God is alive or something. But that's not the question. You want God to be a friend—how come he allows us to go through all this? How come he has a little girl come into the world, daughter of a whore, and then the whore gets murdered and she's alone? And that's not the worst of it. A lot more, a lot more goes on. So if you don't mind, God as friend really doesn't do it for me."

"You want to talk or you want to rant? If you want to rant, I'll shut up. If you want to talk, I'll tell you what I think."

"Fine, tell me what you think. You gave me a fine cigar. It's the least I can do."

Father Bob took a languid puff, then said, "My good friend McNitt likes to say that a good God would never allow evil to exist. So when I ask him if it could be that a bad God exists, he clams up. Don't you see the irony of it? The argument against evil really admits there is a God."

"Not necessarily," I said. "You can say there's evil, period, and that means there's no God at all."

"You sure you want to make that argument?"

"Yeah."

"Then let's see where it goes. If the world is evil but there's no God, where do you get your definition of 'evil'?"

Verbally circling me. And sounding like he was having fun. Got me a little mad. "Good and evil are self-evident," I said.

"I'm sorry, Ty, but they're not. Without the Cosmic Ump, you can't settle anything."

"Say what?"

"The Cosmic Umpire. The one who calls the game. If you say something's evil and I say it's not, how are you going to settle it? If there's no ump, there's only might-makes-right."

"So?"

"So you can't claim that the existence of evil is an argument against God, because just making that argument supposes the Cosmic Ump. Am I making sense?"

"How 'bout those Dodgers?"

"Shall we continue?"

"Not tonight. My brain hurts. If we're going to duel, I want to be fresh."

"You know where to find me."

We sat in silence, listening to the night, and I was glad that I knew where to find Father Bob. What he believed in didn't matter to me much at all. What mattered is that he was a friend, that he was somebody who cared about what I did and what I was thinking, and it's good to have somebody like that around.

For a few minutes there, I was happy.

You're always happier when you don't know what's coming.

76

FRIDAY MORNING I called on B-2.

Jonathan Blake Blumberg, better known as B-2 around town, is the electronic devices entrepreneur I'd helped once. In a bitter custody dispute during which his ex-wife had managed to float false accusations.

Blumberg, despite all his money, couldn't fight the power of a lie. That's where I had come in.

So now he liked me. And he was a self-made man who knew ways to get things done that weren't always going to show up on a radar screen.

I was on the 405 heading south when I called JatDome, Blumberg's company that he built from scratch. His gatekeeper put me on hold, then came back and immediately put me through. Blumberg told me to come in, that he would drop anything he was doing to give me some time.

Fifteen minutes later I was in the Blumberg Building, in B-2's expansive office with the killer view of the ocean.

The guy was as in shape as ever. He has thick black hair and a boxer's body. Energy to burn. He wore blue jeans, Adidas shoes, and a yellow pull-over shirt. I don't think I ever saw him in a tie.

His desk, as big as an aircraft carrier, had all sorts of electronics on it. I knew from before these were products, prototypes, and sometimes just something one of his R & D people threw together at his behest.

He gave me a hug and a slap on the back. The slap took some of my breath away.

"How are you, boy?" he said.

I coughed. "Aces."

"That's the ticket."

He looked a little looser than when I'd first met him. That's when he had the heavy weight of false accusations over him. His ex-wife, a woman named Dyan, made Lucrezia Borgia look like Florence Henderson. She had poisoned the mind of their only daughter, Claudia, to the point where a false memory of sexual abuse was implanted in her brain.

We didn't sit. B-2 liked to pace around. Sitting in his presence felt like sleeping in anyone else's.

"How's life out of the law firm?" he asked.

"Humane," I said.

"You still living with the nuns?"

"You make it sound like I'm some explorer among a strange race."

"Your point is?"

"Yes, I'm still living with the nuns," I said. "It's peaceful up there. I get the occasional case, too. Right now I've got a client accused of murder. I've also got a little girl whose mother was murdered. At the Lindbrook Hotel downtown."

"How did you get involved with that?"

"The mother came to see me at my office."

"Office?"

"I rent a chair at a little coffee place in the valley. She came in with her daughter and they were trying to give her a fast one down at the Lindbrook. Get her out of the building because they want to develop it into lofts."

"Who does?"

"The DeCosses."

"Oh yeah. Quite a little family. The old man did all right for himself in the wife department."

"I've met her."

"No fooling?"

"I got invited up to see them. When I filed a temporary restraining order on their little eviction, it rippled its way up to the top. Quite a nice house he's got."

"Almost as big as mine," Blumberg said.

"Anyway, I want to have a little talk with Junior. He's speaking down at the Staples Center this afternoon."

"What's down there?"

"Big success show, you know, where a bunch of people come and tell you how good they are at making money?"

"Oh yeah. Then make their money selling you stuff that promises to make you money. What a racket. Ty, how can I help you out?"

"I was thinking," I said, "of putting a little tail on the kid. I've seen his car. I figure I might get lucky and find it down there somewhere, and maybe you know the best way to put a tracker on it."

"You need a GPS to stick under the car, gives you real-time location every fifteen seconds, and maps it on your phone. Gee, if only we made something like that."

Smiling, he tapped his own phone and gave some instructions. Turned back to me.

"No time at all," he said.

"You're kidding, right?"

"I got you covered. Hey, take a look at this." He snatched a cylinder off his desk, black and a little larger than a lighter. He pushed with his thumb and the thing made a snapping noise. "Cute, huh?"

"What is it?"

"EWT. Electroshock weapon technology. A mini stunner."

He held it up so I could see the twin prods. They looked so innocent.

"This baby delivers four hundred K," he said.

"Volts?"

"A quarter second on the neck, and your guy's muscles contract. One to four seconds and he's on the ground, confused as a Democrat with a tax break. Five seconds, he starts thinking he's Al Gore and the earth is melting."

"You're going to sell these things?"

"I'm thinking of calling it the iProd, but Jobs'll probably come after me. Let him. I've wanted to take him on for years. I'm also working on a new, very hot pepper spray."

"Don't tell me," I said. "The iFog?"

"That's not bad! But I was thinking 'Face Melters.'"

"You're the genius."

He put the iProd in my hand.

"You're giving this to me?" I said.

Blumberg nodded.

"I'm speechless," I said.

"But not sparkless. Hey, you know what? I'm your Q."

"My what?"

"You know, in all those Bond movies? Bond'd see Q and get all his toys before going out on his mission. That's me. I'm supposed to tell you not to play with anything, and you're supposed to press a button and set the office on fire."

"I'll skip that part," I said.

"I'm glad," he said.

77

AFTER Q, I went to learn the secrets of success.

Staples Center is on South Figueroa, down the street from one of my favorite eateries, the Original Pantry, where you can still get surly waiters and an honest breakfast. I treated myself to the pancakes and then prepared to have my life transformed.

A hundred years ago there was a large ad in the *L.A. Times* from a woman named Romanya, "the Gypsy Queen." In her dive on Main Street she promised to: "Tell all. Settle lovers' quarrels, reunite the separated; tell whom and when to marry; how to control and win the one you love; how to overcome enemies. A visit will convince all. Skeptics and unbelievers invited!"

I think Romanya would have been at home in today's L.A. The selling of false hopes is a big business here, and every now and then a dog and pony show at Staples attracts thousands of the sweating masses aching to find the one secret they've been missing in their lives, the golden door to riches.

I wandered into this circus at about two-thirty in the afternoon. The lobby was packed with tables and the tables packed with all sorts of swag—coffee mugs with pithy sayings, T-shirts, mouse pads, posters, books. Lots and lots of books and tapes and CD and DVD programs.

Behind these tables were slim women in black dresses or guys in their twenties trying to dress and look like executives in their forties. Little success wannabes, working on behalf of this or that huckster or company.

One of these guys saw me looking and called me over, the way a used-car salesman would verbally net an Okie with a fat roll on his way to Las Vegas.

"How you doin', sir?" he said.

"Me?" I said.

"You look like you're here to reshape your world."

"Do I? I thought I looked a little pasty."

A forced laugh. "That's a good one. Are you willing to invest in an unlimited future?"

"How much?" I scanned his table of wares. The smiling face of Oz Julian jumped out from books and CD cases. He was a thin, multitoothed, black-haired bundle of joy.

"Oh, I'm not talking about dollars," the young man said. "I'm talking about life itself. These principles apply to everyone, without regard to income."

"How much for the books, I mean?"

"Fifteen dollars. Today they're on special. The CD series is eighteen dollars."

"Eighteen? And for that I get what?"

"You get Oz reading his own book. Unabridged."

"Oz the great and powerful?"

Another laugh. "Oh, we get that all the time, sir. That's a good one. Would you like a book?"

"Sure. You have anything by John Grisham?"

He stared blankly, then plastered on a big grin. "This book will show you how to turn failure into finances, disappointments into diamonds, and a stinkin' attitude into mountaintop altitude."

"All that in one book?"

"It's a promise."

"I'm actually looking for ways to make less money. You have any books on that?"

Blank. Then grin. "That's a good one."

"Give my best to the great and powerful Oz and remember not to look behind the curtain."

I went looking for Junior.

78

THE SCHEDULE HAD him down for a four o'clock talk. So I got to sit with the teeming masses and listen to a pitch from Pug Robinson. He'd been a pretty good fighter in his day. Peaked about the time I went to law school. Fought past his prime a couple of matches and blew through about fifty million dollars over his career.

I remembered Pug from his fight with Mike Tyson—one of those fights in which Tyson didn't try to chomp his opponent's ear off. Pug had Tyson on the ropes in the fifth but got careless and almost had his head hooked into the press box. He didn't come to until thirty minutes after the fight was over. When he woke up he thought he was a shoe salesman named Frank.

His brains unscrambled, though, and he knocked around awhile after he retired. His money ran out and he was down, seemingly out.

Then he got into skin cream products for men and built up a major business just as the metrosexual craze made *Time* magazine. The commercials of this former boxer putting cream on his cheeks as gorgeous women fawned were part of popular culture now.

He bounded out to the theme from *Rocky,* shadow boxing, smiling. He did the "Pug two-step" a couple of times, a boxing move he made popular (though it grew less popular after the Tyson fight because it's what he did before the left hook that turned him, momentarily, into a shoe salesman).

"How y'all doin'?" Pug shouted when he got to the lectern. I could see teleprompter screens in front of him.

"I wanna knock the 'can't' right out of you today! I'm gonna jab your doubts and uppercut your fears." And then he unloaded his catch phrase: "You can't be beat if you stay on your feet!"

At which the crowd cheered.

I groaned. How much of this horseradish would I have to sit through before Junior?

A lot, as it turned out.

Pug was followed by the Key couple. They started with a slick movie showing how George Washington had used the Key at Valley Forge and Thomas Edison used it to invent the lightbulb.

It has something to do with the universe being made of vibrating spheres of attraction, and how you could tune your body to be in harmony with them.

Then the black-clad duo zipped onto the stage to the old Fleetwood Mac tune about yesterday being gone. She was a blonde and he was of darker hue. Both pumped their fists. Causing vibrations in the universe, no doubt. Both wore head mikes, so their hands could keep causing them.

The man said, "You can have more than you've got because you can become more than you are!"

The crowd cheered wildly.

Then the woman said, "If you can think, you can attract. Think gold, attract gold. Think love, get love. Get anything you want!"

"Five years ago we were living in a one-room apartment," the man said. "Beans on the table, moths in my pocket! And then one day I looked in the mirror and I said to myself, Enough! I made a decision. That is the essential first step. You need to decide to be rich. Have you decided?"

Five thousand voices shouted *Yes!*

"If life gives you lemons," the man said, "don't just make lemonade. Make it, bottle it, sell it, and turn it into a lemonade fortune. We are going to tell you how."

No doubt, I thought. Look what they did with manure.

It was all I could take. I made my way down toward the floor, where a ring of blue-blazered security guards stood facing the seats. They looked bored. I walked around the ring toward the tunnel where the power couple had emerged. I figured that might be the bullpen, key word being "bull."

Maybe I could get a word in with Junior before his talk. Get him all pumped up with questions about his fleabag hotel and throwing people out on the street to avoid the law.

But a security guard stopped me when I tried to walk into the tunnel.

"May I see your pass, sir?" he said.

"Pass?"

"No access without a pass."

"Oh, I'm just a fan. I wanted to see if I could get an autograph."

"I'm sorry, sir, this area is restricted."

"But I want a mountaintop altitude."

He did not change his face muscles into a winning smile. "I'm sorry, sir."

"Darn," I said. "I guess I'll have to go back to selling pencils again."

I scanned the seats in the arena, saw an empty about the third row. Went for it and sat between two guys. The black-clad couple were still pumping fists. The guy on my left leaned over to me and said, "This is a pile of you-know-what, but she's a babe."

A formula for success in America.

79

FINALLY, MERCIFULLY, THE Key couple was through. Another slick video played on the jumbo screens, reminding people of all the great success junk they could buy in the lobby. A commercial for a "fail-safe" way to build an empire based on "distressed properties" played.

I thought all the people taking this stuff seriously *were* distressed properties.

Then it was time for Sam DeCosse Jr. to take the stage.

After a glitzy video intro, of course.

In the space of about ninety seconds, we were given a window into the lifestyle of this rich and famous developer. They showed some of the projects he had overseen, and naturally showed him walking along in a hard hat on a project. Like those candidates who run for office always show themselves in a hard hat, never having been on a site like that in their lives. Except when the cameras were rolling, of course.

Then the lights came up and out walked Junior, looking sharp in his Italian cut.

He smiled and pointed at the audience in response to their applause.

Then said, "Let me tell you how to get rich beyond your wildest dreams."

And I thought, *Make sure you have a daddy who is rich beyond your wildest dreams.*

He started in with some story I didn't believe for a second.

"I bought my first property when I was nine," he said. "It was my friend Dave's front lawn. He gave it to me for nothing down, and a flat fee deferred, to come out of the profits from the lemonade stand I was going to put there. Why? Location, baby. His house was on one of the busiest streets in town. And I cleaned up. Gave Dave the dollar I promised him, and kept the profits for myself."

Applause. Any sentence with the word *profit* in it and these people would clap. You could say, "Four hundred baby seals were slaughtered today, and the fishermen who did it made a profit," and they'd cheer.

"And that's how I learned about finance and negotiation," Junior said. "And that's what I want to teach you today, in my DVD series, which is on sale for the first time anywhere in the lobby."

I thought I heard crickets chirping.

"Now, let me continue with my story," Junior said.

Not interested, I tuned out the rest and started scanning the people near the stage.

Then saw someone I recognized. He had the look. The lawyer look. The lawyer who'd been up to see Sister Hildegarde.

I slipped over to him and bumped his shoulder slightly. He cast a quick glance my way and moved a little.

I said, "This guy know what he's talking about?"

"Yes," he snapped.

"Then this is a guy I definitely have to talk to."

The lawyer said nothing, kept his eyes straight ahead. He was about six feet tall, impeccably dressed in a dark gray pin-striped suit.

And a great big diamond-studded tie clip.

"I have some questions I really want to ask him," I said. "What do you think?"

"Please, I'm trying to listen."

"You think you can arrange that for me?"

"Arrange what?"

"To meet with Sam Junior."

"He's a very busy man."

"I think he'll want to talk to me—"

"Are you a reporter?"

"No."

"Mr. DeCosse has a full schedule. Now, I'd like to finish—"

"Busy with the Lindbrook Hotel?"

The guy whipped a glare at me. "Who are you?"

"The name's Buchanan."

"What do you want?"

"A few minutes with Junior."

"Why?"

"I have some questions for him."

"Who cares?"

"Maybe the tenants at the Lindbrook. Maybe some nuns."

His jaw twitched at that one. "What are you talking about?"

"The little development you're planning in the Santa Susana Pass. The piece of ground you're going to purchase from St. Monica's. Nice property. You're one of Junior's lawyers, right?"

For a moment he said nothing, but I sensed a vibration. Was he trying to call in all the forces of the universe? Make lemonade? At the very least there was an instant weighing of options. Maybe a single bead of sweat forming in a random pore somewhere.

He turned to face me fully. "Who are you?"

"We passed like ships in the night in Hyrum Roddy's office the other day."

He looked like he was trying to remember. "Who do you work for?"

"I'll talk to Junior about that."

"You'll talk to me."

"I don't have any reason to talk to you."

"This is as close as you're going to get to Mr. DeCosse."

I handed him one of my cards. "You tell Junior to get in touch with me. You tell Junior that people dying in his hotels is not a good thing. And tell him a lot of things can go wrong when you try to buy land from nuns. You tell him that for me. Tell him Daddy would want him to see me."

He looked at the card. Then he crumpled it and dropped it on the ground.

"Now is that any way to reach the mountaintop?" I said.

"I can have you forcibly removed," he said.

"You guys seem to like forcible removal. What if I forcibly remove our whole matter to the courts? You think Junior would like that? The public spectacle?"

I looked at the giant monitors and saw the smiling face of Sam DeCosse Jr. He looked so happy. I was looking forward to doing something about that.

The lawyer gave me the silent stare. I smiled, nodded, and went to look for some popcorn. My work here was done. I'd probed and hit something. I'd be hearing from Junior, I was sure.

80

OUTSIDE I MADE my way around toward the back, where all the limos and security guys were. The celebrity entrance. Private parking. It didn't take me long to spot Junior's Ferrari.

Guy has a car like that, he drives it. It's part of his image. And something told me Junior was all image. An empty suit. Sam Senior, at least, was a self-made man. Ruthless, yes, because you can't be a slug in commercial real estate.

But he made his way up by fighting and clawing.

Junior had everything handed to him. Probably including this Ferrari.

I walked with purpose through the cars, fumbling with my keys. Wanted it to look like I had a car here.

At the Ferrari I dropped my keys. Bent over. Took out Blumberg's GPS from my pocket, peeled off the tape, and stuck it under the car. Solid.

Stood up and continued my walk. Got to the other side of the arena and circled all the way back around to my car.

81

I STOPPED OFF at the Ultimate Sip. Pick McNitt made me what he called a Darwinian. "If you can survive this, you're one of the fittest."

It was like all the espresso beans in Los Angeles in a single cup.

"Wow," I said.

"Exactly," McNitt said. His big moon face was beaming under his snowy beard. "You think it'll sell?"

"Oh yeah. What're you going to charge?"

"Five bucks."

"A little high, isn't it?"

"All the writers will buy it. I'll tell 'em they can be the next Balzac."

"Balzac?"

"You know Balzac. Guy drank about forty cups of black coffee a day. Had his servants wake him up at midnight, got to his writing table, and wrote until exhausted. Then he'd start with the coffee and keep going. Wrote a hundred books that way. Before the age of fifty-one."

"What happened when he turned fifty-one?"

"Died."

"How?"

"Caffeine poisoning."

"Ah." I took one more sip and started to feel like I could jump over the Los Angeles Memorial Coliseum.

McNitt handed off the coffee bar duties to Megan, a student from CSUN. McNitt only hires students to work for him. His way to have an opportunity to teach because he'll never be able to get another teaching gig again. He took me to the back room where he keeps his butterflies.

Barton C. McNitt may be a rabid atheist and recovering mental patient, but he lovingly raises monarch butterflies for funerals. He feeds them, inspects them, and constantly talks—some would say, lectures—to them. Then he packs them in little triangular cardstock boxes, puts them in another box with bubble wrap, and ships them overnight to the bereaved, who order off his Web site, Barton's Butterflies.

"Heat is the enemy," he said as we entered the room he keeps at sixty-eight degrees exactly. "You've got to keep them out of the heat. I had a hysterical woman call me from Phoenix one time, dead summer. They opened the boxes and all the butterflies went straight down. It was 110 degrees and they kept my beauties in the back of their gas-guzzling, Middle East–supporting Suburban! I almost booked a flight to Phoenix so I could set up another funeral myself."

"You love your work."

"Coffee and insects. There are no two purer things in this wide world. They are the top of the evolutionary chain."

"Higher than man?"

"Way higher than man! Do you think a world of Insecta Lepidoptera would have invented war?"

"No," I said. "But also no Bach."

"They have their own music. Bach to them might sound like gangsta rap does to me! By the way, a sniffer came by."

"Sniffer?"

"Guy asking about you. When you might be in."

"What'd you tell him?"

"I said, I don't know anyone by that name." McNitt reached into one of the mesh cages and lightly touched a butterfly wing with his fingertip. The wing fluttered.

"And did this fellow believe you?" I asked.

"He copped a little attitude on me, so I just quoted Marcus Aurelius to him."

"You did what?"

"Stoic philosophy, son. I said to him, 'Do the things external which fall upon thee distract thee? Give thyself time to learn something new and good, and cease to be whirled around.'"

"That must have changed his life."

"I don't think so. He didn't look pleased." McNitt faced me and touched his head with his index finger. "He was not fully in control of his ruling part. Are you, Ty?"

"In control of my ruling part?"

McNitt nodded. "You see, for some men, the ruling part is not in the head, but south of the equator, and that is what gets them into trouble. You'll recall that was the point of the exchange in *The Republic* between Socrates and Cephalus."

I cleared my throat. "I have to admit it's been a while since I've cracked *The Republic*."

"Cephalus is the old man reflecting on his youth. He finds a calm in his age because he is no longer a slave to, as Sophocles called it, that mad and furious master. You see?"

"So, Pick, what did this guy look like?"

"Cephalus? No one knows. He—"

"No, the guy who came sniffing around for me."

"Ah. Black, dressed fine, about your size, maybe a little bigger."

"He say what he wanted with me?" I said.

McNitt shook his head. "He gave me a few choice words, then left. But the words did not bother me." He touched his cranium again.

"You make a fine receptionist," I said.

"You gonna chase me around the desk?"

"First," I said, "that's a sexist remark. And second, it wouldn't be much of a chase."

"I move a lot faster than you think," he said, then ambled back to the store with all the speed of an excited mollusk.

I opened my phone and checked out the program Blumberg had given me. Came up with a road map and a blinking red dot. That was DeCosse the Younger.

A couple of clicks got me closer, so I could read street names. The dot was heading south on the 710 Freeway. Every fifteen seconds the map and location refreshed.

I sat there feeling powerful and paranoid. That I could spy like this on a private citizen was stunning. But also the mark of our age, when privacy was an ever-decreasing commodity.

Which was one reason I was glad, but also a little nervous, about being at St. Monica's. Kept thinking I was like Harrison Ford in *Witness*, hiding out in Amish country.

Until the bad guys found him and showed up with guns.

82

BEFORE I COULD get in my car I got stopped. By a guy fitting the description McNitt just gave me.

"Hey," was all he said.

He was a little taller than me and about my age. Either his eyes were naturally narrow or he was glaring. Whatever, he didn't look happy.

"Hey what?" I said.

"I need to talk to you."

I studied his look, tried to think of what business he would have with me. Then I said, "You wouldn't be James, would you?"

His eyes opened wider, so I guess the original look was a glare. How very observant I am.

"How'd you know that?" he said.

"And Lana talked to you. That's how you found me."

"That's pretty good, man."

"Yeah, well, I imagine things aren't pretty good for you right now."

He looked at the ground as he shook his head. "I didn't do it. I didn't kill her. I loved Avisha."

"You talk to the cops?"

"No way. They'll take me down. I can't go down. I got two strikes. That's why I'm talkin' to you."

I looked around the parking lot. Like I expected to see a deputy sheriff or Brosia, or even a security guard named Petey watching us through binoculars.

"Let's go inside," I said.

"Where?"

"You drink coffee?"

83

HE DID. MCNITT fixed him up with a regular cup and left us alone at a back table.

"I really loved her, man," he said. There was real pain in his voice. "I wasn't there to protect her."

"Where were you?"

"My brother's, Inglewood."

"You have a last name, James?"

"Kingman."

"How'd you find me?"

"Reatta told Avisha about meeting you here."

I nodded. "What do you do, James?"

He hesitated, wrapped his hands around his cup, and wiggled his fingers. "Don't laugh."

"Hey, I'm a lawyer. I get abuse all the time. I won't laugh."

"Standup," he said.

I laughed.

"See?" he said.

"But you want laughs. You're a comedian."

"I'm tryin'. You know how hard it is?"

"What do you do in the lean times?" I asked.

"That's like all the time. I pick up jobs. That's how I met Avisha. She and some of the girls at Night Silk had a party. I did some catering for it."

"How long had you been with her?"

"Over a year. She was gonna quit the trade."

"Why were you at your brother's the night she was killed?"

"We had a fight. She was nervous lately. She wouldn't tell me why. I wasn't working. She didn't want to do what she was doing anymore. She said she was working on something, but she wouldn't say what. I got mad at her for that. I wish I didn't."

"You don't know anything about what she was working on?"

"She said it was a score. That's all. It was gonna be a score."

"Drug deal?"

"No way. She never did any of that. Me neither."

"Anything else she might have said about it?"

He thought for a moment. "She called it an operation. Like Operation Spice Deal or something like that. Pepper or ginger or something."

"Spice Girl thing?"

"Spice Girls? They still alive? No, that's not it."

I said, "When's the last time you saw her?"

"It was Wednesday. We had a big fight and I was yellin' and screamin' and she was givin' it right back to me and I left and drove to my brother's place."

"How long were you there?"

"Three days, I think. Yeah, three."

"Can you account for your time there?"

"Like how?"

"Anybody besides your brother see you?"

"Some guys came over that night. I tried out some material on 'em."

"How many guys?" I said.

"Three, four maybe."

"No maybes. I want a definite answer. You have to think definite from now on."

He nodded and gave it some thought. "Four guys. One guy left early."

"I hope he didn't walk out on your routine."

"I wasn't too on. Hard to make people laugh when you just had it out with your woman."

"Show business, huh? Now, do you know the names of these guys?"

"A couple I remember."

I rubbed my eyes. "Did you try to call Avisha?" I said.

"Nah. I was waiting on her. I wasn't gonna make the first move."

"Very male of you."

"What do I do now?"

"You want my advice?"

"Yeah."

"You need to turn yourself in."

He shook his head.

"You're an obvious suspect in a murder," I said. "You stay outside, it'll look like you're guilty."

A sound came from his throat. Muffled anguish.

"Look at me, James."

He did.

I said, "You tell me you can cover yourself, where you were at, with more than your brother doing the talking. Think real hard before you answer."

There was definitely thinking going on, for about a minute. Then James said, "Yeah. I can."

"Because they will check out your every move."

"You gonna help me?"

"I don't work for free."

"Oh man, I don't have lawyer money."

"What kind of money do you have?"

"Chump change."

"How much of a chump are you?"

"You serious?"

"When it comes to my fees, I'm very serious."

He frowned and reached for his wallet. Opened it and fingered the contents. "Like thirteen bucks," he said.

"Give me ten."

James hesitated.

"Give me ten dollars," I said.

He took out two fives and handed them to me. I put them in my shirt pocket. "Now it's official. Now I'm your lawyer."

"Just like that?"

"You're going to help me out, too. You're going to try to come up with some names for me. You're going to think real hard. Do you think you can think hard for me, James?"

"I can try, man."

"Good. Write out your brother's name, address, and phone number. Tell him I'll be talking to him. And here's some free advice. You lie to your lawyer and it's very bad. Do you understand that?"

"Yeah, man, you don't—"

"Are you lying to me, James? In any way?"

"No!"

"Okay then. Now we call the deputy at Malibu station and we take you in. You are going to say that you didn't kill Avisha, and that's all. I'll take it from there."

James nodded.

84

DEPUTY BROWNE SAT us in an interview room and James told him he was innocent. I told Browne I would do some checking and when I found out some useful information, I'd let him know.

"Sure," he said, like he didn't believe me.

And why should he?

Browne requested that James not leave the county.

I thought they only said that on TV.

Then I took James to his car outside the Ultimate Sip and went back to St. Monica's ten dollars richer.

What a roll I was on.

85

THE NEXT MORNING I took on Sister Mary again on the court.

This time I brought my A game.

I was hot. In a zone. When I played high school ball I was deadly from fifteen feet. Automatic. Had a silky shot I modeled after Larry Bird. A little fadeaway that was unstoppable.

Today it was going in, and Sister Mary didn't like it.

We played one on one and I took her down, eleven to four.

"Just thought you should see the game when it's played right," I said afterward.

Sister Mary, in her gray sweats, said, "I'm ready. Show me."

"You didn't see the sweet jumpers? The perfect spin on the ball?"

"Was that you?"

"What does a guy have to do to get appreciated around here?"

"Eat more fruitcake."

"I'll take the dis instead, thank you very much."

"Okay," she said, "I can handle that."

She bounced the ball a couple of times. I kept wondering what she would have been if she hadn't given her life over to the church. A reporter maybe, one who could dig out facts, a bulldog.

Or maybe a cop or private investigator. She could get people to open to her. She had a way of making you feel comfortable and when she listened, she really listened. She didn't have a personal agenda.

Maybe that's what they make you pack up when you get here, your agendas. Leave them behind for God.

Which brought to mind Sister Hildegarde.

"Come with me a minute," I said.

Sister Mary paused, then rolled the ball to the side. The basketball court backs up against the hill at the edge of St. Monica's. There's a dirt path up the hill to the perimeter wall, which has a wooden gate they keep unlocked. Something about trusting St. Benedict and his devotion to hospitality.

Which worked for me.

I opened the gate and that brought us to the crest of a hill. From here we looked out over the northern section of the Santa Susana range. Undeveloped land. About sixty acres of it was owned by St. Monica's.

"It's pretty today," Sister Mary said.

"Imagine what it'll be like when the development goes up just over there."

"What development?"

"Homes, of course. Big, new, jammed together, designer McMansions. Dogs and kids and cars."

"What are you talking about?"

"The dream village of Sam DeCosse Junior, with the cooperation of Sister Hildegarde."

She faced me. "Can you get to the point?"

"Sister Hildegarde has made, or is about to make, a deal to sell off some of this land. To the DeCosses, so Junior can get into home development. They want to make money. Apparently Sister Hildegarde does, too. Now why would she do that?"

"You know why. To pay for health care for the older ones. Like Sister Perpetua. But we are supposed to take care of our own, not sell off assets and hire somebody else to do it."

"Can Sister Hildegarde just decide to sell?"

"Oh, it has to go through a council vote, and technically the archdiocese has to approve. But in reality Sister Hildegarde can pretty much have her way. I'm just sick about this."

"What if I talk to Sister Hildegarde?"

"You?"

"Yeah. Lawyer talk. Get her all confused."

"That would be pouring gas on the fire, Mr. Buchanan. Best not."

"Is there anything you can do? Protest? Take it to the cardinal or the pope or something?"

"Maybe I'll write a letter. To Sister Hildegarde. And a copy to the archdiocese."

"There you go. A little protest."

She shook her head. "No protest is little to Sister Hildegarde."

"Now, that I can believe," I said. "But don't let it be said that a nun who can throw an elbow on the court—"

"I don't throw elbows! I use them judiciously."

"Fair enough. You don't strike me as someone who'll back down from anything if she believes in it."

"Neither do you."

"Then think this through with me. How does a woman living at the Lindbrook Hotel, a DeCosse property, come to connect with Father Bob, who happens to live on the grounds of a monastery that owns land about to become *another* DeCosse property? And then end up dead?"

"Because she found something out?"

"It would have to be something big enough to put a contract out on her. I mean, she was getting evicted illegally. So what?"

"Or maybe it's a coincidence. I mean, it's not surprising that DeCosse owns properties all over."

"Think about it," I said. "After we play another game. The irresistible force versus the immovable object."

"Which one are you?"

"Irresistible, of course."

"And I shall not be moved," Sister Mary said. "I'll even let you take it out."

86

SISTER MARY AND I brought Kylie to the Ultimate Sip on Monday morning. I got them both hot chocolate with whipped cream and had a Darwinian for myself. I was starting to get hooked.

I made some calls. One of them to Detective Brosia. Left a message.

Sister Mary said, "We need to talk about Kylie's schooling."

"Do we?" I said.

"I want to go to school," Kylie said.

"You ever been?"

Kylie shook her head.

"We need to get her caught up," Sister Mary said. "I want to undertake tutoring for a time."

"What's cootering?" Kylie said.

"It's something nuns do with rulers," I said.

"I ought to slap *you* for that," Sister Mary said.

"Slap who?" Kylie said.

"No one," Sister Mary said. "If Mr. Buchanan can focus for a moment, I would like to ask him a legal question."

"Oh, goody."

"Goody!" Kylie said.

"My question is as follows, Mr. Buchanan."

"Ty, please."

"Mr. Buchanan, what are the legalities involved in private tutoring vis-à-vis the truancy laws?"

"Did you just say *vis-à-vis*?"

"What if I did?"

"That's good. Usually I have to write those kinds of words down."

"Your answer?"

"I don't know the answer."

"Can you find out?"

"It's what I do. What about public school?"

"In Los Angeles? Are you out of your mind?"

"Touché. Parochial school?"

"Yes, when she is brought up to speed."

"Speedy," Kylie said.

"I don't think it will take long," I said. "Go for it."

87

BROSIA CALLED ME back. "What have you got?"

"Maybe we can trade a little information."

"I don't do that. You can tell me what you have and I'll let you know."

"That doesn't sound exactly fair."

"I'm not interested in fairness."

"You don't sound like you like me anymore," I said.

"I don't like the fact that there are two dead women and you're involved with both of them."

"You call what I'm doing 'involved'?"

"What would you call it?"

"Interested."

"There's nothing worse than an interested lawyer. You're not an investigator or a cop. You're going around sticking your nose in places it shouldn't be. And you're not licensed to do that."

"Detective, you know as well as I do that a license is not required when working as a lawyer. Now, I could hire an investigator, but I figure with the money I save doing it myself, I can go to Starbucks."

"If you end up making things tougher on me, that could mean obstruction."

"I know what I'm doing. The question is, do you?"

"Listen—"

"Have you talked to any of the people at the Lindbrook yet?"

"That's none of your business."

"Have you figured out how somebody could get in wearing a big rainbow hat and get out and nobody saw him?"

"Mr. Buchanan, I'm giving you a friendly warning."

"Those never work for me. You have to make it mean."

"Consider it done."

"Those don't work for me, either."

Long pause. "You called me, remember?" Brosia said.

I was operating on too much caffeine. I didn't need to make him angrier. At least I knew that much. Sometimes I'm a real clear thinker.

"Sam DeCosse, the old man," I said. "He's interested in buying a piece of property adjacent to St. Monica's monastery. That's where Reatta went to see the priest."

"Are you suggesting Sam DeCosse had something to do with her murder?" Brosia asked.

"I'm exchanging information with you," I said. "Which, by the way, means it's your turn."

He didn't respond.

"How did Reatta die?" I asked.

"Her neck was snapped," Brosia said.

I thought of Kylie then, asleep in the closet as this happened to her mother.

"Thanks for calling," Brosia said. "Let's do this again soon."

88

I DROVE BACK to the Lindbrook to take it one floor at a time. The same little man with the wheat pasta hair was behind the Plexiglas. His eyes got round like lollipops when he saw me.

He started shaking his head.

"I have some questions for you," I said.

"You get out!" he said. "Or I'll call the cops."

"Listen, Bashful, I represent the tenant in 414. I have the authority to go in and spend the night if I want to, which I would if I wanted to train a cockroach."

He picked up the phone.

As long as he stayed in his aquarium, there was not much I could do. So I turned my attention to the guys sitting in the lobby.

Disco Freddy was nowhere to be seen. The one guy I recognized was the man named Oscar. He was sitting near the window reading a newspaper.

I joined him.

"How you doing?" I said.

"Oh. Hey. What's up?"

"Mind if I sit?"

"Take a load off," he said. "I just been reading about our wonderful mayor and his little dogs."

"The mayor has dogs?"

"Did I say dogs? I meant the city council."

"Whoa."

"That's what I said. I used to be a cop, you know. Back in the day when they'd stand up for the troops. Back when the public was on your side."

"Glory days?"

Oscar closed the paper. "Just the days when a cop didn't have to look twelve ways before doing his job, thinking he might get videoed doing his job and then getting reamed for it. But you didn't come here to listen to me jabber on, did you?"

"Matter of fact, I wanted to ask about the murder in 414."

"You're workin' for the girl, right?"

"That's right."

"Cute little thing. She okay?"

"All things considered, not too bad."

He leaned over the table like a conspirator. "You want to know if the cops talked to me, don't you?"

"Did they?"

"Not very much. Like they were just goin' through the routine. I guess somebody dies here, it doesn't rate much attention. Not the way I woulda handled it."

"Why'd you stop being a cop?"

He paused, looked out the window at Sixth Street. "I went into the Turkey Stress Relief Program. Finished first in my class."

"Turkey Program?"

"Wild Turkey."

"Ah."

"Had a wife. She left. Being married to a cop's no life. No kids. Here I am."

"Oscar," I said, "would you help me out with this case?"

The dark eyes cast a little glow. Then he smiled, showing a lost upper tooth, a gap where old memories might leak out.

"What do you want to know?" he said.

"Where were you on the night the woman was murdered?" I asked.

"I was right down here, where I always am. I was sitting and watching Disco Freddy—I watch out for him, see, make sure he doesn't wander into the street too far—and played some cards with Ricky."

"Who's Ricky?"

"Third floor."

"Might he have seen anything?"

"Don't think so. We talked after—he couldn't recall. Course, the way he pickles his brain, it's kind of hard for him to remember much."

I was kicking around in my mind how much to tell Oscar. For all I knew, he could have done it. Unlikely, but this was beginning to sound like an inside job. People in Rasta hats don't just waltz in unnoticed, do their thing, and leave without being seen.

"How long did you and Ricky play cards?" I asked.

"Till about eleven or so. I remember 'cause the TV news started. Eleven's about when I get to bed."

"What room?"

"I'm 207."

"You went to bed after that?"

He smiled. "In a manner of speaking."

"You had company?"

"That's none of your business, counselor."

"It could be police business."

He narrowed his eyes at me. "Are you trying to say you think ol' Oscar has to have an alibi?"

"Do you?"

"You know, you're a funny guy. I've done nothin' but try to help you, help the cops. Help the little girl. That's all I've done and you think I could do that? You can leave right now, Mr. Lawyer, and take the train right to hell."

He pushed himself away from the table and stood up.

"Wait," I said. "I didn't mean anything by it. I'm flying blind here."

"You just flew into a wall."

"I'm sorry," I said.

Before he could answer, the lights of an LAPD patrol car flashed through the front window. It pulled up to the curb and two uniforms got out.

They walked into the lobby where the Munchkin had come out from his lair. He pointed at me, and the officers walked over.

"Can you tell us what you're doing here, sir?" the younger of the two cops asked. He was tall and skinny. His partner, older and fatter, I figured was his trainer. Letting the kid take a stab at questioning.

"No," I said. "What I'm doing here is my business."

The cop blinked so hard you could almost hear his lids clacking.

"You're trespassing," the cop said.

"I'm not."

"Do you rent a room here?"

"My client does."

The cop frowned and looked at the Munchkin, who shrugged.

I produced a card, gave it to him. "You can call Lieutenant Brosia at Central if you want to check it out. There's currently litigation over the tenancy. I have authority from the tenant to be on the premises. It's just that simple."

"He's causing trouble!" the Munchkin said.

The older cop shook his head, like he'd just placed the Munchkin in the nut category.

"Hickman, is that you?" Oscar had come up from behind me.

The older cop squinted. "Oscar?"

"Hey man."

Smiles and a handshake.

Oscar said, "Me and Hickman rode together a long time ago."

"Back when men were men," Hickman said, mostly to his young partner. "How you doing?"

"I'm alive."

"That's great," Hickman said.

The Munchkin said, "Hey."

"Much ado about nothing here," Oscar said to Hickman. "Me and Mr. Buchanan been talking quietly. I can vouch for him."

That was that. The Munchkin stormed off like a child who got his toys taken away. Hickman and Oscar swapped a couple more jovialities. The young cop looked at me and I looked at him.

That's when Disco Freddy burst into the lobby with a shriek.

The young cop spun around, his hand going to his gun.

"Easy," Oscar said.

Disco spun around and put his hands out. "Mr. John Travolta!" he said.

"Time to roll," Hickman said, giving Oscar a clap on the shoulder. The cops left, walking quickly past Disco.

I looked at Oscar. "Thanks," I said. "How come you backed me?"

"Because you said you were sorry," he said. "Everybody deserves another chance. I'm talkin' from experience."

Disco Freddy strutted across the lobby like Travolta in *Saturday Night*

Fever. Well, not *really* like it, but if you tried real hard, you could almost pretend to see it.

"Mumbuddynomakenomubbamind," he said to us.

Oscar said, "Not now, Disco. Got business."

Then Disco said, "You want to find the guy that killed her?"

89

OSCAR'S CHIN DROPPED. "What'd you just say?"

"I seen the guy, yeah, I seen him, mumbuddy."

"You can talk?" I said.

Disco flashed a hard look at me. "Mumbuddy!"

"Better let me," Oscar said. To Disco: "What are you telling me, Freddy? That you saw the guy who killed 414?"

Disco Freddy nodded.

"What did he look like?" Oscar said.

"Mr. Buddy Ebsen!"

I shook my head. Buddy Ebsen? I thought I recalled him from an old movie I watched with Jacqueline once. Maybe a Shirley Temple. He was a dancer. That's why Disco Freddy was saying this.

"Nice try, Oscar," I said.

Disco Freddy did a turn.

Oscar grabbed Freddy's shoulders to stop him. "Freddy, listen to me. What do you mean you saw a guy who looks like Buddy Ebsen?"

"Buddy Ebsen! The greatest dancer of all time! Loosey goosey!" Disco Freddy started to flap his arms. He looked like a heron made of rubber.

"I think he saw somethin'," Oscar said to me.

To Disco Freddy I said, "Hey, man, was the guy white or black?"

"Buddy Ebsen..."

"Yeah, Buddy Ebsen. Was he white or was he black?"

Disco Freddy shrugged. "Saw him from the back."

"Okay," I said. "What did he have on his head?"

"Head?"

"Yeah. Was he wearing anything on his head?"

Disco Freddy frowned, took a step back, spun around one time. "Over the rainbow!"

"Whoa," I said. "You mean a rainbow hat? Different colors?"

Disco Freddy nodded. I looked at Oscar. "Now I think he saw something, too."

"Where'd you see him?" Oscar said.

"Mumbuddy."

"Come on, Freddy."

"Mumbuddy!"

I looked at the ceiling.

"Why don't you just show us?" Oscar said.

Disco Freddy jumped, then crouched, then went into a soft shoe. Leading toward the stairs.

Oscar looked at me. "Let's go," he said.

90

FREDDY DANCED UP to the second floor, shouting "Mr. James Cagney!" all the way.

Yankee Doodle Freddy.

We came to the second-floor corridor. It was long and narrow and gray, except for the white wainscoting that spoke of an earlier era. Most of these downtown hotels had been fashionable once.

A music mix blared. Somebody was pumping out gangsta, and somebody else had Tony Bennett on full blast. So a lovely street ode to ho's and weed was bucking right up against Tony telling everybody to forget their troubles and, come on, get happy.

Sitting against the corridor wall was a young African-American woman with a child, a boy about eight, who was rolling a fire engine back and forth on the floor. She looked our way with sleepy eyes, and then I knew it wasn't sleep that was in them. She'd had her morning fix.

Disco stopped and pointed to the end of the hall.

Oscar said, "Down there is where you saw him?"

Disco nodded.

"Show us."

Disco started dancing down the corridor in little circles, left arm out, saying, "Dancing with the lovely Leslie Caron! Mumbuddy."

It was hard to imagine him dancing with Leslie Caron to the tune-stew of gangsta rap and Tony Bennett. But by this time I knew Disco had his own inner band. The question was, could he communicate with the outside world? Meaning me.

The boy with the fire engine looked at us with suspicion. The mother—I assumed she was his mother—just stared, not focusing.

At the end of the corridor was a window and an exit door. Out the window was a fire escape. The window itself was locked. Didn't look like it had been opened since the fifties.

I pushed the bar on the exit door, opened it to the stairwell. "Are these doors locked on the outside?"

"No," Oscar said. "Some secure building, uh?"

"So this guy you saw," I said to Disco, "was he going out or coming in?"

"Dancing!" Disco said.

"He was dancing?"

"Everybody dances in Disco's mind," Oscar said. "Some are just better than others."

I watched Disco bow, back away, then do what can only be described as a Bizarro World buck and wing. He shot his legs out at the same time, his arms akimbo.

Then he winced and fell to the ground, grabbing his groin.

Oscar grunted, shook his head, then knelt down to help Disco up. "Fred Astaire pull a muscle?"

"Mumbuddy," Disco said.

"That's right," Oscar said.

"Is there anything else you can tell us, Disco?" I said.

"Owweee."

"I'm gonna take him to his room," Oscar said.

"I'll be in touch," I told him.

Oscar held Disco's arm and the star of the Lindbrook ballroom limped off with him.

I went through the exit.

91

I TOOK THE stairwell all the way down, then pushed open the door. It opened up to an alley that ran behind the hotel, emptying out into Sixth Street to the right. The door locked and denied access from the alley.

So what was accomplished? Not much. If Disco Freddy had indeed seen the killer, it was likely he'd seen the guy on the way out. The question would then be, what was he doing on the second floor?

Or, the guy could have been coming in, which would mean having access from the alley.

Or Disco Freddy could have been on his own little dance floor in his own little universe, taking us all along with him.

Whatever it was, it wasn't much. Not anything you could go to the cops with.

I went back to the entry and this time the Munchkin didn't do a thing. I went back up to the second floor. The woman and child were gone.

I knocked on a couple of doors and talked to a couple of guys—one a young actor from Iowa, the other an ex–city parks worker. Neither one saw anyone in a Rasta hat. Both told me Disco Freddy was not the most reliable source.

Like I needed to be told.

92

ON MY WAY out I found Oscar back in the lobby, frowning at a newspaper.

"Oscar, you loved being a cop."

"I did."

"Then do me a favor. Question folks. Casual. See if they saw anyone come in or go out with a Rasta hat on. Would you consider doing that for me?"

He smiled and tossed the paper aside. "I been looking for something to do besides this Sudoku, which is from the pit of hell."

"Thanks."

"Good to be back in the saddle."

93

I DROVE TO Inglewood and talked to James Kingman's brother, Silas. He was a teacher at Inglewood High, history. I met him at the school, where he was expecting me. He had a fifty-minute break. We sat in his room and, with Washington and Jefferson and Lincoln looking down from posters, I grilled him.

I had to grill him. I had to ask him about the times he was with James and the other people who could provide that information.

The nice part was that Silas would make a very credible witness for his brother. The not so nice part was that might not be enough. James spent Wednesday night at his brother's house. There were witnesses to that. But on Thursday Silas was teaching. There was a long stretch James would have to account for.

I didn't think James killed Avisha. But I had to get some good alibi evidence together.

That or find the real killer. Because my thought, the one that wouldn't go away, was that the killings were related.

Reatta. Avisha. Same guy maybe did both.

94

AMONG THE THINGS I care least about in this world are the travails of Britney Spears, sumo wrestling, and being seen in the hottest clubs in L.A.

If NASA engineers could design the greatest waste of human time and energy, it would be a lot like trying to look cool enough to be seen as not trying to look cool.

Even though here it becomes a battle of hip, and there's nothing sadder than being an unhip hipster in L.A. Sort of like showing up at the prom with an unzipped fly you never notice.

So people stress over the hippest clubs to go to.

Sunset Strip used to be hip but has fallen on hard times. It's "maturing," some say, which, to hip, means death. Now Hollywood is giving the Strip a run. The dive bars have been cleaned up and the architecture is cooler, so it's getting a younger crowd these days.

On the Strip, even thrash metal venues get the yuppies in button-down shirts, which the rockers deplore. They migrate east to avoid yuppie cooties.

They go over to Hollywood, join a crowd that considers itself more authentic, outfitted in true rock-punk-hip-hop-new-wave-techno-glam style. Avoiding the open fly at all costs, for to lose an ounce of hipness here is to die a little.

Todd McLarty, Sister Mary managed to find out, preferred the Cahuenga corridor to the Strip, even though he was now pushing forty. Going Hollywood was a way to keep the edge for him, I guess.

And his favorite hangout was the Ninth Circle, just off the boulevard.

So that's where I went, fighting the crush of cars and getting into a parking lot near Franklin. Clubbers everywhere. All trying hard to look as if they know what's going on.

The line was long, but I wasn't going to wait regardless. I went to the velvet rope where a wrestler with a dome for a head stood with his earpiece and look of practiced venom.

He gave me withering look #4.

"That's good," I said.

"What is?" Withering voice #3a.

"You. You're good at your job. Ben and I need to see a guy."

"I need to see Ben."

I gave him the hundred. He asked me to open my coat. Looked me over and then let me into the Ninth Circle.

95

THE BEAT WAS fully amped. There was dancing and grinding and the smell of the hormonal. Booths lined two walls, lit in low copper color. I went to the bar and squeezed between two stools and ordered a Coke. I wasn't here to party or loosen up or get warm.

The first sip didn't make my lips. It made the front of my shirt. A woman on my left had snorted a laugh and reared back, hitting my elbow.

To her credit, she immediately turned around and, with the laugh still passing from her face, said, "Sorry!"

"Must have been a good one," I said.

"What was?"

"The joke."

"Oh that." If she was twenty-one, it was barely. She had short dark hair and olive skin. "We were just talking about that vid on YouTube, the CEO who dropped his pants during the board meeting. Seen it?"

"Darn, I missed that one."

"Oh, it is out there."

"Note to self."

"You'll love it," she said. "So what do you do?"

"I'm a weaver of dreams."

"Huh?"

"Lawyer."

"Cool."

"Sometimes."

"When is it not cool?" She leaned her head in her hand and put her elbow on the bar top.

"Well, you know what a lawsuit is, right?"

"Sure."

"It's where you go in a pig and come out a sausage."

She stared at me. "Really?" It sounded like "Rilly."

"Metaphorically."

"You talk funny."

"I've been told."

"I want to go to law school someday."

"Rilly?" I said.

She nodded.

"That's one thing this society needs," I said. "More lawyers. You can never have too many lawyers."

"How do you do it? How do you get to be a lawyer?"

"Well, first you have to go to law school. Have you graduated yet?"

"Yeah. Three years ago."

"Pretty young for college, weren't you?"

"High school."

"Ah. Where are you doing your undergrad?"

"You mean college?"

"That's what I mean."

"I have to go to college first?"

"Uh, yeah."

"Rilly?"

"Rilly."

"That is not fair."

I took a sip of Coke and considered my answer carefully. I am a weaver of dreams. "You'll make a good lawyer someday."

"What's your name?" she asked.

"Buchanan. What's yours?"

"Nora." She stuck her hand out. I shook it.

"You know this place pretty well?" I said.

"I come here all the time."

"You ever see Todd McLarty here?"

"Oh yeah. And Heather and Brit and Brad and everybody."

"Let me buy you a drink," I said. "While I wait."

"Are you Todd's lawyer?"

"Not yet, but who knows?"

"You're the leaver of dreams," she said.

That seemed to be a better fit, so I let it stand.

96

I BOUGHT NORA a martini and she made me talk about being a lawyer, which I can do even without alcohol. Five minutes after that she looked at the door and said, "There he is."

McLarty was with his retinue—a blond mannequin model type hanging on to him, almost wearing a tight black dress. Another couple of the same ilk was with them, laughing it up as they got shown to a booth.

A large African-American male with a proportionally large head full of hair, dressed all in black, stood near the booth, scanning the crowd. I watched him for a minute. A couple of giggling young ladies scurried up to the booth and the large man put up his hand. It was the size of a canned ham. He talked to them and they looked like they were pleading. He shook his head and talked a little more and the ladies hung their heads and walked away.

"He's always got the big guy with him," Nora said. "You never know."

"I left my bodyguard at home," I said.

"You have a bodyguard?"

"Doesn't everybody?"

"You're funny. What's he look like, your bodyguard?"

"She. A nun."

"Now you're just playing me."

"Only a little," I said. "I think this nun can take care of herself. I play basketball with her."

At McLarty's table a server came by with a silver bucket and champagne. McLarty started on the cork.

"Nice meeting you, Nora," I said.

She slipped me a card. "Call me."

That hadn't happened in a while. I tucked the card in my pocket and made my way across the dance floor and up to the large man with the hair. I nodded at him. He glared at me. I handed him my card. He looked at it, handed it back. Said nothing.

"I need to talk to him," I said. Shouted actually.

The man shook his head.

"He'll want to talk to me."

Shook his head again.

"Let's ask him," I said. I didn't even get a full step in before the big hand thumped my chest and pushed me backward.

"Let the man have a good time," he said.

"I have some news. Very important to him. Tell him."

"Tell him what?"

"Just say Tawni."

He pulled back and looked at me without comprehension.

"Tawni," I repeated. "Go ahead."

"What's Tawni?"

"He'll know."

Behind the guy I could see the champagne being poured. It was Cristal.

The big man shook his head again. He was really good at that.

"Trust me," I said. "He will want to know."

The guy turned around and gestured at McLarty. Then he leaned over and talked into his ear. As he did, McLarty looked at me. He did not look happy. He said something to his bodyguard. The guy turned back to me and said, "Let's go outside."

"I don't think so," I said.

"You can talk out there."

"You can break my fingers out there."

Then he smiled and nodded. He could nod, too. "Not gonna, though. He'll talk to you out there."

McLarty downed his champagne in a big gulp and started talking to his mannequin.

The big guy encouraged me with a hand on my arm. It felt like a skip loader.

97

THERE WERE SOME smokers out in the back, and another big guy at the door checking on those who went out. The big guy at the door nodded at the big guy who was with me. They were probably in the same union.

A minute later McLarty came out and immediately lit a smoke. He seemed nervous. He had an ex-addict look to him. His forearms were a little too thin, sticking out of his striped polo like, well, a couple of thicker stripes.

"So what's this all about?" he said.

"You want to talk with your man here?" I said.

McLarty thought about it. "Maybe you better let me take this alone."

The big guy said, "You sure?"

"It's okay."

The guy went back to talk with his twin at the door.

"So," McLarty said to me. "You got my attention. What do you want?"

"Then Tawni rings a real bell with you."

"I didn't say anything like that. Who's Tawni?"

I smiled. "You're a good actor but not that good."

He eyed me through a haze of smoke. "I repeat, why am I listening to you?"

"The name Tawni must mean something to get you away from the Crissy for half a second and out here with me."

McLarty sucked smoke, blew it out fast. "You got something to say to me, let's hear it."

"I'm looking for information," I said. "Here's what I know. I know you and Tawni were kind of tight for a while."

"Who's Tawni?"

"You want me to just go to the blogs with the information I have?"

He waited, then said, "How do you know anything?"

"As they say, I have my sources."

"What's it gonna take to get you to the point?" He puffed again.

"You're still listening, so there's something there. I've never seen your show, by the way, but I hear you're pretty good in it. I hear you turned your life around. I hear you've got a family audience that's pretty big now. Congratulations."

"Do I care what you think?"

"Yeah, you do."

He waited.

"So here it is," I said. "You knew Tawni back there in your bad old days, knew her pretty well. Or should I say, used her pretty well?"

He threw down his cig and fished for another. Stuck it in his mouth. "Do I need to tell you what you're full of?"

"Tawni's dead. Somebody murdered her. She had a kid. Your kid."

That froze him. The nail in his mouth was shaking a little. "You want money, is that it?"

"How'd we get from murder to money so fast?"

"That's what it comes down to."

"I just want to know if you're the father of the kid, that's all."

McLarty looked as if he'd snorted Tabasco. He spun around in a little circle. Like Disco Freddy's more talented cousin. He shouted a couple of choice words and that got Bodyguard over in a hurry.

"Bax," McLarty said, "tell this guy I'm not interested and make him understand. Tell him my lawyers are smarter than he is, okay?"

He legged it back to the club.

Bax said, "Mr. McLarty is not interested and his lawyers are smarter than you. Understand?"

"You don't even know me, Bax. I might be another Einstein."

"If you were smart, you wouldn't be here." He put his ham hand on my shoulder. "Mr. McLarty gets all sorts of grief from people—requests, paparazzi, all that, you know? And he hires me to be kind of like a buffer."

"You're a buffer, I'll give you that."

"So I'm buffing you, man. Let's leave it at that."

"Your boy will want to give me a call."

"He says no."

"Ask him if he'd like to have a paternity test done. Ask if he'd like to come to court and tell a judge the story. Because, see, when guys don't step up to the plate for what they've done, you have to haul 'em to court. I hate to do that, I really do."

"He's gotten sued before."

"Not by me."

"What makes you so special?"

"Bran," I said. "I eat lots of bran."

"Hey, I'm into fiber, too."

Unbelievable.

"A lot of legumes," he said. "Really like legumes."

"I never thought I'd be discussing health with Todd McLarty's bodyguard."

"Most natural thing in the world," he said. "You want to stay healthy, stay away from Mr. McLarty." He poked my chest with his finger. "And eat plenty of cruciferous greens."

98

I WALKED BACK to my car thinking about the word "cruciferous" and what Todd McLarty was hiding.

Of course, I had no idea if Kylie was McLarty's. And maybe I didn't want to find out. What if he turned around and said he wanted her?

There's no way I would let that happen.

But if she was his, maybe there was a connection with Reatta's death.

What if Reatta was trying to hold him up for money? Would it be beyond the realm of possibility for McLarty to send someone around to silence her?

99

TUESDAY MORNING I stopped by the DA's office in Van Nuys. Mitch Roberts had a packet of discovery for me.

In California we have reciprocal discovery. The prosecutor has to hand things over like police reports and notes, witness statements, and the list of witnesses themselves. The defense has the right to interview prosecution witnesses, though you can't compel them to talk.

The defense has to hand over stuff, too. That's how the judiciary took some of the creative element out of criminal trials. No more surprise witnesses. No last-minute twists. Too bad. Those seemed like so much fun in old movies.

Roberts met me in his office. He had a file box on his desk. No doubt my reading matter.

"You still thinking of taking this thing to trial?" Roberts said.

"My client keeps telling me this strange thing, that he didn't do it," I said.

"Pretty strange."

"What if it's true?"

Roberts shrugged one shoulder. "The jury says what's true."

"I'm for that," I said.

"Capital jury for the first time, pretty rough."

I said, "What if you took off your prosecutor hat for just a second here and looked at it from the standpoint of a reasonable man."

Roberts cracked a smile. "You saying we DDAs aren't reasonable?"

"You know what I mean, that old law school standard. The reasonable man. Look at what you've got in the witness statements. The IDs. They're all over the map. And this Nydessa whatsername, she's got a reason to lie."

"So you say. You'll have to convince a jury of that."

"Think that'll be so hard?"

Roberts shrugged.

"Don't be pulling a Nifong on me, okay?" Roberts knew exactly what that meant. A reference to the odious Mike Nifong, disgraced DA of Raleigh, North Carolina. The guy who thought he could prosecute three Duke lacrosse players for rape when he knew the victim's story was a load. But he wouldn't back down. Prosecutorial macho. Only he got caught by the national media, backed further and further into a corner until he had to crawl out in shame.

Problem is, when prosecutors pull a Nifong, most of the time there's no media. No one to hold their feet to the flame. Then they dangle the prospect of long sentences in order to get your client to cop a plea.

Even innocent ones take the deal because they know if they don't and get convicted, they'll spend a lot more years in the slam when they're sentenced.

Roberts said, "That what you think I'm doing?"

"Just search your heart," I said, trying to sound sincere.

"I have, and it's a cold, dark place," he said with a smile.

"Oh, I have a message for you from my client."

"From your client? And it's not a plea?"

"No."

"I'm all ears."

"He told me to tell you he's sorry that he told you that you were scum."

Roberts sighed. "I'm comforted. I was really worried there."

"Thanks for the load," I said. "Of discovery."

I picked up the box and left.

100

OUTSIDE THE COURTHOUSE I heard a guy yelling. He had a scraggly black beard and was using his hands like a mad Italian. No one was listening to him. People in suits on their way in or out of court hurried by.

Still the man went on. He was raving about the Antichrist, who happened to be the pope.

Nice.

Then he started shouting that everyone who took a mark of the Beast was going to hell forever and ever. There would be no rest, day or night, he said, where the worm dieth not.

It was all about resisting the Beast, he said.

I wondered what I would do if the Beast came to me and asked for legal representation.

Get the fee up front, that's what.

101

ON WEDNESDAY MORNING I appeared in the Superior Court of Los Angeles County, downtown, in the courtroom of Morris Page. He was a judge I'd been in front of before, but that was back when I was a real trial lawyer with a law firm behind me.

He gave me a nice hello in chambers anyway. I was there to talk about the temporary restraining order with him and Al Bradshaw before we went and put everything on the record.

Al had brought along a little friend, Hyrum Roddy.

"Double-teaming me?" I said.

"You can give up now," Al said.

"Might be a good idea, Ty," Judge Page said. He was gray haired and slightly built, maybe sixty years old. Wore old-fashioned wire-rim glasses. He had a college professor look to him, mild mannered. But in his day he was reputed to be one of the most fearsome trial lawyers you'd ever run up against. He spoke softly but carried a big briefcase.

As a judge, he liked things calm in his courtroom and his lawyers prepared.

The lawyers sat in leather chairs in front of the judge's immaculate desk, and he said, "Ty, what are you doing with this thing? Scraping the bottom of the barrel?"

"Not a nice way to talk about a six-year-old girl," I said.

"I mean legally speaking."

"No, it's not the bottom of the barrel. Because if you scrape off what's on the bottom of the barrel, you get the crud underneath, and that's where you'll find Orpheus Development doing the twenty-eight-day shuffle."

"Your Honor," Al said, theatrical disdain dripping from his voice, "this is just Mr. Buchanan trying to poison the well."

"Me being the well?" Judge Page said.

"Yes, Your Honor."

"Exactly," Hyrum Roddy said.

"I can take care of my own water supply," Page said. "But thanks for looking out for me." The judge looked at me. "Ty, is that what you're really after? Stop the practice of shuffling tenants?"

"I'm appearing on behalf of a client. I want it stopped for her sake."

"And if it is, my ruling could apply to all the tenants."

"Maybe."

"Which would be just fine by you," the judge said.

I smiled.

Judge Page sighed. "All right. Let's get down to it. You've got to show me that the moving party here, this Kylie with no last name, will suffer irreparable harm if I don't grant relief. So just how will that happen, Ty?"

"She'll be out on the street," I said.

"Is she occupying the premises?"

"Not at the moment."

"Where is she?"

"I've got her."

Page blinked. "You're taking care of her?"

I nodded.

"If you're taking care of her, how can the harm be irreparable?"

"Once she's evicted, she won't be able to get back in," I said.

"Come on, let's be real here. She's not going to live in that place by herself."

"She might," I said. "But that's not your call, it's hers. And I'm her guardian ad litem, so I'm making the claim on her behalf."

Al chuffed like an impatient dog and shook his head.

"Even if I found irreparable harm," Page said, "you also have to show that monetary damages would be inadequate. Has there been a settlement offer?"

"Mr. Buchanan does not seem disposed to that," Al said.

"Now, that doesn't seem very sporting," Judge Page said.

"I don't see this as a sport," I said.

"And you and Mr. Bradshaw used to be such good friends." The judge smiled.

I did not smile.

Al and Hyrum Roddy did not smile.

So Judge Page stopped smiling and cleared his throat. "What about harm to Orpheus, Mr. Bradshaw?"

"Clearly," Al said, "there's harm here. The right to control one's premises, to set rents, to take full advantage of the free market."

"What about this twenty-eight-day shuffle business?" Page said. "That's clearly illegal, isn't it?"

"We deny engaging in any such action," Al said.

"Wouldn't a hearing on the merits help us figure out if that's true or not?"

"Sounds good to me," I said.

Al shot me a look. His eyes showed a sudden fear, that the judge might actually be considering granting this thing.

"Your Honor," Al said, "this is just a simple matter of a sham tenant being used by a lawyer to harass my client. That's really what this is about."

"Is that what this is about, Mr. Buchanan?"

"It started with a tenant," I said. "But it's more than that now. One of the considerations for a TRO is the public interest. Well, here's your public interest. The Lindbrook is the last stop for a lot of people. Like vets. Guys who came back from Nam and got spat on. They don't need that again. Like ex-cops who put it on the line out on the streets every day. I don't think they should be put out there every twenty-eight days. But maybe that's just me."

To Al, Judge Page said, "What about that?"

"When was the last time you ever granted a TRO for the public interest?" Al said. "That never happens."

"Why shouldn't it?" Page said. "I think the public interest here is pretty strong, don't you?"

Al's lips fluttered but no sound came out.

"You know what?" the judge said. "I'm feeling a little interested in the public this morning. I woke up and saw a story in the paper about the folks they want to evict to expand the freeway. You know, people with homes, people who've lived there for years. Something about that sticks in my craw. So we're going to go out there and I'm going to grant the TRO, and then we'll all come back and make our case for an injunction. Shall we?"

"I'd like to make a phone call," Al said. "Five minutes."

"Four," the judge said, standing and putting on his robe.

102

AFTER THE RULING Al stopped me in the corridor. Hyrum Roddy had apparently scurried for the nearest exit.

"Mr. DeCosse would like another meeting with you," he said.

"When?"

"Now. I've got a ride waiting."

"Yeah? Where we going?"

"A golf course."

"I don't play golf."

"Not that kind of golf course," Al said. "This one you won't believe."

103

I DIDN'T BELIEVE it. Because it was a floating golf course. It was on the Pacific Ocean, west of Catalina.

Not looking out at the Pacific Ocean. *On* the Pacific Ocean.

It happened this way.

Al took me to a heliopad at one of the buildings DeCosse owns downtown. We coptered down to Long Beach and set down at a private mooring.

Where Sam DeCosse had his yacht.

A 205-footer called *Lady Ariel*.

Two large crew members met Al and me. Al said a few words to one of them. Then we boarded.

I said nothing. This was something I just had to see.

We went downstairs and into a room that would have been a stylish studio apartment in Beverly Hills. It was all teak and brass. A polished bar ran along one wall, complete with a mirror behind it.

"A guy could have a pretty good weekend here," I said.

"You have no idea," Al said. "Wait here."

He left, along with the two monster stewards.

I went to the bookcase, which was enclosed in glass. Two shelves of books that looked like collectibles. First editions, no doubt.

The Sun Also Rises, by Ernest Hemingway.

The Grapes of Wrath, by John Steinbeck.

Slaughterhouse Five, by Kurt Vonnegut.

The Naked and the Dead, by Norman Mailer.

I tried to open the case, but it was—

"Locked," Ariel DeCosse said.

She was wearing workout clothes and a slight sheen of perspiration. Had gloves on her hands. Some kind of boxing workout, I guessed. She crossed the room, taking off her gloves, and shook my hand. "Welcome aboard."

"Nice boat," I said.

"Hardly a boat." She tossed her gloves on an end table. "Do you like art, Mr. Buchanan?"

"I haven't got a lot of room for it."

"Oh? What sort of house do you have?"

"I live in a trailer."

"Oh my. Are you intentional about the interior?"

"If you mean, do I throw my socks on the floor near the bathroom, then yes."

She smiled. "You're a funny one. Don't you care about money and love? Don't you want to have more of both in your life?"

"Should I?"

"Of course. What else is there?"

"Chimichangas?"

The smile left. "Don't you want to be happy?"

"It beats the alternative."

"Happiness is always a part of it. Did you know you can divide your quarters into eight sections?"

"Really? Doesn't that make about three cents each?"

"No, your living qua—you're making fun of me."

"Go on. I'm interested." I was, too, because I was trying to figure out whether she was serious about this.

"You can actually make these sections right on your desk," she said. "One of the sections is for wealth, and if you want to, you can put a crystal in that section and attract wealth."

"It's that easy?"

"Of course. You're tapping into the chi, the universal force. When you drive your car, for instance, you can drive in the direction of your career, and use your mirrors to fend off bad luck."

"Mirrors fend off bad luck?"

"Yes."

"Not when I shave. I have to look at myself."

Now she ignored me and went on. "You must also remove all the clutter from your life. Clutter doesn't do you one ounce of good. There's so much to learn. Do you have ducks?"

"Excuse me?"

"You should display two mandarin ducks, which symbolize happiness and love. But do not display a solo mandarin duck, because that means you will be single forever."

"Check. Two ducks."

"You're making fun of me again. I understand. This is new to the Western mind."

"Are you saying I have a Western mind?"

"Don't you?"

"I do like John Wayne movies. Also Randolph Scott."

She said nothing. She did frown. I was obviously causing her stress. Unfenging her shui. Thought maybe that would be a good mission for me in this life. I could call it duck hunting.

Sam DeCosse came in. "Is my wife after you again?"

"At least she's not throwing punches," I said.

"She can do that, oh yes."

Ariel went to DeCosse and pecked his cheek. "Are we heading out now?"

"We are," DeCosse said.

"Ah. Nice to see you again, Mr. Buchanan. You're about to get a real treat." She snatched her gloves and left the room.

104

"YOU ENJOY THE game?" DeCosse said.

"I watch it from time to time," I said. "If Tiger's playing."

DeCosse had an Astroturf mat on the stern of his yacht and a bucket of golf balls. Out about a hundred yards was a buoy with a little flag on it, and a circular surface the size of a trash can lid. About fifty yards to the right, a couple of guys on a smaller boat were dropping another buoy. DeCosse's personal golf course.

"You like this?" DeCosse said as he pulled a wedge out of his golf bag.

"The water hazard's a little treacherous," I said.

He laughed, then took a ball from the bucket and dropped it on the mat. He took his stance and gave the floating hole a look. Waggled the club. Whacked the ball.

The ball arced through the sea air, with a slight draw, then plopped about five feet over the target.

"Need to take a little off it," DeCosse said. "Want to give it a try?"

"I'd just embarrass myself," I said. "If you have a windmill to putt at, I might go for it."

"You never get anywhere unless you try, Mr. Buchanan."

"I try cases," I said.

"I love the way golf focuses the mind." He used his wedge to flip another ball from the bucket onto the mat. "It's peaceful, contrary to what people think. If you know how to approach it."

He hit another shot. This one clanked on the metallic surface of the buoy. The guys in the other boat clapped.

"Great shot," I said.

"You see, if I hit a bad one, I always know there's another shot to come. I don't let the bad ones ruin my game. I'm always looking ahead."

He took another shot. It hit the water. He smiled. "I've already forgotten that one." He slapped the wedge on the mat. Like he was killing a bee. "Remember that old rule I gave you? When you're in trouble, get out of trouble. The thing is to just get the ball back into play. You always have another shot coming."

DeCosse sent another ball to the buoy and hit it. His little grounds crew applauded again.

"I'd like to see you get out of trouble," he said to me. Then he looked over my shoulder and his face went stone cold.

I turned around.

Ariel DeCosse was strolling along the port side almost wearing a thong bikini.

If I had been a cartoon, my eyes would have popped out. They almost did anyway.

I turned around, embarrassed for Sam DeCosse. Al and a couple of the crew were all out there, and they had eyes, too.

DeCosse did not move. His jaw muscles throbbed.

I heard a splash and took it to mean Ariel had gone for a dip.

Sam DeCosse snapped the club across his knee. Then threw the pieces into the water.

"Come with me," he ordered.

105

BACK IN THE lounge he offered me a drink. I said no thanks. He poured himself one. He said, "You tried to talk to my son." Direct and sharp, like he expected answers fast.

"Sure," I said.

"Why?"

"Thought he might be able to help me."

"How?"

"With information."

"What kind of information?"

"That's between him and me, isn't it?"

DeCosse shook his head. "When it comes to my family, I take an interest in everything."

"Good policy."

"This'll be a short meeting. Shorter still if you just tell me what you've got in mind."

"Mind?"

"You think you're going to make some trouble here? Interfere? Why? What good's it going to do you?"

"I don't care about my good."

"What do you care about?"

Good question. I wasn't really sure anymore, except that something in my gut had to get some people down a peg, and others up. DeCosse's son had to come down. Legally, but certainly.

"Your son is planning on developing a piece of land in the Santa Susana Mountains," I said.

DeCosse tensed. I'd scored on him. A guy who prided himself in never showing his cards had flinched.

"Not bad," he said. "The currency of negotiation is information. You have it, somehow. I don't know how, but now it's on the table. We have to deal with it."

"What's so secret about this?" I asked. "And what's so hard about letting tenants have their rights?"

"Mr. Buchanan, you need to drop this whole line about rights. That

doesn't even figure into it. Rights have no value whatsoever. Nobody believes in rights. They never did. The powder heads who wrote it into the
Constitution, they owned slaves. They allowed rights only up to the point
of their bottom line. It's still the same, so drop the pose and tell me how
much money it's going to take to make you go away."

If this had been a reality show, I'd be a star. A guy who actually got Sam
DeCosse to make an open-ended offer. This was a place unoccupied by
anyone on the planet, as far as I knew.

Felt great. I was all powerful.

For about ten seconds.

"I don't need any money," I said. "But there's a girl, the daughter of the
woman murdered at the Lindbrook. Maybe you could see your way to do-
nating a significant amount in trust, for her education and all."

"Interesting," he said. "Anything else?"

"I still want to know who killed the woman."

DeCosse didn't flinch. He took a sip of his bourbon. He swirled the glass
a little, then said, "That's a police matter."

"It's a family matter."

"Well, then, I hope you find out who did it."

"Any ideas?"

Sam DeCosse sighed. "Mr. Buchanan, you're a sharp guy, and I admire
sharpness. I think your best days are ahead of you." He put his drink on
the table. "But if you go around making false accusations, that doesn't help
anybody."

"I haven't made any accusations."

"Oh, come on, you want to know if I had something to do with this
woman's death, right?"

I swallowed. My Adam's apple felt like a volleyball.

"You know," DeCosse said, "my favorite show when I was a kid was *Perry
Mason*. Ever watch *Perry Mason*?"

"I've seen a few of them."

"Raymond Burr. The greatest! And at the end of every show, he'd get
some poor sap to break down on the witness stand and confess to the murder. I thought for a long time about becoming a lawyer, because I wanted
to be able to do that. But then I found out that never happened in real life.

It was fiction, but fun fiction. What you're suggesting now is fiction, but I don't find it fun."

"So no tearful confession?"

DeCosse laughed. "You know, I really like you. You can be irritating, but I like you. And if you'll just think before you speak, I'll like you even more. I have no motive to do some poor woman harm just because she wanted to stay in one of our hotels. What would that possibly accomplish?"

"Did you know this woman at all?"

"Of course not. I don't want anything to do with the day-to-day down there. I leave that to others."

"Your son?"

"And that's another thing. I don't like you sticking your nose through his fence. I would really appreciate it if you wouldn't interfere with things anymore. See, we have family matters, too. Just take some money and run."

"I'll have to think about it," I said.

"Well, isn't that just what I've been saying? Thinking is a good thing." DeCosse looked at his watch. "And since we're just about to head back, I'd like to help focus your thoughts."

106

DECOSSE CALLED SOMEONE on his cell phone, and a minute later Dev the bodyguard was in the room with us.

"You know Dev," DeCosse said.

"Oh, yeah," I said. "Hi."

DeCosse asked Dev to close the door.

"Now, it's just the three of us," DeCosse said. "What we say here stays here. Agreed?"

I looked at Dev, who was looking at me and not responding to the question. So I shrugged.

DeCosse said, "Dev, give him the information."

Dev, with a cat smile on his face, came over to me and plowed a fist into my solar plexus.

It was a pile driver.

All air left me. I collapsed to the floor. Sparkly lights glittered behind my eyes.

I don't know how long I was on the floor, but they stood by until my breathing normalized. They didn't say anything or move. Just waited until I got to my feet.

"He's pretty good," I said. "When a guy's not ready."

"And I hope that helps you to think this all through," DeCosse said.

My intestines were doing a Samoan fire dance. I put my left hand on my stomach. With the back of my right I smacked Dev across the face. Hard.

I loved the look in his eyes. Shock. A moment of confusion. Then anger.

DeCosse put a hand on Dev's chest to keep him from doing what he wanted to do.

"Don't worry," I said. "What happens here stays here."

"What you lack in brains," DeCosse said, "you make up for in moxie. I like that. But moxie will get you hurt."

"Let me," Dev said through his teeth.

DeCosse said, "You can go, Dev."

With obvious reluctance, Dev walked out.

DeCosse said, "You showed me something, Mr. Buchanan. Up top, when my wife made her…appearance, you didn't gawk. You turned around. I think that was out of respect."

I said nothing.

"Your instincts are good. Listen to them."

Hand on my gut, I said, "Take me back."

"We're on our way."

107

THE TRIP BACK was agony and was supposed to be. My stomach was inside out, like a gym sock taken off fast. Dev was deadly. He knew exactly where to hit to do enough damage to get the message across. And leave the rest of me for another day.

One of the other "stewards" was stationed in the room. I was collapsed on a leather chair.

At some point Al came in, looking sheepish. He told the steward to leave us alone for a minute. The guy looked happy to leave.

"You okay?" Al said.

"What do you want?" I said.

"Ty, I'm sorry."

"Save it."

"This is not something I approve of."

I felt sorry for him. "Al, do you know what a whore is?"

"Ty—"

"Do you?"

"Why are you doing this? You were always a pig head, but you could be talked to. You could be reasoned with."

"Al, I'd be real glad if you never talked to me again. Unless it's official. Now kindly get out of my face."

They dropped me on the dock and offered me a ride back. I said no and called a cab. That was a ride worth paying for.

108

WHEN I GOT back to St. Monica's it was almost evening and I was in a foul mood. As I made my way to my trailer, bad waking dreams kept kicking my can.

When I was a kid I had a hot temper. Didn't like getting hit. When I was nine or so I pounded the snot out of kid bigger than me after he thought he could intimidate me with a punch to the face. I went to a different place that day at school. I surprised myself as much as the kid, whose name was Donny.

Before it was over I had him on the ground and was sitting on his chest. I bloodied his nose—broke it, I found out later—and puffed both his eyes. My friend Yale Hutchison said Donny was screaming, but I don't remember that. The pulse hammering my ears kept all other sound out.

The beating caused a little scandal for a while. I was called in with my father and there was talk of a lawsuit by Donny's parents. But in the end I was let off with a suspension.

When the dust died down my dad took me on a fishing trip, and when we were good and quiet he told me that he almost killed a boy once when he was thirteen. He called it the Buchanan temper and said it came from his grandfather and just got passed down. And if you didn't learn to deal with it, you would end up in prison and there they'd give you the same treatment every day.

After he was killed I told myself I'd do everything I could to make him proud of me. And I did work hard at it, real hard.

But the Buchanan temper rose from the grave when Dev hit me.

And I wasn't caring if it came back. That was the scary part.

That was my wonderful frame of mind when I got to the trailer. Father Bob was in his priest clothes, coming out of his own trailer. Getting ready for mass or prayers or something. I didn't care.

"Ty, you look all in," he said. "Anything wrong?"

"The world's my oyster."

He laughed. "Why don't you tell me about it?"

"Why don't you go pray or something?" I reached for the handle of the door. A fresh pain froze my arm for a minute.

"Hey." Father Bob came to me. "What's up, my friend?"

"Nothing."

"Talk to me."

"Don't you have to go hear some confessions or something?"

"It might not hurt for you to…"

I grabbed my stomach.

"Hey, what happened?" Father Bob said. "Come in and tell me."

So we went into his trailer and I told him. The whole deal. DeCosse and Dev and the punch. And my desire to put serious hurt on both of them.

109

FATHER BOB WAS silent for a long time. Finally, he said, "You need to learn how to protect yourself better."

"I thought you only dispensed spiritual advice," I said.

"You need that, too. But you're also running around getting involved with bad people. You're out on the street. People are going to try to mess you up, yeah?"

"Yeah."

"You want to try to hurt me? See what happens?"

I looked at the face of true religion and couldn't believe he just said that. "Is that your bad self talking?"

"Come on. Come at me."

"Maybe you could describe it to me instead."

"Good answer," he said. "I don't want to break any of your small bones."

"Got to tell you," I said, "I wouldn't have pegged you for talk about breaking bones."

"Let me tell you a little story," Father Bob said. "Story of a black kid in Hawthorne whose daddy got shot by a white cop who thought he was going for a gun when all he was doing was trying to get the ID that showed he was employed as custodian for L.A. Unified. Then his mama decided life was too much to take, and she did to herself what the white cop did to the boy's daddy. The boy gets shipped off to the archipelago known as Los Angeles County foster care. After four horrendous experiences he's placed with a Catholic family. Latino. By this time the boy was headed for a life of crime and gangs. He was sixteen now, ripe for the picking, living out in Compton. He had to learn to survive on the street, and he did."

I tried to imagine Father Bob as a gangbanger. Couldn't do it.

"And then one day he met a black priest, which he never knew existed. This priest saw something in the kid, took him under his wing. It was a real Spencer Tracy moment."

"What's that mean?"

"The movie. *Boys Town.* Tracy played the priest who thought you could always get through to the boys if you showed empathy and kindness and a little love."

"Sounds rose-colored glasses to me."

"Well, he got me playing baseball instead of bashing heads. And then somewhere along the way got me thinking about God, and the next thing you know, I had a new desire in life. It was to totally and completely get out of the world I was living in and get into a world where God was real and I could serve him for the rest of my days. So I went to Xavier College in New Orleans." He paused, then said, "And I ended up back in L.A., doing what I loved. Parish work. I still had to know how to survive on the street, though."

"But aren't you supposed to be nonviolent?"

"Self-defense is long established in Catholic moral teaching."

"Violent self-defense?"

Father Bob nodded. "Each person has the right to defend himself against the attack of an aggressor. You may use whatever means are necessary—and that's the key word, 'necessary'—to defend your bodily integrity."

"Even kill?"

"Only if necessary."

"You? Do you think you could ever kill somebody?"

He thought about it. "When somebody's coming at you, you don't always have time to think it through. Still, you're responsible, and that's that. Do the best you can. If you sin, that's what grace is for."

"You are a surprising sort of priest," I said. "So what exactly is your advice concerning my self-defense? How about I just carry a gun? Any rules about having guns here?"

"It's not part of the Rule of St. Benedict, if that's what you mean. It doesn't exactly go along with the idea of hospitality."

"St. Benedict never lived in L.A."

Father Bob got up and came to me, squeezed the back of my arms. "First thing, you need some muscle back there. I want you doing a hundred push-ups a day."

"Did you say a hundred?"

"Between chairs, you know?" He mimed a deep push-up. "You can work up to it. Start doing ten. Then rest and ten more. See how you do. Maybe one month you do a hundred a day."

"Anything else?"

"I'll tell you one thing. Let's say you have a shot at me. What do you do?"

"A shot?"

"Mano a mano." Father Bob stood and faced me. "Come on."

I got to my feet. We were about two feet apart.

"Show me what you'd do," he said. "In slo-mo, please."

I thought about Jean-Claude Van Damme and Chuck Norris. I made a fist and motioned toward Father Bob's jaw.

"No," he said. "That's a good way to break your hand."

"John Wayne never broke his hand," I said.

"The Duke never hit a guy in his life. Look." He put his hand out so the heel of his palm was up. "Best thing to do hand to hand is this…"

He shot his hand up, as if he was doing an uppercut with the palm. "Catch him right under the chin. You'll mess his jaw up and have a second for a follow-up."

"Follow-up?"

"As fast as you can, and as hard as you can, kick him in his sacred documents."

"Ouch."

"And I mean hard. Then you either disable him or get away as fast as you can. Are you in running shape?"

"I run away?"

"Always a good idea if you can. It saves needless carnage."

"What if I *want* carnage."

"Then you come to me. I'll talk you down."

I shook my head. "What would happen if Sister Hildegarde found out you were teaching this stuff?"

"Let's not let that happen, huh?"

110

THE NEXT DAY Kylie was antsy and I needed some rest.

So I packed Sister Mary and Father Bob and Kylie in the car and drove to Disneyland.

It was worth it.

Kylie had never been. That was a sin. That had to be remedied.

Seeing her face in the car was almost reward enough. She was absolutely giddy. Sister Mary was a close second, but second nonetheless.

We got to the park around eleven. Kylie held my hand as we went in. It was magic. The train was just coming in to the Main Street station. In the town square Mickey and Pluto were waving and posing for pictures.

Kids were everywhere, some smiling, some crying—no day at Disneyland is complete without some kid screaming for Mickey-ear hats or an expensive stuffed character.

A girl about Kylie's age came up to Sister Mary and said, "Who are you?"

Sister Mary looked down. A woman, presumably the girl's mother, came up from behind. "She thinks you're a Disney character," the mother said sheepishly. But just to make sure, she added, "You're not, are you?"

"She most certainly is," I said. "Didn't you ever see *Snow White and the Seven Nuns*?"

The mother frowned.

"Yes," I said. "This is Slappy, the nun with the ruler."

Sister Mary slapped my shoulder.

"See?" I said.

The mother forced a smile.

"Who's Slappy?" the little girl said.

"Let's go, Brianna." The mother took the girl's hand and led her toward Pluto, a safer bet.

"Slappy?" Sister Mary said. "You named me Slappy?"

Kylie tugged my hand.

"Let's go," I said, and started for Main Street before Slappy could give me more grief.

We stopped to listen to the Dapper Dans, the barbershop quartet. Kylie was transfixed by the harmonies.

Then it was off to Fantasyland, through the castle, and all the rides. We went on Snow White—finding no nuns, no Slappys—and Mr. Toad, Peter Pan, and Alice in Wonderland.

We did the flying Dumbos, then walked over to New Orleans Square, where I bounced for warm, sugary fritters for all hands. You don't go to Disneyland without packing in the snacks.

Sister Mary ate hers with almost as much enthusiasm as Kylie. It was her first time, too.

Father Bob was the veteran. He used to bring poor kids here when he had a parish. Before the false accusation of pedophilia got him canned.

As we were sitting there, a kid walked by in a Mad Hatter hat. He was maybe eight years old. The hat was teetering as his mother yanked his hand. Then it fell off. The kid had a buzz cut.

And a thought hit me. "I've been making assumptions," I said.

"What's that?" Father Bob said.

"The Rasta hat. The killer. That it was a guy in a Rasta hat with a bunch of hair. At the Lindbrook. Maybe it was just a hat. Maybe there was nothing underneath."

"We're supposed to be having a good time," Sister Mary said.

"This is how I have a good time," I said.

"I'm having a good time, too," Kylie said.

They had fireworks that night. We stood in New Orleans square watching. I loved the colored lights on Kylie's wide-eyed face. Father Bob seemed peaceful, and Sister Mary entranced.

The only one who wasn't fully into it was me.

Because I was looking at Sister Mary and wishing she did not wear the habit. That she was someone I met at a party or at the grocery store where I asked her if she knew where the salsa was and she laughed and said she'd better show me personally, and now here we were at Disneyland on a magic night.

I hated myself for thinking that, because I'd just lost someone I loved and this was too soon to be happening—let alone happening with someone I could never have.

I realized my jaw was clamped and that Father Bob was now looking at me, in that way he has, with X-ray vision into your skull.

And then Sister Mary said to me, "Thank you. It's been a wonderful day."

Gold and silver exploded in the sky.

111

FRIDAY MORNING I went to see Firooz Roshdieh at his place of business, Baskin-Robbins, the place where his wife was shot.

Roshdieh had black hair, skin like coffee with a dash of cream, and nervous brown eyes. He was behind the counter showing a fresh-faced Latina how to scoop ice cream.

When he saw me he smiled, like I was a customer.

Then his face went colder than the Rocky Road. "You that lawyer!"

"Mr. Roshdieh, if I could—"

"You get out of here! You get out of my store!"

The fresh-faced girl looked scared.

"How about a scoop of mint chip?" I said.

"Out!"

"Mr. Roshdieh, I need your help."

His eyes narrowed. "Why I should help you?"

"I'm after the truth," I said. "Like you are."

"The truth I know!"

"You think my client killed your wife."

"I know it! Now you get out!" He came out from behind the counter, waving his arms. As if he were shooing away locusts.

"I want to find out who *really* killed your wife," I said.

"You lawyer! All you want is for getting your client to get out! Now *you* get out!"

"Please." I pulled a photograph out of my inside coat pocket. "Would you just make sure?"

I held up the photograph.

He started to nod. "Yes! I tell you yes! It is him, I tell you!"

"No doubt?"

"No!"

The girl was still looking scared. I went to the counter and showed her the picture. Her wide eyes took it in.

"What you doing?" Roshdieh said. "Leave her out. Now you get out. Get out or I call cops."

I put the photo back in my coat pocket. "I'm sorry for your loss, Mr. Roshdieh. Believe me."

I walked out.

112

AND SAT IN my car, listening the radio, watching the Baskin-Robbins from the far end of the parking lot. I wanted to have a conversation with the young server, away from Mr. Roshdieh.

For the next hour and a half I listened to classic rock, news, some jazz, and thought about my case.

It all came down to lousy eyewitness testimony and shaky IDs. People get convicted that way all the time. Most of them guilty. The way Gilbert might be guilty.

But *might be* isn't supposed to be good enough in our system of justice. A lot of people want it to be. They'd like to loop the rope around the necks, too. Around both the accused and the criminal defense lawyers.

Question was, was I good enough to stand up to a vet like Mitch Roberts? He was right that criminal trials, especially capital cases, were a different thing from what I was used to. I wanted to believe I was Fast Eddie, but maybe I was more like George Costanza. I was running around posing like a criminal lawyer. I was looking impatient and annoyed to give the impression I knew what I was doing.

Finally, the girl emerged from the store and started walking toward the street. I was glad to get out of the car and walk, for obvious reasons. Actually, I did a little jog so I wouldn't lose sight of her

She ducked into a Petco.

I followed her.

Inside, it was all barking and tweeting, with the smell of cat litter and dog fur strong in the air.

The girl went down an aisle of fish food. I slipped down the facing aisle and took a position at the end. I picked up a package of aquarium cleaner and started reading the label. The first word was "Warning."

The girl came around a moment later.

"Oh," she said.

"Oh," I said.

She looked confused and a little frightened. Unsure what to do.

"Hey," I said, "I'm sorry about the thing in there. I hope I didn't upset you."

"It's okay."

"It's just part of my job. I'm on your boss's side, you know. Just want to get at the truth."

"He knows who killed his wife. You showed him."

"Yeah." I held up the cleaner. "You have fish?"

She nodded.

"I'm just getting into them," I said. "I don't know where to start. What would be a good starter fish?"

"Starter fish?"

"Something easy."

"I guess a goldfish is always good."

"Yeah. Goldfish. Good call." I put the cleaner back and took out the photo I'd shown Roshdieh and the girl. "I guess his identification wraps this thing up."

"I hope so," she said. "It's been so hard on him. He's a good man. It's so sad. He's really been struggling."

"You'd like to help him out?"

"Yes."

"I'll take this photo to the DA right now."

She frowned. "Aren't you the lawyer for this man?"

"I want the truth. The DA wants the truth. The sooner we get there, the better. In fact, would you talk to the DA if he called you?"

"Well, I guess."

"It would help your boss."

She thought a moment, then nodded.

"Here," I said, handing her the photo, with the back toward her. I held out a pen. "Just put your name and phone number there and I'll have him call."

She hesitated. "I don't want to sign anything."

"I understand. Would it help to talk to the DA? I can call him right now." I took out my phone.

"No," she said. "But can he call me at the store?"

"Sure," I said.

She wrote her name and a number on the photo, gave it back to me along with the pen. I looked at what she wrote.

"Thank you Ms. Esparza," I said. "Your boss is very upset, so don't mention this until the DA calls, all right? If you need to talk to me, call this number."

I gave her a card.

113

SATURDAY WAS WORKDAY on the gentle grounds of St. Monica's. Various tasks were attended to by the sisters and Father Bob, and I joined in the festivities. Kylie liked working in the garden, so she went with Sister Jean to do the roses.

For Sister Mary and me, it was painting the exterior of the wing where the older nuns lived.

Sister Perpetua sat outside with us, in her wheelchair, under the shade of an old pepper tree. It made her happy. She looked like someone who deserved to be happy.

At one point she tossed out, "Are you a Catholic?"

"No, Sister," I said.

"Protestant?"

"Not anything at the moment."

"You don't belong to a church?"

"No."

"Oh, we all need a church. Without it, we're dying embers."

"Embers?"

"The love of Christ is lived out through the church. Inside, the fire keeps you warm. But if an ember falls out on the hearth, it quickly grows cold."

"Love is a good thing, Sister, but I don't think you have to be in a church to do that."

"Ah, but how do you know what love is without the church? For love comes from God, is manifested in Christ, and embodied by the church. No one would know what love is without the church."

"Why not?"

"No ancient civilization knew about love. It was God who brought that to us."

I tried to think of one. Couldn't. Sharp little nun.

"What makes you tick, Mr. Buchanan?" Sister Perpetua asked. It wasn't offensive the way she said it. It was as if she just wanted to know.

"Yes," Sister Mary added. "That's a good question."

I shot her a look. "I like butterflies and rainbows, and little children and rabbits."

"That's nice," Sister Perpetua said.

"And piña coladas and walks in the rain—"

"Oh, stop it," Sister Mary said.

Sister Perpetua gasped. "Is that any way to talk to our guest?"

"It's okay, Sister," I said. "That's one of the nicer things people have said to me over the years."

"Who influenced you most growing up?" Sister Perpetua asked.

"My dad. He was a cop."

"Ah."

"After my dad, I'd have to say Thomas Magnum."

"I don't know him," Sister Perpetua said.

"He was a private investigator in Hawaii."

"A television show," Sister Mary said.

"Oh," Sister Perpetua said. "I remember Bishop Sheen. Now *that* was a television show. You don't get that kind of thoughtfulness anymore, I can tell you that. Such charisma he had! And could he ever command a stage. What a voice. What an intellect. You strike me as having quite an intellect too, Mr. Buchanan."

"Well, Sister, I use what I've got and hope for the best."

"You have gifts, given to you by God. Do you think you were made out of random parts?"

"I sometimes wonder when I try to do a spin move."

"Amen," Sister Mary said.

Sister Perpetua shook her head. "I like what Ethel Waters once said. 'God don't sponsor no flops.' Not one of us is junk, Mr. Buchanan, if we get together with our Creator."

Another voice cut the air. "How is it going?" Sister Hildegarde squinted at us in the sun.

"Like the guy said falling off the Empire State Building," I said.

"Excuse me?"

"So far, so good."

Sister Hildegarde did not crack a smile. A smile did not get within a hundred yards of cracking Sister Hildegarde. Sister Hildegarde could have gone to a Julia Roberts impersonators' convention and the collective toothiness therein would not have made a dent in her granite cheeks.

Instead, Sister Hildegarde turned to Sister Mary and said, "I would like to see you in the office. Immediately."

In the ensuing pause, looks were exchanged between the sisters—Mary Veritas, Perpetua, and Hildegarde—as I watched. Then Sister Mary dutifully descended her stepladder. Sister Hildegarde turned and walked away.

Sister Mary put her roller in the drip tray and followed.

When the two nuns were out of earshot Sister Perpetua said, "That doesn't sound good."

114

AS I PUT the paint roller in the pan, Sister Perpetua said, "I'm sorry if I offended you, Mr. Buchanan."

"When?" I said.

"When I asked what makes you tick."

"It takes a lot to offend me, Sister. I'm a lawyer, after all."

The nun smiled. "I try not to offend people. It's a better reflection on the church that way. I haven't always been successful."

"You? I can't imagine you offending anybody."

"I once said 'crud buckets' to a cardinal."

I laughed. "You wicked woman."

Sister P gave me a long look. "I like you. You don't put on airs."

"I wouldn't even know where to find airs."

"Let me ask you this then, Mr. Buchanan. What do you yearn for? I used to ask all my students that."

"Yearn?"

"When I was your age I yearned to go to Africa, to serve the poorest of the poor there. But that wasn't God's will. Instead I ended up with sixth-graders. Only now do I see why. It was fitting for me."

I wiped a little sweat from my forehead with the back of my hand. "I don't know what I yearn for, to tell you the truth."

"Think about it," Sister P said. "Here's a little secret. What was it you loved to do when you were twelve?"

I folded my arms and it came to me right away. "Basketball. I wanted to be a professional basketball player."

"And you never realized your dream?"

"Didn't have the hops."

"Hops?"

"Jumping ability. White men can't jump."

She shook her head.

"That was a movie," I explained. "Also my autobiography."

"But you loved playing basketball?"

"Oh yeah."

"Now tell me why. Why did you love it?"

"I don't know, I just did."

"No, no. Go deeper."

For a second I hesitated. What was this old nun after? And why? What business was it of hers? But then I felt this little door open up in me. Like Sister Perpetua held the key that unlocked it. And I found I actually wanted to talk about it.

"All right," I said, "there was this one time, in high school, we had a game against the city champions, a monster team. They had a guy named Pierpont Wicks, six-eight, the city player of the year. He actually did make it to the NBA for a few years. He was the leading scorer and just an amazing player."

And he was. I can see him now. He looked like a sequoia.

"We were playing in their gym, and we were warming up doing layups when they came out. The music pounding, everybody cheering, and they did their layup drill and the last four guys slam-dunked."

"Were they all right?" Sister P said.

"Oh, more than all right. A slam-dunk is a good thing, slamming the ball down through the basket. You have to be very big or be able to jump."

"Have hops?"

"Now you're catching on. Anyway, Pierpont Wicks was the last guy, and when he slammed it seemed like a bomb exploding. So they tried to intimidate us right off the court, but that night we played the game of our lives. Me especially."

"This is exciting."

"It was for me. I went into the zone."

"Where's that?"

I pointed to my head. "It starts here and your body follows. For a few minutes I felt like I could fly. You know, sort of float over the floor, and around people, without my feet making contact with the wood. And not only that, I could put the ball up with either hand. Little jump hooks, whatever, and I had complete confidence. I went through the middle once and it was like being in a forest, these guys were so big. Pierpont Wicks was one of them. I saw his eyes. It was Ahab looking at the face of Moby Dick."

"Oh, my."

"I should have passed the ball away as fast as I could, but I remember having this complete calm, and turned my back and threw up a three-foot no-looker."

"What is that?"

"I wasn't looking at the hoop. I was looking at the stands and I threw the ball up back over my head. Thing was, I knew exactly where I was, I knew the ball would go in. And it did. I was past the zone. I was in hyperspace. I was Star Trekking. I was boldly going where I had never gone before. I scored thirty-nine points that night, my all-time high."

"And you won the game?"

"Uh, no. Unfortunately this wasn't a Hollywood movie. But we only lost by five points, our little school, and it was more than anybody expected. But the thing that got me…"

I stopped a second. I couldn't believe this thing was getting caught in my throat. Sister Perpetua just waited, an understanding look on her face.

"The thing that really got me," I said, "was as we were leaving the floor for the locker room, Pierpont Wicks ran up to me. He went out of his way to find me. He puts out his hand. He says to me, 'Man, you were on fire. Great game.' You know what? I don't think anything anybody's ever said to me since meant as much as that."

I came back from the past and looked at Sister P. "That's why I loved basketball. And I guess I'd like to feel that way again sometime. Something I do, where I feel like I'm flying, and I know where everything is, and I make the shot."

Sister P nodded. "You will, Mr. Buchanan. I'm quite sure of it."

115

LATER, I FOUND Sister Mary kneeling and praying in the chapel. Below the big crucifix, candles were lit near her. The rest of the place was in darkness.

She continued to pray. I sat and looked at Jesus on the cross, then cleared my throat.

"I heard you," Sister Mary said, without turning around.

"Can we talk?"

She stood up, crossed herself, turned, and came to me. She slipped into the pew.

"Can what I'm about to say be confidential?" she asked.

"Of course. I'm your lawyer. I hold whatever my clients say in complete confidence."

"You're my lawyer?"

"You need it, Sister. The way you play basketball is criminal."

"This isn't funny. Not this time."

"Go ahead."

"I've been designated 'rigid' by Sister Hildegarde," she said.

"What's that mean?"

"It is a term of discipline. It goes on my record, so to speak. If I do not reform my ways it could mean a greater discipline. I could even be asked to leave the community."

"So what did you do to deserve this?"

"Sister Hildegarde says it's because I wanted to wear my rosary."

"Isn't that a good thing for a nun to do?"

"The community wants the sisters to present themselves a certain way. To move with the times, so to speak."

"You're talking about the beads, right?"

"Yes. At first it was optional. Now it's mandatory that we not wear them. I said something about this to Sister Hildegarde a few weeks ago. And about the change in the community prayer book."

"What change was that?"

"Oh, she wanted to take out some of the quote-unquote sexist language. I don't think that's a good reason to change the prayers of the church. So I reviewed the constitutions of the community, and the process for change, and it wasn't followed. Sister Hildegarde acted alone. So I wrote her a letter. And in the letter I questioned the decision about selling the land. I said we should be taking care of our own, that this is what St. Benedict would have wanted. That's why she called me into the office today."

"What did she say to you?"

"The first words out of her mouth were, 'Who do you think you are?'"

"She said that."

"She did."

"A little harsh."

"So I'm rigid. I'm on probation. I must accept it."

"Why?"

"Keep your voice down," Sister Mary said.

"Let's do something about it," I said.

"What are you talking about?"

"I'm your lawyer, remember? What can we do about Sister Hildegarde?"

"Nothing. I'm telling you—"

"I'll talk to her, I'll—"

"You don't really have any authority in our community, Mr. Buchanan."

"But I can persuade," I said. "I'm a great persuader."

"Oh yes?"

"I'll tell her, 'Look, you treat Sister Mary right or I'll…go Protestant.'"

"Ooh, that'll really get her attention."

"You think?"

She didn't answer. She looked forward. "Sometimes…"

"Sometimes what?"

"Nothing," she said. "I need to go."

"Where?"

"Back to work. And you, too."

She got up and left, not looking back at me or Jesus.

116

THAT WAS SATURDAY.

Sundays were quiet at St. Monica's. In a relative way, of course. It was the Lord's day. Their day for deep prayer and mass and being about the business of knowing God.

Which left me to be about my own business, which was finding out where Nydessa Jackson was and why she was so determined to pin her ID on Gilbert Calderón.

"In fact," he told me, "that's when I got religious. Until I met her, I never believed in hell."

So be it.

According to the witness list, Nydessa Perry lived in Hollywood, in an apartment building on Ivar. In the twenties this was a fashionable neighborhood. The buildings were high end then. After World War II most of them had become transient nests.

It was in one of these buildings that Joe Gillis, the screenwriter in *Sunset Boulevard*, was avoiding the repo men. As I parked on the street I wondered how many of the people inside were avoiding the law in one way or another.

The building was three stories, squat and white, with a little courtyard visible from the street. As I entered into the courtyard I almost stepped on a dead squirrel. I wondered why nobody had bothered to clean it up.

Nydessa's apartment was on the ground floor, facing the courtyard. I knocked and got a voice from behind the door.

"Yeah?" A woman's voice.

"Candygram," I said. I wanted it to work once.

The door opened with a chain across it. A young black woman, thin in the face, said, "What did you say?"

"I said candygram."

"What's that?"

"It's a gift people give, with candy. But this one comes with a condition."

"Who are you?"

"I'm a lawyer. I represent people like you."

"Whattaya mean people like me?"

"People with troubles."

"Ain't got no trouble."

"You may."

She said nothing.

"Can I come in for a moment?" I said.

"No."

"Then tell me about Gilbert Calderón."

Pause. Then: "You're his lawyer."

"You and Gilbert used to be together," I said.

"So?"

"I'm just trying to find out what happened between you two."

"You can just get yourself outta here now. I'm not talking to you. I'm talking to the DA."

"And he's told me all about you. All about your past."

"You lie."

"No, Ms. Perry, it's the law. It's called discovery. Prosecutor has to give me your info, including your little brushes with the law."

"I cleared my parole."

"You have a record. A pretty long one."

"So, that don't mean I told a lie."

"Did I say anything about lying?"

She slammed the door. As was her privilege. But it gave me enough information to know I was on the right track, that she'd make a lousy witness. At least I'd be able to cross-examine the effectiveness out of her.

But something told me there might be more here for me. Nothing makes a lawyer's day, or year, like finding some helpful bombshell in the prosecutor's own bunker.

So I went back across the street and got in my car. I moved it forward to a spot where I could see into the courtyard and view Nydessa Perry's door. And waited.

Listened to the radio, local news. Sports. Kobe Bryant was whining again. What else was new? Whining had replaced the work ethic in sports, and Bryant was making a play to be the best at that particular aspect. Words like *big, stupid, overpaid, ungrateful, jerk* floated across my mind like a big, stupid jerk going in for a slam.

A little while later a guy came out of Nydessa's door, wearing a dark blue hoody. He walked out the front and north on Ivar toward Franklin. I paused a moment, then got out and followed him.

The day was hot and Hollywood steamy, the way it sometimes gets. The sun likes to park itself on the stars on the sidewalk. A burning Cary Grant, a sizzling Bette Davis, Henry Fonda on a hot plate. Kate Hepburn boils and there's no wind for relief. The sea is forty-five minutes away, give or take.

Hoody was strolling, taking his time, not exactly looking like he had any appointments. A hoody on a hot day. That didn't make sense. I wasn't able to catch his face.

He crossed Selma, continued down to Sunset. The old Cinerama Dome building was across the street. On the other side of Ivar was Amoeba Music. I watched Hoody cross Sunset and go inside Amoeba.

It's a huge two-story behemoth, row upon row of CDs and DVDs and unhelpful help. Hoody strolled into the hip-hop section and started flipping through the CDs. I went a couple of aisles over, so I could look at him.

He looked a lot like Gilbert Calderón.

117

THEN HE LOOKED at me.

If he recognized me he didn't show it.

He looked away and walked down the aisle. I kept him in view with the old peripheral vision. My basketball coach in college was convinced that peripheral vision could be developed. He used to have us walk across campus trying to identify things without looking directly at them. He said Bill Bradley used to do that when he was growing into a basketball legend.

He may have been right, because my side view was good.

I spent about twenty minutes tracking Hoody. He went up the stairs once. I waited awhile, then followed. Watched him with the DVDs. Came back down before he did, waited. Picked him up again when he came back to the first floor.

I was standing by a Velvet Revolver display as he walked by.

And heard behind me the screech of the damned.

"Get out of my face!"

It was Nydessa Perry. She was running to Hoody but looking at me. She filled the room with obscenities, which blended perfectly with the song now playing.

She kept the fire as she grabbed Hoody. "That's the lawyer! He followed you!"

Hoody turned and ran for the front. I started to follow but Nydessa grabbed my shirt and tore at my face with her nails.

Like Muhammad Ali—not Pug Robinson—in his prime, I pulled my head back. That made her swipe superficial.

She bared her teeth and came at me again. I grabbed her wrists and held them. She had skinny arms but with tensile strength. It was like holding a squid from a fifties sci-fi movie.

A squid that screamed. Which finally got the attention of a security guard, a lardy college dropout type with sandy hair.

"Let go now!" he said.

"Take her from me," I said.

He looked lost.

"She's on the attack," I said.

Nydessa screamed I was lying, all in a language where "K" is the primary sound. She laced so many of them together in such a short time—with the term *mother* making several noted appearances—I thought I was in a speeded-up Mamet film.

"Sir!" the guard said.

I pushed Nydessa back a step and let go of her.

"Now—" the guard started to say. Then Nydessa flew at me again. Her hands were talons.

This time the guard had the presence of mind to intervene. She turned her claws on him. Got him flush on one of his pink cheeks.

Three red stripes appeared on his face.

Nydessa stopped, looked at her work, then ran for the exit. The guard was too stunned to do anything. Blood was running down his cheek now.

"You guys have a first aid kit?" I said.

"I think so," he said. "What was that?"

"I got a name and address if you want to press charges. You got a boatload of witnesses."

Several people were looking at us.

I gave the guard my card and made sure he got to the bathroom.

118

MONDAY I WENT to see Mitch Roberts. He'd just come back from court and said he only had ten minutes to talk to me.

I told him ten minutes would be enough. He showed me to his office, one of the corner pens with a window overlooking the backside of Van Nuys.

"I want you to dismiss against Calderón," I said.

He smiled. "And I want to play quarterback for the Colts."

"Do you have an arm?"

"Not like that."

"You don't have a case, either."

"Please." He put his coat over the back of his chair and loosened his tie. "You've now got seven minutes."

"You know the case is wack. You got shaky IDs all over, and one very bad druggie who hates my guy."

"She made a positive ID," Roberts said. "No question."

"I have a feeling you're going to have real trouble with this one," I said.

"You let me worry about that."

"I'm telling you, she's one loose rivet."

"So you can cross-examine her."

Oh, I would cross-examine her. I decided not to let him in on the little incident in Amoeba Music. There are not a lot of surprises trial lawyers can spring anymore, but this was going to be one of mine. As long as Nydessa didn't tell Roberts what happened.

I thought she wouldn't. I decided she wanted to have as little to do with the proceedings as possible. Because the guy who really did the shootings could very well be her boyfriend.

Yes, Mitch Roberts would have a little surprise if he put her on the stand. I'd bring in a certain security guard to testify about her little friend in the hoody. I didn't know if it was the shooter or not. But I didn't have to know. All I had to do was put that picture in the mind of the jury. They'd take care of the rest through the magic of deliberations.

"I got the vic's husband looking right into the guy's eyes," Roberts said, "and making another positive ID."

"You sure about that?"

He said, "I got a call from Mr. Roshdieh. He says you invaded his store."

"That's the word he used, 'invaded'?"

"He was upset that you would do that, that you would come in and harass him, show him photos. Did you do that, Mr. Buchanan?"

"I did my job," I said. "I'm a working lawyer, Mitch."

"Don't call me Mitch."

"Mr. Roberts?"

"That'll do."

"You don't seem to like me."

"I don't. I think you're arrogant."

"Just because I think I'm better than everybody else?"

He shook his head in disgust.

"Kidding, Mitch—I mean, Mr. Roberts. If we can't have a little collegiality here—"

"I'm not interested in collegiality or conviviality or yucking it up. I have a job to do."

"Which is to seek justice, right? That's what the canon of ethics says, am I right?"

Roberts took a fuzzy green tennis ball off his desk and bounced it once on the floor, caught it, and squeezed. "Your point?"

"Don't make this personal with me," I said. "Don't make me think prosecutors aren't really interested in following exculpatory evidence to a dismissal. Just think about it, will you? You have a murder to prosecute, but your case is thin. That means the real guy may still be out there, right?"

"We have the right guy." Roberts bounced the ball again. "By the way, did you show Mr. Roshdieh a business card?"

"Did I what?"

"When you went to see him? Did you show him a business card?"

"No."

"You mean you violated 1054.8?"

I tried not to look lost. He was referring to the penal code, which, not being a career prosecutor, I hadn't memorized.

"Disclosure rules when you talk to one of my witnesses," Roberts said. "You didn't do that, sanctions may follow."

"He knew who I was pretty quick."

"Maybe we'll let the state bar figure that out."

"You're threatening me?"

He smirked.

119

SMIRKING IS SOMETHING trial lawyers like to do. We are all egos on wheels. You can't try cases without a healthy concept of your own self-worth.

That's why trial lawyers can be hard to live with. We have to win all the time, even if it's just what restaurant to go to, what DVD to watch. We start to see all the exchanges of life as little sessions of the one big game, which is winning.

Yeah, we can sometimes have a drink after a day in court. But even then we're watching. Can I outdrink him? Does she have what it takes to play with the big boys and girls?

It's better not to open your mouth too much at opposing counsel. But Mitch Roberts annoyed me. Prosecutors, of all the practitioners among us, are supposed to be the ones who can set ego aside for the cause of justice.

Mitch Roberts was not the type to do that. And I'm not the type to keep my pie hole shut.

Which can get me into trouble.

Especially when you're invited to see a hot Hollywood actor in his native habitat. I was outside heading to my car when I got the call.

"This is Mr. Baxter." The voice on the phone sounded eerily familiar.

"Who?" I said.

"Cruciferous greens."

"Oh. Hey. Really good to hear from you."

"What?"

"I was just about to fry up some bok choy. Wanna come over?"

Pause. "Mr. McLarty would like to clear up any misunderstanding."

"I shouldn't deep-fry bok choy?"

"You interested or not?"

120

MILLIONS OF VIEWERS tune in each week to watch the high jinks of Barry and Kyle, two divorced guys living in a two-room apartment with Barry's seven-year-old daughter. How the courts, or a good God, would have allowed this girl to be there was a question dealt with in the first show. I guess.

The taping I'd been invited to was at the Warner Bros. Studios in Burbank. They shot *Casablanca* here. Now it was home to *Men in Pants*.

Here's lookin' at crud, kid.

They had a VIP pass waiting for me as I drove on the lot. McLarty's peeps set it up, and I was given prime treatment. Hollywood. Glamour. Bring your autograph book.

The shoot was on a Tuesday evening in one of the big sound stage buildings. A line of audience members was waiting outside as I was escorted past them by a guy in a navy blue coat.

Inside I was intro'd to a tall woman with headphones and a clipboard. She was expecting me. Her name was Starr. Last name Brite.

I am not kidding.

"We're so happy to have you," Starr said, smiling. She had prominent cheekbones and smooth skin. Auburn hair and brown eyes. About twenty-five.

"Are you a fan of the show?" she asked.

"I've seen it."

"Just a couple of times?"

"Once. That I can remember."

"Oh, well, we'll have to remedy that, won't we? Something to drink?"

Starr Brite showed me the set and gave me a front row seat. She brought me a Coke and a *Men in Pants* T-shirt, along with a press kit. The crew were getting ready for the shoot, setting lights, positioning cable, checking cameras.

Big headshots of the actors beamed from the back wall. The other star, Wayne Chesterfield, was a Broadway actor whose big break came after he posted a fake commercial for Preparation H on YouTube. It became a comedy sensation, and he was cast in the show a few weeks later.

The little girl in the cast was named Madison Martell. She was blond and cute and had been a hit in a cereal commercial.

A little before seven the doors opened and the teeming masses stormed in. Took seats in anticipation. A rotund family of four was sitting on my right. Two kids, a boy and a girl, between larger versions of themselves. On my left were three teens chattering and laughing about one of their friends who wasn't there.

Starr Brite came out and gave the audience some instructions and warnings—cell phones and all that. She said she hoped they'd all enjoy the taping. The large mother on my right told one of her kids she was going to march him right out if he didn't shut up.

Then the warm-up guy came out. He was about thirty and he did a few jokes about Hollywood and then the president and a few people laughed. Not enough to get him out of being a warm-up guy.

Then it was time for the taping.

In this particular episode, McLarty was trying to get a pizza delivery girl into bed. He kept ordering pizzas. Chesterfield and he fought about it. Madison Martell kept eating pizza and got sick.

Then hurled into McLarty's underwear drawer.

What great writing these shows have.

McLarty, for what he was doing, was fine. Professional.

The taping came to an end and the cast members were introduced. They came out and bowed.

Then it was over.

The teeming masses headed out.

Starr Brite asked me to join McLarty in his dressing room.

121

"I'M REALLY SORRY about the other night," McLarty said, lighting a cigarette. "You know, you show up, I'm trying to have a good time, you know how it goes."

"Do I?" I said. "Why don't you tell me how it goes?"

His dressing room was nicer than most homes in East L.A. There was a fully stocked bar and a mirror table, a treadmill, and two plasma TVs. The place smelled like cold cream and smoke.

We were alone, which surprised me. I expected his bodyguard to be there.

"Dude, you have any idea what it's like to be me? Come on, I'd like you to be me for a while. I mean, you've got paparazzi and hotties one after another who come around, saying he did this, he did that. You know how many times I been accused of rape?"

"Seven," I said.

He blinked. He had his shirt unbuttoned and a white towel around his neck. "No. Two. Where'd you come up with seven?"

"It's a lucky number."

"It's not funny! I got all sorts of things happening. You wonder why I had to go into rehab? You wonder about that?"

"I don't."

"Don't what?"

"Wonder."

He wiped his face once with the towel. "Let's cut this short, huh? What exactly do you want from me, Mr., what is it, Buchanan? Solid name."

"I had an Irish cop father."

"Sweet."

Sweet?

"I would love to play an Irish cop someday. Do I look Irish to you?"

"You're not Pat O'Brien," I said.

"The TV guy?"

"No, the actor. Don't you ever watch old movies?"

"Oh, that guy. What was he in again?"

"*Knute Rockne, All American*," I said.

"Canoot who?"

"Never mind."

"Drink?" He got up and headed for the bar.

"No thanks."

As he poured some Svedka in a glass I said, "What I want to know, Mr. McLarty, is whether you fathered a child with Tawni."

"You want to hold me up for some money, that it?" He took some ice cubes from a little freezer and plopped them in his glass.

"So you're telling me you did father a child?"

"No, man." He flipped a switch on a console and the place filled with music. Rock. Nirvana.

He smiled and rocked his head a few times. "The classics, huh?" he said.

"Right," I said. "Along with Cole Porter."

"Cole who?"

"Not important."

He took a seat in a director's chair, facing me. I sat on the only other chair in the room.

"Look, my friend," he said. "I know you have work to do, you're a lawyer, and that's all good. It's all good. But I'm asking you and telling you at the same time. I'm asking you to drop this whole deal, because I'm telling you I don't have any kids."

"You do have a past. With women, I mean. It hasn't been exactly a secret."

"Hey, you know how it works. This town. The pressures. The fame. The money. You know what it's like."

"I never went to an escort service."

"It's sort of like an A rating at a restaurant, right? I have a favorite sushi place. I know when I go there I'm going to get the best. So it's the same with women. I don't see anything wrong with that as long as you can pay for it. As long as you're not spending the milk money. Am I right?"

"Does anybody have milk money anymore?" I asked.

"But the girls all get checked, I get checked, and there's always protection, you know. To keep those little items from happening."

"Items."

"You know what I mean." He took a sip of vodka.

"You're a romantic guy. So you're saying you never had a little *item* come along?"

"And if I did," he said, leaning forward. "I'd take care of the problem, you know?"

For some reason, I wanted to grab his drink and throw it in his face. I wanted to splash it all over his self-satisfied expression, his secure-in-his-own-juices look.

Instead I said, "What was your relationship with Tawni?"

"She was one of many."

"You spent a lot of time with her. You were seen out with her on a couple of occasions."

"Yeah, there were a couple of stories in the tabs. You do that sometimes. Generate a little publicity. Back then I needed some."

"You needed that kind of publicity?"

"Thought I did," he said. "It's a whole different environment now. I got one I want to hang on to."

"An item?"

He frowned. "No, a woman."

"Was she with you the other night? At the club?"

Now he smiled. Bobbed his eyebrows. He need that vodka facial. "Not that particular night. That was more of a pub deal, too."

"I can't keep track of the pub you like or don't like."

"You don't have to. Only I have to."

"Are you telling me your relationship with Tawni was nothing more than commercial?"

"That's what I'm telling you." He tossed back the last of his drink. "You sure you don't want anything?"

"There's a simple way to figure out what we've got to figure out," I said.

"Figure out what?"

"If there's a little item in your life you don't know about."

He stared at me.

I said, "Let me run a DNA test. I have a private lab. We can rule you out as the father, and that would be that."

He stood up, his hands clenching the ends of the wooden chair arms. "You're not taking anything from me. I try to be nice. I invite you down here."

"Sometimes, you schmooze, you lose."

"Go now."

"You won't give me some spit?"

"In your face, maybe."

"That'll do, too."

He went to the door and called out. The big guy from the club appeared at the door, like a storm cloud over Tulsa.

"Time to go," McLarty said.

"Can't I get an autographed picture or something?" I said. "For the item?"

"Get out!"

122

BACK AT THE ranch, as they say, I heard some rapid-fire *tink tink tinks* coming from Father Bob's trailer. I knew what it was and let myself in.

"Join me, Ginger?" he said, referencing one of the all-timers, Ginger Baker of Cream.

Father Bob was drumming coffee cups and jars on his kitchen table.

We share a passion for great drummers. I did some rock drumming in high school. Father Bob was into the jazz side. But he had some sticks and I think that's what he does for therapy. Me, too. A little "Moby Dick" (as if anybody can do "Moby Dick" but the great Bonham) and I'm good for a couple of days.

I sat down at the Formica table and the father handed me a couple of stems and we tapped some table, jar, and cup. Got going pretty good there, smiling. Egging each other on the way Buddy Rich and Animal did on *The Muppet Show* once. You can YouTube it.

When we took a break I said, "Man, you still got it."

He laughed. "Never had it, but thanks." He looked down, a little sadness washing across him.

"So what is it?" I said.

"What's what?"

"Experience tells me you play when you've got something on your mind."

"We all have something on our minds," Father Bob said. "Only some people just aren't in touch with it. That's my theory about drums, by the way. It was how people got in touch. With each other, with themselves. It was the earliest form of community. It was therapy before Freud. Religion before gods."

"And what are they now?"

"Missing. More drumming would mean more communication."

"Maybe we should tell that to the talk shows."

"You got an idea there. All they do is yell over each other now. Why not drum solos to determine who's right? We could get Arianna Huffington and Ann Coulter together and they could drum it out."

"How do you know about Arianna Huffington and Ann Coulter?"

"What good can I do for others if I don't know about where they live and who they listen to?" He paused and said wistfully, "What good can I do anyway?"

"That's it," I said. "What is going on?"

He didn't answer.

"Listen, Padre, you get people confessing to you all day. Who do you get to talk to? Me, that's who. What is it?"

He paused, then reached for a trifolded paper under the salt and pepper shakers. Handed it to me.

I unfolded it. It was a letter on the official stationery of the Archdiocese of Los Angeles.

To: Father Robert Jackson

Greetings in the name of our Father and His son Jesus Christ.

After further review of your case, it is the considered judgment of the council that the facts do not warrant a re-opening of this matter. We are sure that you will agree the greater good to the Church should be our ultimate concern.

With one voice we commend your piety and obedience. It is a model for which we are truly thankful.

May the Lord be gracious unto you.

Sincerely,
Monsignor Michael O'Malley, J. C. B.

"What's a JCB?" I asked.

"Juris Canonici Baccalaureatus," Father Bob said. "A law degree. Canon law. The law of the church."

"Which is a fancy way of saying they're gonna let you hang."

He shrugged. "What's done is done."

"What's done is they've shelled out over half a billion dollars in damages to settle all the abuse claims, and they don't want any more publicity. They don't want any reporters crying that they've restored a priest they got rid of, even if he happens to be innocent."

"The church has suffered enough."

"Maybe not," I said.

He frowned at me. "Don't go there."

"What about justice? Doesn't the church believe in that?"

"You're an outsider. You don't know what you're talking about."

"I have eyes."

"So does a blind man. Doesn't mean he can see."

I folded my arms. I was holding in an anger I didn't want to unloose. Or maybe I did. "What kind of a church is it that treats one of its own that way?"

"Look, Tyler. You don't go into somebody's house and start tearing down their mother. She may be a crank. She may be a loon. But she's loved, and it's none of your business."

His face twitched then and a little cluck came out of his throat. Like he was choking on some words. Or on emotion.

"I want to be alone now," he said.

"Come on—"

"Please."

"I didn't mean—"

"Please!"

A flash in his eyes like distant lightning. I could see the street kid he used to be, forty or so years ago. Confused kid, too.

I could tell it was gnawing at him but, like he said, the church wasn't my mother. So I left. I could hear him drumming fast when I got outside.

123

THE NEXT DAY I drove all over L.A.

One of the things I like about this place is, you can drive a mile and be in a different world. Even though driving a mile can sometimes take half an hour, you deal with it. If you care to look, you see things. L.A. is about being alive to the possible.

If you were free to drive, of course, as Gilbert Calderón wasn't. My first stop was at the Twin Towers to see him.

"Where you been, man?" he asked.

"Oh, here and there."

"Yeah? You got busy with stuff?"

"Yeah. Stuff. How you doing?"

"Great. I'm doing real good. I been having visions."

"Yeah? Of what?"

"You, man. Winning my case. We're gonna win this thing."

"Gilbert, I appreciate your faith in me but—"

"Faith! Yeah!"

"But let me tell you, this is not an easy win, for either side. I want to give you a chance to hire another lawyer."

"Huh?"

"I want to make sure you have somebody who knows what he's doing."

"I don't have money for that."

"There are good public defenders. They—"

"No! You're the best I'm gonna do." He paused, smiled. "Sorry, dude, that came out funny."

"Gilbert—"

"If you don't rep me, I'm gonna rep myself. I mean it."

Now I smiled. "In that case, Gilbert, you're better off with me."

"That's what I been trying to tell you!"

"Got it. Then I figure we make Roberts go to trial right away."

"Can we do that?"

"Sixth Amendment. Speedy trial. We don't have to wait. The less time Roberts has to prepare, the better."

"I like that. See, you're already paying off. "

"That's only to get to trial, Gilbert. It's not a win until the jury says it's a win."

"How they not gonna like you, huh?"

"Experience tells me there's always a way."

124

NEXT I WENT to the Lindbrook and found Oscar in the lobby, reading a newspaper as usual. Disco Freddy was rehearsing a new number in the far corner. A couple of other guys played chess near the window.

I sat with Oscar and asked if he'd found anybody who'd seen a guy in a Rasta hat.

"No one," he said. "Or they're not telling. But I been thinking about this case. Thinking about it 'cause they're not giving it a lot of priority, are they?"

"The police?"

"This ain't what you'd call a high-profile case. But it's a dead woman, same as any other. A stiff in Beverly Hills doesn't have any advantage."

"Except money."

"Last time I looked they don't put U-Hauls on the back of hearses."

"So nothing to report?"

"Think this out with me for a second." He leaned forward, his eyes intense. "Somebody goes to 414, knocks on the door, talks quietly, then kills Reatta. That has to mean a couple of things."

"She knew him," I said.

"Let him in. Now, the girl's in the closet."

"It's her little room, where she goes to play or sleep."

"And she doesn't make any noise."

"Kylie didn't think much of it. She sees the guy through the door, but nothing seems strange. Which means guys have come and gone before. Maybe it was a buy."

Oscar shook his head. "She didn't look like a user to me."

"Turning a trick?"

"That could very well be." He said it sadly, like it was something that happened all too often at place like the Lindbrook.

"You found anyone who saw a guy come in matching the description?" I asked.

"Nope. Not even the elf in the window." He nodded toward the Plexiglas.

"It was someone with access," I said. "Came in from the alley, then went up the stairs. Coming in through the front, somebody would have remembered."

"So who'd have access?"

"People who own the place, or the people they hire."

"Which probably means a lot of people."

Before I could say anything else I was aware of a guy standing next to us. He was maybe sixty, wore jeans, cowboy boots, and a T-shirt with a very unflattering word attached to a certain prominent Democratic senator.

"This the guy?" he said to Oscar.

"That's him," Oscar said. "This is Clyde. Clyde, Ty Buchanan."

He shook my hand.

"Clyde was in Nam," Oscar said. "Then was an electrician. Been hard times lately."

"I'll get something soon," Clyde said. "I just wanted to tell you thanks."

"For what?" I asked.

"For putting the squeeze on the owners. I know you don't have to."

Oscar tapped the newspaper. "Know what it says here? Says one in four vets are homeless. Not just the older ones, the ones from Iraq and Afghanistan, too. That ain't right."

"No," I said.

Clyde said, "Thanks for stickin' up for us."

125

THE MAIN ADMINISTRATIVE offices of the Los Angeles Archdiocese were downtown too, and as long as I was here I thought I'd pay a call on the monsignor who sent Father Bob the keep-quiet letter.

I showed up unannounced, was polite to the receptionist, an older woman with actual blue hair. I always thought that was a myth.

A few moments later a bespectacled priest in his early fifties came to the foyer. He could have been a college history professor.

"I'm Monsignor O'Malley," he said. "How may I help you?"

"Is there somewhere we can talk?" I said. "I'm from St. Monica's. I'm a lawyer, and a friend of Father Robert Jackson."

He cocked his head, studying me. Then he nodded and showed me to his office. It was wall-to-wall books. I made a comment about them and he made a comment about Jesuit education and then said, "I wasn't aware that Father Robert had consulted an attorney."

"He hasn't. I'm here on my own."

"You're familiar with the facts, then?"

"Very. What I'm not familiar with is canon law."

He smiled then, like this was his favorite subject. "Would it surprise you to learn that it is the oldest system of law in our culture?"

"Not really. You Catholics go back a long way."

"And just as English common law developed over the centuries, so did our canon law. 'Canon' is from a Greek word meaning 'measuring rod,' or 'ruler.'"

"That explains it," I said.

"Explains what?"

"The nuns' weapon of choice."

The monsignor laughed and said, "That is a cliché, Mr. Buchanan. Although I will tell you this, I had nuns like that in school. And it did me a whale of a lot of good."

"And now here you are."

"And now here I am. My passion and mission are the same. To use the divine gift of the canon law to serve the church, to keep things on a smooth course. This, by the way, is a charge from Christ himself."

"Big charge."

"Our system must be a bit mysterious to you, but only because you are not of our faith and have not studied our codes. That is why this particular situation is best left to us."

"Maybe you could explain it to me, lawyer to lawyer."

"Gladly. According to the Code of Canon Law, Mr. Buchanan, if the good of souls or the necessity or advantage of the church demands that a pastor be transferred from a parish, the bishop is charged with persuading him to consent to it out of love for God. This is precisely what happened in this matter."

"Now, from an outsider's perspective, it sounds like you put pressure on your people not to make waves."

He put his fingertips together and tapped them a few times. "I would say we're all in the same boat. We are all under the direction of Christ."

"And you think he's for this?"

"Who?"

"Christ."

"I do."

"That an innocent priest, accused of the most vile act imaginable, has to sit back and just take it? Help me understand that." My tone was on the hot side. What was I doing? Father Bob didn't want me here. I was indeed an outsider. But it just seemed to me that fundamental fairness was the basis of the law, whether it came from church or not.

"I'm not sure I can help you understand," O'Malley said. "Except to say that we do not operate according to the dictates or codes of the world."

"So what about an appeal?"

"Father Robert has chosen not to. It is the right choice."

"I know the church hasn't exactly had the best publicity the last few years." Monsignor O'Malley said nothing.

"And you've had to shell out hundreds of millions and sell a bunch of your assets. It's easy for one priest to get lost in the shuffle."

"But he is not lost," Monsignor O'Malley said. "He is in service to Christ. He is where he should be."

"I guess you're right," I said. "I don't think you can help me understand."

126

I WASN'T EXACTLY upping my batting average this day. I decided to make one last stop before heading back to St. Monica's. It was late afternoon, and traffic showed it.

A little after five I got to the address on Owensmouth in Canoga Park. Brown stucco house. I knocked on the door. Something moved behind the peephole. Then a woman in her mid-twenties opened up. She was on the short side, with a pleasant face.

"Yes?" she said.

"Heather Dowling?"

"Uh-huh?"

"My name is Ty Buchanan." I took out my business card, to please the prosecutor's office, and gave it to her. "I'm the lawyer representing the man accused of robbing your flower store."

She looked at the card, then at me. "Am I allowed to talk to you?"

"You're absolutely allowed to. But it's your choice. I just wanted to ask you a couple of questions about what you saw."

"I already talked to the police and to the deputy district attorney."

"That's right, you did. All I wanted to do was—"

"Honey, who is it?" A man's voice from behind her. He came up to the door and I saw he had a young, aw-shucks sort of face, a Huck Finn type.

She showed him my business card. He looked at it, frowned, then broke into a big smile. "Wait a minute, you're Ty Buchanan."

"Guilty," I said, then wished I hadn't.

"Honey, he's that guy."

"What guy?" Heather said.

"Remember? That lawyer who was accused of murder? He was in the news."

"Oh, yes," she said. "Now I remember."

"Man," the guy said. "A real celebrity."

"Would you mind if the celebrity stepped inside?" I said.

It was a modest interior, filled with the sorts of things a couple in their twenties would have before they had kids.

"I hope you'll give me an autograph," the man said.

"I'm awfully shy about that," I said. "You understand."

"Tell me what it was like in jail."

"If you don't mind, I'd just like to ask your wife some questions."

"Just this one thing. See, I practice law, too."

That didn't seem quite likely. He looked too young. He looked like he should be working at In-N-Out. "What kind of law do you practice?"

"Estate planning."

"So I guess you never get to see the inside of a jail," I said.

"Is it really as bad as they say?"

"Well, every night my cell mate sat on the edge of his cot and played 'Swing Low, Sweet Chariot' on his harmonica."

"Now you're just playing with me." He stuck out his hand. "My name's Jack Dowling."

I shook his hand. "Now about those questions . . ."

"Should I call Mr. Roberts?" Heather asked.

"No, honey. It's all right. I'll stay here and listen to the questions and if there's something inappropriate, I will give a shout-out to Mr. Buchanan. We understand each other."

"Thank you," I said. We all sat down, very informal. "I just want to ask you about that day in the flower shop. According to the police report, you saw the Hispanic man behind the counter, is that right?"

"Yes," she said. "I was taking a short break and went out back, and when I came back in the store, he was there."

"About how far away were you from him?"

"I don't know, maybe twenty feet or so."

"And you said, I think, that he pointed the gun at you."

"Yes, he told me to stop where I was and just stay there."

"That must have been pretty scary."

"Of course it was. I was really afraid he was going to shoot somebody. Denise, she was behind the counter right next to him."

"Then he walked out of the store and I believe you said that you saw some tattoos on the back of his neck."

"Yes. It looked like a name."

"Can you tell me any of the letters in the name?"

"I don't think so. It happened so fast."

"Are you sure they were letters? Could they have been numbers?"

She thought about it. "I don't think so."

"Think or know?"

"Honey," Jack said, "think about it very carefully. Think about what you'd say in court. Mr. Buchanan here is just doing his job, but he is a lawyer." He snorted a laugh my way.

I didn't snort. I try not to when questioning wits.

"I'm just not sure, okay?" Heather said, an edge to her voice. Like she didn't want any more advice from either one of us.

There was a pause. Heather was rubbing her hands together, looking at them.

"Where'd you go to law school, Ty?" Jack said.

"UCLA," I said.

"Good school. I went to LaVerne."

"Ah."

Heather was still working her hands.

"Did you see anybody get shanked?" Jack said.

"Shanked?"

"In jail."

"Jack," I said, "to tell you the absolute truth, I'm trying to put that episode behind me, if you know what I mean."

He put his hands up. "Sure, yeah, understand completely."

"Is that all, Ms. Dowling?" I said.

"Yes, that's all," she said.

"What about drugs?" Jack said.

I got up, thanked them, and left. The day had pretty much accomplished nothing.

127

AND THAT WENT for everybody else. Sister Mary told me Kylie'd had a bad episode, crying for her mother.

So I said we were going out. To throw an unbirthday party for Kylie, like in *Alice in Wonderland*. Father Bob, he would be in the Mad Hatter role. Sister Mary was more like the Cheshire Cat.

Which left me as what? I shudder to think.

We went to a little place I knew on Ventura. Neighborhood joint with a great chef. Got a booth near the window.

Just as we settled I saw an older woman at the next table point at her salad and say, "There are no cranberries here!"

The man next to her said, "Those are cranberries right there, Mother."

"Those aren't cranberries!"

"Yes they are, Mother."

Kylie whispered, "Why are they fighting?"

"The lady is making a mountain out of a molehill," I said. "Do you know what that means?"

Kylie shook her head.

"It's what lawyers do, honey," Sister Mary said.

I threw a bread stick at her.

"Food fight?" Kylie giggled.

"Fine example," Sister Mary said.

Father Bob tried to hide his smile.

"All right," I said. "Who is hosting this dinner, anyway? A little respect here would be nice."

Kylie asked if she could have roast beef. "Like that knight of the Round Table!"

Sister Mary asked what that meant.

Kylie said, "Ty told me a story about a knight of beef."

"Sir Loin of Beef," I said.

"I see," said Sister Mary.

"He sat right next to Sir Osis of Liver."

Father Bob put his head in his hands.

"All my best stuff I get from cartoons," I said.

"Best stuff?" Sister Mary said. "I'd hate to hear the rejects."

And so it went, with Kylie laughing a lot. Having a great time. She had a steak, ate about one-quarter of it, savoring every bite.

Then I had them bring out four slices of chocolate cake, with ice cream, a lit candle on Kylie's. Her unbirthday.

She didn't know about making a wish. I told her to close her eyes and make a wish and then blow out the candle, and if she could blow out the candle the wish would come true.

She closed her eyes, paused, then blew out the candle.

She should have wished harder.

128

AS I TURNED up the road heading to St. Monica's, headlights flashed behind me. Coming fast. Valley kids like it up here, rodding on these back roads. I pulled to the right slightly to let him pass.

Pass he did, then pulled right in front of me and hit the brakes.

I almost rear-ended him.

A second vehicle, an SUV without lights, stopped on my left. Which meant I couldn't turn left and go around the first car. On the right was hillside. I was hemmed in.

"Get down," I said. "Everybody down."

"What is it?" Sister Mary said.

"Just get down."

Silently they did.

A man in a ski mask appeared at my window. Out of nowhere. He had a sawed-off shotgun. Pointed at my face.

"Get out!" he shouted.

Another masked gunman was at the passenger side, pointing his weapon through the window.

I opened my door. I was hoping all they wanted was money or the car. But the weaponry and obvious planning here didn't leave much room for hope.

Gun to my face, the masked guy said, "Them too. Everybody out."

"Look, take what you want," I said, "but leave them out of this."

He turned the sawed-off around in his hands and jammed the butt in my stomach. I doubled over, breath gone.

"Everybody out or they're dead," he said.

"It's all right," Father Bob said from inside the car. "We're coming."

Still folded, I looked at the ground, at the guy's boots. In the dark it was hard to see, but they looked big. Like they could do a lot of damage if he cared to do it.

I waited for the other boot to drop.

It did. After a gun butt to the head, a boot kicked me in the side.

A sense of falling. Looking up at the sky and stars for a moment. Then lights-out.

129

NEXT THING I saw was the face of a monster.

A dream. Or whatever it is that comes to you when you're out cold.

This face had horns and nostrils with smoke coming out. And it closed in on me from the sky, coming down down down to have a look at my sorry self.

In some distant place I was thinking or feeling that I'd let everyone down. That they would all be dead. Kylie and Sister Mary and Father Bob. And it'd be my fault.

The demon head got closer and opened its mouth, laughing and mocking, and I was sure I was destined for that maw. And I was scared.

Then the head exploded, soundlessly, all traces of it disappearing.

I heard a voice. Familiar, but I wasn't sure if it was real.

"Easy," Father Bob said. "How do you feel?"

It was still night. I was lying on my back. My head felt like it was in eight sections.

"What happened?" I said.

"Anything broken?"

"Get me up."

"You sure?"

"Get me up."

He put one hand under my head and the other under my shoulder. Helped me to a sitting position. I tried to blink some of the gravel out of my brain.

"What'd they do?" I said.

He didn't answer.

I knew then it was bad. "Tell me."

"They took Kylie," he said.

130

A BLINDING LIGHT shot through my head. White flame. I grabbed both sides with my hands.

"Sister Mary?" I said.

"She's all right."

"Where?"

"Up at the car. Praying."

I fought the hot and cold in my brain. The world started coming back into focus. Lights in the sky, lights down in the distant valley.

Took Kylie.

"They said something," Father Bob said. "They said don't talk to the law. If we talk to the law she's dead."

"Anything else?"

"They said they'd make contact. Tomorrow night."

I stood up. My head was spinning. "Who are they going to contact?"

"They didn't say. We need to get the police involved."

"No way. Not yet."

"We can't just wait," Father Bob said.

"They wouldn't go to all this trouble just to harm her," I said. "We wait to hear what they want. It'll be money. The only question is how much and how to deliver it."

"She must be so frightened," Father Bob said.

"She's got some grit," I said. "You and Sister Mary pray to your God that she keeps it."

131

WE HAD TO break it to Sister Hildegarde. And then everyone in the community. Once it was learned Kylie wasn't there anymore, there'd be questions. And questions could leak out of a monastery and into a cop station.

Sister Hildegarde was not pleased. We met with her in the front office.

"Absolutely you must call the police," she said.

"Not yet," I said.

"You do not have the authority here, Mr. Buchanan."

"I'm telling—asking—you not to say anything to anyone. It's critical that you don't give out any information."

"Mr. Buchanan, you have imposed yourself upon us, in good faith I have no doubt, but nevertheless—"

Sister Mary said, "Sister Hildegarde, would you consent to a period of prayer before making a final decision?"

Sister Hildegarde snapped her a look. "What is that supposed to mean, Sister?"

"Nothing, I—"

"Your piety is becoming something of a problem here. And—"

"Please," Father Bob said. "This is not getting us anywhere. As your priest, Sister Hildegarde, I am advising you to wait."

"And you do not have authority," Sister Hildegarde said, though she sounded the least bit unsure.

"But I do. If you'll recall, this was my appointment by the archdiocese. I am here at their behest."

"The decision will be made through vote of the council," Sister Hildegarde said. "In accord with the constitutions of the community. And that's all I have to say on the matter."

132

YOU CAN'T SLEEP, so you think about things.

You think about your life and your powerlessness.

You think about being alone in the world.

You think about angst and the absurdity of life. How little control you have over anything. And even when you choose to do anything, it's pointless because there's no ultimate meaning, so what does it matter? What does anything matter? So what if a little girl gets iced? If anyone does? What does it matter, because we're just accidents of nature and when it's over, it's over. No life after death, no singing with harps—that's what you think about at night when you can't sleep.

And then you wonder what makes you go on, what makes you care, because it's in there somewhere, the caring, even if you don't know why, even if you don't know any reason for it. It's just there and that's why you don't sleep.

You look out at the dark, you walk around in it, you think maybe there'll be a big insight, a sudden realization. And then everything will all add up. That's the hope part, the part the absurdists call a fool's game.

Are you just a fool like everybody else?

You think of the girl and you think of her being scared and you can't stand it, and caring becomes torture.

If God was in the room right now you'd scream at him.

That's what you think about when you can't sleep.

133

THE MORNING WAS no better. The community went about its business, but the word gradually spread. Faces looked at me with concern, but a little something else, too. Like maybe I'd brought an infection to this place.

Like I'd overstayed my welcome.

I was a mess and I looked it.

So I cut weeds on the outside of the wall. I worked in the sun. The heat felt good on my body.

Father Bob came out and made sure I had Gatorade. But I kept clearing the weeds. Every hack was one less thought.

Around four I knocked off and took a shower in my trailer. Got out, dried off, fell on my bunk and fell asleep.

It was dark when Father Bob shook me awake.

"They called," he said. "They want to talk to you."

134

SISTER MARY WAS waiting for us in the office. We didn't say anything. Like a voice would snap whatever thread held hope for Kylie.

The office phone rang five minutes later. I took it.

"Buchanan," I said.

"I know." The voice sounded electronic. Purposely masked. "The girl is all right."

I waited.

"Did you hear me?" the voice said.

"Yes."

"Good. You know that if you go to the police or the federals, you will never see her again?"

"Yes."

"This doesn't have to end bad. It's all up to you. You and the Catholics."

"What's that mean?"

"You'll find out. A little at a time. You can't trace this. Don't try."

"I want to talk to Kylie."

"You don't get to make up the rules."

"This a game?" I said.

Pause. "Don't question me."

"Let me talk to her, then we'll go on."

"I'm not gonna tell you again."

"We're negotiating here," I said. "A little give on each side."

"You want me to give you something?"

"Just so I know she's okay."

Another pause. Longer. "If this is going to be a problem, I'm gonna get upset. And you don't want me upset. I sort of lose control when I'm upset. Now you just hold on."

I heard a sound like the wind blowing across the microphone of a cell. Then silence. Then a scuffing sound. And low voices.

Then I heard her. "I wanna be with Sister Mary and Ty." She said it in a low voice, a scared voice. Trying hard to be brave.

It ate my insides up.

Silence again, then the sound of the wind. He was going outside.

"That's all you get," he said. The electronic voice was mobile. It now sounded like one of those vibrating things people hold to their throats when they've lost their voice. Simple. "There's a pay phone at the Thrifty gas station on Foothill. You take the 118 to the 210, get off at Ocean View. Turn left, then left again on Foothill. You'll run into it in about a mile. You getting this?"

"That's on the other side of the Valley."

"Wait at the phone. I'll call you. Come alone. I'll be watching. If you come with anybody, the girl is going to get hurt. You have one hour. One. If you're not there, the girl will feel some pain."

135

THE THREE OF them looked at me, waiting.

"I have to go," I said. "I have an appointment."

"I'm going with you," Sister Mary said.

"I have to go alone. This is only the beginning. I don't want to get any of you or St. Monica's more involved. Whoever they are, they want to deal with me, so I'll let them."

"Will they hurt her?" Sister Mary said.

"Yes," I said.

136

I HAD TO burn some tire to get there in time. The 118 jammed up at Balboa, so I broke the law. I hopped into the diamond lane, reserved for cars with two or more. I was taking a big risk, that I'd be spotted by the CHP or a cop. But a bigger risk was not getting to that pay phone in time. The thought of Kylie getting some harm done to her was almost choking me.

It was forty-seven minutes by my watch when I took the turn onto Foothill. I followed it until I saw the yellow and red sign for the gas station.

And the pay phone, under a blue sign.

With a guy taking up the space.

I pulled into the station and swung around and parked just beyond the phone. The lights of the station cast a yellow glow. I could see that the guy on the phone wasn't dressed too sharply. His long hair was greasy. He was jittery, moving around as he talked.

He eyed me as I approached. "I need to use the phone," I said.

"What? Wait…Billy…wait a second." He put the phone on his chest. "What'd you say?"

"Sorry, I need to use this phone. I need to have it now."

"I'm talking."

"I'll give you five bucks if you hang up now."

"You crazy?"

"Five bucks."

He rejected the offer with a few words about what I could do with my five dollars. I took the phone out of his hand and hung it up.

"Hey man!" he said. Looking at me. Sizing me up.

I put the fin in his pocket and said, "Leave."

He hesitated.

"Now," I said.

He google-eyed me, as if he wanted to scare me off. But he had nothing on me. I was more than half crazy at this point. I pushed him hard. His back slammed into the phone.

It took the google right out of him. He walked away fast.

There wasn't much traffic at this hour. It felt like a desert town at night in some B movie.

But the phone ringing made it real.

137

"THAT WAS JUST great, the way you handled that guy," the voice said.

I looked around.

"Don't bother," the voice said. "You can't see me."

He could have been anywhere out there, with night vision optics. Or on a roof, or right behind me.

"What now?" I said.

"Okay, here's what I want you to do. I want you to bend over and grab your ankles."

"What?"

"Don't make me repeat this. Bend over now and grab your ankles."

That's what I did, leaving the phone hanging from the wire. I stood up and took the phone again. "Happy?" I said.

"Real happy. You're doing what I want you to do. You see how easy that is?"

"Let's get to it," I said. "You want money?"

"Yeah. I want money. Lots of money. How much you got on you?"

"I don't know."

"Find out. Right now."

I took out my wallet and looked inside. I had two twenty-dollar bills and a couple of singles. "Twenty-two bucks," I said.

"Any credit cards?"

"Yeah."

"How many credit cards?"

"Two," I said.

"American Express? Visa?"

"Both."

"Great. Here's what you do. Take out the bills and credit cards. Wrap the bills around the credit cards. Do that right now."

"Twenty-two dollars isn't going to—"

"Do it right now. Don't question me again."

I shut up and did what he said.

"Now, walk that over to the fence. You're going to see a can of Campbell's Bean-with-Bacon soup there. An empty can. I want you to put the money and credit cards in the can, put the can back down where you found it, then come back to the phone. I'll wait."

I let the phone dangle, walked over to the chain-link fence that sided the gas station. There was enough light for me to see the can. I picked it up and put the money and credit cards inside. I put the can back on the ground.

I turned to walk back to the phone. It wasn't dangling anymore. The guy I gave the five dollars to was standing there, holding it, looking at me with a half smile.

"Don't hang up," I said.

He hung up.

138

"WHAT'S IN THE can?" he said.

"Get out of here," I said, approaching. I took two steps toward him. Something flashed. He had a knife, holding it flat against his belly.

"Get me the can," he said. "I wanna see what's in it."

"Listen," I said, "you don't know what's happening. You're being watched."

"Right." He started walking toward me, slowly, tapping the knife against his chest. "Tippy tap, tippy tap," he said. "I like to play with knives and forks and spoons, and I like to cut things."

I looked around. If the guy came at me, I didn't have many options.

"Tippy tap, tippy tap," he said, closer now. I had to start backing up.

Knife guy kept coming and I didn't think he was serious about sticking me, but I wasn't going to test him. He backed me up past the fence, then looked down. Saw the can and edged toward it, keeping an eye on me and another on the can. He kicked it slightly.

It fell, some bills flapping out.

"Muh-nay," he said. "What is up with that, Doc?"

"I wouldn't touch that," I said.

"Yeah, you wouldn't do a lot of things, probably. I like to do things." He held the knife in his right hand as he squatted and reached for the can with his left. He pulled out the bills and the cards. Stood up and looked at them.

"What're you doing this for?" he said. He shot a look at the phone. "Who you talking to?"

"Publishers Clearing House," I said. "Congratulations. You win. Now you better get out of here because some bad dudes are around and they can see what you're doing."

"What are you talking?" He looked at my cards. "Tyler Buchanan. You a rich guy?"

"Shut up. Put the money and the cards back."

He smiled, put the items in his shirt pocket, and pointed the knife at me. "You got any more on you?"

I sized him up. Pure punk. Then I remembered what I had in my pocket.

"I ask do you got any more," he said.

"Yeah," I said. "I do."

"Then give it to me."

I have never been in a knife fight. The closest I came was in seventh grade, when I faced a guy down with a bread stick.

But so much adrenaline was pumping through me now it didn't matter. I put my hand in my pocket and pulled out B-2's iProd. I held it out for the punk.

The moment he looked at it was my window.

In the split second it took him to blink, I kicked him in his classifieds. Kicked him square. A Butch Cassidy move. Paul Newman would have been proud.

He doubled over. I thumbed the iProd and pushed the business end into his neck. He screamed and dropped the knife, then dropped to his knees.

I kept it there until he was on his back and in spasm. I picked up the knife.

The phone rang. I ran to it. Put it to my ear.

"Way to go," the voice said. "How'd you do that?"

"What now?" I said.

"This place is too much trouble. Give me your cell phone number and get going."

I gave him the number. He hung up. I went back and fished out my credit cards and money from the punk's shirt.

His eyes were wide and frozen, like he was Bambi and I was halogen headlights. I thought about strapping him to my hood. But I just left him to contemplate phone etiquette and got to my car and left.

139

BACK AT ST. Monica's I met with Father Robert and Sister Mary outside the trailers, near the basketball court. Fitting, as I was being played big-time.

When I told them what happened, ending with the knife incident, they gave me an appropriate breathless response.

"Yeah, I'm okay," I said. "Let's talk about the call. When I heard the voice the first time, it sounded like he was in a windy place. It could be anywhere. He altered his voice, and he has Kylie. Now, can you think of why he would tell me to drive out there to the pay phone, do this thing, and hang up on me?"

"Testing you?" Father Bob said.

"Yeah, a test run maybe," I said. "To see if I'll follow directions and not give him any back talk."

"About the guy with the knife," Sister Mary said.

"He'll be all right," I said. "His hair might be a tad frizzier."

"What do we do now?"

"He's got my cell. He'll call me back. That's when the real deal will be made."

"What kind of deal do you think it will be?"

I shrugged. "Monetary, but the how and when of it is up for grabs. I mean, it's not easy to get a ransom anymore. There are too many ways money can be traced. I'm going to assume this guy knows that."

Assuming and waiting. Two uncertain things. It was the not knowing, and the not knowing how long it would take, that was so bad.

I've always thought I could work my way out of anything. Grit teeth, put in more hours than the next guy. But what do you do when you can't even see the next guy?

Then he called.

140

"ALL RIGHT," THE voice said. "Get ready. I'm only going to say this once. Here it is. The price is five million dollars."

"Five," I said tonelessly.

"Now, this is how it's going to be," he said. "You talk to the Catholic church and you tell them to transfer the funds to the Sister of Divine Mercy in Guadalajara. They will be expecting it there. No worries—transactions between churches are out of the reach of the feds."

"How do you expect—"

"Shut up. You always do that. Five million is not much for the church. You use your lawyer skills and convince them to do that. You let me worry about getting it out of them down in good old Mexico. I'll take care of that part. And that's it. The little girl comes back to you all safe and sound."

I waited. He said nothing. I said, "What if they don't—"

"Make sure they do."

"How much time do I have?"

"I'll call you tomorrow to check on your progress. There better be some."

He hung up.

Sister Mary and Father Bob waited patiently for me to tell them what was what.

"He wants the Catholic church to pony up five million dollars. He wants it transferred to the church in Mexico. That way he avoids the feds. Is there any way to do this?"

"Five million?" Sister Mary said.

"That's right," I said.

"So we try to get the money," Sister Mary said. "We talk to the superior."

"Oh, that will be fun."

Father Bob said, "Who would want to do this?"

"What are those seven deadly sins?" I asked Sister Mary.

"Lust, gluttony, avarice, sloth, wrath, envy, and pride."

"Avarice," I said.

"An inordinate love of riches," Father Bob said.

"But maybe this is just the tip," I said. "Someone wants something out of the church. Money. But maybe it's more."

"How so?" Sister Mary said.

"Maybe it's just my intricate criminal mind, but what if the DeCosses are behind this? They put financial pressure on the church, the church answers out of concern for Kylie."

Father Bob rubbed his head. "You're saying that the whole thing is a plan to move some land deal?"

"I'm saying that's one thing that springs to mind. I know I haven't got any evidence to prove it. But somebody knew a lot about Kylie, about me, about this place, about where the best place to pull the snatch was."

"There couldn't be that many people who fit," Sister Mary said.

"No," I said. "There couldn't."

My cell bleeped.

141

"THIS IS LIEUTENANT Brosia. I'm not disturbing you any, am I?"

I looked at Father Bob and Sister Mary. "No, not at all."

"I'd like to talk to the girl again. How's she doing?"

"Fine."

"Well that's just great. Where is she?"

"Someone's watching her."

"I'd like to come see her."

"Not right now," I said. The rule from the Voice was no cops, and I wasn't ready to violate that rule yet. Not with Kylie still out there.

"Why not?"

"I don't want her disturbed yet, that's all. Maybe later. Maybe I can—"

"Mr. Buchanan, I have this feeling that you're not being—"

"Talk to me later."

"I want to talk to the girl."

"I'll bring her to you when she's ready."

"Are you her doctor now?"

"I'm whoever it is that's looking out for her, that's who I am."

"I can force the issue, you know."

"I'm asking that you don't."

"I don't like it when I think somebody's hiding the ball."

"I'll hand you the ball, Lieutenant. I'll hand you a whole playground-full. Just give me time."

He paused. "I'd really like to believe you will. But I'm having trouble with that."

"We've all got troubles," I said.

142

IT WAS A little before five in the morning. I'd managed to get a little more sleep, dreaming about monsters with big teeth. Seeing Kylie in the middle of them. They were monsters drawn in crayon.

I woke up to a pounding on my door.

Groggy, I opened it. Thought it might be Father Bob.

It was Sister Mary, standing out there in the dark. "Listen," she said. "There was no wind in most of the city last night. I checked the weather reports, the National Weather Service, all the local news stations."

"So maybe he's far away?" I tried to shake the sleep out of my head. It stayed. I realized I was standing there in a T-shirt and boxers. I said, "I'm not decent."

"It's just like a basketball uniform. A bad one. Don't worry about it. But if there wasn't any wind, I mean around the city, I thought I'd check outlying areas."

"It could be anywhere. But you're on the right track."

"I wish I had more resources. All we've got is a single desktop."

I rubbed my eyes. "I know a guy," I said. "A guy who can help."

143

I TOOK SISTER Mary with me to DuPar's. I needed pancakes and plenty of coffee. At eight o'clock we were back in traffic, heading to the west side.

To the offices of Jonathan Blake Blumberg.

He saw me immediately. I introduced him to Sister Mary.

"We use your security cameras at the abbey," she said.

"My stuff?"

"It's the best," she said. "I was the one who picked it out."

A big smile spread across his face. "I like you," he said.

"You're two for two, Q," I said. "Your tracker is tracking and that little iProd worked wonders." I had him sit down—not easy to get him to do—and told him everything. His face remained impassive as he listened. Like this was not something surprising or outrageous.

There was a rumor that Jonathan Blake Blumberg had once been a shooter for the CIA. He told me as much himself. The CIA would never confirm this, of course. But I couldn't help feeling that it was true.

When I finished he tapped his lips with his index finger a couple of times. He swiveled in his chair and looked out his office window toward Santa Monica and the ocean.

He stayed that way for half a minute, then swiveled back.

"I'm going to give you something," he said. "A digital stick to record your calls. I want you to get this guy's voice, then bring it to me. The moment he calls you and you get the voice, I want you to contact me. Because time is running out on the girl. Tell him you can only get eighty-five thousand right now, but you'll keep working on the rest. I will arrange the transfer of the money. It will come from offshore right into the coffers of that church in Mexico."

"I can't ask you to do that," I said.

"I'm not asking you to ask me," he said.

144

BLUMBERG SHOWED ME how to attach the device to my phone. Now it was a matter of waiting for the call.

I drove to the beach, near the Santa Monica pier. If Sister Mary and I had to wait, why not wait where there was some life going on?

We found a bench and looked down at the sea. Rollerbladers and old couples passed in front of us. On the sand people threw Frisbees, while the pier buzzed with tourists. Life was going on. I envied all of them.

Sister Mary was pensive. Silent.

"We've got to believe we'll get her back," I said.

She managed a smile.

"Look who I'm telling to believe," I said.

"There's hope for you yet."

"I'm not taking that to the bank just yet, but thanks."

The breeze was nice and it wasn't too warm, and we sat for another hour or so. Then the call came.

145

"WHEN CAN I expect a transfer?" the voice asked.

"A couple days," I said.

"That's not soon enough."

"You're talking about a lot of money. You can't just walk up to the cardinal and say, 'Do it, please.' And this abbey doesn't have the resources on its own."

"That's why I had you drive out to the pay phone," he said. "I saw what you can do when you put your mind to something."

"I want to talk to Kylie."

"We've been over that—"

"You want money? Give me Kylie. You're going to be a rich man. You can be benevolent."

"I can be what?"

"You can throw me a bone. Come on."

"Shut up."

"You shut up." I said it before I thought about it. "Let me talk to Kylie and I'll get you money. I can get you eighty-five large right now. You owe me an exchange."

"I don't owe you a thing, man."

"You want the money, I talk to her now."

He hung up.

146

"I HOPE I didn't blow it," I said. "And I hope I got his voice on this thing."

I handed the digi stick to Sister Mary.

"He didn't understand the word 'benevolent,'" I said. "We're not dealing with an educated guy."

"What do we do with that?"

"It's just more data to put in the pan." I stopped because of the picture in my mind. "If anything happens to her…"

Sister Mary put her hand on mine. A good, strong hand.

My phone buzzed again.

"I'm going to be right here," the voice said.

Then I heard, "Ty?"

"Kylie, are you okay?"

"I don't like this place. Come get me."

Voice said, "That's all."

In the background I heard Kylie yell, "No!"

"Six o'clock," Voice said. "If the eighty-five isn't there, well, then that'll be that."

I sensed he was bluffing. He was this close to getting some serious money and wasn't going to kill Kylie. Yet.

"What about the big money?" I said.

"I'm going to give you a couple of days longer for that," he said. "If you come through now."

"You're not going to get anything until we decide how the exchange is going to take place."

"I'll tell you that later."

"Just so you know, just so there are no surprises, you're going to bring Kylie to a place where I can see her. I will okay the transfer, and then you will let Kylie go."

He clicked off.

147

I CALLED B-2 with the transfer numbers. Then he told us to meet him at his house in Marina del Rey.

House? That's like calling Disneyland a playground.

The elaborate security system outside looked like a TV studio. Made me think of Sam DeCosse's place on steroids. Inside the walls it was a juiced Steven Spielberg movie. Part landing pad from *Close Encounters* and landscaping by Indiana Jones.

Inside it was *A.I.*

A young guy in black jeans, who said he was part of Blumberg's R & D team, let us inside the ultramodern abode. He took us to the second floor, where B-2 had about a thousand square feet of office space designed in techno. You got the feeling the world was controlled here, by touch screen.

"Welcome," B-2 said.

I gave Blumberg the stick and he plugged it into a laptop that was sitting on a desk that could've roofed a single-family dwelling. He told us to look up at the flat screen monitor on the wall.

Up popped a screen with tracks and lines and something that looked like an equalizer.

"This is a voice analysis program the FBI doesn't even have yet," Blumberg said. "It's still in development, but watch what it can do."

Blumberg tapped and moused his way across the screen. In a few moments, after a colorful screen or two, we were back at the main screen. It showed several waves of sound.

"Looks a little like GarageBand," Sister Mary said.

"I can make Buchanan here sound like Plácido Domingo," Blumberg said, "but that's not the point. If this guy is changing his voice on the cheap with an artificial larynx, we may be able to get something. If he's using a digital voice changer, we won't be able to get much. So let's give it a shot."

We waited as he tapped a couple of keys. Then a voice came through the speakers, much clearer: *That's why I had you drive out to the pay phone. I saw what you can do when you put your mind to something.*

"Did you hear that other sound?" he said.

"What sound?" I said.

"Listen." He replayed the clip.

"Yeah," I said. "A little squeak right there in the middle."

"I'm going to isolate it," he said. "Let's see what it sounds like."

He played the section with the squeak. Stopped and enhanced it, played it again.

"Sounds like a door opening," Sister Mary said.

I looked at Blumberg. His look told me he didn't agree. I didn't either.

"Can you isolate the voice now?" I asked.

"Yeah baby." He worked the keyboard. As he did I looked at Sister Mary. She gave me a reassuring smile. Like a coach's pep talk without the audio.

A year ago I was a partner at a major law firm getting ready for marriage. The phrase *settle down*, which my grandfather might have used, kept running through my mind. And I liked it.

Now I didn't know what to like. Or if I should like anything again. What I had to do was find the girl.

"Ready," B-2 said. The voice came through again, this time with a more normalized tone. *That's why I had you drive out to the pay phone. I saw what you can do when you put your mind to something.*

Something clicked in my head.

"You got anything that can help me see at night?" I asked.

B-2 said, "You want night vision?"

"Do you?" I said.

"Ask me something hard."

148

DRIVING BACK TO St. Monica's, Sister Mary said, "I don't like the look in your eye."

"Who asked you to look?"

"I see darkness there."

"You got a pretty keen sense of sight."

"I know something about light and darkness."

"And I know all about gray."

"Maybe, but no one can stay in the middle. We all drift toward one side or the other. The idea is to go toward the light."

I said nothing. Kept my eyes on the freeway. Kept thinking about what I was about to do. Planning in my head for something that could land me in the slam for a long time.

"Do you know Genesis?" Sister Mary said. "The creation?"

"I wasn't there."

"In the beginning, God created the heavens and the earth. But the earth was without form and void, and darkness was upon the face of the deep. And God said, 'Let there be light, and there was light.' The light was good. God divided the light from the darkness. And that is a picture of what God does for those who seek him."

"Does what now?"

"Get rid of the darkness."

I was on the verge of a comeback, but the words got stuck on my tongue. We ran into some traffic and it hit me then that having a discussion about something that mattered more than the flow of cars in L.A. was not a bad thing.

We finally came down the other side of the Sepulveda Pass. Clouds covered the tops of the mountains on the other side of the Valley. The sun reflected off them, making everything bright and silver.

Sister Mary mentioned the homesick-for-heaven thing again and I said I wasn't homesick for anything.

That seemed to make her upset. She didn't say anything else after that.

I dropped Sister Mary off and drove away, waiting for night.

149

WHEN IT CAME, I was waiting somewhere else.

The odds were not good any way you looked at it. The Voice had every advantage and I knew that.

I was on a bluff looking down at the mobile home park near the ocean. Watching for the lights.

It was a shot in the dark with a pea shooter, but I was going to blow. The sound I heard on the voice track sounded like a seagull. And the voice, normalized, sounded like a certain has-been rocker.

The wind whipped, like it always did here at the beach. I was in weeds, with night scopes, courtesy of J. B. Blumberg.

The ocean waves whispered.

An hour or so went by. I imagined all sorts of things crawling through the weeds, looking for some fresh leg to bite. This was a habitation of snakes. They were here first. They had property rights.

But I didn't care. If I got bit, I was going to bite right back. I was in that kind of frame.

I could see the lights of Santa Monica all the way down the coast, where the curve of the land headed right, toward the Palos Verdes Peninsula. In the distant sky, like a string of neon pearls, were the planes coming into and going out of LAX.

Life was happening and I wasn't close to any of it—and didn't care.

Not much happened down below. If life was happening in the park, it was mostly on the inside.

The mobile home I was looking at had no lights on. No car in front. How long I'd have to wait didn't matter to me.

I kept thinking I could hear Kylie crying. It was only my mind, of course. The question I started to have was whether I could get it to stop. Maybe I was losing it, going a little over the edge here. Not telling the cops, not telling anybody.

Brosia was not going to be pleased. I was a little sorry about that. I was getting to like Brosia. He knew what he was doing. He was a cop who liked what he did. That's how I remembered my dad.

I wondered what he'd think of what I was doing. Wondered what he'd say. I'd tell him I was out there on a wire, I know it, and I can't go back. I have to try to make it to the other side.

Then the car pulled up. I followed the headlights from the front of the park entrance, past the kiosk, and in front of Fly's single-wide.

And I had a vision. I saw everything that was going to happen, I knew where everybody in the world was, who was watching and who wasn't. I knew that he would get out of his car and go into his trailer and all would be right with his world.

Knew that I would shuffle down from the weeds without being seen by anyone. That I would knock gently on his door, and Fly would answer, and his eyes would go wide. And he'd try to close the door and I would know for certain he did it. That certainty wouldn't stand up in a court of law, but there wasn't a courthouse within shouting distance. That's all that mattered.

It happened exactly that way.

When he tried to close the door I plowed right into it. Fly landed on his bass.

I jumped on his chest. He wasn't that big. I put my hand on his throat.

"Don't bother to talk," I said. "Don't try to move or to make a noise, because if you do I will surely make you sorry."

I waited until I saw the fearful understanding in his eyes. It was instantaneous, and the rage and fire inside me made my body hot.

"I know you did it," I said. "I know you have her. I know it was your voice on the phone. You don't need to know how I know, but I do. You're going to tell me exactly where she is. Am I getting through to you? Oh, before you answer, I'm packing a neat little stun gun, and I won't stop, even if you scream 'Don't tase me, bro.'"

I slowly let the pressure off his throat.

"Where is she?" I asked again.

Fly said, "She's close by. Back in the hills."

"How many watching her?"

"Just one."

"How much is he getting?"

"Fifty thousand."

"You, too?"

"Yeah."

"And the five million? Who's getting that?"

"Look, man, I'll go away. I'll go to Mexico. You won't get any trouble from me. I'll give you the girl if you let me get out of this place."

"Who hired you?"

"Come on—"

I put my hand back on his throat and made his eyes bug out. His face turned a bright shade of pink before I let it off again. He coughed a couple of times.

"You're a lawyer!" he said. "You can't do this."

"We can go all night."

"Wait, wait." He coughed again. "I don't know who, man. I'll give you the girl and I get out."

"That's your deal?"

"That seems fair."

"Fly, who's on top of you right now?"

"You, man."

"You're not in a good bargaining position. Now, you get me the girl. How's it supposed to go? You call when the transfer's been made?"

"Yeah. I'm supposed to call and he brings the girl to me. I bring her to you alone."

I thought about all this.

"Can I get up?" Fly said.

"No," I said. "You have a piece?"

"No, man."

Hand back on throat. Big fly eyes. "I'm going to knock you right out and search the place," I said. "And I find out you're lying to me…"

I let the pressure off.

"Okay…the bedroom," he said.

I controlled him with an old-fashioned arm bend behind his back. He had a shotgun under his bed. Double-barreled, sawed-off, break action. Mean. I hadn't fired a shotgun since my dad took me shooting as a kid. I forced Fly to the floor, facedown. I cracked the gun. It had two cartridges. I took them out, shook them the way Steve McQueen does in *The Magnificent Seven,* put them back in and closed the gun.

"Fat lot of good living with nuns did you," Fly said.

"Here's what I want you to do," I said. "You're going to make the call that the transfer's done, and take delivery of the girl. You're going to have her brought right here and dropped off. I am going to listen to every word you say and watch every move you make, and if anything goes wrong I'm going to blow you and your friend away."

"What about our deal?"

"Time to make the call. Do not let your voice shake. Do not say anything that would put the girl in any danger."

"Nobody wants to kill her, dude."

"And don't call me *Dude.* Not while I'm holding this gun."

150

HE MADE THE call. His voice did not shake. It was an amazing show of vocal control. Like in his glory days.

And so we waited.

I had Fly sitting in a beanbag chair in front of me. I held the gun on him. Just so it would be a reminder.

"Now it's time for you to give up the boss," I said. "Who was it?"

"And I walk out of here?"

"It's your one chance, let's put it that way."

"Man, you got no idea what I been through. What they call music now? The whole rap thing? The whole airhead-blonde-with-the-nasal-drip-voice thing? The music died, man, like 'American Pie' said. Trash bands, grunge. It's all nothing. So don't sit there and judge me. A man's got to do what he's got to do."

"That's some philosophy of life you got there."

"And what about you? Sitting here with a gun. How did you get so low?"

"I'm tired of people close to me getting hurt."

"Happens all the time, man."

"Talk to me, Fly. Time's wasting. Who hired you?"

"I don't know the dude's name."

"Fly…"

"I'm being straight with you. There was a middle guy. I never saw number one."

"You ever see this middle guy?"

"Once. But it was dark."

"Where?"

"Malibu Canyon. Little side road up in the hills. It was like *Deliverance*, man. I thought there was banjos playin'. I hate banjos."

"What did the guy look like?"

"I don't know."

"You didn't get a look at his face?"

"He didn't want me to."

I shook my head and waved the sawed-off his way.

"I'm tellin' you the truth, man!" Fly said.

"When the car comes up," I said, "you stand at the door. You don't open the screen door. You tell them to leave the girl at the steps and get in the car and drive away. If you don't, you will be the first to go and then I'll take care of the other guy."

"What about the girl? She might get it, too. You ever think about that?"

"That's all I'm thinking about."

I heard a car driving up, coming to a stop on the gravel outside.

"This is your moment, Fly. A chance to redeem yourself. Don't blow it."

He got up and flipped his braids behind him.

151

FOOTSTEPS APPROACHED, THEN came up the wooden stairs. A knock.

Fly opened the door, keeping the screen closed. I stood off to the side, by the closed, shaded window, ready with the gun.

"Here we are," a voice said.

"Where is she?" Fly said.

"In the car. She's okay. Crying a little. She wants to go home, I told her that's where we were takin' her. I want to get out of here. You got a beer?"

"No. Let's get—"

The guy outside pushed his way in. "Come on, man, you always got beer."

He was twice the size of Fly. A denim-jacketed behemoth with a mis-shapen head. It looked like one side had been kicked in. Or he was in a serious accident without a helmet.

There was nowhere for me to go. Nowhere to hide in the little home. The behemoth was all the way in when he saw me.

"Who…?" He focused on the shotgun I was holding.

"On your face," I said.

He didn't move. Not a twitch.

"Better," Fly said. "Dude's crazy."

"Don't call me 'Dude,'" I said. "I really can't stand that."

A long moment passed as the big guy stared me down. His lizard eyes were cold, almost lifeless.

Then he said, "This guy's not gonna shoot anybody."

"Down," I said. "Now."

The behemoth said, "Look at him, Fly. This guy's not hard-core."

"Try me," I said.

He didn't move.

"Now!" I put the gun butt to my shoulder. I could feel the wet on my right wrist and palm. I finally knew what they meant by "itchy trigger fin-ger." I was this close to letting them have it anyway, for what they'd done, for who they were. Whatever held me back was thin. But it worked.

"It's okay," Fly said. "All he wants is the girl."

"Last time I ask," I said. "Or I will put a hole in your mad and furious master."

"What is he talkin' about?" the behemoth said.

I yelled a word they'd both understand and pointed the rifle below the belt.

The two of them slowly got to their knees and spread out on the floor, facedown.

And then a visitor showed up.

152

"WHAT IS GOING on here?" I recognized the high whine of the security guard. He was outside the door, where he could only see the two on the floor.

"Petey!" Fly said. "Help!"

The guard stepped through the door. He was holding a big flashlight. He started to say something, then saw me. And the gun.

"Don't move, Petey," I said.

"He's crazy!" Fly said.

"Easy, Petey." I could hardly believe I said that. I actually felt sorry for the kid. He looked completely out of his element. As I was.

"Put the flashlight down," I said.

Petey hesitated.

"Now," I said.

He put it on the ground.

"Now kick it toward me," I said.

Petey did like I asked him. "Please, sir, don't shoot anybody."

"Listen carefully, Petey. The car in front, look inside. There's a little girl in there. She's a kidnap victim. By these two."

"Don't listen to him!" Fly yelled.

"Go look, Petey," I said. "I'll be right here. You're about to become a hero."

"I know who you are," the behemoth said, but I wasn't sure who he was talking to.

"Go now!" I yelled, and Petey moved. I took a couple of steps so I could see out the open door. Petey looked through the window of an SUV. He turned around.

"She's tied up," he said.

"Come here, Petey," I said.

"You tied her up?" Fly said to his companion.

"Shut up," Behemoth said.

"Both of you shut up," I said. To Petey I said, "Call the sheriff. Now."

That seemed like a good idea to the security guard. He made the call on his cell and that seemed to generate, finally, a little good faith.

"They're on the way," he said.

I handed Petey the shotgun. "If either one of them makes a move, shoot to wound."

"Where you going?"

"There's a scared little girl," I said. "She comes first."

"Petey!" Fly screamed. "Shoot him!"

I walked to the SUV.

"Maybe you should stay," Petey said.

"No," I said.

Fly screamed at me. "We had a deal!"

To Petey I said, "Tell him that a verbal contract isn't worth the paper it's written on."

"Petey!" Fly yelled.

"Now, you just be quiet," Petey ordered, and I knew all was well. A boy becomes a man.

153

THE DRIVER'S-SIDE DOOR of the SUV was unlocked. I hit the unlock button. Kylie was in the backseat, hands tied in front of her, gagged with a scarf. She'd been crying, and her nose was stuffy. She could barely breathe. I took off the scarf and untied her hands.

The second I did, she threw herself to me and wrapped her arms around my neck. And started crying big-time.

"I'm here now," I said. "I'm not going to leave you."

I carried her all the way down the drive and back up toward where I'd parked the Taurus.

Kylie stuck to me.

"Did they hurt you?" I said.

"When he tied me. I was scared."

"Are you sure you're okay?"

"I have a tummy ache."

"Are you hungry?"

"He gave me tacos."

"The big guy?"

"He said I was going to be okay, but I was still scared."

"You don't have to be scared now. You're all right."

"I told him he was going to get in trouble," Kylie said. "But he didn't listen."

"He's listening now, sweetheart. He's going to get in big trouble. We'll make sure, okay?"

"Okay."

154

I CALLED SISTER Mary and told her I had Kylie and that she was all right. She and Father Bob were waiting for us in the parking lot when we pulled in.

Kylie gave them both hugs, then Sister Mary took her to get her cleaned up and to a warm bed.

"What happened?" Father Bob asked.

"Some other time," I said. "I feel like I need to sleep. Say some sort of prayer to the saint of sleep, if there is one."

"How about I skip that and go directly to the Father?"

"You're the priest."

155

MY SLEEP WAS cracked by a call from Deputy Sheriff Mike Browne. It was a strained, law enforcement tone. He requested the pleasure of my company at the station. I told him the pleasure would be all mine.

And it would be, because two bad guys had been caught. Kylie was safe. A few items were still outstanding, like who killed her mother and who was behind the nab, but for now I was counting it as the start of a good day.

Always a dangerous thing.

I got to the Malibu/Lost Hills station a little after ten. Browne was waiting for me. This time I got to sit in his office.

He sat behind his desk. I sat in a leather chair in front of his desk. He folded his hands and said, "Do you want to tell me what happened?"

A little clipped. "Didn't you get the statement from the security guard?"

"Do you mean the security guard who is now in the hospital?"

"What?"

"That's right. When my deputy got to the trailer park he found one Peter Burnett bloody and unconscious. When Burnett was able to speak to us in the hospital, early this morning, he mentioned your name. That's why it might be good for us to talk."

"Where are the guys he was holding?"

"Nobody knows. Maybe you do."

"Why would I know that?" I stood up. "When I left last night the guard had a sawed-off shotgun in his hands and two suspects on the floor. How did they get away from him?"

"I haven't determined that yet. Burnett is not doing so well."

"Did he tell you anything at all?"

"He mentioned something about a little girl."

"Yeah. A kidnap victim. The guy whose mobile home I left last night was in on it. And now the girl is safe."

"Do you want to explain a little bit about why you broke into this mobile home? Was there some sort of probable cause?"

"Wait a minute. Are you leveling some accusations at me?"

"I'm just trying to determine what happened."

"When Mr. Burnett is able to talk, he'll tell you. Right now you need to get people out looking for Mr. Fly Charles, the tenant in that mobile home. And a very large man who was with him. These are dangerous people."

"Can I talk to the girl? Who is she?"

"She is six years old and she's been through hell. I will arrange for her to talk to you later. But right now I'll give you a description of the two suspects so you can hop over this."

"That'll be very helpful, Mr. Buchanan."

156

I TRY TO be helpful. That's why I stopped off at the little hospital where Burnett had been taken.

I checked in at the front desk, where an old gentleman asked who I was. I said I was Peter Burnett's lawyer. That seemed to me the shortest distance between two points. The old gentleman must have agreed. He issued me a visitor's pass and gave me the room number.

Burnett didn't look good. He had gauze around the top of his head and his face was puffy and black and blue. It probably didn't do him much good when I walked up and he saw me. He grimaced.

"How you doing?" I said.

"Why are you here?" The high voice was even higher.

"I sort of feel responsible that I got you into this."

He rolled his head a little back and forth. "I just messed up."

"No, I did. I should have stayed with you. I was concerned about the girl. What happened?"

"The big one, he tackled me. I was afraid to shoot. That's all I remember. I woke up in here."

"I'm really sorry, Pete."

"Were they really kidnappers?"

"Yes, they were. I gave it all to the deputy sheriff. The girl will back everything up."

"Did they catch 'em?"

"Not yet."

He groaned.

"But listen," I said. "The girl is safe. You made that happen."

He stopped groaning and looked at me hopefully.

"That's right," I said. "Now is there anything you need?"

"A new face, probably."

"I'll stop at the gift shop."

A weak smile. Then: "You didn't have to come here."

"And you didn't have to believe me last night. But you did. I'm going to make sure your bosses know you went the extra mile."

157

A LOT OF people were going the extra mile for me. Father Bob and Sister Mary. McNitt. Even Brosia.

Who I called on my way back to the Valley.

"I've been holding out on you," I said.

"I had that feeling for quite a while," Brosia said.

"Would it help to know that I've had a few things to take care of lately? Like, I've got a client who is facing a capital murder charge and I'm taking care of a little girl who was kidnapped."

Pause. "Are you talking about Kylie?"

I gave him the story, up to poor Petey in the hospital.

Brosia whistled when I finished. "So this guy Fly and the other one, they're gone?"

"I suggest you contact to Browne out at Malibu. You need to talk to this guy."

"I'd love to."

"And Sam DeCosse," I said. "Junior and Senior."

"I need something to question them about," Brosia said. "There's nothing that connects them to the killing except the location."

"What if I get you something?"

"Does it involve breaking the law?"

"Me?"

"What I said."

"I love you, too," I said. "I'll be in touch."

"Wait—"

I clicked off.

158

SISTER HILDEGARDE HAD her arms folded. That is the universal sign of trouble. She was standing at the edge of the parking lot.

Sister Mary was next to her, holding Kylie, who was holding Sister Mary tightly around the neck.

"What's up?" I said. The moment I did Kylie turned and wiggled out of Sister Mary's arms and ran into mine. She put her face in my shoulder, like she wanted to hide.

"I've called the Department of Children and Family Services," Sister Hildegarde said.

"Oh you have?" I said. "And you were going to tell me when?"

"I'm telling you now. It had to be done. I'm sorry."

"I thought I explained that I was her guardian," I said.

"That's something that the department will have to sort out, Mr. Buchanan. I felt it my responsibility—"

"I appreciate it," I said. "But Kylie is not going anywhere."

"She cannot stay here."

"Of course she can," Sister Mary said. She faced Sister Hildegarde like a lion eyeing a water buffalo.

"Excuse me?" Sister Hildegarde said.

"May I speak, or am I too *rigid*?"

"Be very careful about what you say next."

"You want me to weigh every word? Okay, here they come. You are not looking out for the best interest of this child."

"Sister Mary—"

"I'm not finished."

"I think you are."

"Then let me go down in flames! We have too long put aside our true religious duties in the community. We are not taking care of our elders as we ought. Now we are not taking care of the least of these, the children. You are content to hand her off to a bureaucracy. We have lost our vision."

"Sister—"

"Maybe *that's* why Mr. Buchanan came here, for this very purpose, to turn us back to what we should be. Maybe God is using this as our moment, to reclaim what it means to be a real community. That includes those who have come to us for help."

Sister Hildegarde made a face that a mother might, sort of *You wait until your father gets home.* "The decision has been made." She turned and stormed to the office.

I looked at Sister Mary, who was breathing hard, and said, "You go, Sister."

"I will probably have to now," she said.

"Let's all three of us go," I said. "Let me make a call."

159

"KYLIE, THIS IS Fran."

Kylie was not ready to let go of me, even after we got into Fran's little living room.

"Hello, Kylie," Fran said.

Kylie said nothing.

"And this is Sister Mary Veritas," I said.

"Welcome," Fran said.

We stood there for a moment, silent.

Then Fran said, "I wish someone would help me feed the cats."

I felt Kylie move.

"You have cats, Fran?" I said.

"Oh yes I do. But I just need help feeding them."

"I wish there was someone who could help you," I said.

Kylie's head lifted from my shoulder. Then she whispered in my ear, "Can I help?"

"Do you want to?" I said.

Kylie nodded. I set her down. "Kylie said she'd like to help."

Fran held her hand out. "Then let's go."

After a moment's hesitation, Kylie took Fran's hand and went with her toward the back door.

When they got outside, Sister Mary said, "Well, now I can think about more stupid things to say to Sister Hildegarde."

"It needed to be said."

"You don't know anything about us. You don't know anything about authority or order or things that last."

"Whoa—"

"I let my mouth and heart lead when it should have been my head."

I said, "Sometimes you have to lead mouth and heart, okay? You're not a head of state. You're not leading us into war. You're not Groucho Marx."

She said, "What on earth are you talking about?"

"You ever see *Duck Soup*?"

"I don't think so."

"Then soon we will watch *Duck Soup*. Groucho plays the leader of a country. An enemy country sends over a diplomat. Groucho says to him, 'Maybe you can suggest something. As a matter of fact, you *do* suggest something. To me you suggest a baboon.'"

Sister Mary smiled a little.

I said, "And after the diplomat looks outraged, Groucho says, 'I'm sorry I said that. It isn't fair to the rest of the baboons.'"

A faint, almost imperceptible laugh issued from Sister Mary Veritas. I put my hand under her chin and lifted it a little. "Now, that is a comment that led to war. You didn't call Sister Hildegarde a baboon, although…"

"Watch it."

"So I think you're in the clear. There's still a First Amendment in this country."

160

OUTSIDE, I ASKED Kylie if she'd be fine staying here awhile while I went on a little trip.

"I'm feeding the cats," Kylie said. Three of them were purring around a bowl. "You can feed them when you come back."

Fran smiled at me, nodded. She looked like she was having the best time of all.

"Sounds good," I said. "You stay with Fran till I get back."

"Okay," Kylie said.

Fran said, "Maybe we'll have some oyster crackers and grapes."

"Oh, boy," Kylie said. "I like grapes."

"So where are we going?" Sister Mary said.

"We?"

161

SISTER MARY DROVE.

"We're going to follow the little red dot on the B-2 bird dog," I told her. "Do a little surveillance."

"Cool."

"You know, I just can't seem to get used to the idea of a nun saying 'cool.'"

"It's all in how you look at it. In some ways, we're the ultimate cool."

"Let's not go into that right now." I took out my phone and brought up the tracking data Blumberg had programmed into it. A map showed up with a blinking red dot in the middle. I hit the info.

"Our boy's in Long Beach," I said.

162

EVERY FEW MILES I checked again. It was steady. I thought I knew why. That's where DeCosse Senior had his floating golf course moored. But we'd checked on Senior earlier, and according to one news item he was in New York for meetings.

Which could mean that Junior was taking the family yacht out for a spin. *Gee, Dad, I didn't mean to beach her. I was just trying it out...*

I knew a spot up high where we could park and watch the boats come in. I used binoculars to find the DeCosse space. It was empty.

So we waited. With windows rolled down and a nice sea breeze coming through.

"Ask you a question?" I said.

"Sure."

"Theological."

"Really?" she looked extremely pleased. "Shoot."

"About nuns. You take vows and all, right?"

"That's right."

"But sometimes nuns stop being nuns."

She said nothing.

"You know," I said. "I've seen it in the movies. What was it, *The Nun's Story*?"

"Audrey Hepburn. I'm impressed."

"Don't be. Jacqueline liked old movies. Her favorite thing wasn't going out to dinner. It was pizza and TCM with me."

"I think that's very cool."

"There you go again. So about *The Nun's Story*. Didn't she walk out at the end?"

"Yes."

"Why? I can't remember."

Pause. Sister Mary looked out the windshield, toward the ocean, as if the answer might be there. Finally she said, "She was torn between what she felt was her calling to serve God as a nun, or in the world as a nurse."

"So let's say you wanted to go out in the world, what would you do?"

"We Benedictines take a vow of stability, to remain in community and obedience to our abbess. And—"

She stopped and looked down.

"I get that," I said. "I don't like authority, either."

"I didn't say that," she snapped. Fire in the voice.

"What did you mean, then?" Heat in mine, and it surprised me. I was more interested in her answers than I thought.

"It's a lot deeper than that," she said. "We're talking about God here."

"I thought we were talking about Sister Hildegarde."

"Who serves at the behest of God, I would remind you."

"Maybe," I said. "And maybe not. I mean, who knows the mind of God, right?"

"That's what you have a church for."

"But the church gets it wrong sometimes."

"How would you know?"

"Agnostics know a few things, too."

"Just don't die an agnostic," she said. "Otherwise they'll have to give you one of those special gravestones."

"What special gravestone?"

"The one that says, 'All dressed up and nowhere to go.'"

163

WE TALKED SOME more and then I saw it. Heading in. No question—it was DeCosse's yacht.

Through the binoculars I had a clear view and didn't see any deckhands. One guy on the bridge.

Junior.

Then I saw someone else on the bridge. A woman in a large-brimmed hat and shades. She put her arm around Junior and kissed his cheek.

"Well," I said, "it looks like our boy has a tootsie."

"Tell me you didn't just say *tootsie*."

"Tootsie."

"Your world is very strange," she said.

"Just get ready to drive."

"Where?"

"Wherever the dot leads us. I want to see where Junior and Tootsie go next."

164

THE DOT LED us north, through downtown L.A., and exited in Hollywood.

We were about five minutes behind them. The dot stopped on Cherokee. Behind Musso & Frank Grill, a Hollywood institution since 1919.

I had Sister Mary park at the curb. "Looks like a little early dinner at Musso's," I said. "Ever been there?"

"No."

"Want to go in? Have a martini?"

"Mr. Buchanan—"

"Ty, please."

"…don't mess with me."

"Not messing. They're famous for their martis. One of those and you'll be so theological you'll—"

"Thank you, no."

"A milk shake?"

"Some other time."

I looked at my watch. Called Fran. She and Kylie were having spaghetti and meatballs. I asked if Kylie might spend the night. That was aces with Fran. She put Kylie on.

"Hi, Ty."

"You having fun?"

"Uh-huh."

"Fran's cool, isn't she?"

"Yes."

"If it gets late, would you like to spend the night? We can come get you in the morning?"

"I like Fran," she said.

"So it's okay?"

"Uh-huh."

"Remind me to buy you some ice cream next time I see you."

"Okay."

I clicked off and turned to Sister Mary. "Let's talk about your case," I said. "We have some time."

"My case?"

"With Sister Hildegarde."

"Oh. There's no case. She is the judge."

"Jury and executioner?"

"We don't have those," she said.

"Not since the Inquisition, I guess."

"This talent you have for insults, is it a gift?"

"No," I said. "I have to work on it."

165

ABOUT AN HOUR later Junior and the woman came out the back door of Musso's making like octopi. Arms all over each other. Sucking face. I saw Junior a little more clearly. He wore a black shirt and black coat with a white handkerchief in the pocket. He fished out a wad of bills and peeled one for the valet.

The valet brought the red Ferrari around and the happy couple got in. Junior pulled out onto Cherokee, then took a right on Hollywood Boulevard.

We followed the dot. Past the El Capitan and Kodak Theater, to La Brea, where it took a left.

And came to a stop at a corner a half mile later.

When we got there I saw the Ferrari in front of a theater, one of the many small venues in the city where actors can show their stuff in the hopes an agent or producer will wander in some night and see them. And then sign them up, get them on a soap or hit series or the new Spielberg. That happens about as often as the Cubs win the World Series.

The theater marquee announced *As You Like It*.

They were going to see Shakespeare? Junior had culture?

I had Sister Mary pull to a stop on the opposite side of LaBrea. We waited and watched. The red Ferrari was empty, parked illegally at the red curb in front of the theater. A few people milled around the entrance.

A couple of minutes later Junior came out the front doors, alone. He jumped in the car and drove off.

"Follow?" Sister Mary said.

"No," I said. "We can pick up his location later. I'd rather see if we can talk to Tootsie."

We found a metered parking place on the street then walked to the theater. At the box office I asked a guy with glasses and tufts of gray hair sprouting around a bald head if the production was worth seeing.

"Yeah, it is," he said. "*L.A. Weekly* loved it."

"Sam DeCosse said I should see it."

"Then you came to see Elinor."

I smiled as if I knew who he was talking about.

"She is absolutely radiant," the ticket guy said.

"Radiant?"

"The theater is all about the suspension of disbelief," he said, getting excited. "When an actor is on, it makes that suspension of disbelief easy. You forget you're watching a play. That's what she does every night."

"Pretty good review," I said.

"How do you know Mr. DeCosse?"

"I'm one of his lawyers," I said. "One of many."

Ticket guy laughed. "I hear you."

"So just between us," I said. "Does she have what it takes to go all the way? You know, to the movies?"

Ticket leaned forward. "Movies, nothing. This is where it's at. Shakespeare. She's great. And it's a great part, of course. Maybe the best for a woman ever. Right? Am I right about that?"

"Better than Juliet?"

"Please! Rosalind is a woman in control of her fate. She would have stepped in and solved the feud."

"Right on," I said, having forgotten most of what I knew about the play. "I'm surprised Sam didn't stick around."

"He's seen it four times," Ticket said. "That counts for something."

"Okay, give me two tickets," I said. "You sold me."

Thirty bucks for Sister Mary and me to sit at the back of the small theater and watch Shakespeare. The program said it was Elinor Hanlon in the part of Rosalind. Her bio was brief, only that she was studying with a noted acting teacher and was thrilled to be making her Shakespeare debut with this production.

As we waited I asked Sister Mary if she knew the play, and she not only knew it, she went on to give me the rundown on its historical significance.

"Rosalind is both witty and wise at a time when this was not thought feminine," Sister Mary said.

"I think it's feminine," I said. "You could play Rosalind if you didn't cheat at basketball."

"Be quiet. I'm lecturing. You want to learn something? Rosalind is one of the great characters in theater. She points us to the joys of true freedom even in the midst of absurdities."

"Such as?"

"Rosalind teaches us that the way of love is irrational and yet…"

"And yet what?"

She was silent, looking at the stage. Then she said, "Necessary."

She looked down and didn't say anything else.

The theater got about three-quarters full by the time the lights went down. Recorded music started, a sort of bucolic theme.

Lights up and the play began. I followed along and was even getting into it when Rosalind made her entrance.

"Dear Celia," she said, "I show more mirth than I am mistress of…"

In the dark my jaw dropped. But Sister Mary must have seen it.

"What is it?" she whispered.

"Rosalind," I whispered back. "I know her."

"An old flame?"

"Hardly. And her name's not Elinor Hanlon. It's Ariel DeCosse."

166

AFTER THE SHOW we went backstage. Made our way past young actors with towels rubbing their faces and chattering. Nobody stopped us. We found the door to the women's dressing room. A female techie was about to go in and I asked if I could speak to Elinor.

The techie went inside. A moment later Ariel stepped into the corridor. She was all smiles, fielding some compliments from other actors. Still wearing her boy clothes from the play.

When she saw me she frowned. Then slapped on a grin. "Mr. Buchanan, isn't it?"

"Nice to see you again," I said.

"Did you enjoy the show?"

"A really interesting interpretation," I said. "What's with the stage name?"

"I just want to act. I don't want to be known as Mrs. DeCosse who got her break because…" She looked over my shoulder at Sister Mary.

"Oh, this is Sister Mary Veritas," I said. "Big Shakespeare fan. Played Puck in an all-girl production of *Midsummer Night's Dream*."

"He jests," Sister Mary said.

I had a copy of the program and held it out to Ariel with a pen. "Would you mind?"

"Flattered," she said. She gave me the autograph and handed the program and pen back to me. I put them in the outside pocket of my coat.

Ariel said, "How did you happen to know I was performing?"

"Is there somewhere we can talk?" I said.

"Well, I do have to get ready to go."

"It won't take too long. I'm sure Junior won't mind waiting."

Her look made me want to put on a jacket. Ice face. "What makes you think—"

"Why don't we find a little place," I said. "Why talk out here in the middle of everybody?"

167

IN A SMALL backstage office, the three of us had some privacy.

"Now, what is it you want?" Ariel said. She was no longer the queen of mellow, the lady of laid back. She faced me like a wrestler.

"I want to talk about you and Sam Junior," I said. "You went out on the yacht today. I don't think it was for fishing."

Her nostrils actually flared. Ricky Ricardo could not have done it any better. "I don't have anything to say to you," she said.

"You should be more careful. What if your husband were to find out?"

"There's nothing to find out." She turned casually and looked at the wall. "Sam's in New York and I asked Sammie to take me out on the boat. We've done that before."

"Like you've tongue-tangoed before?"

"I have no idea what you're talking about."

"You were more convincing as Rosalind," I said.

"Get out."

"Sure," I said. "But what's to stop me from getting hold of your husband with this sordid little—what's the word I'm looking for?"

"Farce?" Sister Mary said.

"Farce," I said.

And then Ariel jumped at me like Bruce Lee on speed. She punched with her right hand, caught me on the jaw. Her left got the other side of my face.

I took a step back, bumped a stool and went down. As I flopped on my back I saw Ariel's foot of fury heading for my face. I rolled and her foot gave me a glancing blow off my forehead. I put my hands up to fend off the next one. But what I saw was Sister Mary Veritas, Benedictine nun, servant of God, executing a beautiful spin move and jamming an elbow into the nose of one crazy actress.

Ariel screamed. Blood spurted from her nose. She put her hands to her face.

Somebody pounded on the door.

Ariel screamed, "Get in here!"

The ticket guy from the box office came in. What looked like most of the cast was assembling behind him.

"What is all this?" he said.

"They broke my nose!" Ariel shouted.

The guy looked at me. Quivered a little. A couple of women rushed in to attend to their Rosalind.

"I'm calling the cops," Ticket said.

168

SISTER MARY AND I waited for the police in the lobby, along with the angry cast. They whispered Elizabethan threats at us. Ariel was still somewhere in the back.

A black-and-white pulled up outside the same time Sam Junior did.

It was quite an entrance. Very theatrical.

Junior's face was as red as the lights over the cop car. He homed in on me. "That guy! He's been harassing me! Coming after me!"

The two uniforms, a woman and her older partner, a man, stayed calm. Good old LAPD training.

"Who made the call?" the woman asked. Her nameplate said "Estevez."

"I did," Ticket guy said.

"So arrest them," Junior said.

"Sir, please," Estevez said. "One at a time."

"They assaulted one of our actors," Ticket said. "Broke her nose!"

"Who assaulted?"

"They." Ticket wagged his finger at us. "Them."

Estevez looked at Sister Mary. "You an actress?"

"No, sir," Sister Mary said. "A Benedictine."

"Can you tell me what happened?"

"Mr. Buchanan is a lawyer," she said. "We went into an office to speak with the actress who calls herself Elinor Hanlon."

"Calls herself?"

"It's a stage name."

"Arrest them!" Junior shouted. "What are you waiting for? Where's Ariel?"

"Who's Ariel?" Estevez said.

Junior followed one of the actors out of the lobby.

"They broke her nose!" Ticket said.

"Sister," Estevez said, "what happened?"

"I broke her nose."

"Whose nose?"

"Ariel."

"And she is who, now?"

"She's in the show," Sister Mary said. "Quite good, actually."

"And you say you broke her nose?"

"With an elbow."

"On purpose?"

"Hard as I could."

"But why?"

"She was about to kick his face in," Sister Mary said. "I don't think paying customers should be treated that way."

Estevez smiled. "You really broke somebody's nose?"

"What is this?" Ticket said. "What are you doing?"

"Sir," the officer said, "I'm trying to get the story. Did you witness the assault?"

"Well, no—"

"Then please be quiet. Who saw it?"

"Only the three of us," Sister Mary said. "Mr. Buchanan, the woman, and myself."

"And you're telling me that this woman, this Ariel, is the one who attacked first?"

"That's right. I just happened to be there."

"And where," Estevez asked with a glint, "is elbowing in the catechism?"

"Defense of the innocent," Sister Mary said. "Equal force may be used to stop an attack. I was the equal force."

"This is unbelievable!" Ticket cried.

"I want to talk to the woman," Estevez said.

"Before you do…" I indicated I wanted a private word.

Estevez took a few steps away. Ticket shouted, "Hey!" But the other cop finally got involved and said, "Please be quiet, sir."

169

OUT OF RANGE of the others I said, "The woman is the wife of Sam DeCosse."

"No way," Estevez said.

I heard Junior's voice coming closer, like a freight train. He burst into the lobby with a weeping Ariel holding a towel to her face.

"You better arrest them right now," he said, "or I will sue you and your whole department, you hear me?"

Estevez said, "Sir, I would like to talk to her if—"

"No," he said. "I need to get her to a hospital."

"Maybe I can help," I said. Before anybody could stop me I went to Junior, right up close, and thought of the best movie cliché I could. "You're goin' down."

It worked. He jumped me. We fell back on the floor. Rumbled around. The male cop pulled Junior one direction. Estevez pulled me in the other.

I heard the cop say, "You're under arrest, sir."

"Do you know who you're dealing with?" Junior shouted.

"Turn around," the cop said.

"Hey," I said, getting up. "Why don't we just chalk this one up to a misunderstanding. I won't swear out on him this time."

The cop looked disappointed. Like he really wanted to slap bracelets on Junior. "All right," he said. "Let's clear the lobby now."

"This isn't over," Junior shouted, and walked out the front door with Ariel.

To Estevez I said, "Well, it doesn't look like there's reasonable cause to detain me and the sister."

"What's he mean by that?" Ticket said.

Estevez nodded. "You have a card?"

I gave her one. She said, "You can go now. I'll be in touch if I need you."

"Unbelievable!" Ticket said.

"Suspend your disbelief," I said.

170

OUTSIDE, THE NIGHT air was moist and warm. We walked toward the car in silence, but I couldn't get in until I asked, "How did it feel smashing her in the nose?"

"I did what I felt I had to do," she said. "You were about to get really hurt."

"She surprised me," I said.

"Don't worry. Your manhood is intact. But we all need a little help from time to time. Even big-deal lawyers."

"Thanks for the press release. And thanks for cracking her in the schnoz. That's not going to endear the Catholic church to the DeCosses."

"Let them take it up with the pope. What's our next move?"

"Our next move?"

"You're not getting rid of me now. Not after I saved your bacon."

I was looking in her eyes and there was a blue and green restaurant sign reflected in them. I wanted to put my arms around her and pull her to me and kiss her. I was this close to doing it, so close my stomach clenched like it was in the grip of Stone Cold Steve Austin. And I hated myself.

I gulped down a dry throat and said, "We call Lieutenant Brosia. I have something he needs."

171

WE WENT TO Fran's to check on Kylie. She was asleep. Fran was still up and said they'd had a wonderful day, baking brownies and watching the sunset.

I told Fran we'd had a less than wonderful night at the theater, and we'd come back for Kylie the next day and did she have a Ziploc bag?

She did. I carefully placed the program Ariel had autographed into the bag and sealed it.

I got Sister Mary back to St. Monica's and said a quick good night, then drove all the way down to Central Division, where the nice detective had consented to wait up for me.

When I handed him the Ziploc I said, "This is either going to be very big or nothing."

Brosia said, "We of the Los Angeles Police Department appreciate your efforts. But if it turns out to be nothing, we will appreciate it even more if you stop trying to help us."

All the way back to St. Monica's, I wondered if it would be big. Or if this was all a product of my fevered brain, rattling around looking for anything certain to land on.

I drove the 101 past the old lights of Hollywood—the Knickerbocker and Capitol Records—and on toward the newer lights of Universal City Walk. And I kept trying not to think of a certain nun, and I kept not succeeding.

172

THE NEXT MORNING I heard the ball being pounded on the basketball court. Sister Mary was up early, doing her workout. I peeked out through the kitchenette window. I took a shower and when I got out she was gone.

Good. I got dressed and went to see my next-door neighbor.

Father Bob was in his civvies, a white T-shirt and jeans, barefoot, holding a copy of a thick book in his hand.

"Need to talk," I said.

"Fine," he said. "Aquinas can wait."

We sat at the kitchen table, where the cup drum set still was. Only now he didn't tap anything. He waited for me to start.

So I did. "I just want to know how bad it is if a guy, hypothetically speaking, of course, has—how shall I put this—*thoughts* about a nun."

Father Bob's gentle features did not reflect surprise. "I've been wondering when we would have this conversation."

"You saw it coming?"

"A guy reading braille could have seen it coming."

"Why didn't you say anything to me?"

"Timing. Like comedy, there is timing in life, too. The time is now here. Tell me, how deep do these thoughts about Sister Mary go?"

"You want the details? It's not like I want to jump into bed with her. No, that's not it. But, yeah, there's attraction there. I think about what it would be like to kiss her. About holding her. About...all right, yes, sometimes about going to bed with her. And here I haven't even stopped grieving about Jacqueline. So there you go. Am I damned? Am I going to burn? Do I need to get out of here?"

"One question at a time. So you want to go with damnation, hell, or whether you have to leave St. Monica's?"

"Let's start with if you think I'm a really bad guy for thinking this."

"No, Ty. You see, thoughts are not inherently sinful. It often comes as a shock to people to hear me say that, so I don't say it very often. But desires or thoughts, in and of themselves, do not constitute sin. You are wired by God for sexual desire, and it can occur at any time. Even after you've lost a fiancée you don't stop being a man. It's only when you allow those desires to control your actions that they become sin."

"So I'm safe?"

"No one is ever completely safe outside of the power of God. So, no, truth in advertising compels me to tell you that doing battle with your desires on your own power is doomed to failure."

"You saying I'm going to end up doing something I will regret?"

"The odds are in that direction."

"What if this is not just sexual desire, but something more?"

"Ty, Sister Mary has taken vows. Vows don't mean much to most people anymore, but to a Catholic they are a solemn matter. She has not taken final vows, but it is still very, very serious."

"What if she left?"

"What do you think would happen if you were the reason she did? Do you think you could live with that?"

"Quit asking me what I think."

"Is that a bad—"

"Forget it."

I got up and left.

And walked.

Walked out the back, out on the land waiting for the DeCosse family to ravage it. Walked fast, trying to clear my head. It was a riot in there. Scenes from Jacqueline's death duking it out with pictures of Sister Mary.

Then I thought about the darkness inside me, not wanting it there but thinking it was not going away.

And what that meant for any future I had among the living.

173

BROSIA CALLED ME a little before noon.

"It's big," he said.

174

I DROVE TO Sam DeCosse's fortress on the hill. Stopped at the King Kong gate, got out, hit the button on the security box. I gave the cameras a wry smile.

A moment later the gates opened. Without so much as a hello.

Devlin was waiting for me at the front of the house. As I got out of the car he said, "You should make an appointment next time."

"There won't be a next time," I said. "And I'm really going to miss you."

I walked by him. And felt a brick hit my kidney. Not enough to do permanent damage, but enough to make me wish I'd gone to the beach instead.

I looked at him. He showed me his brass knuckles.

"You're a real hero with those things on your hand," I said.

"Just want to impress you with my resources," he said. "Save your energy for Mr. DeCosse."

175

SAM DECOSSE WAS in his library, putting golf balls into a little machine. I watched as a ball rolled in and the machine punched it back.

"You're intemperate, Mr. Buchanan," DeCosse said.

"You're doing it all wrong," I said.

He looked at me. "What?"

"Your grip is all wrong. Look." I walked over with my hand out. He gave me the putter. He must have felt awfully secure with Devlin standing in the room. I kicked one of the balls toward the door, where Devlin was stationed.

I walked to the ball. Then I put the putter in my hands like a baseball bat and swung like A-Rod.

Taking out Devlin's left knee.

He cried out. His face contorted and he went down. He grabbed his knee with both hands.

DeCosse's face tightened.

"I just wanted him to be impressed with my resources," I said. "Thanks for the putter." I threw it on the floor.

"You're going to be sorry you did that," DeCosse said.

"How's your wife?"

"Not good public relations to bring that up. But I do know my wife, despite her best efforts, has a temper. Is it true a Catholic nun did that to her?"

"It's true."

He shook his head. "The world is changing. Now, what do you want?"

"I'm ready to settle with you," I said. "But we have to do it my way."

"With putters at high noon?"

Devlin was still on the floor. Probably wondering why nobody was paying attention to him.

I said, "I want you and your whole legal team, in the conference room of Gunther, McDonough. We are going to have a sit-down and hammer out a settlement once and for all."

"You drove up here to tell me that?"

"You're the quarterback. I didn't want to go through your filtering system. This is between us."

Devlin was starting to get to his feet.

I said, "Are we on?"

"I'll call Pierce McDonough and set it up."

"Thanks," I said.

"Anything else?"

"Tell Mr. Devlin I don't want to see him again."

"I'll see what I can do," DeCosse said. "He has a mind of his own."

"He has a mind?"

176

I COULDN'T GET down off that hill fast enough. Away from the stink. Down to where people got up every day and went to work and fought the fight and tried to do good things for their kids.

Yeah, there's the other kind, too, who don't care about the kids they father. Who leave their idea of manhood scattered on the streets, spawning boys who will become lousy fathers someday, and the wheel goes round.

Back at St. Monica's, the sky was cloudy, the grounds sleepy, I walked around the hill outside the walls. A hill that was pretty much the same as when the Gabrielino Indians walked over it, dreaming not of Hollywood stardom but of altered states. They smoked weed. Jimsonweed to be exact, in a ritual for moving young men into adulthood.

I walked up a knoll. From here I could see no buildings or cars or people. Not even a plane in the sky. The grasses were light brown, dotted with some plants deep green and scrubby. I wondered if any of this was jimsonweed. If there was a wildfire, maybe this whole side of the Valley would get high.

I thought about Sister Mary and how I shouldn't think about her.

I thought about how it was cooling off in the hills.

And how everything else was heating up and needed to blow.

It didn't take long.

177

WHEN SAM DECOSSE wants something to happen, it happens.

The next day at ten-thirty a.m. Sister Mary and I were outside the building that houses Gunther, McDonough & Longyear.

Waiting for Lieutenant Brosia, who was prompt.

"Nice to see you again," Sister Mary said.

"I can't believe I'm doing this," Brosia said.

"I guarantee that you'll find this of interest," I said.

"That's not what you guaranteed. You guaranteed new evidence."

"It's inside," I said. "At least, I hope it is."

The detective sighed.

I put on a slight Marlon Brando godfather voice. "Someday, and that day may never come, I will ask you to do me a service."

"Let's just go up and get this over with," he said.

178

THEY WERE WAITING for us in the conference room. Seated at the table with their backs to the windows were Sam DeCosse and his son, along with their legal team—Al Bradshaw, Hyrum Roddy, and my old boss, Pierce McDonough.

What a surreal experience that was, entering that room again. I'd done many a deposition there. Now I was, in a manner of speaking, the enemy.

They looked surprised at my guests. "This is Lieutenant Tim Brosia, LAPD," I said. "And Sister Mary Veritas of the Benedictine Order."

Pierce McDonough said, "What is this supposed to mean, Ty?"

"They're my support team," I said. "And may have some relevant information for all of us."

"Forget this," Junior sputtered. "We don't have to sit here and—"

"Shut up," Sam DeCosse Senior said. Junior shut up. Then, to me, Senior said, "Let's get this over with. I don't want to do this again."

Brosia, Sister Mary, and I took chairs on the other side of the conference table. Al and Roddy had pads and pens ready. The others glared. This was something. Legal and business power on one side. The cops, the Catholic church, and me on the other.

It was a toss-up who'd walk out bloody and bowed.

"Well, thanks," I said. "Nice of you to consent to this meeting. I think, as Mr. DeCosse says, we can settle this thing and not have to do it again. So let's review how we got here. It started with a client of mine at the Lindbrook, who was about to be shuffled out, contrary to law. Then she ends up dead, and her daughter motherless and that bothers me. See, I don't like my clients to end up dead."

"Come on, Ty," McDonough said. "This isn't about a dead woman."

"Oh, but it is, Pierce. Whoever it was that killed her had to have access to the hotel. Came up the back way, where the door is locked. Also, had to be someone who knew Reatta, also known as Tawni. Formerly an escort with an outfit called L.A. Night Silk. Does that ring any bells?"

Looks were exchanged all over the place until Pierce McDonough said, "What does this have to do with settling the tenancy dispute?"

"Maybe everything," I said. "Nine years ago one of the escorts for L.A.

Night Silk was charged for misdemeanor prostitution, under section 647. Her name was Ginger Lambelet. I went down to the Hall of Records and found the court file. I was able to find that file because Lieutenant Brosia here found the docket number in the LAPD database."

The two DeCosses looked the same at this point. You could tell they were father and son. Staring straight at me, not moving, cheeks beginning to show pink.

"He found the name because he got a set of fingerprints, very nice ones, too. On slick paper."

I nodded at Brosia and he pulled a plastic bag out of his inner coat pocket.

Inside was the program from *As You Like It*, the one Ariel had signed for me.

Brosia slid it across the table to Pierce McDonough. Junior grabbed for it, but Senior's hand slapped down on top of it, trumping everybody.

He kept his hand on the bag, not bothering to pick it up. "So what?"

"The print from the program matches that of Ginger Lambelet," I said.

Junior jumped out of his chair. Arms flailing he screamed, "Are we gonna sit here and let him do this?"

"Sit down," Senior said.

But Junior didn't sit down. He backed away from the table, started walking away.

That's when Daddy stood up. His voice boomed like Thor's hammer, and he ordered his son, in words and phrases that no nun should ever hear, to get back in his chair.

Junior looked like he was going to cry. Maybe he did. He was sure breathing hard. Then he said, "No. Not this time."

Senior now dropped his voice to almost a whisper. "You think you're ready to go it alone?"

That was all he needed to say. Whatever resolve Junior had managed to work up melted away like snow on a stove. He was practically liquid when he slid back to his chair. I almost felt sorry for him.

"I apologize," Sam DeCosse Senior said. "Please get to your point, Mr. Buchanan."

179

"MY THEORY," I said, "is that your wife killed Reatta in the Lindbrook Hotel. The question is, why? And the answer is that Reatta was into some sort of blackmail. Maybe she was threatening to expose Mrs. DeCosse, who is trying so hard to go legit. I don't know, but whatever it was, I think it was a freelance idea."

"What do you mean by that?" Senior said.

"Reatta had a connection to both the Lindbrook and St. Monica's. The hotel is owned by Orpheus, and there's also a pending deal on the land adjacent to St. Monica's that Orpheus is interested in. Now, either that's a very great coincidence or a setup. I think it was a setup. I think Reatta was a plant, in a very nice scheme to squeeze some very big dollars out of Orpheus."

"Planted by who?" DeCosse said.

"That's the really interesting part," I said. "On the Lindbrook matter she talked about getting a TRO. Not temporary restraining order. TRO. I don't know, but in my experience, right here with good old Gunther, McDonough, very few people toss that term off the cuff, like lawyers do. It sounds like she either went to law school or got prepped by someone who did."

I opened my briefcase and pulled out a copy I'd made. "Here's a copy of the court transcript in the 647 prostitution matter, which records the appearances of counsel. Ginger Lambelet had two lawyers that day. One of them I don't know, but the other name I do."

I slid the paper across the table.

Hyrum Roddy was already standing when the paper reached Senior. He knew his name was on the document.

I said, "So here we have a DeCosse lawyer appearing at a prostitution misdemeanor. Now, why?"

Brosia said, "I wonder if I might have a few words with Mr. Roddy alone."

"No," Roddy said. "You may not."

"I think Mr. Roddy may know something about the murder of an escort named Avisha Jones," I said. "And the kidnapping of a six-year-old girl named Kylie."

Roddy's lips moved but no sound came out.

"Avisha was working on a score," I said, "and it had something to do with Ginger. I think she knew Ginger, and maybe she wanted in on the action Reatta had found."

"This is ridiculous," Roddy said.

"Is it?" Senior said. To Brosia he said, "Maybe Mr. Roddy can have a talk with me and a Mr. Devlin."

Hyrum Roddy laughed. "This is such a joke." He grabbed his briefcase and walked around the table, headed for the double doors.

Brosia got up and said, "We're going to have that talk now."

"I'm not talking to you or anybody," Roddy said.

"Call your lawyer," Brosia said. "Tell him to meet you at Central Division."

180

AS SOON AS Brosia escorted Roddy out, Sam DeCosse looked at me and said, "You're pretty smart."

"I try," I said.

"He really does," Sister Mary said.

"What is it you want?" he said.

"Maybe you can see your way clear to give the Lindbrook residents the full tenancy rights they deserve. The guys there don't have much left. A bunch of them fought so you and Junior can keep on living and keep on making deals. I think it would be a nice gesture, don't you?"

"Don't tell me *that's* what this has been about."

"It's been about a lot of things, Sam."

"Don't give him anything," Junior said.

"Now, Junior," I said, "don't be getting in the way of your dad's best interests."

"Don't talk to me," he said.

"Shall I talk to Dad? Tell him about the yacht party and the intimate scene at Musso and Frank?"

Junior looked at Dad. Dad looked at Junior and seemed to know everything. Or else was thinking that he soon would.

"I think that's all the information I need," Senior said. "I'll talk to Mr. McDonough and Mr. Bradshaw and we'll get back to you."

181

"YOU WERE VERY effective in there," Sister Mary said in the car as we drove back to St. Monica's.

"Partly," I said. "There are still some threads dangling. I'm hoping Brosia can help me weave them together."

"Maybe I can help, too."

"You have a theory?"

"A hunch. The sin of pride. There are things going on in the past here that people don't want to come out."

"Good theory," I said. "We all have things from the past we don't want people to know about."

"Even you?"

"Even me."

"Like what?"

"If I told you," I said, "then you'd know."

"Very logical," Sister Mary said. "You ought to be a lawyer."

"No money in it."

"The best things are never done for money."

"Tell that to Donald Trump."

"I'd like to tell a few things to Donald Trump."

And I wanted to tell her a few things, but I clammed up. Maybe the right time would come. Maybe it wouldn't.

And maybe I had to get used to the idea of never seeing Sister Mary again.

182

IT HIT THE news the next day.

Sam DeCosse Senior was going to war. With his wife. With his soon-to-be ex-wife. He was going to cut her up and feed her to the fish.

Metaphorically speaking, of course.

He had an ironclad prenup. The prenup of all prenups. Better than the Massey Prenup from that movie with George Clooney. It was the iron-jaws-of-death prenup.

At least that's how his lawyer put it in the paper.

But Ariel DeCosse would soon have a greater problem than this.

183

THE MURDER TRIAL of Gilbert Calderón lasted a week.

Mitch Roberts was very good. Workmanlike. Professional. Deadly.

The jury we'd picked could go either way. Like most lawyers in trial, I got the sick feeling they'd go for Mitch.

Gilbert kept putting his hand on my arm to cheer me up.

Terrific.

I had two major moves to make, and the judge, an old veteran named Paul Lowe, could stop them both.

To lay the groundwork for the first move, I cross-examined Detective Sean Plunkett, the lead detective, and asked him only three questions.

"You took a statement from Nydessa Perry, is that correct?"

"Yes."

"She was the last witness you interviewed, is that right?"

"That's right."

"And you did not consider any other suspects after that, did you?"

"Our investigation was complete."

"Thank you."

I questioned him that way because Mitch Roberts did not call Nydessa Perry as one of his witnesses. She was too volatile.

So when the prosecution rested and it was my turn, the first witness I called was Nydessa Perry.

Roberts objected. At the bench he told the judge, "She's not on the defense witness list!"

"She's on the People's list," I said. "Don't they know their own witnesses?"

"It doesn't matter," Roberts said.

"Can you cite me a case?" Judge Lowe asked.

Roberts said he could try to find one.

"Not on my dime," Lowe said. "Objection overruled. The witness can testify."

She did—and blew up, just like I'd hoped. She insisted Gilbert did it, but she looked like a nut saying so. The judge let me treat her as hostile, so I got to impeach my own witness with her drug record. Roberts kept objecting but to no avail.

When closing argument came, I'd tell the jury that Detective Plunkett should have discounted Nydessa Perry's statement, and kept the investigation going.

But that was not the big move.

184

THE BIG MOVE was when I called Leonora Esparza, the woman I'd cornered in the fish food section of the pet store.

Roberts objected and wanted an offer of proof.

Up at the bench I showed the judge the photo that Ms. Esparza had signed, the one I'd shown to Mr. Roshdieh, the one he'd ID'd as definitely being Gilbert Calderón. Only it wasn't a photograph of Gilbert Calderón but of someone named Rolando Santiago. A fact I could establish by another witness.

"He violated 1054.8 to get that," Roberts pleaded.

"So what?" Judge Lowe asked. "You want sanctions?"

"No, I want to exclude this evidence."

"Seems like relevant evidence to me, Mr. Roberts. The remedy of exclusion does not seem apt here."

Roberts looked at me. He seemed incredulous.

"Just like pool," I said. "It's a table and it's balls."

"What are you talking about?" the judge said.

"It's a Paul Newman thing," I said.

So I got the photo evidence in. And then it all came down to closing arguments.

This is usually where I want to be. Give me a jury. Give me twelve in the box I can talk to. It helps to believe in your client. Defense lawyers almost never get to do that. We have to argue the Constitution and the presumption of innocence and all. Nothing wrong with that.

When you really think your client is telling the truth, though, it's like getting an espresso in your coffee. But that jolt also makes you nervous. Because when it's an innocent guy on the line you really better be good.

Be your best.

Mitch Roberts was at his best. In California the prosecution leads off with its summation. Then the defense gets to argue. And the prosecution gets to have the last word.

Roberts would get two bites at the apple to my one.

I had to make mine a very big bite.

I got up to argue at 11:05 a.m. on a Friday morning. I thanked the jury for their attention. And I started in on my prepared statement.

But then something happened. Some words came to my head. And I had to say them.

"You, ladies and gentlemen, stand between the government and Mr. Calderón. It is you, and you alone, who judge the facts in this case. Not the prosecutor. Not the judge. You. And that, ladies and gentlemen, is what makes this country different from almost every other country on earth."

I engaged several sets of juror eyes. And got this funny feeling. It was like I was flying almost. Yes, that was it. As if Mitch Roberts was Pierpont Wicks and I was in his home gym. But flying through the middle, throwing the ball up backward, a no-looker, knowing it would go in.

"In our country it is not the prosecutor who gets to vote. He has to prove his case to you beyond a reasonable doubt. *Beyond* a reasonable doubt. If he does not, you must find Mr. Calderón not guilty. Because, ladies and gentlemen, throughout the history of the criminal law there runs a sacred trust, which is now placed in your hands. I am talking about the presumption of innocence."

I talked about a lot more, sat down, and listened to Mitch Roberts go.

He was good again.

Judge Lowe instructed the jury on the law and sent them off to deliberate.

And the lawyers home to stew.

Then called us back two hours later. It was 5:15 p.m. when the jury came in with their verdict.

When one of them, number six, a woman from San Fernando, smiled at me I knew what it was.

Not guilty.

Gilbert Calderón threw his arms around my neck. "I told you you could do this!"

"Easy—"

"You got a friend for life, man. Me!"

"You can let me go now," I said.

"No way, man!"

"Go hug your mother."

"Oh, yeah." He let go, but not before planting a kiss on my cheek.

Mitch Roberts walked over. "Don't expect a kiss from me," he said.

"I'm hurt, Mitch. I mean, Mr. Roberts."

"Mitch. Nice job."

"Thanks," I said.

"I hope you know I really thought it was your guy," he said.

"You mean, nothing personal?"

"That's what a trial is for," Roberts said. "If I didn't think I could prove it, I wouldn't have brought it. But I brought it and the jury said I didn't prove it. I accept their verdict."

"For what it's worth, you're very good."

"So are you. I didn't think that sacred-trust stuff worked anymore. You made it work. You ever think of giving up the solo life, you'd make a good DA."

"Me?"

"Why not?"

"I guess I'm not the company type."

He put out his hand. I shook it.

"Now maybe we can all get some sleep," he said.

185

A COUPLE OF days later they caught Fly Charles trying to cross the border into Mexico. Brosia sent a detail down to pick him up and cart him back to L.A.

When he got a chance to question him, Fly Charles sang like he hadn't since the breakup of Detritus and the Electric Yaks.

The song was pointed at Hyrum Roddy.

Brosia invited me to have lunch with him at a Mexican place on Figueroa.

Over some great carnitas he told me about his grilling of Hyrum Roddy. "The guy hates the DeCosse family. Doesn't think they give him the respect he deserves. He did all this work for them over the years, but then they gave most of it to that big firm you used to work for."

"Gunther, McDonough," I said.

"And all he got was cleanup and table scrap work. He didn't seem to like that."

"I wouldn't, either."

"So one day this Reatta woman shows up at his office. She saw Ariel's picture in the paper. She also knew Sam DeCosse Junior."

"What?"

"He was apparently a Night Silk regular. That was how Ariel, then known as Ginger Lambelet, met Sam Senior. He found out about the dalliance his son was having, broke it up, but in the process he fell for Ginger himself. Love, huh?"

"And another one of Sam DeCosse's reclamation projects."

"Meanwhile, Ginger gets nabbed for a misdemeanor. Roddy is sent to help make it go away."

"What does this have to do with Reatta?"

"She thought she could squeeze some money out of the DeCosses by claiming Kylie was Sam Junior's kid. Roddy told her there was a better way. She'd check into the Lindbrook and go for an injunction against getting shuffled out. Refuse to settle. Ariel would eventually find out who Reatta was and then *she* would offer a major payout for Reatta to go away. Before any publicity hit. Roddy would broker the settlement and split the money with her, eighty-twenty. Eighty for him."

"Hyrum Roddy told you all this?"

"He's cooperating. He doesn't think we can get him on any of this, and he's probably right. He didn't murder Reatta. Though he had a motive. Reatta decided she would go for more on her own. Reatta found out about the DeCosse interest in the land owned by St. Monica's. Reatta went there to see what she could find out. Maybe she thought she could find a way to inject herself in that deal, too."

"That's how she found me," I said. "She met Father Bob, who had her talk to me."

"There you go," Brosia said. "Hiring you would cut Roddy completely out. She could keep all the money that way."

"Very nice."

"Roddy denies hiring Fly Charles for anything. He says Charles came to him trying to extort money. He'd found out about the Reatta scheme from Avisha."

"Loose lips sink ships," I said.

"Charles says Roddy hired him to kidnap Kylie, but that doesn't sound plausible to me. More likely it was Fly's own idea."

"So who did Avisha?"

"Both of them deny it. The investigation, as they say, is ongoing."

When the check came Brosia picked it up. "I am doing you a service," he said. "I am no longer in your debt."

186

TWO DAYS LATER Brosia arrested Ariel DeCosse for the Lindbrook murder.

She was still living in DeCosse's mountaintop home. Brosia served a search warrant for the place. It turned up all sorts of items, including a large cache of books on spiritual matters. Everything from feng shui to Buddhism to, interestingly, Rastafarianism.

Why did she kill Reatta? To stop a claim against Junior for paternity? Was Reatta threatening to spill all the details of Ariel's sordid past at the same time Ariel was trying so hard, with a new name, to be taken seriously as an actress?

Was that even enough of a motive? Then I thought of the woman who poisoned her husband so she could use the life insurance to pay for breast implants.

Motives are cheap currency in this land of the sun.

Ariel was nailed and did the only thing she could. She played the arrest for the publicity bonanza it was. She was now where every actress wanted to be. The spotlight was on her. The talk was Ariel DeCosse, 24-7.

Wronged wife of Sam DeCosse.

Former call girl escaping her past.

Murderer.

She denied the latter, of course. She was going to fight.

Didn't really matter. Even if convicted, she'd be a star for the ages.

Only in Hollywood.

187

SHORTLY AFTER ARIEL'S arrest I got a personal call from Sam DeCosse.

"I just wanted to tell you the agreement's done," he said. "It makes the Lindbrook full residency. That satisfy you?"

"That satisfies me," I said.

"I am moving forward on the land deal near St. Monica's. You want to come work for me?"

I was too stunned to answer.

"I have a little hole in my operation," he said. "Mr. Roddy is no longer part of my team. You're smarter than he is. Smart enough to come on board."

"I didn't expect this."

"Then say yes. Come down from your hill and rejoin the living. Make some real money again."

"Thanks, Mr. DeCosse. But the best things are never done for money."

Long pause. "That's a sentiment I don't understand, Mr.Buchanan. I will have the agreement messengered to you."

"And I'll go down to the Lindbrook Hotel."

"Why?"

"It'll be nice to deliver some good news."

188

THE LOBBY OF the Lindbrook Hotel was as lively as always. Somnolent men sitting in front of streaked yellow windows, watching the traffic and life itself pass by.

Oscar saw me and threw down his ever-present newspaper.

"How's the Sudoku?" I said.

"Still from hell," he said, motioning me to sit down.

"I have a little news for you."

"More news? You been busy."

"It just came in," I said. "Orpheus is going to make this place a full-residency hotel."

Oscar's mouth dropped open a little. He teared up. "Well that's just…that's just fine, Mr. Buchanan. How's the little girl?"

"Doing great. I think I may have found a real home for her."

Oscar smiled. "I'm glad when something works out. Kind of restores my hope for the human race."

"That's worth celebrating," I said. "How 'bout I buy us a couple of Cokes?"

"If the machine's workin'," he said.

"Be right back." I stood and turned around and headed for the stairs. I was going to go down to Candyland.

I never made it.

189

HE STEPPED OUT of the shadows from the corner near the stairs. Devlin.

He wore a black jacket and had his hands in the pockets. "Let's go outside," he said.

"If you came to apologize, you can do that right here."

"Outside."

"How's the knee?" I said.

"We won't talk about that."

"We won't talk about anything."

Devlin pulled back his jacket so I could see his gun.

"What, you're going to pop me right here?" I said.

"You don't come with me, yeah."

I put my hands up. "What can I say?" I shot the heel of my right hand up under his chin. I heard the sound of clacking teeth. His head went back and I kicked him in the groin.

He buckled slightly, then came back at me with his left hand. I saw the brass knuckles flash. I moved enough so the blow only glanced off my side. I backed up, into the light.

I heard Oscar shout, "Hey!" and start moving toward me.

Devlin shouted, "Back off!" and pulled his gun. His eyes were wild now. He had the somebody-is-going-to-die look.

It could be anybody.

"All right," I said. "We go outside."

"What is this?" Oscar said.

Devlin pointed the gun at Oscar. "Stay where you are, old man. Goes for the rest of you."

"Don't do anything," I said. "The guy'll shoot."

"That's right," Devlin said. "That's so right."

"So come on." I started backing toward the front doors.

Devlin pointed the gun back at me.

That's when I saw Disco Freddy spinning toward Devlin from behind.

It was a moment frozen in deadly time. A nightmare beat where you couldn't move, couldn't talk.

Devlin turned his head toward Disco.

And then I saw what is still the most magnificent, poetic move I've ever seen, and I've seen Magic Johnson.

Disco Freddy made a final spin and leaped, and as his left foot came down his right foot went up.

He kicked Devlin solid in the mouth. The smack echoed through the lobby.

Devlin went straight down.

"MumbuddynomakenomubbamindRiverdance!" Disco Freddy shouted.

Oscar and five or six other guys hurried over. They had Devlin disarmed and incapacitated in about two seconds.

I called Central Division and told them to come collect a multiple felon packing a gun.

Oscar got some duct tape and he and the boys got Devlin's hands secured behind his back. He was still groggy from Disco Freddy's kick.

As we waited for the police to show, I approached Disco, who was doing circles in the middle of the lobby. He stopped when I got to him.

"You're beautiful," I said.

He looked at me. And winked. "Beautiful?" he said. "MumbuddynomakenomubbamindRita Hayworth!"

Then he waltzed across the foyer.

190

KYLIE WAS FEEDING the cats in Fran's backyard when I went to see them on Saturday. Brought them a tub of mint chip ice cream, too. You just can't have enough of that around the house.

"I'm going to get her enrolled in school," Fran said, watching from the kitchen window. "She wants to go. She's excited about it."

"Can you do this?" I said. "Do you want to do this?"

"I want to."

"We can try to find a couple."

"I know I'm older. Is that selfish?"

"No."

"Some kids are raised by grandmothers, aren't they?"

"Happens all the time," I said.

"Can we make it happen?" she asked.

"I'll take care of the legal hoops," I said.

"Will we ever know who her father is?"

Kylie was petting the gray tabby. And talking to it, as if the cat was one of her best friends.

"I doubt it," I said. "But it doesn't matter. In this case blood means nothing. Love means everything."

"Then she's home," Fran said.

191

I HAD NO home. My things were packed to leave St. Monica's. What things I had with me in the trailer, that is.

I'd come to appreciate a certain freedom up here. Was I ready to go back to how I lived before?

Well, what else was there? Continue to practice law in the offices of the Ultimate Sip?

Professionals just didn't do that.

Why didn't they?

Somebody knocked on the door. I opened it.

Sister Mary stood there in her sweats, holding a basketball. "One more game?" she said. "For the road?"

"I don't know," I said. "I want to leave on good terms. I don't want to have to hurt you."

"So you're refusing to play?"

"That's right. Don't make anything out of it."

"I just thought the big-city lawyer would rise to the challenge, but I've been wrong before."

Talking smack again. She was so good at it.

And I did want to play her. I wanted the game to last forever.

"You're on," I said.

I got my togs from the suitcase and suited up.

Sister Mary wasn't as on as she usually was. A lot of her shots clanked off the rim.

I guess I wanted her to beat me, but she didn't this day.

It was my game, eleven to six.

"Let that be a lesson to you," I said.

Sister Mary bounced the ball a couple of times, looking at the ground.

"Okay?" I said.

She kept looking down. I went to her. She looked up.

"I don't want you to go," she said.

She dropped the ball and walked quickly away.

Leaving me standing in a doorway between two worlds.

At least that's what it felt like to me.

And then I ran after her.